CLASS REUNIONS

CLASS REUNIONS

By
Alexander Gregory

GRIFFIN PUBLISHING

Disclaimer

Notice: This book is a work of fiction. All characters in this book are products of the author's imagination. Any resemblance or similarity with any actual person is purely coincidental.
Some locations in this book are also creations of the author. Actual places mentioned here are used fictitiously and may be altered in this book to suit the author's needs.

The City of Griffin is fictitious but would be in the approximate location of Amery, Wisconsin. The author chose to replace the real city of Amery with the fictitious city of Griffin so he could create the town, its history, businesses, and people to suit his needs.

ISBN 979-8-9903288-0-8 (e-book)
ISBN 979-8-9903288-1-5 (paperback)
ISBN 979-8-9903288-2-2 (large print paperback)
ISBN 979-8-9903288-3-9 (Hardcover)

Library of Congress Control Number: 2024903852
First Edition: 2024 (e-book, paperback, large print, and hardcover)

Published by Griffin Publishing

Dedication

This book is dedicated to the Amery High School Class of '72. All characters in this book are completely fictitious, but the friendship and camaraderie shown at their reunions were inspired by the real-life AHS class of '72. It was during our twenty-year class reunion that the idea for this book came to me. That was when I first thought of writing a book about a couple and telling their story through the five-year intervals of their class reunions.

I would also like to mention the Unity High School Class of '72. I began high school in Unity and was a student there when I decided I would one day become a writer and chose my pen name. You do not need to graduate with a class to be part of it; you need only to have been a part of it at some time. I now attend reunions for both schools and enjoy the friendships that both classes eagerly share.

Acknowledgements

For their assistance with the cover photo, I would like to thank Jack Davis, Hannah Monson, Clair Diethert, Alex DeRosier, Preston Jones, Breanna Burstad, Seraphina Johnson, Morgan Monson, and Steve Anderson for the loan of his cars.

For her assistance with the author's photo, I would like to thank Susan Avery.

I also wish to thank Sara Ciccia, and Sheryl Hallen Kieselhorst for their editing and proofreading assistance. Your contributions are greatly appreciated.

Table of Contents

PART 1: GRADUATION

Chapter 1: Graduation Morning

I will begin by stating that I am a member of the Griffin High School class of '72. Having attended all our class reunions and events, I have been able to personally witness much of what I will be telling you. Naturally, there are many parts of this story that I could not have witnessed personally. For those events, I interviewed or had conversations with those who were present at those times, allowing me to mentally reconstruct those moments to our satisfaction. My friends not only helped with missing details, but some even recalled and shared their very thoughts and feelings as they remembered them. People mentioned in this book have already read my previous draft and agree that this is an accurate telling of their stories.

Unfortunately, even though I was present for much of this story, I played no real or significant part in it. For that reason, I will not bother to introduce myself and will simply remain an unnamed narrator who happened to be a member of this class.

I'll begin this story in the bedroom of Rachel Davis, on the second floor of an old country farmhouse a few miles north of Griffin, Wisconsin. I should mention that Rachel is not the main character of this story, but for some reason things often seem a little more interesting when Rachel is involved.

* * *

It was graduation day, the third Sunday of May 1972. An old-fashioned alarm clock ticked annoyingly on the nightstand next to Rachel's bed. It was a typical alarm clock, with a round face, metal skin, and twin alarm bells on top. It was cordless, had no battery, and kept excellent time when its springs were properly wound.

Minutes ticked by until five o'clock, the time the clock had been set for. The clapper instantly began banging between the twin bells, sounding reminiscent of a school fire alarm.

A feminine hand shot out from under the blanket, slapping down on the nightstand, with fingers just brushing the clock. With a bit more reach, Rachel grabbed the clock, sat up in bed, and brushed the red hair away from her eyes so she could read the hour. She looked across her bedroom to see that she had indeed left her window open when she went to bed, approximately three hours earlier. In an instant the clock was flying through the window as the alarm faded to a small murmur, which slowly died as its spring unwound.

Satisfied, Rachel pulled her blanket over her head and returned to her slumber.

* * *

In the next farmhouse down the road, Scott Severson hurried through the kitchen on his way to the back door. "I must have slept through my alarm this morning. I'm surprised the girls aren't calling for me by now."

"Morning chores are already done," his father said from the kitchen stove. "You didn't oversleep; I shut your alarm off before I went out. Just wash up and pour some coffee while I get breakfast on the table."

A surprised Scott washed his hands in the kitchen sink while his father explained, "I woke up early and figured this would be my last chance to do morning chores alone. Besides, this is a big day, and you deserve to sleep in for a change."

"Thank you." Scott removed the basket of grounds from the percolator and poured two cups of coffee.

Tom Severson carried two plates to the table, each with a thick waffle covered with whipped cream and cherry pie filling.

"Belgian Waffles." A feeling of warmth and comfort came over Scott when he saw what his father had prepared.

"I figured that's what Ellie would have made if she were here." Tom stepped back to the stove and returned with two plates of

2

bacon and eggs. "You're graduating, so we should celebrate with your favorite breakfast."

Scott thanked his father as he picked up his fork to begin eating.

"The guy buying the farm called after you went out last night." Tom cut into his waffle. "They're all packed and will be leaving this morning; they should be here this afternoon. They'll use the empty bedrooms upstairs until we're gone. I told him we could do the chores together for a day or two; that'll help him and the cows get to know each other. I'll show him around the farm a little more and then we can both move on."

Scott took a bite of waffle. "I'm pretty much ready. I have my toolbox and camping supplies in the trunk. I have a suitcase and duffle bag for the rest of my clothes. I don't think there's anything else that hasn't been moved already."

Tom sipped his coffee. "Same here. I finished packing my clothes and the family pictures last night. The only other things I'm bringing are the cabinet you made for Ellie, and her mother's dishes. Dale's house should have anything I need."

Scott nodded. "Dale's house should have everything, but you may replace some things to suit your taste."

Tom shook his head. "I never dreamed I would retire in New Mexico."

"Uncle Dale did suggest it last time he was up."

"Yeah! But leaving his house to me is a sneaky way of getting me to do it."

"How's the fishing in New Mexico?"

"I don't know. Dale loved fishing almost as much as he loved the cigarettes that killed him, so there must be something worth catching." Tom ate another bite of waffle. "Did you have a good time last night? You weren't out very late."

"I know better than to stay out late when cows need early milking." Scott took a bite of bacon. "Rachel's brothers are home for graduation. Yesterday was her eighteenth birthday, so they all celebrated at the Pike Lake Resort. I stuck around until the music started so I could have a birthday dance with Rachel."

"When you were little, I used to wonder if you two would get together when you grew up. Maybe merge the two farms into one."

"No," Scott shook his head. "Rachel is like a little sister to me, and she always will be. And she'll always see me as an extra brother. Besides, the farm is already sold, so it's time for both of us to move on."

"You could o' kept the farm," Tom reminded. "I did offer it to you."

"I was tempted, but I think I should move on."

Tom lifted his cup to sip coffee as he thought. "I didn't really have any choice. When I was young, it was just expected that the oldest son would stay on to run the farm. I almost left once. Then Dad died, so someone had to look after Mom and keep things going. Then the war shot down any chance of my brothers taking over."

Scott looked thoughtful as he ate another bite. "I used to dream of marrying the perfect girl and running the farm with her, like you did with Mom. Unfortunately, she's taken, so it's better that I move on. Then I don't have to see her with somebody else."

Tom nodded with understanding. "I met a perfect girl once. I knew she couldn't be interested in such an old man." He paused and shook his head. "Then she went and married me anyway."

Scott nodded with a smile and said, "She told me she thought she was going to grow old waiting for you to ask her." Scott watched his father smile with memories before changing the subject. "The Davis boys said they were staying until closing time last night. Lou said she was getting everyone up early for church anyway. I'm betting there are a lot of hurting heads next door this morning."

* * *

When Rachel Davis was little, her mother woke her for school each morning. As she grew older, her brothers would simply yell, "Rachel, time to get up!" Time moved on, and she was finally given her first alarm clock. That was the first of many alarm clocks for Rachel. Rachel found that she did not especially care for alarm clocks; a more accurate statement would be that Rachel had an extreme hatred for alarm clocks.

Rachel learned that alarms came with bells, buzzers, pulsing tones, and annoying beeps. She discovered that if you threw a clock while it was still plugged in, the cord would sometimes hold on to snap the clock back at her. Eventually, the cord would come loose from either the plug, or the clock, allowing the clock to die, sometimes with sparks! Rachel learned that if you cut the clock's electrical cord with wire cutters or tin snips, the wires would arc and burn a big notch in the cutting part of the tool. Smashing an electric alarm clock with a hammer or mallet usually resulted in sparks, along with a blown fuse and no lights on the second floor. Bumping the clock off the nightstand, causing it to land in a bucket of mop water, would blow the same fuse, but with fewer sparks. Clock radios were more peaceful. They allowed her to wake up to music. Of course, in winter months the radio was set to WCCO, so she could hear the school closing announcements which came with foul weather. Unfortunately, she might also wake up to the hog report, which was all the encouragement Rachel needed to smash the clock with a rubber mallet.

Rachel's latest clock was spring powered and had a sturdy metal skin. The alarm pin rested halfway between five and six, so the clock would begin ringing at 5:30 a.m.

At the first sound of the alarm, Rachel's hand shot out from the blanket and slapped down on her empty nightstand. A confused Rachel sat up in bed, looking for the source of this noise. She saw that the clock was ringing from the other side of her room, defiantly sitting on her windowsill.

Rachel considered three possibilities for what she was seeing: one, throwing the clock out the window earlier was merely a dream; two, her mother heard the clock land, retrieved and rewound it, and reset the alarm before setting the clock on the windowsill; and three, the clock was possessed by an evil demon and had climbed up the side of the house to challenge her. Rachel was betting on number three. Sitting on the windowsill was the clock's most evil move, as it required getting out of bed before turning it off. Everyone knows that you can turn an alarm off while in bed, but when your feet hit the floor, you are up, and there is no going back.

Rachel looked down, confirming that she was indeed still wearing the same clothes she had worn to the bar last night. She flipped her blanket aside enough to grab her left foot, and removed the tennis shoe she was still wearing. In an instant, the shoe bounced off the evil clock and landed safely on the floor. The demonic clock, however, fell outward and frighted the unsuspecting dog that was sleeping below.

Rachel felt satisfaction and victory as she snuggled into her blanket, closed her eyes, and returned to sleep.

* * *

In yet another farmhouse, a few miles south of town, Lois Vanderzee was wide awake and fully dressed as she descended the stairs. Her long blonde hair was freshly brushed and hung lightly behind the shoulders of the spring dress she wore.

"Good morning," her grandmother greeted when Lois came to the bottom of the stairs.

"Grandma!" Lois hurried to greet her grandmother with a hug. "When did you get here?"

"Early this morning. Your grandfather wanted to get here in time to help your father with morning chores. That means they'll do a lot of talking and breakfast will be cold by the time they come in. Alice didn't want any help with breakfast, so we have time to visit."

"Great!" Lois and her grandmother seated themselves on the living room couch. "If Grandpa enjoys chores so much, does he regret retiring?"

"No. I think he just likes spending time with Storm. It's good when a man gets along that well with his son-in-law. I hope you find someone like that when you marry."

Lois looked skeptical. "I don't know. Mike and I have been dating for almost two years, and Dad still doesn't seem to like him."

"Well, you are his only daughter, so he'll always be protective of you. My father was the same way when I started dating, at least he was, until I met Wayne. He and Dad just hit it off from the start." She gave Lois a questioning look. "Why doesn't your dad like Mike?"

"I don't know. Dad's big on family, so maybe it's because Mike's parents are divorced. Maybe he thinks that because Mike's father left them, Mike might walk out on me."

"You never know. Maybe he sees something in Mike that you don't, or maybe you see something in him that your father doesn't. Some people take after their parents. What's his father like?"

"I've never met him, but Mike thinks the world of him. They take trips together every summer, and he stays with his dad in Minneapolis so they can work together a few times every year. Tomorrow, Mike's leaving to work with his father for a few weeks."

"What kind of work does he do?"

"I don't know; he never says anything about the work. I get the impression the work must be boring, because spending time with his dad is the only thing he talks about."

"So, he's leaving you for two weeks. What will you do without him?" Grandma paused as something occurred to her. "As a matter of fact, you're graduating today, so what are your plans?"

"I'll be going to college in Eau Claire in the fall," she said proudly. "There's not a lot of jobs around here, so I'll see what Eau Claire has to offer. If I can find a job where I can keep working part-time after school starts, that will be great. Of course,

I'll have to find an apartment too. Griffin is too far from Eau Claire to commute."

"Supporting yourself with your own apartment. You sound so independent." Grandma looked thoughtful. "Or... will you be alone?"

Lois chuckled at her grandmother's question. "I might find a roommate later, but it's just me for now. Mike and I aren't ready to move in together. I didn't want to get too serious in high school, so there's no reason to rush into anything. Mike says he has a steady job lined up, but he doesn't want to jinx it by saying anything."

Grandma nodded. "A steady job should give your father a better impression of him. Being a good worker shows responsibility."

"That's true. I just wish I knew what Mike was planning, so I could tell Dad before tonight's party. Dad's still leery about me going there with Mike."

"What party?"

"You haven't heard?" Lois thought her mother might have mentioned the party. "Rich Lester and Danny O'Brian are throwing a big party for the whole class, or as many as can come anyway. There will be music, a bonfire, hot dogs, beer or pop, and breakfast in the morning." Lois noticed her grandmother's eyes widen at the mention of breakfast. "Danny's bringing a keg of beer; he said no one drinking would be allowed to drive until morning. Mike can sleep in his van, and Vanessa has tents set up for some of the girls. Or Rachel may let me sleep in the front seat of her car."

"Rachel will be there too." Grandma seemed pleased. "That's nice. She can help watch out for you." Grandma thought for a moment. "Or you could keep an eye on Rachel. That may be a better idea."

Lois nodded, knowing what her grandmother meant. Her cousin Rachel wasn't a wild person, but she could be unpredictable. Lois may have had other plans too, but there was no reason to mention them to her grandmother.

* * *

Rachel Davis woke once more to the sound of her alarm clock. It was quiet at first, only to become louder when her bedroom door opened, and her mother entered with the ringing clock. After turning the alarm off, she reset the time, rewound the alarm, and set the clock back on the windowsill.

Rachel uncovered her head with annoyance. "Mom! It's Sunday! School's over. We can sleep in now."

Irritated, her mother said, "School is not over until after graduation. Father Mathew wants the graduates to wear their caps and gowns to church this morning, so it's time to get up."

"I can't go to church. I have a headache."

"You have a headache because you closed up the bar last night, which is all the more reason for you to go to church this morning."

"I had to drink." Rachel groaned as she tried to cover her eyes with the back of her hand. "It was my eighteenth birthday. It's a rule in Wisconsin. It might even be a law."

"It's not a law, it's not a rule, and you didn't need to drink that much. At least now you know what drinking feels like the next morning." She pointed to the clock, "It's set for six o'clock. You need to shower, eat, and get ready for church. You know you'll change clothes half a dozen times before you decide what to wear, so when the alarm goes off, you need to get up."

Rachel pulled the blanket over her head as her mother walked out the door. "It doesn't matter what I wear; no one will see it anyway. I could be naked under that robe, and no one would know." With that thought, Rachel grinned and laid her head down, closing her eyes once more.

It seemed her eyes had barely closed when Rachel sat up again, hearing the incessant ringing of the alarm clock. She tossed back her blanket, pulled her right foot up, and removed her remaining shoe. This time, the shoe followed the clock out the

9

window. "Great! Now I'll have to go outside for my shoe." Satisfied that her feet had still not touched the floor, Rachel lay back down and closed her eyes.

"Crap," she cried, as she opened her eyes and sat up in bed. "I have to pee." Flipping the blanket aside, Rachel sat up, turned, and put her feet on the floor.

* * *

Moving on to a small house within the city limits of Griffin, Mike Burman and his mother had just finished having breakfast together. As she rose to clear the table, his mother looked out the window and noticed a car stopping in front of their house. She recognized the passenger as he retrieved a duffle bag from the back seat and closed the door, allowing the driver to pull away. Frank, her former husband, had stopped coming to Griffin shortly after Mike got his driver's license. Life became much simpler after Mike began driving to Minneapolis, and she no longer had to see Frank.

Nervous, perhaps a bit fearful, she glanced back at Mike. "You've got company. I'll take care of the dishes so you can visit out here." Hurrying to the kitchen, she had the dishwater running in the sink before she heard the knock on the front door.

She could hear the surprise in Mike's voice when he greeted his father, and invited him in. Mike came into the kitchen just long enough to refill his coffee cup and pour a fresh cup for his father. Sitting at the dining room table, they could not see his mother by the kitchen sink, but she could hear everything they said through the open doorway.

"Will you be coming to the graduation ceremony today?" asked Mike.

"No." Frank shook his head. "There's no telling who will be there, and I don't want anyone recognizing me."

Mike could tell something was bothering his father. "Dad, is everything okay?"

Frank shook his head with irritation. "I had some trouble last night. I managed to get my bank book and a few things from home, but I won't be going back to Minneapolis. It's time to relocate to another state." He paused long enough for that to sink in. "The problem is, I left in a hurry and had to leave my van. Now I need new wheels, preferably another van."

Mike nodded with understanding. "And since I'm going into the army tomorrow, I won't be needing my van."

"I don't want to leave you stranded either," Frank assured him. "Kevin doesn't have anything on hand now, but he promised he would have something ready before your basic training's over. I told him to make it something sporty enough to be a good graduation present. I already paid him, and he's never let me down. Just give him a call when you get your first leave, and he'll get it to you."

"That's fine Dad, but can you wait until tomorrow? I kind of need the van tonight."

"What's going on tonight?" It was easy to hear the annoyance in Frank's voice.

"Tonight's my last chance with Lois. She's been saying, *'Not while I'm in high school'* since we started dating, but that excuse expires the moment we graduate. We're going to an all-night party tonight. Plenty of beer, and no one expects her home until tomorrow morning. One way or another; tonight's the night." He gave a hopeful look to his father, "It would be a lot better in the van, than the back seat of Mom's car."

"If she's been holding out like that, why'd you put up with her? You never had any trouble with girls when you stayed with me."

Mike shrugged. "There's a few around here who are never any problem either. I just made sure Lois never knew about them. There's one I really go for." His grin grew as he thought about her. "She's been poked more times than a pin cushion, but she still leaves you feeling brain dead and exhausted when she's done. Unfortunately, she won't even get in the car if you're already dating someone else. I know a few outside of town too, but Lois is different. She's beautiful, and I'll be her first. Even better, Scott

Severson has been waiting for his chance for years, but he won't make a move on her as long as she's wearing my ring.

"That's the guy you told me about last summer. The one whose mother..."

"Yeah, he's the one. Also, back when you worked on the farm, his dad and him were talking to old man Sorenson, and the next day the cops were looking in your shed."

"I remember that. I always figured someone said something to get him to look in that shed. It fits that it was a nosy neighbor."

Mike's mother exhaled with relief when she heard that. She felt much safer hearing that they suspected a neighbor, rather than considering that she had talked to Mr. Sorenson about what was in that shed. She listened as Mike continued.

"I've been trying to get one-up on Scott ever since then, but somehow he always comes out on top." Satisfaction filled his voice as he gloated, "As long as Lois is wearing my ring, what he wants is mine! So, he loses."

"But you're joining the army tomorrow. Is she still going to wear your ring after you're gone?"

"She doesn't know I enlisted." Mike sat back, obviously pleased with himself. "I told her I'll be working with you for the next few weeks. His dad just sold their farm, so he'll be gone before either of them knows I'm not coming back. Even if he does come back, after tonight, he'll always know that I had her first."

Frank was silent for a moment, no doubt feeling proud that his son thought so much like him. "Okay, how about this? I'll borrow your mom's car this week. Then I can still find a new place. I'm thinking maybe Iowa or Illinois. That way, you will still have your van for tonight. Next Saturday, I'll come back and swap her car for the van. When you get your first leave after basic training, Kevin will have a car ready for you."

"Sounds like a plan." Mike was pleased with this arrangement. "I'll sign the title and leave it with Mom."

He hurried into the kitchen with a vague explanation to his mother. She listened, showing no sign that she had already heard everything as they discussed it. She gladly gave Mike her car keys, feeling grateful that she did not have to speak with Frank. Being in the next room was as close to him as she ever wanted to be.

When his father accepted the keys from Mike, he said, "Son, don't count on the beer tonight; some girls don't like it. Keep some wine on ice in the van too."

Watching Frank drive away in her car, Mike's mother let out a sigh of relief and began to relax. She considered all she had heard. She wondered if she could say something to Lois; but knew she would not have the courage to do so. Mike was becoming so much like his father, and she began to fear him too. Even if she couldn't say anything to Lois, she would still avoid seeing Frank when he returned. She decided that after Mike leaves for the army, she would pack whatever she could fit into the van. She did not know where she would go, except that it would not be in Illinois and Iowa. If Frank was going to disappear and start somewhere new, there was no reason she could not do the same.

* * *

It would be more than twenty years before Mike's mother returned to Griffin, and then only for a brief stay. I happened to meet her during that visit, and we had a very good chat. She could not recall what she had made for Mike's graduation breakfast, but she still remembered every word of the conversation she overheard. Neither Mike nor his father ever saw or heard from her again.

Chapter 2: Graduation

Morning passed and the time came for us to head to the school for graduation. Scott Severson parked his car on the street and began walking to the school. He was almost to the building when he met Rachel's father, Don Davis, who was talking with another man.

"Where's your dad, Scott?" asked Don.

"The family that's buying the farm showed up just as we were ready to leave. Dad's talking to them, but he'll be here soon." Looking around, Scott asked, "Where's your family?"

"They went in to save seats with my in-laws. Storm and I wanted to visit before going inside." Don gestured to the man with him, "Scott, this is my brother-in-law, Storm Vanderzee. Storm, this is my neighbor, Scott Severson."

Scott extended his hand to Storm, "Lois's dad."

"That's me," Storm accepted and shook Scott's hand. "It's a pleasure to meet you." Scott's short hair and flannel work shirt gave him the look of a working man, which impressed Storm.

Don looked at Scott. "So, the farm really is sold?"

"Lock, stock, and machinery. They're taking the house, farm, and everything with it. We're not taking much more with us than our clothes. We'll stay a few days to help him get started, and then we're gone."

Don asked, "Where to next?"

"Dad's brother died and left him his house in New Mexico. He gets to retire in a land without winter. I'll be working road construction and living on the road all summer."

"Why didn't you take over the farm?" asked Don.

"I thought about it, but then Dad would have stayed to help me, and that wouldn't be much of a retirement. Now he can afford to retire without any worries, and he deserves it."

"Well, we're going to miss you both, Scott. You were great neighbors. Be sure to stop by and see us before you go."

"I couldn't leave without saying goodbye."

"Before you go," Don glanced to Storm before looking back to Scott, "what can you tell me about the party tonight?"

Scott looked around to be sure no one else was listening. "It's a typical keg party for graduation. There'll be beer, pop, hotdogs, bonfire, music, and breakfast tomorrow morning."

"So, it *is* an all-nighter?" asked Storm.

"It is for anyone drinking. They can bring tents, sleeping bags, or sleep in their cars, but no one drives after they've been drinking. If anyone needs to leave tonight, they'll have to stick to pop. Car keys are collected before they get any beer."

Don nodded. "I guess that makes sense."

Storm looked concerned. "So, everyone's sleeping in their cars?"

"Unless they have other plans. Vanessa borrowed my tent, and a few more from other people. She has those set up for some of the girls. Some plan on just laying their sleeping bag on the ground."

"Are there any chaperones?" asked Storm.

"None officially, but it should be a big enough crowd so that no one will really be alone, if that makes you feel any better."

"Lois, my daughter, is planning on going with her boyfriend, Mike," Storm said with concern. "I just don't know if I trust him keeping her out all night."

Scott was pleased that Storm was not fond of Mike, but wondered how Storm would feel if he were the one dating Lois. "I understand. I'm not in Mike's fan club either, but he'd have more privacy at a drive-in theater than he would in a field full of classmates. This could be the most public date they've ever had."

Storm nodded. "I guess so. It's just... She's my only daughter. I worry about her, especially when she's with him."

"I understand," said Scott. "If it makes you feel better, I'll try to keep an eye on her."

"Thanks. I'd appreciate that." Storm looked at the box under Scott's arm, recognizing it as one holding his cap and gown. "You'd better be going. You've got a graduation to get to."

"Yes, I do." Scott nodded with satisfaction. "It's been a pleasure meeting you, Mr. Vanderzee."

As Scott hurried to the school, Don looked back to his friend and said, "I'm going to miss that boy."

"So, he was a good neighbor?"

"The best," Don answered without hesitation. "His whole family was. When I was laid up after that accident a couple years back, Scott came over and pretty much ran the farm until I was on my feet again."

"Really? I thought Tommy took care of everything."

"Tommy was the youngest of the boys, so he was used to his brothers handling most things. Scott was the only son of an aging father, so he was used to doing the same work as all my boys put together. Tommy might have managed the cows by himself, but I don't know if he would have gotten any crops in. We might not have made it without Scott's help."

"I'm glad he was there for you."

Don nodded. "And his mother died in that same accident."

"That was his mother in the car with you?" Storm asked with surprise.

"Yep," Don nodded. "Rachel got invited to prom, so she needed a dress. I was going to take her shopping in the Cities that day, but Lou had already promised to do something with the church. I don't know anything about buying dresses, so Ellie offered to go with us. She never had any girls to fuss with, so she was happy to go. We shopped, found a dress, and got dinner at Country Kitchen. All in all, it was a nice day, except for the shopping." Don paused as he remembered driving home that night.

"It was getting dark when we were on our way home. I was heading up a hill on highway 65 when some asshole tried to pass us. We were going up a hill, so I slowed down to let him get around. Another car came over the top of the hill, and he zipped back into my lane, pushing us off the road. The last thing I remember was the car rolling ass over tea kettle down the side of a hill. I woke up in the hospital, Rachel was rolling around in a wheelchair, and Ellie was dead."

"Did they catch the other driver?"

"They found the Trans Am he was driving wrapped around a tree, not too far from home. It had been reported stolen in Minneapolis a week earlier. He'd been bar hopping around the country, but everyone remembered the car more than they did him." Don took a deep breath and sighed. "When I asked Lou how Tommy was doing with the farm, she told me Scott was helping with the cows, plowing fields, and pretty much taking care of everything. His dad was doing everything on their farm, so Scott started working ours."

"Working through grief."

"I think so." Don looked over to where Scott had parked his car. "He wouldn't accept any pay, but he did accept that car when I offered it."

"Which one?"

"That brown '65 Rambler over there." Don pointed. "Rachel got her license, so I thought that would be a good first car for her. First thing she did was sit down and pull the lever on the side of the seat, and the back dropped down like a double bed. I never even thought of that car having Nash seats. I love and trust my daughter, but no father in his right mind can send his teenage daughter out in a car like that."

"I know what you mean," Storm said with a small laugh. "With him living next door, did you ever worry about him dating Rachel in that car?"

"No. Scott would be a great son-in-law, but he was like another brother to the kids. Besides, Rachel tells me that he only has eyes for one girl," Don grinned, "and you just asked him to keep an eye on her tonight."

* * *

While the school auditorium filled with friends and family, the graduating class gathered in the large second-floor study hall. All had either worn their gowns to the school or brought them to put on after they arrived. Name tags had been set on the desktops so we would be seated in the order our names would be called for graduation. If everyone found their desk and lined up as they were seated, they would be in the correct order for everything that followed.

When it was time to name the class valedictorian and salutatorian, the school principal looked at the lists of students as they were ranked by their grade point averages. When he noticed that their ranking was in boy/girl order, he decided to move the honor students to the lead so they would be called in order of class rank. Because of that change, everyone who had planned on walking with those honor students had to find new walking partners.

* * *

Peter Baker saw Rachel seated with her head on her desk. Seeing his name on the desk in front of her, Peter sat and turned to ask, "Rough night?"

Rachel slowly lifted her head and blinked. "It was my birthday. You're supposed to drink when you turn eighteen. Then Mom wouldn't let me sleep this morning. She even made me get up and go to church."

"That's not so bad. At least there wasn't any thunder when you walked in."

"No. The thunder was between my ears." Rachel looked to Peter, "Will you do me a big favor?"

"Like what?"

"Take notes and wake me up when it's time to leave for the gym. Until then, don't let anyone wake me."

"What's in it for me?" he asked jokingly.

"I'll let you in on a big secret: my last act of high school defiance."

"Sounds interesting." Peter found himself wondering if Rachel was really planning anything. With Rachel, you never knew what to expect.

* * *

Randy Richards entered the study hall and looked around, realizing he did not know the person he was looking for. He said, "Excuse me," as Eve Johnson was walking by.

"Yes?" Eve turned and immediately smiled when she saw him. He was of average height, slim build, but not too skinny. He had long sideburns and wavy blond hair that covered his ears, and eyes she would have gladly lost herself in.

"I'm looking for Richard Lester. Could you point him out for me?"

Eve brushed her long blonde hair back with her fingers as she turned to look around the room. "There he is." She pointed to the first row of desks on the left. "He's talking to Peter Baker." Realizing this man had no idea who Peter was either, she added, "standing by desk in front of the sleeping redhead."

"Thank you." Randy nodded with gratitude and headed in that direction.

"Any time," she said softly as she watched him walk away.

"Who's that?" Scott asked as he joined her.

Eve turned to see him. "There you are!" Looking back to watch Randy, she said, "Just some guy with dreamy eyes and a cute ass. He's looking for Rich." Looking back to the desks she said, "I already checked for our names in the first three rows from the right, so I think we'll be somewhere in the middle."

"Okay," Scott said, "I think the first row is all honor students, so we should be to the right of them."

Scott and Eve found their names on desks near the center of the study hall. Scott pulled his gown from its box, pulled it over his head, and set the graduation cap on the desk before sitting down.

"By the way, Scott," Eve began, "I want to thank you for asking me to walk with you."

"No problem. I'm just lucky you were still available when I asked. Vanessa asked me at the beginning of the year, but when the top ten got moved to the head of the line, she got stuck walking with Dave Masters. I just lucked out that you were available."

"Well, that was a lucky break for me." Eve sighed. "You know, at one time or another, I've dated most of the guys in this class. You'd think that one of them would have been willing to be seen with me at graduation."

"Well, it's their loss."

"It is now," Eve confirmed. "I realize that I may not be the kind of girl you want to bring home to meet your mother, but they didn't have to run and hide whenever I mentioned walking at graduation. If I'm not good enough to be seen with them when their families are watching, they're not good enough to ask me out when they want to go parking." Eve blushed when she realized how boldly she was speaking.

Scott wasn't sure how to respond. "Well, at least you were still willing to walk with me today."

"We've never been out together, so you don't count. You don't use someone just because she's easy. You're holding out for Miss Right, and I'm cool with that." Eve looked to see Lois Vanderzee with Mike Burman, as they looked for the desks with their names. "I admit, when you first asked me to walk with you today, I found myself wondering if you were interested. Maybe it's just the way I'm wired or something. Anyway, I've seen the way you look at Lois, and it's alright. I'm just glad to have someone to walk with."

Scott felt a warm blush when Eve mentioned Lois. "Well, there's not much chance of anything ever happening there anyway. Mike is her one and only, and there's nothing I can do about it." Looking to where Eve had glanced, Scott also saw Lois and Mike looking for their desks. Scott thought many couples looked right together, but he could never see that with Lois and Mike. Lois's long blond hair seemed to shine as it danced on the back of her green graduation gown, while Mike's brown hair hung stiffly from his cap to his collar, reminding Scott of a horse tail that had never been trimmed or brushed.

Eve said, "Don't be so sure. When Mike's in the army, Lois might start looking around. I'm sure Mike will do his share of looking when he's away."

Scott looked up with surprise. "Mike's going in the army?"

"He took some early enlistment deal, along with Alvin Murphy. They go in this week." Eve paused, before adding, "But that's supposed to be a secret, so forget I mentioned it."

Scott looked to where Mike and Lois were sitting together, wondering if Eve could be right. They did not look like a couple that was about to separate.

* * *

Mr. Opus, one of their class advisors, stepped to the front of the study hall and called for everyone to take their seats. He explained how we would soon leave the study hall, lined up as we were already sitting. He then gave us a brief rundown of the upcoming ceremony. When the ceremony was over, we were to leave the gym in the same order and return to the study hall, where we would return our rented caps and gowns. Peter woke Rachel when everyone began standing. We all marched two by two, out the door, down the stairs, and through the halls. The band began to play as we entered the gymnasium.

Graduation went as typical graduations go. The school principal, superintendent, and others who would be speaking sat at the rear of the stage. Among those speaking was Randy Richards, a popular Disk Jockey from the Twin Cities. A key speaker was needed for graduation, so our class asked Randy. No one had recognized him in the study hall earlier because we knew him only by his voice.

Not being used to a live audience that looked back, Randy planned to focus on one or two students, rather than the mass of people in attendance. When he noticed the red-haired girl who had been sleeping in the study hall, Randy decided to focus on her while he spoke. She was sitting up like everyone else, but

Randy could see that her eyes were closed, even though she sat up as if paying attention. He could not help but picture her looking alert as she slept in class.

Those who were seated on the stage arose in turn to make their brief, or not-so-brief, speeches. The school band played a song or two. Finally, Randy heard the flattering words of the person who introduced him as the most popular Disk Jockey in the Twin Cities area. That was Randy's cue to rise and walk to the podium.

"First of all, I want to thank you for inviting me to be here today," he began. "Second, I want to apologize. You see, I had a long well-written speech prepared, but after talking to some of you this morning, I realized that my speech does not fit this class. For that reason, I will disregard my planned speech, and I'm just going to wing it." After a slight pause, he continued, "That's okay. Winging it, or talking off-the-cuff, is pretty much what I do for a living. I must not be too bad at it, because it got me invited here."

Focusing on the still-closed eyes of the girl with long red hair, he said, "In the speech I had prepared, I planned to talk about how all of you have been together for twelve years and are now ready to move on in separate ways. This morning, I found out that many of you came from one room country schools, so you did not all come together until the schools merged several years ago. This surprised me because I grew up in a city that apparently lost touch with country life. We knew about one-room schools, but they made it sound like they were only something from pioneer days. I suspected they may have continued through the depression years, which still seems part of the distant past. I had no idea that we still had one room schools halfway through the 1960s. After talking to some of you earlier, I realized just how common those little country schools were, and still are. I guess that shows just how little some city schools know about what's going on in the world around them. We're not so far from our past as some might think."

Rachel's head began to tip, but she subconsciously shot up straight again.

"Even though you came together as a full group only six or seven years ago, you are all together now. All those little schools may have disappeared, but I'm sure the bond those students share will remain forever. Now you have the additional bond of this entire class. All those country schools have united, making you the Griffin High School class of seventy-two. You will soon be moving on in different directions, but each of you will always remain a part of this class."

Rachel began to lean to the side slightly; her head eased onto Peter's shoulder. Peter tipped his head with satisfaction.

"I recently attended my class reunion," Randy continued. "I realized that my class has a little bit of everyone. Rich man, poor man, beggar man, thief; doctor, lawyer, justice of the peace. However the poem goes, we were all there. Just about anything you could think of, we had it. Regardless of our differences, when we got together, we were still the same group that grew up together. We had all moved on with our lives, but when we got together, we were still us. We were still Eagles!"

"On that note," Randy shifted direction, "I must admit, being a Griffin is a whole lot cooler than being an Eagle. I mean, I don't think you could come up with a cooler mascot. Part lion, part eagle, and maybe a few other animals in there as well. How can anybody ever defeat a griffin? Okay, if the next school down the road were the dragons, they might have a chance?"

Rachel smiled in her slumber as if she were happy with Randy's words.

"You worked hard to get to where you are today. Some may think your education is over, but in truth, you've only just begun. Whether you are going on to college, trade school, or on-the-job training, you will continue learning. No matter what you decide to do, your education never ends. In work or home life, we are still always learning in one way or another. Someone once told me, 'When you meet someone who has nothing to teach you, it means you are not paying attention.' School only laid the groundwork for you to begin; your real education will never end."

Rachel leaned a bit more against Peter, which did not seem to bother him in the slightest.

"Last week, I read your local newspaper, The Griffin Gazette. It had all your pictures, and it said a little about everyone's plans. Some of you will be staying here, keeping life going in your own hometown. Some of you are going on to college, furthering your education before moving on in the world. Some are entering our armed forces to keep America safe. The different roads you take are all important. You are all individuals, finding your own roads. You are making your own lives and finding your own way. Your graduation today brings an end to one chapter of your life, so you will now simply move on to the next. You will now step out to make your own mark in the world."

Rachel shifted in her chair and nuzzled her head more comfortably onto Peter's shoulder.

"Whatever road you take, enjoy it and make it your own." Randy looked over the rest of the class and continued, "You may be doctors, ditch diggers, or president of the United States, but you will still remember the wonderful city you came from. I congratulate you all today. You are the Griffin High School, Class of seventy-two! GO GRIFFINS!" With that, Randy stepped back from the podium as the gymnasium broke out in applause. Rachel sat up to join us when she awoke to the sound of clapping. I cannot say if it was because Randy really inspired us, or if we were just glad the speeches were over, but every one of us did applaud.

Blinking her eyes, Rachel turned to Peter and said, "I feel great now. This is even better than church."

After Randy's speech, those on stage prepared to call names to hand out diplomas. Students would walk up in pairs, cross the stage one at a time to accept their diploma with a handshake, and step down from the stage. With diplomas in hand, they would pair up again and march back to their seats. Peter and Rachel were among the honor students who would be called in order of class rank. They stood together and began walking to the stage as the first names were called.

"Dave Masters," the voice on the public address system called.

"So," Peter turned to Rachel as they walked, "what's that big secret you were going to tell me?"

"What?" Rachel was confused until she remembered her promise to Peter.

"Vanessa Winters," the voice called the next name as Vanessa crossed to get her diploma.

"Oh, that," Rachel leaned close and spoke in a soft voice, "Underneath my gown today, I'm wearing my gym sneakers."

Names continued being called as they walked to the stage.

"Your sneakers are your big secret?" Peter was puzzled. Dave and Vanessa began their walk back to their seats. More names were called.

"That's it."

Another name was called as Peter began climbing the steps.

"Your gym sneakers are a secret?" he puzzled aloud as he turned to face the diplomas.

"That's it," she repeated as his name was called.

Peter pondered that as he crossed the stage to accept his diploma with one hand while shaking hands with the other. Rachel's name was called.

"That's it," echoed in his mind while Rachel was accepting her diploma. He began to descend the steps at the other end of the stage when he looked back to see how Rachel's gown hung on her. Her words echoed in his head once more as Peter finally understood her meaning. *"That's it,"* was her secret. As in, gym sneakers, and *"that's IT!"* Stepping on the edge of the step, Peter stumbled and fell, landing face down with his graduation gown sliding nearly to his waist as he sprawled onto the gymnasium floor.

Rachel was quickly by his side and helping him up as she said, "Boy, I'm glad I didn't do that."

Peter stood straight and held his diploma high to show that he was alright. Recovering from the embarrassment of falling, Peter smiled as he marched back to their chairs with Rachel by his side.

"Well, this is it," Rachel said as they retook their seats. "We're almost out of here."

"Almost," Peter agreed with a smile. "First, we go back to the study hall... to return our caps and gowns. Remember, they're only rented." Peter's grin grew as he watched Rachel's eyes widen at his words.

* * *

As graduates, we left the auditorium paired up the same as when we arrived. Rachel was at the door waiting for Scott when he and Eve arrived.

"Scott," Rachel pleaded, "I need help! You're smart, so tell me you'll think of something!"

"Whoa!" Scott looked at her with concern. "What's wrong?"

"We can't leave until we turn in our robes. I told them that I have to go home for pictures first, but they said we were supposed to do that before coming. They won't let me leave until I give them my robe!"

"Robes," mused Peter, "I like that. Everyone has been calling them gowns. Somehow robe sounds so much more masculine. Or is it just me?"

"That was the deal," Scott reminded her. "No one wanted to pay what they charge to buy the robes. We only needed them for the ceremony, so we rented them. Now we give them back, but we do get to keep the tassels. What's the problem?"

"The problem is, I forgot we have to turn them in!" Rachel turned to look at Peter for help as she tried to explain.

"The problem is," Peter explained, "in Rachel's excitement, sense of rebellion, or just hung-over feeling this morning, she neglected to wear anything but gym sneakers under her graduation gown."

Scott nodded with a growing grin. "It's like skinny dipping at graduation. I like it. That is so Rachel. In fact, I think this is the Rachelest thing you have ever done."

Rachel cried, "Don't laugh at me; think of something. You're good at that, so think."

"Okay," Scott spoke in a calm voice to relax her. "First thing we have to do is go to the library."

"Why?"

"Because you have to use the bathroom, and the closest one is in the library."

"Okay Scott, but if you try to wrap me up in toilet paper and tell everyone it's a dress..." Rachel's voice trailed off as they walked away.

Eve tried to stop Scott, but they were already heading for the door which connected the study hall to the school library. She turned to Peter and said, "I'm going to turn my robe in and run home for a second. Tell them to wait in the library. Or ... just have them wait .... And tell me where they went when I get back!"

Mr. Opus stopped Scott and Rachel at the library door, saying, "The library is closed today."

Scott said, "I know, but she has to use the bathroom, and I need to get something from the prop room."

"There's a bathroom down the hall," said Mr. Opus.

"I can't make it that far." Rachel crouched slightly, showing signs of urgency. "That ceremony lasted longer than my body expected."

"Okay," Mr. Opus opened the door. "I'm coming in too, to watch the library while you're in there. And what exactly did you need to get?"

"It's in the back room." Scott pointed as Rachel hurried to wait in the library's restroom. "The one where you store all the props from the school plays. We did that play about a detective this year, and I brought in an old trench coat for the play. I was hoping I could still get it today."

"That was a good play. I remember you bringing it in, so ... Let's see if we can find it." As he unlocked the storeroom door, Mr. Opus said, "I thought you were donating that coat, in case they ever do another play like that."

"I was, but something came up and I have a friend who needs it."

"Okay." Mr. Opus picked the trench coat out of other costumes, which hung on a small closet rack. "Thank you for the loan. That coat was perfect for that play."

Coming back through the library, Scott stopped by the restroom. Knowing Mr. Opus wasn't about to let him walk into the ladies' room, he said, "Okay, here's the thing. Rachel wore very tight pants today, and... did you see when she bent over to help when Peter fell off the steps?"

Mr. Opus nodded suspiciously.

"Well, when she bent over, she could hear and feel the back side of her pants rip out. Now she can't take her robe off until she has something to cover her backside." Scott leaned close to whisper, "She's not wearing any underwear."

Mr. Opus smiled in understanding. "I knew this would happen when girls started wearing their pants so tight. Okay, but don't go in. Just call to her and toss it in the door."

One minute later, a smiling Rachel emerged with the coat buttoned up and her graduation gown hanging loosely over one arm. The trench coat covered her almost as well as the gown had.

After turning their gowns in, Scott and Rachel stepped out of the study hall together. Rachel said, "Now all I have to do is explain the trench coat to my parents."

Peter met them at the door and pointed to Eve, who hurried toward them with a cloth shopping bag in hand.

"Nice coat, but I think we need another bathroom break." Eve took Rachel by the hand and pulled her to the bathroom down the hall. Once in the restroom, Eve handed Rachel the bag.

"Fortunately, I live practically across the street, so it only took me a minute to get this."

Rachel looked into the bag. "Eve, you're a lifesaver."

Taking the bag into the end stall, Rachel took off the trench coat and put on clean underwear, a loose-fitting bra, short sleeve white shirt, and a denim skirt. Once dressed, Rachel looked at herself in the bathroom mirror. "I think I used to have an outfit like this."

"You did. I found it in the Thrift Store. I took the hem down a little, but I think it's the same one you used to wear."

"I don't know how to thank you. I'll give this back at tonight's party."

Eve shrugged. "Keep it. I think I can spare one of your old outfits. I'm not sure if I'll go to the party anyway."

Rachel rolled the coat into a ball. "Why not?"

"I don't know if I should. I've sworn off most of the guys in our class." She held the bag up so Rachel could fit the coat into it. "Scott offered to bring me, but I know it wouldn't be a date or anything. He said he's going to be busy guiding people in for quite a while anyway."

"So come hang out with me. If you don't want to ride out with Scott, I can bring you. It's the least I can do. You can even sleep in my car. You're taller, so I'll let you have the back seat. Just you though. I don't want to listen to any companions. Who knows? Maybe you'll meet someone new tonight."

"Maybe I should go there with Scott. There is something I'd like to talk to him about. If I can sleep in your car, could you give me a ride home tomorrow? I don't expect anything to click with Scott, so I shouldn't be counting on him for a ride home."

Chapter 3: Getting to the Party

There is one thing I should explain to those of you who were born in later years. In March of 1972, Wisconsin passed the eighteen-year-old minority law. This law gave everyone in Wisconsin full adult rights at age eighteen. We could sign our own contracts, marry without parental consent, and be responsible for our own debts. Basically, everything previously reserved for twenty-one-year-olds became legal at eighteen. Most noted of those rights, we could now buy, sell, and consume alcohol. The drinking age went back to twenty-one in 1984, but all other rights remained at eighteen.

Many of us had graduation parties with friends and family. Some would stay at those parties well into the night. Others would delay their parties for another date or end them early so they could attend Rich and Danny's all-night party. A small fee, something like five or ten dollars, covered admission to the party. That was to cover expenses and hopefully leave some profit for them.

Danny was first to arrive, bringing two kegs of cold beer from his uncle's bar. An old cattle tank had been partially filled with water and surrounded with baled hay and straw for insulation. He set the kegs into the tank and added several blocks of ice, and cases of Shasta pop. After tapping the first keg, he poured a large bag of ice cubes over its top. More ice blocks were added with new arrivals, as some of us had been freezing milk cartons of water at home in anticipation of this night. Scott's home freezer had been filled with nothing but ice blocks, all of which were now added to this water tank. When beer cups were finally set up, the tank was overflowing with ice water.

Greg Peterson arrived and backed his pickup to the edge of our party area. Greg had graduated a year earlier, but he was friends with many in our class and was engaged to Donna Strong, one of our classmates. Her parents no longer wanted to delay the wedding, as Donna had already begun wearing maternity clothes.

Greg opened the tailgate of his truck and Donna removed picnic coolers and other supplies, setting them on a table made of covered hay bales. She set out paper plates, buns, condiments, and roasting sticks, along with marshmallows, graham crackers, and chocolate bars for s'mores.

A pair of large speakers stood in the back of Greg's truck, which he connected to his truck's stereo. When he turned on the radio in his truck, the music could be heard throughout our party area. We listened to AM radio when the party began. When the signal began to fade, we switched and listened to Greg's 8-track tapes.

* * *

Rich Lester arrived, followed by a white '62 Ford Thunderbird convertible. Randy Richards got out of the Thunderbird to greet the others. He smiled when he heard his station playing on the radio. If he had not traded shifts to get this day off, it would have been his show we were listening to. Rich had contacted Randy in advance, asking him to meet before graduation. When they met in the study hall, Rich invited him to the party.

Randy looked around, surveying their party grounds. A river ran alongside their main party and camping area, not too far from the water tank holding the beer and pop. There were a couple of picnic tables and many hay bales provided seating throughout the area. There were two stone-ringed fire pits, a large one for a bonfire and a smaller one for roasting hot dogs and marshmallows. A special grill Danny and Rich had made in Metal Shop stood not far from the picnic tables. This grill had a large griddle for cooking pancakes, eggs, and sausage for tomorrow's breakfast. Next to the camping and party area, a large hay field, not yet ready for cutting, provided plenty of open area for parking.

All of this was surrounded by woods, with a wide driveway leading to the road.

Rich unloaded party supplies from his car before showing Randy around.

Randy said, "So, this is a field party."

"It will be when people start coming," said Rich. "In older days, someone would get a keg, find a field or someplace the cops wouldn't show up, charge admission, and drink until the keg was empty. Now most of us are eighteen, so getting raided wouldn't be such a big deal. Still, it's best to keep the location secret."

Carol Murphy quickly joined them, holding up an open envelope with Rich's name.

Rich dropped his car keys into the envelope. "How do you like that? I throw a party, and my keys are the first to go."

Carol sealed the envelope with the keys inside and handed Rich a paper name tag to stick to his shirt. "No keys, no name tag. No name tag, no beer. No exceptions!" Carol produced another envelope with Randy's name and held it open for Randy's keys.

Randy said, "I need to leave early in the morning. How will I get my keys back?"

Carol said, "I'll give everyone's keys back during breakfast tomorrow morning."

"I've got the morning shift tomorrow. I should leave between four and five a.m."

Carol thought about that. "As long as you don't get shitfaced, that should work. Donna isn't drinking, so I'll let her be the judge. We'll come up with a way to get your keys to you before then."

"Alright." Randy dropped the keys into the envelope. When Carol gave him his name tag, he peeled the paper off the back and stuck it on his shirt pocket. "Far out! Name tags, just like at my class reunion."

"That's right," Rich said. "This is our Five Hour Class Reunion!"

* * *

"So, how's this work?" Eve asked Scott as they sat in the front seat of Scott's Rambler. They were parked at the Polk County Park and Campground. Eve wore a white peasant blouse that showed off her assets, knowing the effect it would have on some of the boys she was no longer interested in.

Scott said, "Only a few people know where the party is, so everyone was told to meet us here. Ray and I will take turns leading them."

"Where is the party?"

"It's part of the Lester farm. Just woods by the road, but a driveway cuts through to a hay field between the woods and Apple River. Rich and Danny cleaned up the area by the river for camping. It's been their private campground for years, so it didn't take too much work to set up for tonight's party."

"Through the woods and facing the river, I think Rich took me parking there once. That's a nice spot." Eve thought about their security. "Do you think we might get raided?"

"Not likely. It's isolated enough to keep anyone from getting in to surprise us. Most of us are eighteen now, but not everyone. If we were raided, it would be easy to just hide anyone who's still underage in the woods."

Eve thought about that, and decided not to mention that she would be one of those hiding if they were raided. She shifted in her seat to face him. "Scott, why does Mike Burman hate you?"

"I didn't realize he did." Scott seemed unconcerned. "If it makes any difference, I never liked him much either. Maybe it's because I like Lois."

"I think it goes farther back. I think it may be more the other way around. I get the impression that he goes with Lois, so he can keep her from going out with you. Does that make any sense?"

"Not really, but neither does Mike. What's he got against me?"

"He said something once, about you breaking his hand when you were in grade school."

"Grade school?" Scott paused to think and remember. "In grade school I was in River Bend, along with Ray, Rich, Rachel, and Vanessa. That was all in our grade anyway." Scott considered what she had said. "You said I broke his hand? That does ring a bell. There was a kid who was one year ahead of us. Maybe that WAS Mike. I think his dad was working on one of the farms in the area. They lived in a trailer on the farm, so he went to River Bend." Scott closed his eyes as he thought back to remember Mike in their old school. "He always acted like he was the boss of everyone. He was the only one in his class. He seemed to think being older meant he was better. He's in our grade now, so he must have been held back a year. I guess he wasn't better than us after all."

Scott recalled the incident with Mike's fist. "He tried to pick a fight with me by the school building one day. I didn't want to fight, but he pushed me back to the wall. When I couldn't back up anymore, he tried to punch me in the face. I shifted to the side, and he punched the wall. Then he was crying because he broke his fist." Scott paused and turned to look at Eve. "I had forgotten all about that. I never even connected him with that school bully, until you mentioned the broken fist. If he's still mad about that, I just turned out of the way. He's the one who punched the wall. Then his mom picked him up, and I never saw him again. At least not until the schools merged in 6th grade."

Eve said, "I think part of it is from things his father said. It sounds like his father was all macho with him. Telling him he needs to be a REAL MAN, settle scores, things like that. That was also the day they arrested his father. That's why he and his mother moved to town."

"How did you come to know all this?"

"Sometimes, Mike talks to me." Eve nervously fiddled with her purse as she tried to explain. "It started when I worked at A&W. He got there around closing time and offered me a ride home. I told him 'I don't go with other girl's boyfriends.' He held his hand up to show me that Lois had given back his ring.

He said he was a free agent. I figured, what the heck, and we went for a ride after my shift was done. We talked a lot. It turns out, we were good at talking to each other. He likes to talk. He's a good listener too. Then we parked ... and stuff." Eve shook her head slightly. "Monday morning, we were back in school, and Lois was wearing his ring again. It was always pretty much like that."

This surprised Scott. "I didn't know they ever broke up."

"They broke up quite a few times. I think it was usually because Lois wouldn't put out. She told him she won't do it while she's in high school, and he doesn't like waiting. So, he breaks up just long enough to get it somewhere else; then he runs back to make up with her before anyone finds out they had a fight. I think he convinces her that he was just sitting at home crying without her."

"And he tells you about this?"

"He comes to me when she gives him his ring. Then it's official, and he talks me into going for a ride. I know I shouldn't, but Mike can be persuasive. We always talk first. I don't think he realizes how much he tells me. It's like we really connect and understand each other. Then we park ..." Eve sighed. "After he got what he wanted, he runs back to Lois."

"And Lois never knows?"

"It's not something I can tell her. I would come off sounding like I was trying to cause trouble or take him away from her. You can bet he never mentioned it." Eve slowly shook her head and looked back to Scott. "I'm not the only one either. He told me about the girls he sees when he spends time with his dad, and some outside of Griffin. They don't know about Lois, so he doesn't even break up when he goes to them."

Scott remembered what Eve had said earlier. "What's this about the army?"

"His dad used to tell him the army would make a real man out of him, so he decided to do the early enlistment thing with Alvin Murphy. I don't know for sure, but I think they go in this week. He said it's a secret, so he might not have mentioned it to Lois."

"Why wouldn't he tell her about that?"

"He never said, but I think I figured it out." Eve held her purse tight and looked at Scott. "Lois won't do *it* while she was still in school, but we graduated today. If she doesn't know he's leaving, he probably thinks he's still got a shot. I think he wants her notch in his belt before he leaves."

"Could you say something to her?"

"Do you think she would believe me? He would say that I was just making things up because I wanted him, which I don't! He is convincing, and she would believe him." Eve turned to look out the windshield. "Still, it might be worth it. Maybe one of us will get a chance to say something tonight."

"Thanks." Scott looked thoughtful. "Maybe one of us will."

Scott looked to see a green, '64 Chrysler New Yorker pulling into the campground. "Ray's here."

Ray Ellis parked his car and walked over to his best friend and Eve. "Check it out." Ray held up his new camera. "Graduation present from Mom. It's a Pentax, K-1000, SLR. Same as the one I used for the yearbook. The viewfinder looks through the lens, so the picture I see is the picture I shoot. Also, I can slow the shutter speed for low light."

Scott could see how happy Ray was with his new camera. "Would you two like to be alone?"

"Not yet." Ray patted his shirt pocket. "I still have my Instamatic, and I haven't told her that she's being replaced. I don't have a flash for the new one yet, so I'll use the Instamatic after it gets dark."

Ray looked up and saw two cars pulling into the campground. "It looks like we have customers."

* * *

Scott led the first two cars to the party field, leaving Eve to join the party when he left. When he returned, Ray left, leading four more cars. They continued this way, one always waiting with new arrivals until the other had returned. It was getting dark when Ray guided his last car. Scott decided to stay a little longer, just in case anyone else showed up.

* * *

When Rachel arrived, her first action was to find Eve and lead her back to the parked cars. "This is Roberta," she said proudly when they stopped by a '62 four door Plymouth Savoy. It was cream colored with reddish primer applied in camouflage-like patches. "I almost got Scott's car, but then Dad realized it had Nash seats. He gave the Rambler to Scott and found this one for me. She may not look like much, but I love her." Opening the back door, Rachel grabbed the cloth shopping bag Eve had given her earlier. "I have your clothes in here. Thank you again! Mom recognized the outfit and never suspected a thing. I had some other laundry, so I did a quick wash and dry, so they're clean and fresh."

"You didn't have to," Eve assured her. "I wouldn't have minded if you kept them."

"It's the least I could do. You saved my butt today." Rachel returned the bag to the car. "If I don't give you a ride home tomorrow, you can get it when you leave. Also, you can have the back seat to sleep tonight. No telling what tonight will bring, but Roberta is here for you."

* * *

Scott arrived, leading a dark blue, '68 Lincoln Continental. "We have our straggler," Scott announced as Dave Masters followed him to the party. Waving a hand to signal Carol Murphy, he said, "Dave, I believe Carol has an envelope with your name on it."

After dropping Dave's car keys into an envelope with his name, Carol gave Dave a name tag, explaining that it would grant him access to the keg.

A surprised Rich Lester walked up to Dave and handed him a red plastic cup. "Dave!" Rich was now speaking with a slight slur, revealing he had already made a few trips to the keg. "Good to see you! I didn't think you came to parties like this."

"School is done, and grades are in. Harvard, Princeton, and the others have my transcripts and applications." Dave smiled with satisfaction. "Now I'm free to relax and enjoy life for the rest of the summer."

Rich gave Dave a pat on the back. "Well, what better way to start than with your first kegger?"

Ray had been watching for Scott and hurried over to meet him, "Do you have your spotlight in your car, and are you going out again?"

"Yes and no. Why?"

"When I was leading that last car over here, another car was following behind us, so I turned into the gravel pit to lose them. I got out to explain why we stopped. I dropped my keys when I was walking back to my car. I think the Instamatic fell out of my shirt pocket when I picked them up. I didn't realize it was missing until after I turned my keys in and started drinking." Ray let out a sigh. "I'll just get up early so I can look for it before any trucks show up in the morning. If I don't find it," he held up his new SLR, "I've still got her."

"That should work." Scott saw Rachel leaving the keg. "I need to talk to Rachel; I'll catch up with you later." As he walked in her direction, Scott called, "Rachel, could I please have a word with you?"

With her freshly filled beer cup, Rachel hurried to meet Scott while he was still out of earshot of anyone else. "I've got your trench coat in the trunk of my car. I knew I could count on you to think of something today. Then Eve came through even better. I owe you both."

"You can keep the trench coat. My car is full, and you may want to take up flashing someday." Speaking softer, he said, "Two things. One: the family buying our farm has three sons, ages 11, 13, and 15. I thought you should be aware of that before heading down to the swimming hole."

"Damn! That's too young. This could put an end to my skinny dipping. I'm going to have to keep my T-shirt and panties on from now on."

"I've seen your T-shirt and panties," he said with a grin. "When they're wet, they highlight more than they hide."

Rachel made a small shimmy before saying, "That's first, so what's second?"

"After all these years, how come you never told me that Lois was your cousin?"

"That's right. Her mother is my mom's sister." Rachel looked up to Scott with a sly grin, "I know you! If I told you that, it would be the only thing you ever talked to me about. I would be swimming naked, and you would be saying, *'How's your cousin? Did you talk to her about me? When are you bringing Lois to the swimming hole? Does she know I'm alive?'* There would be no end to it." Glancing down for a moment, she added, "And admit it. If you ever thought about Lois while you were at the swimming hole, you'd never come out of the water."

Scott let out a small laugh, "You're probably right. So why didn't you ever bring her to the swimming hole?"

"Too much competition." Rachel turned to walk away. "She might look better without a swimming suit than me." She looked back to Scott saying, "Besides, you couldn't handle it. Look at you. Just thinking about it is making you weak in the knees. You would die of a heart attack if you ever saw her there."

"It would be worth it," Scott called as she walked away. "You could both wear T-shirts. I would even loan her mine."

Scott walked to where Carol waited with his envelope and name tag. Looking into the crowd, he said, "Mike Burman has a pop can in his hand. Isn't he drinking?"

"No. He said he might have to bring Lois home, so he's drinking pop."

Scott saw the red cup in Lois's hand. "But Lois is drinking?"

"Yes, but he's driving. If you see her sharing her beer with him, let me know and I'll get his keys." Carol held the envelope up to Scott.

Scott looked at the envelope and said, "Not yet. I think I'll just stick to pop for now."

Chapter 4: Five-Hour Reunion

Eve was refilling her beer cup when Rachel asked, "Who's the cute guy with the guitar?"

"That's Randy Richards," said Eve.

"Randy Richards, the guy from the radio?"

"Yeah! He gave the speech at graduation today. Rich talked him into coming tonight."

"And I thought he was someone's date."

"As far as I know, he's available." Eve leaned close with a slight grin, "I planned on being good tonight, but for him, I could make an exception."

Randy sat on a bale of hay, holding his guitar as if he were about to play, occasionally fingering notes along with the music on the radio. He was feeling the music, but not actually playing anything. Several classmates, both boys and girls, sat on hay bales near him as they talked with our celebrity. Randy looked up to see Rachel, who was wearing a short loose-fitting pullover shirt with a tan print. Randy smiled when he saw her and said, "Aurora! It's so nice to see you."

"Excuse me?" Rachel was confused.

"I wasn't sure if I should come here tonight, but I realized that this was probably the only chance I would have to meet the Lovely Aurora." Standing up, Randy held his guitar to the side with his left hand, while extending his right hand out to Rachel. "Randy Richards. It's a pleasure to meet you in person."

"Yes. I know who you are." The confused Rachel shook Randy's hand. "I listen to you on the radio, and you gave a speech at the school today."

Randy grinned, "Did you enjoy my speech?"

"I loved it," she bluffed.

"Wonderful!" Randy set his guitar down, leaning it against the hay bale he had been sitting on. "You see, I've been asked to make another speech for a rotary club, and I was wondering if I could just recycle the same speech for them. Do you think it would work for a group like that?"

"Oh... that should work." Rachel had no idea what Randy had said in his speech, but why not?

"And the following week, a Ladies Aid Society wants me to speak there too. What do you think? Would they like the same speech?"

"Totally different groups, but why not? I'm sure they'll all enjoy it just as much as we did."

One of the girls sitting nearby said, "Go Griffins!"

"Oh yeah," added another. "He should definitely leave that part in."

Randy nodded, "Thank you, Aurora. That means a lot to me."

"Why are you calling me Aurora?"

Peter Baker answered from the haybale he was sitting on, "I think that was the name of the Princess in Sleeping Beauty."

Rachel blushed and looked down. "You could tell? I mean, you were up on the stage."

"I don't think anyone else noticed." Randy leaned close to say, "It's just that I have a good eye for drool. And don't worry. I spoke louder when you started to snore, so I don't think anyone noticed."

"I did not snore!" Rachel stated with certainty. "And I'm pretty sure I never drooled either."

Peter chimed in with, "Hey, it was the drool running off my shoulder that made me slip off the steps."

"I know why you slipped!" Rachel stopped, not wanting to say any more about that.

"It's okay," Randy assured her. "You were out before I began, so I know I wasn't the one who put you to sleep. I think it was just my soothing voice that made you so relaxed in your slumber."

"Okay." Rachel nodded.

"The only real drawback," Randy explained, "is that now Peter can truthfully tell people that you slept with him."

Rachel glared at Peter. "He wouldn't dare." She turned back to look at Randy's guitar. "Do you really play that?"

"Not much, but I do pick at it a little. It's mostly just a prop to make me look cool. Also, it keeps my hands busy, so I don't drink too much. Phil took my shift today, so I need to leave early and cover his shift in the morning."

* * *

We mulled about and enjoyed the party. Some danced to the music from Greg's stereo. Most gathered around the bonfire with conversation and beer. The smaller campfire was usually surrounded by classmates roasting marshmallows or hotdogs.

Ray Ellis wandered about taking random pictures with his new camera. When we saw Ray's pictures at later reunions, we enjoyed the memories he had captured. Ray lost his light with the setting sun, but he continued taking pictures by slowing his shutter speed and relying on light from tiki torches.

* * *

"I thought you might be getting hungry." Rachel offered Randy a freshly roasted hotdog.

"Thank you." Randy set his guitar down behind him and accepted the hotdog.

"To be honest, that one burned more than I like, so I roasted another for me. I figured I could unload that one on you." Rachel took a bite of the dog she had kept for herself.

"Or maybe, you just want to show me that you can cook." Randy bit his hotdog with a smug grin.

Eve looked over to Danny and said, "You know what makes hotdogs even better? You put a slice of cheese in the bun first.

Then the hot dog melts the cheese just right, and the ketchup doesn't soak into the bun so much."

Dave Masters said, "That sounds good. I'll have to try it."

Rich Lester said, "So before our next party, we'll have to get a good block of government cheese."

Eve glared at Rich, knowing that was meant as an insult, referring to her single mother relying on welfare programs, such as cheese and other food commodities.

Randy looked down the hill, seeing the tiki torches reflecting in the water. "It's nice here. The river's a nice touch."

"That's the Apple River. It's the same river everyone goes tubing down in Somerset. Although, if you began up that way," Rachel pointed upriver to the north, "you could start at the Polk County Campground, and you would pass by here." She turned to point downriver. "Continue a little farther down, and you'll come to the old River Bend schoolhouse. I used to go to school there."

"That's the one room school Rich told me about this morning. I mentioned that in my speech."

"It's really two rooms. People forget about the pullout divider that separated the younger grades." Rachel looked back to the river. "That would be a good ride by itself. Then if you kept going, you'd eventually come to the swimming hole between Scott and my family's farms." She looked back to Randy with a devilish smile, "I think you would like that swimming hole."

Donna wore an anxious expression as she approached Danny. "Great party. Greg said you guys had everything we needed, so... where's the ladies' room?"

Danny stood up to point as he said, "See those tiki torches along the edge of the woods? Follow them and they'll take you to an outhouse. There's a lantern with a new battery lighting it inside. And we have water buckets sitting on haybales outside, so you can wash your hands when you're done. It's hardly ever used, so it's still nice inside."

Donna thanked Danny and turned to head for the outhouse, and several other girls immediately got up to follow her. Peter looked surprised, as he was talking to Eve when she suddenly stood up to walk away with the others.

Randy laughed when he saw Peter's expression. "Get used to it Pete. I think the last girl to go to a Ladies' room by herself was Eve. The original Eve!" Randy looked up to see Rachel was still standing by him as she finished her hot dog.

Rachel noticed that Randy was looking at her and said, "I went before I came. I'm good for at least another beer. The line should be down by then. I hear it only has one hole, so I've got plenty of time."

Peter stood and was about to follow the girls when Carol stopped him. "That's the ladies' room Pete." She pointed to the woods in the other direction. "See that torch out there? It's next to a tree with a sign that says, 'MEN'S ROOM.' Just watch out for wild animals."

Rachel took the last bite of her hot dog and looked beyond the fire, to the river. Ray Ellis brought his camera up to focus on Rachel. The light from the Tiki torch seemed to cascade off Rachel's long red hair. Ray adjusted his stance, so his camera would be looking up at Rachel. Being the shortest in her class, it wasn't often that Rachel had pictures taken from that angle. After snapping the first picture, Ray stood level with her face and snapped another. Ray then stood at his full height, so he was looking slightly down at her for his last shot. Randy had watched Ray closely as he snapped each picture. Getting Ray's attention, he asked, "Could I get one of those?"

"If it comes out," Ray said. "I'm working without a flash tonight, so good shot or blur depends on how steady my hands are."

As most of the remaining crowd migrated to the campfire to roast their own hot dogs or marshmallows, Randy noticed that he and Rachel were alone. "Rachel, could you sit here for a moment? I have a question for you." Randy moved over, leaving room for her on his hay bale.

Rachel sat next to Randy and said, "Okay, but if this is a proposal, you have to get down on one knee."

"No, we just met." Randy looked around to see no one else was currently within earshot. "I just had to know. At the graduation today, were you naked under that gown?"

"That does it," she snapped. "I'm going to kill Peter." She saw the surprised look on Randy's face. "Scott?" Seeing no change of expression, she said, "Eve?"

Before she could name anyone else, Randy explained, "Rich asked to see me before graduation. He wanted to talk to me about coming here tonight. While I was talking to him, you were sleeping on the desk. Your hair settled down so that your neck was uncovered. The collar of your gown was standing up, just enough for a clear view of your back. I only got a quick glance before I looked up. I didn't want anyone to see me staring down a girl's gown. Now, I'm still wondering if I really saw the naked back that I thought I saw."

"Okay," Rachel stood so she could look down at him as she confessed. "Yesterday was my birthday, so I was hungover when I got dressed this morning. I forgot we had to give our robes back, so I had to leave the study hall wearing Scott's trench coat. I went to bed with my shoes on last night, I swim in the buff, and I kill alarm clocks. Am I missing anything?"

Randy looked at her with a smile. "Happy Birthday."

"Thank you." Rachel handed him her red cup. "Save this for me. I need to talk to my cousin."

* * *

Donna stepped out of the outhouse feeling relieved. "I really needed that. I think someone was standing on my bladder." As soon as Donna was out, the next girl in line raced in and shut the door.

"How is it?" someone asked.

46

"Nice. It may stink by morning, but right now it's good." Donna was washing her hands in one of the buckets when Rachel arrived.

Rachel walked straight to Lois, and said, "Okay! You're my cousin and I love you, but I gotta ask, why the hell are you still with Mike? Is he hung like a horse or what?"

Lois, who was already a little drunk, looked back with surprise. "What? Mike is my boyfriend, and ... I don't know."

"I know he's your boyfriend. You dated Bill, and when you broke up with him, Mike was on you before Bill had a chance to cry about it. I can understand you going with him then, but it's been, what, two years now? He's such a dick sometimes, so the only reason I see for you staying with him, is because he has a big one and knows how to use it. Is that it?"

"I don't know." Lois blushed. "We never..."

"You never, but he has." The words were out of Eve's mouth before she had time to think, but she was glad she said it.

A confused Lois looked at Eve and back to Rachel. "Mike's been my boyfriend for two years, and he's so patient and understanding."

"Not the whole two years. There were times he was showing his ring off and saying he was a free man." Eve wasn't as drunk as Lois, but she was drunk enough to speak more freely.

"But he always came back and apologized," said Lois, surprised that Eve had known of their breakups.

"Only because he got what he wanted somewhere else. He just wanted his brand on you before you went back to school. And how much has he told you about when he stays with his dad?"

"Sometimes he works with his dad. It's only a week or two, and he missed me the whole time." Even as Lois defended Mike, part of her began to wonder how Eve could have known any of this.

Eve let out a snort. "He was never alone long enough to miss you. There's a lot he never tells you about the trips with his dad too."

Lois snapped back, "How would you know? Mike barely even knows you!"

Eve wanted to say just how well Mike really did know her, but somehow lost her nerve. She simply closed her mouth and held up one hand in surrender.

This exchange surprised Rachel, so she waited until they were finished before saying, "I'm sorry cousin, but I have a friend I love like a brother, and he's been in love with you since sixth grade. Mike always seems like such a dick, so why are you still with him?"

"What?" Lois's mind was clouded with beer, and now Rachel's comments confused her even more. "Who...? Nobody's in love with me."

Vanessa chimed in with, "If you believe that, you really are blind. He just won't say anything because you always had a boyfriend."

"It doesn't matter." Eve regained some of her courage. "Mike's going in the army this week, so he'll be out of the picture anyway." Everyone stopped to look at Eve, who lowered her voice to say, "But that's a secret, so pretend I never mentioned it."

Rachel gave Eve a confused look before turning back to Lois. "I just want to know, are you with Mike because you love him? Or are you with him because you like having a boyfriend? If it's option B, just look around before it's too late. You do have options, but he's about to leave town, and there's nothing left to bring him back."

Vanessa said, "I bet he would stay here if someone gave him a reason."

Rachel looked back to Lois. "I'm being selfish. My favorite like-a-big-brother is about to leave, and I'm going to be all alone at the swimming hole. I just wish I could see him happy before he goes."

"Swimming hole?" Carol looked at Rachel with curiosity.

Rachel sighed, "Yeah, but he says a bunch of toddlers are going to find it, so it will never be the same anyway?" Having slightly distracted herself she said, "I wonder if they'll take down our *'Clothing Optional'* sign?"

Lois was even more confused. "I really don't know what you're talking about."

"Most of the time I don't either." Rachel looked into Lois's eyes. "Listen, just talk to Scott before it's too late. Talk to him. You might forget what you ever saw in Mike."

Carol waited. When Lois didn't respond, she looked back to Rachel, asking, "So, are you going to fill us in on that swimming hole?"

Rachel turned back to Lois. "That too! Go swimming with Scott for one minute. Then you'll wonder what you ever saw in Mike."

The door opened, allowing the girl who was in the outhouse to step out. A confused Lois stepped in and quickly pulled the door shut.

"I tried." Rachel turned away with a sigh.

"Wait a minute, Rachel." Vanessa stopped her. "You started something. Now we want details."

"Whaaat?" Now it was Rachel who looked confused.

"Tell us about the swimming hole!" demanded Carol.

"Oh, that." Rachel looked around and saw all eyes were on her. "There's a big swimming hole off the river where our farms meet. It's a fantastic place to swim, like a big deep wart on the curve of the river. After a long day of farming, the guys would jump in to cool off. When I was little, I would trot out there and go swimming with my brothers. When Mom realized that we never brought swimsuits, she said I was getting too big to go skinny dipping with my brothers. She was firm on it. We all had to either wear suits, or swim separately. It's one of the drawbacks of being the only girl."

"And Scott?" implored Vanessa.

"Mom never even thought about Scott swimming there too. She just made sure my brothers weren't there when I went. Scott would be cooling off in the water, and I'd jump in. We've been swimming out there since we were little, so we never thought anything of it. It did seem odd a few times as we got older. We just stayed in the water more and tried not to get caught looking." Rachel realized all the girls were staring at her. "All we ever did was swim. It was fun, but nothing ever happened. Scott only has eyes for Lois, so it was like he couldn't even see me."

Vanessa asked, "And how much do you see?"

Rachel looked at her with a grin, "Enough for you to regret blowing me off when I asked if you wanted to go swimming last summer."

"So," Carol asked, "nothing ever happened out there?"

"No, we stayed in the water and talked a lot, but only as friends. Now if I had gotten Lois to join us ... then he would have paid attention." Rachel let out a big sigh. "That was just our clothing-optional getaway. We were just good friends who had nothing to hide."

"Literally," Vanessa said with a grin.

Rachel looked back to Vanessa, "You should have joined us. You know, next year when you're Peace Corpsing it in some jungle, your bath day will be skinny dipping in the nearest river."

Carol said, "She'll be waiting for Tarzan to dive in and join her."

"Not for four more years," sighed Vanessa. "Being Salutatorian came with a good scholarship, so Peace Corps wants to wait until I get another diploma. They even helped pick some of my classes."

Eve asked, "Any classes on how to catch a Tarzan?"

"I haven't seen as many Tarzan movies as Nessa," said Carol, "but didn't Jane just go swimming until he noticed she wasn't as hairy as the monkeys?"

Eve said, "That sounds like fun. Is the water deep enough to go swimming here?"

"Maybe, but can you imagine skinny dipping with Rich on the sidelines?" Rachel looked to the outhouse. "Now, if we could get Lois to ask Scott, to take us to the swimming hole..."

When Lois stepped out of the outhouse, Vanessa looked at her and said, "Lois, will you ask Scott to take us swimming?"

"And I thought I was getting drunk...." Lois shook her head in confusion as she walked away.

Chapter 5: The Party Winds Down

Scott spotted Alvin Murphy sitting near Greg's pickup truck, along with Greg Peterson, Danny O'Brian, and Ray Ellis. Donna and Carol sat on another hay bale, looking through Greg's case of 8-track tapes to decide what we would listen to next.

Seeing the beer in Greg's hand, and that his truck was running, Scott asked, "How did you get Carol to let you keep your keys?"

"He needs to run his truck to recharge his battery. We need the music, so I took his shift knob." Carol looked at the pop can in Scott's hand. "I see you're still sipping cans, so you're good."

Greg looked up at Scott. "Ray tells me you're going to be working for Stanley Steamer. And here I thought he went back to Alaska after graduation."

Donna gave Greg a puzzled look. "I don't think they make those anymore."

"He means Stan Severs," Scott said with a chuckle. "That nickname is the reason he only uses his last name now."

Carol asked, "Who's Stan Severs?"

"He graduated with me last year," said Greg. "Big guy with blond hair."

"He used to hire out for farm work, and we worked a few hay crops together," said Scott. "He's in road construction now, and he offered me a job. He said he needs some farm boys who know how to work. I'll be jobless and homeless in a few days, so I'll try it for the summer." Scott shrugged. "It's good pay, and I'll see little more of the state."

"You're homeless?" asked Alvin.

"Dad sold the farm," Scott explained. "He's ready to retire, so I get to try something new. I'm not completely homeless. I'll just be living on the road with no address this summer."

"You could join me in boot camp," suggested Alvin. "Another guy is supposed to be going, but he's trying not to say anything about it now. It's like he owes someone money and doesn't want them to know he's skipping town."

"When do you go?" asked Scott.

"We report for basic training tomorrow."

Scott looked over to the bonfire and saw Lois was now talking to Rachel and Randy with no sign of Mike. "I was going to ask you about that. He really did enlist with you then?"

"We signed up when the recruiters were here last fall."

Scott glanced out to the tiki torch by the men's room tree and handed Ray his pop can. "Will you hold this for me? I need to take a walk."

"No problem," said Ray.

Scott was crossing the field to the men's tree when he met Mike on his way back. Scott asked, "How's Lois feel about you going to the army tomorrow?"

"What?" Mike stopped to face Scott.

"You know, when I saw you two at graduation, you just didn't look like two people who were about to separate. I guess she had a lot of time to get used to the idea after you enlisted last fall."

Mike stepped close to face Scott. "You just keep your mouth shut about that."

Scott shook his head in disgust. "So, it's true. You enlisted six months ago, and still haven't told Lois? Do you want to tell her now, or shall I?"

"I'll tell her," Mike paused with a smirk, "when it's time."

Scott no longer had any doubts about anything Eve had told him. Before he could say another word, Mike surprised Scott with a strong kick to his groin. Scott bent forward in pain as Mike launched a left jab to his side, followed by a right hook to the side of his head. Scott landed on his side, still gasping from Mike's kick.

Mike wanted to keep beating Scott, but that could have brought unwanted attention. He turned with a look of satisfaction and headed back to the party.

When Scott felt he could breathe again, Ray Ellis was helping him to his feet. "What the hell was that about?"

"I needed to learn a lesson." Scott stood with a deep breath and exhaled. "If you ever confront Mike, stand sideways."

"Are you okay? Can you walk back to the group?"

"In a minute." Scott took another deep breath. "I still gotta' pee. I'd like to get that out of the way before confronting him again. Also, I wanna know if anything still works down there. He nailed 'em good." Scott turned and continued heading to the men's tree.

As he made his way back to the party, Scott was still thinking about what he would say to Lois. As much as he wanted to attack Mike, that would only make Lois see him as the villain. All that really mattered was exposing Mike's deceptions. She needed to know that Mike had enlisted, and deliberately kept that from her for six months. Maybe Eve would be willing to tell even more.

Returning to the group, Scott looked, but saw no sign of Lois or Mike. He looked at the parked cars, hoping to see Mike's van.

"They left!" Rachel said as she approached. "Mike just grabbed her hand and told her it was time to leave. I tried to get them to stick around, but Mike was suddenly in a big hurry. He acted like his van would turn into a pumpkin or something. I have no idea where they were going."

Angry and disappointed with himself, Scott looked out to the driveway. He should have known that Mike would simply grab Lois and leave. Now she was gone, and he had no idea where they went.

"Can I get you a beer?" Ray asked as he joined them. "Your reason to stay sober is gone, and I'm guessing you could probably use a good drink."

"No," Scott said with despair. "I think I'll call it a night. I don't feel much like a party now. I might as well head home so I can help with the morning chores." He turned to Rachel, "Can you give Eve a ride home in the morning? She said she was planning on sleeping in your car."

"No problem," said Rachel. "We were pretty much planning on that anyway."

* * *

When the music began to slow, Greg knew his battery was running down again. Instead of starting his truck this time, he simply turned the stereo off and removed the key. He was about to call out an apology but saw that no one seemed to have noticed.

When Greg rejoined the others, Randy looked up and said, "It was good while it lasted. That was good music; I like your tapes."

"Thanks!" Greg felt good to have his music complemented by Randy Richards.

Eve was refilling her Solo Cup when Rich staggered over to her. "Hey Easie! Did I ever show you, my tent? I've got it set up over there."

"No," Eve turned to face him, "and NO!"

"Whaht?"

"No, you never showed me your tent. And NO, I'm not goin' there with you. Not tonight. Not ever. You aarre, off limits. Off-limits and done. And DON'T CALL ME THAT!"

"Wha's the matter, Easie?" He slurred.

"I ssaid, don't call me THAT!" Her slur wasn't as strong as his, but it was noticeable. "I know you call me Easy Eavie, and I DON'T LIKE IT!"

"But Easssie..."

"Screw you!" Eve threw her cup into the dying fire and walked toward the cars in a huff.

"Easssie." Rich watched her walk away, before dropping his voice and saying, "Tha's what I had in mind."

"You're a real Dick Rich. You know that?" Rachel waited until Rich turned to see her before she continued. "Eve is a real

55

nice person, and you hurt her with your name-calling and rude comments."

"Whaa..." Rich turned to face Rachel.

"Why do we call you Rich anyway? You're not rich, so you must be Richard. You know, that's not what most people call someone named Richard. Most people call Richards, Dick. That's what you are. You're Dick Lester. Lester is kind of long too. Let's shorten that. Most people named Lester are called Less. Okay, mister name caller, from now on, I will refer to you as Dick... Less."

Doris Jensen patted Rich on the back, saying, "Hey Dickless, how about a beer to drown your sorrows?" as she handed him her empty red plastic cup.

Rachel did not notice Randy pointing at his watch and nodding to Carol and Donna, nor had she noticed them smile and give him a thumbs up in return. What Rachel did notice was that Randy suddenly got up and began walking toward his car. She hurried to catch up with him. "Okay, I'm sorry I was being such a bitch to Rich back there, but he was mean to Eve. She's a sweet girl and doesn't deserve to be treated like that."

Randy stopped next to his car and looked back with confusion. "What? Oh that! No, you weren't being a bitch. You're right. Eve is nice, and Rich needed to be put in his place."

"Oh!" Rachel looked surprised. "The way you walked away, I thought I upset you or something."

Randy reached over the passenger door of his car to open the glove compartment and removed what looked like a two-inch square cigarette case. "I just need to set this to wake me in the morning." He pushed a button on the side of the case, and it opened into a three-sided travel alarm clock. He wound and set the clock before placing it on the dash of his car before turning to face Rachel. "I traded shifts to get today off, so I work the morning shift tomorrow."

"Oh. That's better then." Rachel let out a sigh of relief. "And you were just going to walk away, without even saying good night?"

"I was curious to see if you would follow me."

Rachel blushed and looked at his Thunderbird. "So, this is your car?"

"This is my baby." He patted the inside of the door. "She was only five years old when I got her after my graduation."

Rachel walked around, admiring the car. "So, this is a '62, the same year as Roberta. What's his name?"

"I never named it. And what do you mean, his? I thought all cars were girls."

Rachel looked the car over. "No, most cars are girls. I think this one has balls, so it's a boy. How come you never named him?"

"I guess it just never occurred to me."

Rachel walked around the car looking. "It looks kind of Randy... wait, that's your name. That would never work."

Randy opened the door, tipped the back of the seat forward and stepped into the back before closing the door. After tipping the other seat forward, he sat in the back seat and slipped off his shoes. Sitting back, he rested his feet on the tipped back of the front seat, leaving the seat next to him empty. "No," he agreed, "my car couldn't be a Randy."

Rachel hopped up to sit on the side of the car, lifted her legs, and spun around to drop into the open seat. Sitting back, she put her feet up as Randy had done. "I think he's a Terry, as in dacto. That's what Thunderbird makes me think of. What do you think?"

"I think shoes can be hard on the upholstery." Randy pointed to Rachel's feet and watched as she slipped her shoes off before putting her feet up again. "You may be right," he agreed, "maybe this is a Terry."

Randy raised his right arm, allowing Rachel to slide in close with his arm around her. She laid her head against his shoulder. "Yep. This car feels like a Terry."

Randy kissed the top of Rachel's head, faced forward, and rested his head against hers. "Terry it is then." Sitting back with his arm around Rachel felt natural. He liked the feel of her in his arm. Neither of them moved. They leaned against each other, feeling comfortable together. Soon, their eyes closed, and they drifted into sleep.

Chapter 6: Parking

Lois raised her head to look around when she realized Mike had parked his van. "Where are we?"

"Just somewhere we can have some privacy." Mike turned off the engine but did not remove the key.

"It looks like there's a little building in front of us."

"That's just an office. There won't be anyone around until morning." Looking ahead, he said, "One time, my dad had car trouble and had to call me. He picked that lock so he could use the phone." Seeing she was surprised, he explained, "It was an emergency. He only used the phone, so no one even knew he was there."

Mike pulled Lois close and kissed her. "Let's go back where there's room to be comfortable."

With no sign of resistance, Lois turned and climbed between the bucket seats to the back of his van. Her hands shook slightly as she settled onto the sleeping bags Mike had already spread over the van's floor. She leaned to the side, allowing room for Mike to join her, hoping he would not realize how nervous she was. Her goal of waiting until she was out of school had been achieved and it was time to reward Mike for his patience. She would have asked him about things said at the outhouse earlier, but the beer at the party washed those questions away.

Mike opened a cooler which sat behind the seat and asked if she would like Wild Mountain or Strawberry Hill.

"What?" Lois tipped her head with a puzzled expression.

Mike pulled a bottle of Boone's Farm Wild Mountain from the cooler. "This is on top, so let's try it first." He twisted the cap from the bottle and offered it to her. "I didn't think to bring any glasses, but drinking from the bottle is less likely to spill."

Lois took a drink from the bottle and passed it back to Mike. "That's good. I could have kept my cup from the party, but you're right, we can just drink from the bottle."

Mike took a big drink and screwed the cap back onto the bottle. "Let's try Strawberry Hill." Pulling another bottle from the cooler, he unscrewed the cap and offered it to Lois.

She took a drink. "I like this more. It reminds me of Kool-Aid."

"Then that's your bottle." Mike opened the first bottle and drank from it.

"You know, with all the beer at the party, you didn't need to bring wine too." Lois took another drink from her bottle.

"I didn't get any beer." He took another drink. "If I had, they would have taken my keys, and we wouldn't have had any alone time." He watched Lois take another sip before recapping her bottle and setting it by the side of the van. After taking another drink, Mike capped his bottle and set it aside too.

Mike leaned in to hold Lois as they kissed. He stretched his legs out so he could turn to lie back, pulling Lois down as he did. She straightened her legs out as he pulled her down, rolling her over him until they were lying side by side. Lois soon lay on her back with Mike facing down to her as they kissed.

They lay kissing for some time. Mike gently moved his hand, caressing, massaging, and unfastening. His strongest kisses came when he wanted her most distracted, with the loosening of a button, the release of a hook, or caressing new skin. He tried to inspire passion, wanting to distract her from any thought of what was happening.

Lois tried not to think as they kissed. She knew where this night was going and felt awkward and clumsy. She moved her hands about his back, holding him tighter when her hand began to shake. She enjoyed the feel of Mike's touch, while trying not to notice what his hands were doing. Alcohol had clouded her mind, and she began to feel her rapid heartbeat as excitement rather than nerves. Lois moved her hands down to the lower area of his back.

Lois's hips began moving with a rhythm of their own, just as Mike's passion seemed to fade. Realizing a change in Mike, Lois opened her eyes to look at him. She watched as he stopped and pulled himself away to face her.

"I'm sorry," he tried to explain. "I don't want to, but I have to take a break."

"Is something wrong?"

"I didn't have any beer, but I did have a lot of pop at the party. Now the wine put me over the edge. If I don't stop and take a leak, I'm going to explode, and not in a good way."

The beer and wine had slowed her thinking, but she understood and wanted to laugh at his timing. "Okay. I thought you went before we left."

He pushed himself up onto his knees. "I was going to, but someone I didn't want to talk to was coming, so I decided to wait 'til we were here. When we got here, the thought of peeing just slipped my mind."

"Okay," she sat up with a coy smile. "I'll wait right here."

Mike hurried out the van's side door, hoping he could be back before her mood changed. If they did have to start over, it would still be worth it.

Mike closed the van door as Lois sat up and took another drink of wine, noticing that the bottle was now much lighter. Feeling cold, Lois realized her shirt was open and refastened the buttons. Her bra was loose, but she decided not to refasten it. Lois pulled one strap out her sleeve and over her hand, so that it was free on that side. Reaching into her other sleeve, she pulled the bra out entirely. A mischievous smile grew at the thought of Mike discovering the absence of her bra, and she looked for a place to hide it.

While looking under the front seat, her hand rested on the top of the sleeping bags. She lifted the top sleeping bag and hid her bra beneath it. While smoothing the top to make it look natural, Lois recalled seeing something when she looked under the seat. Reaching to see what was there, she brought her hand back with a white envelope. Having felt something else, she reached again and came back with a large barrette. The barrette looked familiar, but it was not one of hers.

She dropped the barrette by her wine bottle and took another drink. Setting the bottle down, she picked up the envelope for another look. The envelope was empty, but there was enough light for her to make out the return address, *'U.S. Army Recruitment Center.'* Lois knew this should have meant something, but she felt drunk and simply dropped it by the barrette without a thought. She lifted the bottle and took another drink.

Realizing that her belt and pants were open, Lois refastened them. She thought that making him start over would serve him right; imagine taking a pee break in the middle of a make-out session.

Lois was taking another drink from her bottle when the back door of the van opened. She capped and set the bottle down. "You know, you didn't have to bring wine. I was already drunk from the beer." Grabbing his bottle, she handed it to him. "But you're way behind." As he took the bottle from her hands, she realized that his was even lighter than hers.

Mike took one big drink from his bottle, then another before setting it down. He did not need to recap it, as the bottle was now empty. "Where were we?" He reached to rest his hand behind her head and pulled her to his waiting kiss.

As Lois felt his fingers brush her hair, she pictured the barrette coming loose with his touch. She had never worn a barrette where he had brushed, but in her mind, she could see the barrette there, on a head of long blonde hair.

As she returned his kiss, Lois felt Mike's hand caressing her back. She watched as he paused to look at her, clearly pleased when he noticed the absence of her bra. Lois smiled with the satisfaction of successfully surprising him.

Mike pulled her close and began kissing anew. As he kissed, Mike brought his hand down slowly, and carefully unfastened buttons as he worked his way up her shirt. With the release of her final button, Mike brushed the hair away from her ear. He kissed her cheek, her neck, and began to gently nibble her earlobe.

When Mike brushed her hair back, Lois imagined the barrette falling loosely to the floor. Lois pictured the barrette in her mind again, but now she saw it on the head of Eve Johnson. She remembered Eve wearing that barrette and saying it was a gift someone bought for her at the art fair last summer.

Mike began kissing his way down to her neck. He gently began sliding the top of her shirt back, so he could kiss his way to her shoulder.

Lois might have relaxed enough for him to continue, but Eve's words echoed in her mind, *'You never, but he has.'* Lois realized that her shirt was sliding over her shoulder and would soon be sliding down her arm. She did not remember bringing her arm down, but she raised it enough to stop the descent of her shirt.

Mike returned to kissing her on the mouth. Lois found her fingers going to the top of his shirt, where she began unfastening his buttons. She thought of how skillfully he had nearly removed her shirt, as if with practice and experience. Again, Eve's words came to her mind, *'He was never alone long enough to miss you. ...There's a lot he never tells you about the trips with his dad.'* All of Eve's words returned to Lois's mind. *'...He got what he wanted somewhere else... showing his ring off, announcing that he was a free man...'* Lois remembered the envelope she had found. *'...Mike's going in the army this week, so he'll be out of the picture anyway. That's a secret, so pretend I never mentioned it.'* Everything Eve had said began to fit, and Lois realized what Eve had been telling her.

Lois's hands were on the middle of Mike's chest, still fumbling with his buttons, when she suddenly pushed him away and yelled, "YOU CAD!"

Mike fell back onto the van floor. "What?" He was both surprised and confused.

"You cheated on me! You've been doing this with other girls."

"Huh? No, you're my only girl." Mike didn't know what had gotten into her, but he needed to calm her down if he was going to recapture the moment.

Lois got up on her knees and began buttoning her shirt. "You had other girls in here! You've been doing this with other girls all along!"

"I don't have other girls in my van. You're my only girl."

"Okay, another girl!" She was sure the barrette was Eve's, but Eve's words had indicated there had been more. "I know at least one girl. What do you do, pick her up every time we argue?" Lois grabbed the barrette and held it up for Mike to see. "I was saving myself, so you've been doing it with Eve. And who knows how many others?"

Mike stared at the barrette. "Where did that come from?"

Even in her drunken condition, Lois could see the recognition in his eyes. "It was under the seat."

"It was probably there when I got the van."

"You've had the van over two years. Eve got this last summer. She showed it off because it was hand-made and one of a kind." Lois finished buttoning her shirt.

"It just looks like Eve's. If someone made one, they would have made more just like it."

"And when were you going to tell me you joined the army? Were you waiting until AFTER we did it?"

This took Mike by surprise. "Who told you that?"

Lois grabbed the envelope and held it in front of him. "Do you want me to read what time you are supposed to report?"

Recognizing the envelope, Mike knew he was caught. "I talked to the recruiter last fall. Early enlistment means we serve our reserve time before we go in, but nothing is final until we take our oath."

Lois tossed the envelope at him and opened the side door of the van. As she climbed out, he picked up the envelope and saw it was empty.

Mike yelled, "NO!" throwing the envelope down and reaching for the van's back door. He ran around to get in front of Lois, grabbed her by the arms, and pushed her back against the van. "I've waited too long for this. He's not going to get you first."

Her eyes widened with fright. "Mike stop! You're hurting me."

"I don't care!" Mike held her against the van. "Will you get back in the van, or do you want it right here?"

"No!" She tried to push him away.

Mike grabbed the front of her shirt and brought his hand down, tearing the shirt as buttons came loose, or popped off completely. Ignoring her efforts to push him back, he grabbed her breast and tried to kiss her. With his strength, he easily held her against the van.

Lois tried to resist, but she was powerless against him, and even more so in her drunken state. Mike had an entire bottle of wine, but he was still not as drunk as her. Lois was much smaller, so she was feeling the effect of the beer and wine far more. She thought it a wonder that her drinking had not made her sick, or had it?

Lois pulled her stomach in and up, blowing out as she bent forward. With her mouth wide open, she made a retching sound as she bent toward Mike.

Mike recognized her actions and jumped back to avoid the expected spray.

When Lois felt Mike release her, she brought her knee up hard between his legs. She saw his eyes close as he moved back, bending forward with pain. Seeing her target even more open, Lois kicked with all her might, striking Mike's groin even harder.

Mike dropped to his knees with a quiet moan.

Lois fell back against the van, recovered, turned, and ran to escape. Coming around the van, she realized that she had no idea where she was, or where she should go. They were parked behind a huge pile of gravel, so she ran to see what was beyond it. She saw more piles of earth, and somewhere ahead a light moved on the distant ground. She ran toward the light, hoping someone would be there to help her. She tried to yell but felt little more than a whisper emerge. Her feet failed to keep up with her movement, and she stumbled and fell.

Lois looked up to feel blinded for a moment, and the light vanished as if it had never been there. She climbed to her feet but could see no sign of the light. She was not sure which direction it had been, or if it had even been real. She turned her head as she looked but saw only darkness and a distant tree line.

"There's nowhere to go." Mike grabbed her arm and began marching her back to his van. "You can yell all you want. There's no one around to hear you!" When she tried to push him away, he twisted her arm behind her back, forcing her back to his van.

At the back of the van, Mike said, "Get in!" and pushed her to the open door. Lois tried to push past him, but he grabbed the back of her shirt and jerked her back, tearing her shirt more as she fell into the open van. When she rose to face him, he grabbed her arms, ready to push her into the van. He watched her repeat the retching motion she had made earlier, but this time he held firm, not wanting to fall for the same trick twice.

This time, Lois was not bluffing. Retching forward, she sprayed Mike with everything her stomach had to offer.

Mike felt disgusted as he looked down to see and smell what she had done. He pulled off his puke-soaked shirt and tossed it aside. "Now it looks like we both need to get naked." Grabbing Lois's shirt, he began to pull it down until he felt a hand on his shoulder. He turned just in time to see a fist coming at him, growing larger until it smashed the cartilage of his nose. Mike bounced off the van's door and landed on the ground.

Blood from Mike's nose ran down his chest. He looked up and yelled, "You!" Climbing to his feet, Mike yelled, "No! Not you! Not here! NOT NOW!" Ignoring Lois, Mike stepped forward with a powerful punch aimed at Scott Severson.

Scott easily blocked Mike's punch and returned with one of his own, which would leave Mike with a bruised and swollen eye.

Mike stumbled and fell back to the ground. Grabbing a handful of sand and gravel, Mike stood to challenge Scott. He threw his fist full of earth at Scott's eyes as he charged, ramming his shoulder into Scott's stomach, and pushing him back. Holding Scott's waist, Mike attempted to use his wrestling skills to take Scott down.

Scott blinked to wipe sand from his eyes as he moved back. He braced himself and managed to stop their movement. He bent forward to wrap his arms around Mike's waist. Shifting his balance, Scott pulled Mike closer and jerked him up with a mighty heave. Mike rose backward as his feet went over his head. His back rolled briefly onto Scott's shoulder, but momentum kept him moving. Scott let go, allowing Mike to drop behind him. Mike landed on his feet, but continued moving forward until he landed face-first in the gravel.

Mike climbed to his feet and turned to face Scott. He was nearly as tall as Scott and had been weightlifting since he first joined the wrestling team. Bringing his fists up, Mike settled into a boxer's stance. Locking his eyes on Scott, he searched for his best line of attack.

Scott slid his foot back for a sideways stance, reconsidered, and shifted to face Mike straight on.

Mike pulled his fist back, as if winding up for a powerful punch. As he came forward, he withheld the bluffed punch and attempted to kick at Scott's groin instead.

Scott shifted back into the side stance and arced his hand around to catch Mike's foot. He lifted Mike's foot up, and forward as he said, "Not this time." Mike took short hops forward as he struggled to keep his balance. When Scott let go, Mike continued moving ahead with his forward momentum. Scott rotated into Mike's advance with a hard punch, just below the ribcage and dead center in his solar plexus.

Striking the solar plexus causes muscles around the lungs to spasm with shock, making them unable to work until they recover from the blow. Many people explain this as having the wind knocked out of them; even though the air is still in their lungs, they are just unable to move or use it.

Mike dropped to his hands and knees as he tried to breathe. Scott no longer mattered; Mike's only concern was his next breath.

Scott turned and walked to the driver's door and returned with the keys from Mike's van. When Mike began to take a few short breaths, Scott jingled the keys so that Mike could hear and recognize the sound. The heavy keyring was heard landing somewhere in the distance, but their direction remained a mystery. Scott said, "That fob will be easy to spot when the sun comes up. Until then, you're in no condition to drive."

Mike stopped gasping and began to show signs of normal breathing.

"Are you okay?" Scott watched as Mike slowly climbed back to his feet. Scott asked, "Can you breathe?"

Mike stood and nodded. He still bled from his broken nose, his eye was already beginning to swell and darken, and his shirtless skin was scraped and bruised from sliding in gravel.

When Scott could see that Mike was breathing normally, he said, "There's just one more thing..." Scott waited until Mike raised his head to look at him. "You hurt Lois." Scott's fist struck Mike high on his left cheek, causing him to spin and fall with an unconscious thump.

Scott took a deep breath and walked to Lois. He wanted to take her in his arms but feared any touch might feel like another attack. In a calming voice, he said, "It's over. He won't hurt you again." Scott held his hand out to her and said, "My car is back in the driveway."

Lois took his hand and began walking with him, but stopped and ran back to the van's passenger door. After retrieving her purse from the front seat, she hurried back to where Scott was waiting. Scott was pleased when Lois retook his hand and held it as they walked to his car.

When they reached his car, Scott turned to face Lois. He released her hand, and quickly removed his long-sleeved shirt, revealing the white T-shirt he wore beneath it. Scott brought his shirt up, holding it so she could slide her arms into it. "I think you're missing some buttons. You may want to wear this."

Lois looked down and realized that she had been braless with her shirt open since Mike first pushed her against the van. With a tearful voice she said, "I'm sorry," and slid her arm into the sleeve.

"You have nothing to be sorry for." He held up the other side of the shirt for her other hand. Scott's shirt was large on Lois, covering her torn shirt like a jacket. As his shirt settled onto her shoulders, Scott began raising his hands up to help her with the buttons.

"I think I can handle this part." Lois stepped to the passenger door as she buttoned the shirt.

"I'm sure you can." He opened the door for her, waited, and closed it after she was seated inside.

Scott lifted the spotlight, which still hung out the driver's window, and set it on the seat between them. After starting his car, he turned on the headlights and asked Lois if she would like to see a doctor, or report Mike's attack to the police.

Lois shook her head saying that she didn't want to see anyone, or for anyone to see her.

Scott nodded. "I understand. If you change your mind, just say so. Is there anywhere you would like to go?"

"Is there anywhere I can clean up without anyone seeing me?"

"I can think of a couple of places, and one is close by." Scott looked ahead and was about to put his car in gear, but instead he turned the car off and got out to retrieve something he saw in the headlight's beam.

Returning to his car, Scott softly said, "I owe you Ray," as he set his spotlight and a small Instamatic camera into his glove compartment.

Chapter 7: Scott and Lois

Returning to the Polk County Campground, Scott parked in front of the cinderblock building that housed its public restrooms. Saying that he would be right back, Scott went to the south end of the building that faced the campgrounds.

Lois sat in a trance-like state and had said nothing since they had left the gravel pit. She found herself reading the word WOMEN on the sign above the door in front of her. Realizing where she was, Lois grabbed her purse, and began heading for the restroom door.

"Lois!" Scott called to her. "We need to get something from the trunk first."

Lois turned, walked to the rear of the car, and she waited for Scott. When Scott opened the trunk, Lois looked and asked, "What is all that?"

"Camping gear. Almost everything I'll need for living on the road this summer. Everything but my tent, anyway. Vanessa borrowed that for the party." Scott removed a white enamel wash pan, and a bottle of green dish soap, and handed them to Lois. He also removed a large canvas duffle bag, hung its strap on his shoulder, and stepped away from the open trunk. "I think this will do." He offered Lois his hand and walked her to the restroom door.

Scott turned on the light as they stepped inside. Looking ahead to another doorway, he led her to the shower room. After turning on that light, he set his duffle bag and the wash pan on one of the wooden benches.

"At first, I thought you could just wash up in the restroom. Then I realized that the campground has showers too. You didn't get sprayed as much as Mike, but enough. I imagine a shower sounds pretty good now." Scott opened his duffle bag and removed a large bath towel and washcloth. "I don't have any bath soap or shampoo, but the dish soap should work." Returning to his bag, he pulled out a pair of cutoff shorts and set them on the bench. "These may be big on you, but your belt should hold them up. We can wash your pants in the wash pan and let them dry overnight."

Lois looked down, realizing that her pants were still wet with pink vomit. "Thank you. I guess they do need washing."

Returning to his duffle bag, he pulled out a clean white T-shirt, another long-sleeved flannel shirt, and a pair of clean socks. "You'll want clean clothes after you shower. Am I missing anything?"

"That should keep me covered. I have my toothbrush in my purse, so I should be good." Lois turned to look at him. "Thank you. I'm sorry to be such a bother."

Scott lifted Lois's hand to kiss its back before covering it with his other hand. "You are not a bother, and I should be thanking you. I got to hold your hand, and I gave Mike some well-deserved payback. This just might be the best night of my life." He picked up his duffle bag and pulled its strap over his shoulder. "Would you like me to wait by the door? In case you need anything?"

"No. Thank you, but I'm doing much better now." Lois looked around and asked, "What if someone comes? Is it okay for us to be here?"

"I rented a campsite while you were in the car. The camping fee is in the drop box, so we're just normal paying guests. Campsites include shower privileges. I'll set up camp and make a fire. Just holler if you need anything."

* * *

Lois was happy to be clean again when she stepped out of the restroom building. Scott's clothes were large on her, but she was covered, and they had a soft, comfortable feel. His car was parked in one of the campsites, so she headed in that direction. When Scott came to take the pan of wet laundry, she said, "I can carry that," even though she was happy to be relieved of it.

72

"I'm sure you could, but this gives me an excuse to walk with you." He lifted the pan from each side, holding one arm out for Lois to hold.

Lois set her hand on his offered arm and walked with him to their camp. She noticed he was wearing another flannel shirt and asked, "Just how many shirts do you bring for a one-night party?"

"None were planned for the party, but I like to pack at least two of everything with my camping supplies. One set of clothes can last a whole camping trip, but if you don't bring extra, you can count on getting caught in the rain, falling in a pond, or something unpleasant. It's called Murphy's defense. Whatever can go wrong, will, but only if you're not prepared. Things you prepare for hardly ever happen. Mike rubbed off on me during our scuffle, so I thought I should change too." He set the wash pan on an army cot between his car and the campfire. "Now that you're all clean, you wouldn't want to sit near me if I still smelled like used beer."

Lois looked to see a metal cooking grate above the campfire, supporting a metal coffee pot and a cast iron skillet. Two campstools sat near the fire and a narrow rope was strung between two trees, just close enough for the heat of the fire to aid in drying clothes.

Scott reached into the legs of Lois's jeans and turned them inside out before hanging them on the line. Lois had also washed the shirt Scott had lent her earlier, because it had been bloodied in Scott's fight with Mike.

Scott held up a can and asked Lois if she liked corned beef hash.

"I don't think I've ever had it."

"Good." Scott began opening the can. "That means this will be the best corned beef hash you've ever tasted." While stirring the hash in his skillet, Scott said, "I figured you could use something to eat about now. You've had a busy night."

"Translation: you lost your supper, so I better get some food in you. Thank you. I am kind of hungry."

When the hash was hot, Scott divided it on two melamine plates and set the skillet on the ground to cool. After pouring them each a cup of fresh coffee, he sat on the campstool next to Lois.

Lois ate her first bite of hash and said, "This is good. In fact, I think this is the best corned beef hash I have ever tasted."

"Thank you." Scott took a bite. "It's a good camp staple. If you don't catch anything for supper, you can always open a can." They continued talking as they ate.

Lois asked, "Do you camp a lot?"

"Some. Dad wanted to do father-and-son things when I was young. He was getting old for sports, so we went hunting, fishing, and camping. After a few years, he replaced the tent with a little hunting shack. Ray and I go camping too. Either pitching tents by the swimming hole, or at the cabin when we're hunting. I'll be living on the road this summer, and I don't know what will be available. I may rent rooms, or I might just camp all summer. Stan said we should be moving quite a bit, so I'll play it by ear."

"You mentioned a swimming hole. Is that the same one Rachel talks about?"

Scott tried not to grin. "That's the one. It's a nice spot on the Apple River where our two farms meet. We've been swimming there since we were little."

"So why does Rachel always get that funny grin when she talks about it?"

"You know," Scott lifted his cup to drink coffee, "until today, I never knew you two were cousins."

Lois looked up. "Why did that sound like you're changing the subject?"

"Has Rachel ever invited you to swim there?"

"Several times. She even mentioned that we might see you out there. And then she kind of... giggled. What's so funny about this swimming hole?"

"It's a great place to swim, and it's private. There's no need to wear anything fashionable when no one will see you."

"So, always-dress-well Rachel has an out-of-style swimming suit?"

"Not a style you would wear in public. It's really nothing." Scott could see Lois was giving that much thought and asked, "Just how well do you know your cousin?"

Lois looked at Scott as her eyes began to widen. "Do you mean...?"

"We never do anything we wouldn't do in front of a beach full of people. We just wear less when we do it. We've been swimming there since we were little kids and never quite grew out of it." Looking into her wide-open eyes, he said, "I swear, we've always kept a safe distance apart. It's just a place for swimming."

Lois let out a laugh. "I remember when she called and said, *'Scott and Ray are camping at the swimming hole. Why don't you sleep over? We can head out in the morning to surprise them.'*"

Scott laughed. "I wish you had taken her up on that. I'm sure Ray would have been surprised too."

Lois laughed and took another bite of hash. "That might have been fun. If I hadn't been going with Mike at the time, I might have said yes." She let out another laugh. "I still don't think she could have gotten me to swim... like that anyway."

"You should try it sometime." He gestured back to the restrooms. "You know, there's a nice beach area down past the building."

"Oh my God!" Lois laughed again. "When I got out of the outhouse tonight, Rachel had been talking to the other girls. Vanessa asked me to ask you to take them all swimming! I think your secret is out!"

"Well, I guess all good things must come to an end." He laughed and ate more hash. "Did they say anything else?"

Lois looked thoughtful as she tried to remember. "Rachel said that Mike was a dick. Turns out she was right. Eve said some things about Mike too. I didn't understand at the time. When I was in his van, everything they said came back to me. Suddenly it all made sense." She looked down at her plate. "I was going to let Mike, tonight. If I hadn't remembered what Eve had said ..." Lois stared into the campfire. "He never even mentioned joining the army. He told me that he was going to help his father for a couple of weeks."

"So, you wouldn't have missed him for two weeks, and I would have been gone by then. I think Eve was right."

"About what?"

Scott shrugged. "Just a theory Eve had about Mike."

"Do you know when he leaves?"

"According to Alvin, they report tomorrow."

Lois shook her head. "And he knew this for six months."

Scott nodded. "I just found out tonight, but I had to be sure. Mike pretty much confirmed it, but I didn't get back fast enough. I should have known he would grab you and run. I'm sorry I was too late."

"You still got there in time." Lois ate another bite as she thought. "Rachel asked if I was going with Mike, just because I wanted a boyfriend. Maybe she was right. Now that we broke up, I find myself wondering what I ever saw in him. In fact, I think I'm relieved that he's out of my life."

Scott smiled. "Me too."

"It seems like I always had a boyfriend. Mom used to tell me it was nice having a man like Dad taking care of her. Maybe that's what I was looking for. Maybe I should just stay single and take care of myself."

"After my uncle Dale's last divorce, he told me that being alone was better than being tied down to the wrong person. Maybe Mike's a good example of that. But please don't rule out another boyfriend completely. Now that I can finally talk to you, I'd like to think I've got a shot at seeing you again."

"I think I would like that." Lois ate the last of the hash on her plate. "You know what? I don't think I'm drunk anymore."

"A lot of excitement, throwing up the alcohol, a shower, followed by food to absorb what's left. That can have a sobering effect."

Scott got up and put their dirty dishes into the wash pan. "There's a faucet by the restrooms. I'll wash the dishes and be right back. Would you like to make your bed while I'm gone?"

"Is that your way of saying, 'Front seat or back?'"

"There's a lever on each side of the front seat. Just move it up and down and the back will lay down like a double bed. There's a sleeping bag, blanket, and pillow in the back seat. Use the sleeping bag as a sheet, and you can cover with the blanket." Seeing her concern, Scott said, "I'll sleep on the cot outside."

"That wouldn't be fair to you. It's your car, so I should sleep outside."

"What's fair?" Scott looked at her. "You've had a rough night, so you should feel safer where you can lock the doors. If you want, you can roll down the window and we can talk."

*　　*　　*

Lois was staring into the campfire when Scott returned. He sat on the stool next to her. "What are you thinking about?"

"I was thinking about things the girls said by the outhouse earlier. I should have paid more attention at the time."

Scott refilled his coffee cup. "Did they say anything interesting?"

Lois giggled and said, "Rachel said something like, I would wonder what I ever saw in Mike if I went swimming with you."

Scott coughed coffee over the fire, giving Lois a good laugh. After wiping coffee from his nose, he thought he should change the subject. "I met your dad today. He seems like a nice guy."

"He mentioned meeting one of my classmates at graduation. I think he liked you, more than he likes Mike anyway." Lois looked down and said, "I don't know what he'll think when I come home wearing your clothes."

"Your pants should be dry by morning." Scott thought for a moment. "We can stop back at the party. Rachel isn't one to wear the same clothes two days in a row. She may have something you can change into."

"That could work." Lois thought about that. "Rachel and I have swapped clothes before. Dad wouldn't give that a second thought."

"Why do they call your dad Storm?"

"It's his middle name. Apparently, an ancestor was born on a ship in the middle of a big storm. They called him Storm on the Sea. In Dutch, it was Storm Van Der Zee. That became our surname. It was a tradition for each generation to name at least one son Storm. The tradition kind of died out, until Grandpa made Storm my dad's middle name. Dad likes it, so that's the name he uses."

"A lot of people go by their middle name, my father included. Otherwise, people would call me Junior. In fact, Dad started using his middle name so they wouldn't call him Junior."

"If I had been a boy, Storm might have been my first name." Lois chuckled. "I was a girl, so I just got the middle name of Raine."

"Lois, Rain on the Sea. I like that."

Scott stood up and felt the pants hanging on the line. He turned them around so the other side would now face the fire. When he sat next to Lois again, she began to laugh.

"What's so funny?"

Lois smirked a bit when she said, "It just occurred to me... after two years of Mike trying to get in my pants, you not only turned mine inside out, but I'm wearing yours. And this is only our first date." Looking at Scott, she realized what she had said. "I'm sorry. I meant, our first time out together ... I mean ..."

"I know what you mean." Scott put his hand on Lois's. "This may have started as a rough night, but it is starting to feel more like a date. Even better, you said, *our FIRST date.* That implies there may be a second, so I get to see you again."

"Do you even want to see me again? After the way you saw me tonight, I can only imagine what you think of me."

"I haven't seen anything I didn't like. You're still the nicest girl with the prettiest smile in the whole Midwest. What happened earlier was Mike's doing, not yours."

Lois blushed. "I was going to let him, so I think some of the blame is mine. After putting him off for two years, I felt like I owed him."

Scott reached over to hold Lois's hand. "I waited more than six years, just for the chance to hold your hand, and you don't owe me a thing. You didn't owe Mike anything either. You should only do that when you are ready. When you want to as much as your partner does, not when someone tries to guilt you into it."

Lois thought about that. "Tries to guilt you into it. That does sound like Mike. So, you're telling me that you aren't like that?"

Scott squeezed her hand, "I'm not really speaking from experience, but I just don't think it would be the same if both people didn't want it the same way."

Lois gave a small laugh, "Just how much experience are you speaking from?"

Scott looked into Lois's eyes. "Basically, THIS is my first real date. So, how am I doing?"

"I'm having a good time. I think you're doing great. You cooked for me. You made a nice campfire. I don't think I've ever talked this well with anyone. You've been both hero and caregiver. What more could I ask for?"

"It looks like the only things missing are dancing and a late-night swim."

Lois laughed.

Scott stood to face her as he lifted her hand. Lois stood and walked with him to the open area in front of the fire. He set his hands on the sides of her shoulders. Lois put her hands on the sides of his waist and said, "Now all we need is music."

"Don't you hear it?" He moved his head from side to side. "Listen close. What do you hear?"

Lois listened. "I hear the river. It's down the bank behind the trees, but I can hear it." She realized Scott was moving his head with the same rhythm of the river and began to sway side to side with him.

"Can you hear the crickets?"

"They're trying to speed up the tempo." She leaned closer as they moved together.

A bullfrog croaked, causing Scott to say, "There's our bass." He slid his arms around to hold her closer.

"I can hear the fire crackling. It's singing back up." Laying her head against him, Lois slid her hands around to his back to hold him close. Listening to all the forest sounds, they softly moved side to side, enjoying a song that did not end. Lois was surprised at how comfortable she felt in Scott's arms. She was relaxed and comfortable, feeling as if she were where she belonged.

Eventually, Lois lifted her head, looking up to see Scott looking down at her. She raised her head as he tipped his down. When their lips touched, all the forest sounds seemed to vanish. Lois could hear nothing but the silent roar of her pulse. She was safe in his arms, and no one was expecting anything from her tonight. Holding him tightly as they kissed, Lois was genuinely happy. She did not want this moment to end.

Chapter 8: Back to the Party

Rachel and Randy slept peacefully, reclining in the back seat of his Thunderbird. They had barely moved after falling asleep hours earlier. Rachel may have nuzzled in for more comfort, or Randy may have held her more tightly in his sleep, but any observer might have thought them frozen in place.

All was silent as everyone was asleep. Most slept in their cars, but some slept in tents, and a few in sleeping bags over bales of hay. The only sounds were those of nature, and the clock ticking on the dash of Randy's car. As the hands of Randy's clock moved to 4:30, its little bell began to ring. It was not nearly as loud as Rachel's clock had been the day before, but in the stillness of the night, snuggled comfortably against Randy, the alarm was still an enormous jolt to Rachel's nerves.

Rachel's eyes opened and she lunged forward to grab the tiny clock, clipping it shut as she pulled it back. In an instant, the clock was flying like a well launched skipping stone on its way to the Apple River. Rachel could hear the double splash of the clock skipping on the water's surface. Smiling, she turned back to see Randy's wide and startled eyes.

Realizing where she was, and what she had done, Rachel slapped her hands over her mouth in shock. She released her hands to say, "I'm sorry!" Hopping over the side and out of Randy's car, Rachel remembered where she was. Everyone was sleeping, so she repeated in a near whisper, "I'm so sorry. I... I didn't realize what I was doing. I'll go get it."

Randy hopped out of the car and hurried to catch up with her. "It's all right," he said in a quiet voice, trying not to wake anyone. "You just surprised me."

Stopping just short of the river, Rachel turned to see Randy was right behind her. She whispered, "I'll get it back."

"It's okay. You don't have to." Randy stopped as Rachel pulled her shirt over her head and pushed it into his hands.

"Hold this," she said in a soft voice. She quickly set her bra on top of the shirt. Before Randy could say anything, she added her pants, panties, and socks to the pile in his arms.

"It's alright," he called softly, but Rachel was already wading into the river. When the water nearly covered her legs, Rachel dove forward and vanished into the water. Randy stood in shock, wondering if he should drop the clothes and go after her. Rachel popped up and stood with the water line at her hips, at least fifteen feet downriver from where she dove in.

With a defeated expression, a shivering Rachel walked back through the river, and over to where Randy stood waiting. "I don't think it sank. I think it floated downstream."

Randy thought of taking his shirt off, to offer it as a towel, but Rachel calmly pulled her pants from the pile in his arms and pulled them on. Next, she took her shirt and pulled it back over her head. Wadding her bra, panties, and socks in one hand, Rachel looked up to Randy and whispered, "I owe you a clock."

"You are amazing." Randy wrapped his arms around her, holding her tight until she stopped shivering.

Rachel looked up to say, "I've got some dry clothes in Roberta." Walking with their arms around one another, she quietly said, "I did warn you? I told you that I kill clocks."

"Yes, you did. I just didn't realize how honest you were being with me. I think you also said you sleep with your shoes on."

"Only once. Please don't tell anybody about this."

"No one would believe me."

"And when you do... tell them that I was still drunk from last night."

"Are you?"

"No. Not now, anyway. That river's cold enough to sober up a priest."

Reaching her car, Rachel looked to the back seat and saw no sign of Eve. She opened the front passenger door, dropped the underclothes she had been carrying onto the floor, and emptied a bag of clean clothes onto the seat. Leaving her car door open, Rachel asked Randy to stand by the open door, blocking the view of anyone who might be awake.

"Would you like me to turn around?"

"It's too late for that," she whispered. "I've already shown you my crazy side, so what difference would it make? But, if you want to, I understand."

Randy only smiled and shook his head. Rachel removed the damp pants she had worn from the river and dropped them on the car floor. She quickly put on the clean underwear and jeans she had dumped on the seat. Rachel pulled her shirt off again, replacing it with a clean bra, and dry shirt. After shoving her damp clothes into the bag, she dropped the bag back on the floor. She grabbed her clean socks, and quietly shut her car door. Holding her clean socks up for him to see, she whispered, "I have to get my shoes from your car."

Randy wrapped his arms around her and held her tight as he whispered, "You are amazing."

"Is that the new code word for crazy?"

They started to walk back to Randy's T-Bird when Rachel stopped and turned back to her car. "By the way, this is Roberta. Some may think she's not as cool as Terry, but she's special to me and I love her."

"I know what you mean." Randy put his arm around her as they walked. "When I was in college, one of my friends drove an old beater. Whenever someone would say something about it, he said, 'Hey, I lost my virginity in that car.' That always shut them up."

"No. Not yet anyway. But don't ever tell anyone I said that. It's none of their business."

Randy blushed and said, "No, I didn't mean..."

Rachel looked up at him and laughed. "I stripped in front of you twice, and it's a slut-free confession that makes you blush. You really are kind of special."

When they got to Randy's car, Rachel put on her socks and shoes while Randy put on his shoes and retrieved his car keys from Carol's file. She had shown him where to find them after they discussed his early departure.

As Randy was about to get into his car, Rachel grabbed his hand and began shaking it. "It's been great meeting you Randy Richards. I had a good time, and I hope you did too."

After shaking hands, Randy leaned down to give her a simple goodbye kiss. "I had an amazing time Party Girl. I hope I see you again."

"Well, you did say something about giving me a tour of the radio station. And I do owe you an alarm clock."

Randy put his arms around her and kissed her on the top of her head before climbing into his Thunderbird. After starting the engine, he turned to look at Rachel.

Rachel leaned in to give him one long serious kiss. She then stepped back and watched as the Thunderbird followed the driveway through the trees and vanished from sight.

* * *

When Scott and Lois looked through the window of Rachel's car, they saw she was sleeping with her legs and feet on the front seat, and her back against the passenger door. Scott tapped on the window to wake her. Rachel woke and turned to see Scott and Lois, together.

Rachel's door flew open as she sprang out to greet them. Looking down to confirm that they were indeed holding hands, Rachel grabbed Scott with a hug. "Welcome to the family, big brother!" Before Lois could open her mouth to respond, Rachel snapped, "Don't even think of arguing. You're already wearing his clothes."

"That's why we're here. Did you, by any chance, bring an extra change of clothes?" Lois could see that Rachel had indeed changed from the clothes she had worn to the party. She was now wearing a white blouse, and her jeans had flared legs with a heart-shaped patch on one thigh.

"Aw, *'Daddy, I lost my clothes and had to wear Scott's.'* I can see where you're coming from." Rachel grinned when she looked at Lois and asked, "Is your hair wet?"

"I took a shower." Lois's cheeks turned red as she spoke.

Rachel grinned as she opened the back door to remove Eve's shopping bag. "My other clothes got damp, but these are clean and dry. I already gave this back to Eve, but I think she'll loan them out again."

"Did I hear my name?" Eve asked as she walked to join them.

"Can I borrow your clothes again? Or rather, can Lois borrow them this time?" Rachel held up the bag.

"Of course! I'm sure they'll fit better than Scott's." Eve grinned. "But Scott's clothes do look good on you."

Rachel handed Lois the shopping bag and held the door open for her to climb in and change. While Lois changed, Scott went to Ray Ellis's car and set the Instamatic camera on the dash where Ray would see it when he woke.

Rachel looked at Eve and asked, "Did you get a good night's sleep?"

"Eventually. Most of the night, we just talked."

"Talked?"

"Just talked." Eve nodded with satisfaction. "I ran into an old friend, and we didn't do anything but talk, all night. It was nice."

When Lois emerged from Rachel's car, she was completely dressed in Eve's clothes, as Rachel had been after graduation.

Rachel asked, "How about you, cousin? Did you get enough sleep?"

"Not a wink." Lois held her hand out to the returning Scott.

They could smell wood smoke coming from the grill. Danny called out, "Coffee's ready!" Scott held Lois's hand as they walked toward the grill together.

Greg's radio came on and they heard a familiar voice. "Good morning, everyone! It is eight a.m. and the beginning of a brand-new week. This is Randy Richards, and I'm filling in for Phil this morning. He took my shift yesterday, so now you all get to enjoy some Randy time. I'd like to send a very special good morning to the Griffin High School class of seventy-two. They let me share in their graduation yesterday and this class is far-out. Now after digging into our archives, I have a special song to send out to the Griffin gang. This is Tommy Roe..." Randy's voice was quickly replaced with that of Tommy Roe singing, "Party Girl."

Rachel's smile beamed as she looked at her friends and said, "Let's get breakfast."

PART 2: FIVE-YEAR REUNION

Chapter 9: Reunion Morning

Our five-year class reunion was on Saturday, July 23, 1977. A page of questions had been sent with the invitations, resulting in a three-page list of classmates, their locations, spouses, children, and general updates on their lives. Only thirty-eight, a little over a third of the class replied that they would come, but nearly everyone had answered and returned the list of questions. The reunion was to be held at The Pike Lake Resort. The bar would be open to the public, but the dance hall was reserved for our reunion. A catered meal was to be served buffet style, after which there would be presentations and a disco, complete with professional DJs.

* * *

Danny O'Brian was the first to arrive. To be honest, Danny came first because he worked for his uncle, who owned the resort, and he had opened the bar that morning. Danny was filling the beer cooler when our reunion committee arrived to prepare for the reunion.

Danny closed the cooler and greeted them as they arrived. "The dance hall is open, but you won't be alone. Pat finally found a carpenter to fix the steps to the stage, so he's working in there this morning."

Carol Murphy asked, "What's wrong with the steps?"

"One of the bands managed to break them a few weeks ago. Pat's been looking for someone to fix them ever since."

Rich set the box he was carrying on the bar and asked, "Anyone I know?"

"Some guy named Seve. He moved here from Alaska and stopped in yesterday. Pat was complaining how no one would return his call. They talked, and now he's working in there."

Doris thought she had heard him wrong and asked, "Did you say Steve, or Seve?"

"Seve. That's what it said on his shirt anyway. He said something about a boss who didn't use whole names or something. I was busy at the time, so I wasn't really paying attention. He's a big guy with blond hair, reminds me of a blond Grizzly Adams."

Carol thought about that, cocked her head and asked Doris, "Why does that sound familiar?"

* * *

Our reunion committee began decorating with a banner that read, "G.H.S. CLASS OF '72." They also hung crepe paper and other decorations. A collage of pictures Ray Ellis had taken at their graduation party filled up three sheets of poster board. Two long tables were set up for the buffet, and another table was set by the dance hall entrance for greeting classmates as they arrived. A mix of round and long rectangular tables were arranged on the outer sides of the room, leaving the dance floor open.

The carpenter Danny mentioned had his pickup parked near the back door, which was close to the stage. After removing the old steps, he cut and prepared boards on the back of his truck, keeping sawdust and scraps outside and away from the dance floor. When his pieces were prepared, he brought them inside for assembly.

The committee and carpenter kept out of each other's way, although the carpenter was some distraction. He was about six feet tall with long wavy blond hair. A thick curly beard covered much of his face, giving him the appearance of a rugged mountain man.   He wore a tight-fitting T-shirt which highlighted his muscular build. Carol Murphy and Rich's wife, the former Doris Jensen, both seemed to enjoy the view he provided. They had to hang the banner twice; the first time, they were too focused on the carpenter and did not realize their banner was upside down.

With their decorating complete, the committee returned to the bar for a drink while the carpenter cleaned and put his tools away. Carol remained behind to admire his work, which was her excuse to study the carpenter a bit more.

The stage was less than eighteen inches high and sat at the end of the dancehall. After removing the old steps, he built out the end of the stage so that it was four feet wider in the back. He replaced the steps with a ramp running along the side of the stage. The new ramp matched the stage and looked as if it had always been there. The ramp was a definite improvement over the old steps, giving the stage easier access while making it handicapped accessible.

Carol said, "I like it. The ramp's a good improvement. Now bands can roll their equipment up and down, instead of dropping them on the steps."

"Thank you. Pat liked the idea. He'll look it over when he gets up." The carpenter looked up from the tool bag he was packing. "He was tending bar last night, so I don't expect him out too early."

"Danny said your name was Seve?" Carol put her hand out, "I'm Carol Murphy."

"You certainly are." Seve accepted and shook her hand, showing a hint of a smile behind his beard. "Seve was a nickname I got while working at a lumber mill in Alaska. I was wearing a shirt from there when I stopped in yesterday. Pat caught the name on the shirt..."

"Carol!" Rich interrupted, as he called from the bar. "Do you want anything?"

"I better clean up my mess." Seve lifted his tool bag. "I'll meet you in the bar."

"I'd like that." Carol turned and began walking to the bar. "It's nice meeting you."

"Of course it is." Seve watched her leave, with an expression somewhere between curiosity and amusement.

Stepping into the bar, Carol called, "Rum and Coke, since Rich said he's buying."

Danny set Carol's drink on the bar. "What's the final turnout look like?"

"Almost forty of us coming," said Rich. "Most are bringing spouses or dates. That should be enough to keep your uncle happy. We had an ad in the paper too, so we may get some crashers from surrounding classes after the music starts."

Danny asked, "Did you find everyone?"

"Pretty much," said Doris. "Almost everyone answered in one way or another."

They all looked up when they heard the front door open, and Seve entered the bar. "I moved my truck to the parking lot, so it won't be in the way when your band sets up."

"That's good. Would you like a drink now? Or should I call Pat to settle-up with you?" Danny gestured to the phone.

"What I would like is to clean up. I don't have running water at my cabin, and Pat said I could shower in one of the cabins when I was done."

"That's right. He mentioned that in the note he left." Danny grabbed a key from the top of the cash register and gave it to Seve. "Here you go. Cabin three, it is booked, but not until three o'clock. Pat's wife will be in to clean after you're done."

"Not a problem; I shower fast. I'm just looking forward to something with more pressure than my camp shower." Seve accepted the key. "About the Seve, that was a nickname I picked up in Alaska..."

"Rachel!" Doris jumped up and raced to the door when she saw Rachel entering with Randy Richards.

Rachel hurried to greet everyone with hugs. When she turned to Seve, he opened his arms for a hug as well.

Rachel paused briefly before hugging Seve. "I don't know you, but you're cute enough to hug, especially when my husband is watching."

Carol stepped up next to Seve. "Rachel, this is Seve. He just built a new ramp on the stage for you."

"I guess that's worth a hug?" Rachel hugged him again.

Seve tipped his head slightly, as if he were watching something interesting. "Okay. I'm going to get that shower now." He glanced back as he opened the door. "I'll be back in a little bit."

"Did you hear that, Carol?" Rich gave her a small nudge after Seve left. "He's coming back."

"Of course he is." Carol glanced back at the door. "How could he resist?"

Danny looked to Randy and Rachel, "Can I get you guys anything?"

Randy sat on a bar stool. "We need to set up, then shower, but how about a Coke to wash off the drive first? It was a long drive."

* * *

When Seve returned to the bar wearing a clean denim shirt, his hair looked even fuller due to the blow dryer in the cabin's bathroom. Carol was still in the bar talking to Danny. Rachel and Randy were in the dance hall getting everything ready for tonight's disco. Most of the reunion committee had left but would return when it was closer to their cocktail hour.

Danny looked to Seve and asked, "Do you want me to call the house to see if Pat's up?"

"No rush." Seve gave Danny the key. "He can sleep a little longer. I'll run uptown and get something to eat. I'll be back later. I think he'll be satisfied with the ramp."

"Food sounds good." Carol set her glass on the bar. "I haven't eaten since breakfast."

"I haven't even had breakfast yet. Would you like to join me?"

91

She pushed her empty glass away and said, "That's the best offer I've had all day."

* * *

In the Side Street Cafe, Carol and Seve seated themselves in an empty booth. They were quickly greeted by their waitress, Eve Johnson.

"Hi guys!" Eve set two water glasses on the table and handed them menus. "Are you ready for the big reunion?"

Carol nodded as she opened the menu. "Seve, this is Eve Johnson. We went to school together."

"I know. I stopped to eat here on my way through town yesterday. It was Eve who suggested I stop at the resort." Seve looked back to Eve. "I worked there this morning. I made a new ramp for the stage."

"Great!" Eve gave him a congratulatory pat on the shoulder. "You're still getting settled, and you already got your first job. That proves it was time for you to come back." Eve looked from Seve to Carol. "I'll give you a few minutes and be back to take your order."

Carol gave Seve a curious look. "You know Eve?"

"I know a lot of people. I used to live around here, but it seems Eve is the only one who remembers me."

"Where are you living now?"

"I have a cabin in the woods, a few miles northwest of Milltown. It's about an hour's drive from here. I've been gone quite a while, but everything is still there and in good shape. It's nothing fancy, but it'll be nice when I get electricity and running water."

"It sounds rustic." Carol looked at her menu.

"It is, but things were rustic where I was living in Alaska too. At least it won't be quite as cold."

She looked up from the menu, "We do get pretty cold here."

"That's what I thought; then I went to Alaska."

Over lunch, Seve told Carol about his cabin, and his time in Alaska. She told him about her job in town and how she often works as a cocktail waitress when the resort has dances. When Eve brought the check for the meals, Seve picked it up before Carol could look to see what her share would be. "It's my treat. I enjoyed the company."

"Then let me make it up to you." Carol looked into Seve's eyes. "Would you like to come to a class reunion tonight, as my date? There will be a meal, dancing, and a good time with fun people. It's already paid for. You see, I was seeing someone when I replied to the invitation. That didn't work out, so I'm already down for me and a guest."

Seve gave a quick nod. "I'd love to. It'll be fun to see if anyone recognizes me."

Chapter 10: Cocktail Hour

Danny was tending to local customers when Carol and Seve returned to the bar. Pat, Danny's heavy-set uncle, greeted them both by name and asked what they would like. After bringing rum & Coke for Carol, and Mountain Dew for Seve, Pat told Seve how pleased he was with the new ramp. He asked Seve to come to the end of the bar so they could settle-up.

After tending to other customers, Danny walked to where Carol waited. "Well, that must have been a good lunch. I was wondering if we should send out a search party."

"Seve had some laundry to do, so I showed him the new laundromat. He offered to bring me back here first, but I enjoyed keeping him company." Carol sipped her drink, enjoying Danny's annoyance. "He's going to be my date for the reunion tonight."

"That was fast. Do you even know anything about him?"

"He grew up in this area but left when his girlfriend got engaged to someone else. He ended up in Alaska and lived there until a few weeks ago. He's worked as a farmer, construction worker, lumberjack, sawmill, and carpenter. He has a cabin up north, but it's pretty rustic right now. Eve remembers him and says he's a good guy. He's a good listener, picks up the tab, and his truck is only a year old. Is that enough, or do you want to know more?"

"Sounds like you got to know each other pretty well over lunch." Danny began washing glasses in the bar sinks.

"That's the nice thing about spending time in a laundromat. There's lots of empty time with nothing to do but talk. Maybe you should start bringing your dates to the laundromat, or would that feel too much like a commitment?"

"Hey Danny." Seve returned from talking with Pat. "How's it going?"

"Just fine." Danny turned to look at the men at the other end of the bar. "Excuse me, I think one of those guys needs something."

As Danny walked away, Seve turned to Carol. "Pat likes the new ramp. He wants me to look over a few more projects he has in mind."

Carol saw Pat was waiting for Seve to return. "Go ahead. I'll be here when you get back. I need to get ready to greet everyone anyway. They could start showing up any time."

"We shouldn't be very long. He's mostly just mulling over some ideas."

Seve stepped out the back door with Pat, as Rich and Doris returned. They joined Carol at the bar and were quickly greeted by Danny.

Rich looked around the bar. "Where's Rachel?"

"After setting up for their disco, they went to their cabin to get ready." Danny heard the door and looked up. "But that was a while ago, and they look ready now."

Rachel and Randy entered, dressed in tight-fitting disco fashion, and looking ready to party. Rachel's hair was styled and stopped above her shoulders. Randy's hair had a fully layered look. His short sideburns looked good with his thin mustache. Randy said, "Two stingers, with two filberts and two straws in each."

Rachel said, "Make that one stinger and one Diet Coke. I want to keep my head clear until I see how much everyone's changed." When Danny left to get their drinks, Rachel looked to the door and ran to hug Greg and Donna Peterson.

Carol looked at Greg for a moment, as seeing him reminded her of something. Jumping up from her bar stool, she hurried over to him. "Who was that guy you were talking about at the five-hour reunion?"

Greg said, "Beats me; which who?"

"You were talking to Scott about some guy. You said he was a big guy with blond hair. That's why it sounded familiar when Danny described Seve that way."

"Sounds like Stanley Steamer? We talked about him that night. Ray was going on about how far Stan would throw a bale of hay when they worked together."

"That's the one! I remember now. What was his real name?"

"Stan Severs."

"Severs. He said something about Seve being short for his last name." Carol pumped her arms and did a small victory dance. "Now I know who he is."

"Is he back in the area?" Greg stepped closer to the bar. "He didn't come to our reunion last year. I figured he went back to Alaska or something."

"He just got back from there." Carol beamed with the satisfaction of figuring out who Seve was.

"He's Carol's date tonight," Danny said in a less cheerful tone.

"Really?" Greg looked surprised at the thought of Carol dating Stan. "Last I heard, Scott was leaving to work with him. Does he know about Scott?"

Carol stopped smiling and settled back onto her stool. "I don't know. He's been in Alaska, so he might not have heard. Now I'm afraid to bring it up."

Greg looked at Danny, "He was friends with Ray too. If he looked him up, maybe Ray told him."

"Don't bet on it." Danny wiped the bar off with a damp towel. "I think Ray's still in denial about Scott's death. The Griffin Gazette isn't a good enough source for him."

"Bill is bringing the original newspaper tonight," said Doris. "He bought it when he recognized Scott's car in the picture. The article identified Scott as the victim."

"I can't blame Ray." Greg laid money on the bar for his and Donna's drinks. "He and Scott were closer than brothers."

Donna turned on her barstool. "All the more reason for Ray to believe it. If Scott were around, Ray would have heard from him."

Carol lifted her glass and looked at it. "Now I'm afraid to mention it to Seve."

"Don't point me out to him; I don't wanna be the one to tell him." Greg turned on his stool and recognized Randy. "Randy Richards! I thought you were just a one-time speaker. Now we have you for reunions too?"

"I'm part of the entertainment." Randy put his arm around Rachel. "My wife and I do discos together on weekends."

Doris said, "Rachel is on the reunion committee, but living in Colorado made it hard for her to help. So, we let her handle the entertainment."

"Rachel Davis and Randy Richards," Donna wondered aloud. "Who would have guessed they would end up together?"

"Anyone who saw them cuddled up in Randy's T-bird after the music stopped," said Rich.

Randy smiled at the mention of that party. "By the way, Rich, thanks for talking me into coming that night. I wasn't sure it was a good idea, but I'm glad I came."

Rachel put her arm around Randy. "That goes double for me Dickless."

"Please don't bring that back." Rich hunched down and looked to see who was listening. "It seems every time I think that name has died, someone throws it out again. Next thing I know, everyone but my mother starts calling me that."

"So should we change it to 'Dickless, with everyone but his mother'?" suggested Rachel.

"God no!" Rich said with a shudder.

"It looks like our guests from cabin four have decided to join us." Danny was looking at the door as Lois and Mike Burman entered the bar.

Lois's hair was straight and just long enough to cover her shoulders. She wore blue jeans and a long-sleeved shirt. Mike's hair was much shorter now, covering the top of his ears and tapering to collar length at the back. He sported a small mustache and medium sideburns. The bend in Mike's nose made it easy to tell that it had once been broken.

"Lois!" Rachel jumped up and ran to hug her cousin.

Lois flinched slightly as she returned Rachel's hug. "I missed you, Rachel."

Carol hurried into the dance hall and came back with name tags for each of them, along with the stapled pages of classmate information. "It looks like the party is getting started. It's time for me to man my table and check off arrivals."

"Great idea!" Rachel looked to the others. "Let's leave the men out here with their guy talk, and we can all get caught up in the dance hall." Mike held onto Lois's hand until Rachel said, "You can let go of her Mike. You can still tell the guys how much you love her when she's in the next room. We've got a lot of catching up to do." Rachel continued talking to Lois as the girls walked to the dance hall together. "Randy and I have a morning show in Denver, and we do discos on the weekends. I missed you at the family reunion last year. I thought you would be there ..."

Randy turned to say, "So, Mike, it looks like we're cousins-in-law."

* * *

Doris and Carol sat at the first table and prepared to greet everyone with name tags and lists of classmates, while Lois, Donna, and Rachel chose the table next to the stage. Rachel noticed that Lois's hand was empty and left to get a round of drinks.

Donna looked to see that no one else could hear before asking Lois, "You don't have to answer, but I'd like to ask, what happened back then? I mean, when you and Scott came back to the graduation party, you said that you never wanted to see Mike again. I thought you and Scott were really in love."

Lois looked around before answering, "I thought we were too. After all that time of putting Mike off, I couldn't keep my hands off Scott. I was all over him. I thought it was real and forever."

"That's what it looked like to me."

"Scott didn't start his job for a week, so he helped me find a job and an apartment in Eau Claire. I was going to work there through the summer and start college in the fall. Scott left to do road work, but he was going to come back before school started. He had to use pay phones when he called, so we started just writing letters to each other." Lois looked up with pleasant memories. "It was nicer getting letters, because I could read them again whenever I wanted."

Donna said, "Being apart is tough, but it doesn't sound too bad."

"When Mike moved into the same building, I didn't even recognize him with his army buzz-cut. He said that the army didn't work out, and he found a job in Eau Claire. He was just as surprised to see me, and he apologized for everything that happened. He said it was the wine that got to him, but he understood that we were through. I wrote and told Scott all about it. Scott wrote that he didn't trust Mike, but he did trust me."

"So, Scott was okay with him being there."

Lois nodded. "I'd been so busy with all that was happening; I hadn't been keeping track of ... my schedule. I thought I was late, but maybe I just went through it without thinking, like I was on autopilot or something. I wrote to tell Scott that we might be having a baby." Lois bit her bottom lip and took a deep breath. "Scott never wrote to me again."

Lois saw the surprise in Donna's eyes. "Mike saw me enough to know something was bothering me. He thought it might help if I had a special me-day. He made an appointment at a spa. He paid for it in advance, so I couldn't say no. I went, I relaxed, and it was nice. When I came home, Mike said that Scott had stopped by."

"Did he see Mike and get the wrong idea?"

"No," Lois shook her head. "Mike said Scott just stopped by to give me something. Since I was out, he left it with Mike." Lois took a deep breath, preparing for her next words. "Mike gave me a check from Scott, for two thousand dollars. He said that Scott told him that he wasn't ready for kids, and that should be enough to pay for an abortion. He said it was up to me. He didn't wait to tell me in person. He just told Mike to wish me a happy life, and he was gone."

Donna stared in disbelief. She could not picture Scott leaving such a message to Lois.

"I refused to believe it, but the check was from Scott. I hadn't told anyone but Scott, so he's the only one who could have told Mike." Lois looked down with a sigh. "I kept thinking Scott would come back to tell me he changed his mind. Then my father came to see me. He brought the newspaper, the one with the story about Scott dying in New Mexico."

Lois took a deep breath and looked at Donna. "Mike convinced me to forgive him. He still wanted me, and I finally accepted his proposal." Lois looked back and saw Rachel returning from the bar. "Please don't tell Rachel. She and Scott were so close; I'd hate to spoil her memory of him."

Donna promised, "I won't tell a soul."

Rachel carried two lowball glasses and a Diet Coke back to their table. Setting the glasses in front of Donna and Lois, she said, "I'm working, so it's up to my friends to drink my stingers for a while." Taking the two straws from Lois's glass, she said, "First, you must learn proper stinger etiquette." Using the two straws as chopsticks, Rachel lifted one of the hazelnuts from the drink and held it up. "A stinger should have two filberts. You use your straws to remove and eat the nuts. You eat one before you drink, and one after. When you can no longer do that, it's time to cut yourself off."

Donna said, "I can't do chopsticks. I'd never get a second drink!"

Rachel dropped the nut into her mouth, saying, "Fortunately, I can eat soup with chopsticks."

* * *

Seve stopped by the greeting table, setting down a rum and Coke for Carol and a brandy sour for Doris. "I figured you two would be getting thirsty by now. Looks like a good turnout." Carol thanked him and sipped her drink. "We even got a few we weren't expecting."

"Speaking of extras," Doris handed Seve a name tag that read, *"SEVE,"* with *"Carol's companion"* written in smaller letters below it.

Seve read the name tag and smiled through his beard as he stuck it to his shirt. "Can I get one of those lists too?"

"Sure." Carol gave him one of the stapled sheets of classmate information. "It looks like we're filling up. Would you save us a table?"

"Sure thing. Do you mind if Eve sits with us? When I saw her in the bar, she asked if she could join us."

"That's fine," said Carol. "They're big tables with plenty of room."

"Good. I'll let her know before I stake out a table and read this."

Doris watched him walk away before turning to Carol. "You're sharing him with Eve?"

"They're old friends." Carol sipped her drink. "I don't think they dated, but if they did, it was years ago."

Seve selected an empty table on the side of the dance floor where they would have a good view of the stage. He waved to Carol so she would see where he sat, and watched as she waved back in approval. Setting his can of Old Milwaukee on the table, he laid the update sheet before him and began reading from the beginning.

Eve entered the dance hall, wearing a short, tight-fitting red dress, which was cut low and revealing. When she picked up her name tag and classmate sheet, she thanked Carol for letting her join them. Turning to see Seve, she waved and hurried to the table.

Doris leaned to Carol and asked, "Are you sure you want to share him with Eve?"

Carol watched with a look of concern. "She told me they were just friends."

Carol smiled when she looked up to see Ray and Sam Ellis standing before her. After giving them their name tags and classmate pages, Carol pointed to Seve at the table and asked, "Is that an old friend of yours?"

Ray looked unsure for a moment, then he grabbed his wife's hand and hurried over to Seve. Ray bent to look into Seve's eyes. In an instant, Seve was on his feet and hugging Ray like long-lost friends.

Carol felt great satisfaction in having correctly guessed Seve's identity, and decided she would resist the urge to call him Stanley Steamer. She looked to Donna, who nodded, confirming that she saw the reunion of Ray and Seve as well. Carol felt even better when Eve, who had been seated between Ray and Seve, got up and moved to the chair on the other side of Sam, allowing Seve and Ray to speak without having to talk around her. Now Carol wondered how long Seve and Ray would talk before their conversation came to Scott and his passing.

* * *

When Bill Spenser arrived, he carried a sheet of tag board with the front page of a newspaper matted onto it. The newspaper was the one he had spotted years earlier, which reported the story of Scott Severson's death. Carol brought the paper over to Rachel so she could refer to it when she made the announcement of Scott's passing.

Lois read the story, and after looking at the date on the paper, she said, "That's about a week after he stopped by my apartment." Feeling an urge to cry, Lois stood up, saying, "Excuse me. I need to use the bathroom."

"I'll go with you." Rachel began to get up.

"No." Lois held up her hand, "I'm going to use the one in the cabin, so I won't have to wait in line. I'll be right back. I promise."

Rachel nodded with understanding.

Seve was on his way to the bar when he stopped by the greeting table to ask Carol if she was ready for another drink.

"Perfect timing." Carol held up her glass. "This one is almost dead." Looking to the door, she saw Dave Masters, accompanied by a tall slender blond woman. "My last holdout just arrived, so I'll meet you at the table."

Seve turned to go through the doorway when someone bumped into him. "Excuse me," he apologized, as he looked down and saw Lois.

"Excuse me. I'm sorry. I wasn't watching where..." Lois froze when she saw the eyes looking back down at her. "Excuse me," she said coldly, and she hurried to the front door.

Dave Masters was dressed in a suit, which was more fitting for an executive board meeting than for a disco or country party. Nadine held his arm as they walked to the last empty table. Originally Nadine had planned on wearing a formal dress. When Dave told her there would be a disco dance, she chose to wear her little black dress instead. Made by a top fashion designer, her dress was tight fitting, short, and displayed generous cleavage. It was designed to leave a lasting impression.

When Nadine seemed surprised that no one showed them to their seats, Dave explained, "This is a small country resort. A cocktail waitress may take our drink orders, but that's about as personal as the service will get." He looked around the room. "I don't see any waitresses yet. You stay and hold our place while I'll get a couple of drinks."

* * *

When Mike saw Lois returning through the front door, he hurried over to ask, "Where did you go?"

"I went to the cabin to use the bathroom."

He grabbed her arm to pull her close. "Why?"

"Because there's no line in the cabin, and it's more private. Also, I hurt and wanted some aspirin for the pain." She looked up and added, "Holding me like that isn't helping." As he let go of her arm, she said, "Don't worry. The only thing I told them about you was how wonderful you are. All the girls are jealous of me."

"I'm sorry." He looked around, "It's almost time to eat. Let's find a table."

"We already have seats; Rachel is saving our places."

* * *

With all attendees present and accounted for, Carol left the remaining blank name tags, pens, and classmate pages on the table by the door. If anyone else arrived, they would be able to make their own name tags. Seve returned with the round of drinks, and Carol took her seat next to him. She had barely sipped her drink when Danny O'Brian approached the table.

Danny asked, "Did you save a place for me?"

"Right here!" Eve pushed out the chair between herself and Carol, before saying to the others. "I hope you don't mind. Danny was working, so I told him I'd save him a place."

"Glad to have you, Danny," said Seve.

Danny took his seat, feeling a bit awkward when he realized that he was sitting between Carol and Eve. "Eve tells me she was hoping to see someone else, but it turns out he was already taken. So, I get to be a happy second place."

"First place now." Eve set her hand on his. "Someone else was only a thought and a distant memory, and that's all I'm going to say about him."

Rachel carried the newspaper onto the stage and picked up her microphone. "May I have your attention please?" She paused, waiting for the room to quiet. "It's six o'clock, and the food is ready, so feel free to dish up at the buffet. While I'm up here, I would like to make one announcement before I put this next to Ray's photos." She held the newspaper up as she spoke. "Bill Spencer is now an over-the-road trucker, so he gets to see a lot of this country. In fall of '72, he was at a diner in New Mexico when he saw this newspaper." Rachel held the paper up. "Bill also sent a copy of this to the Griffin Gazette. The Gazette did some editing, which caused some to doubt the story, but now Bill brought us the original."

Seeing the newspaper, Seve turned to Carol and said, "Excuse me. There's something I need to do."

Rachel turned the paper around so she could reference it as she spoke. "I'll just sum this up for now, and you can read the article at your convenience."

Greg noticed Seve walking across the room and leaned close to ask Donna, "Who's that?"

Donna looked and replied, "That's your old friend. Stanly Steamer."

Greg looked puzzled and said, "Not unless someone squeezed him until he was six inches taller. When I said he was a big guy, I meant he was heavyset and built like a bull."

Rachel continued, "A local man with a history of drunk driving ran a red light and crashed into a 1965 Rambler, which was going through the intersection at the time." Rachel looked down at the paper as she read aloud, "The driver of the Rambler, one Scott Severson, who had recently arrived from Wisconsin, was killed instantly." She turned the page around for others to see. "Those of us who remember Scott's Rambler will have no trouble recognizing it in this picture. That's what caused Bill to..."

"Excuse me." Seve tapped Rachel on the shoulder. "Before you go any far..."

Rachel quickly turned and lowered her mic. "What are you doing up here? I'm in the middle of something important. Get off the stage!"

"But there is a problem..."

"Yes, there's a problem. Scott was like a brother to me, and your interrupting isn't making this any easier."

Seve leaned forward and looked Rachel in the eyes. "I never thought that you, of all people, would fail to see me. Would it help if I took my clothes off and jumped into the swimming hole?"

Rachel's opened her eyes wide when she heard that. Lowering her microphone, she looked up into his eyes.

Seve pulled a new name tag from his shirt pocket, peeled the paper off the back, and slapped it over the previous tag on his pocket. Rachel looked at the tag that read, *'Scott Severson.'*

Bringing her hands up, Rachel pushed the long hair back and away, so she could see more of his face. When she looked into his eyes, Rachel yelled, "Scott!" loud enough for everyone to hear. She quickly wrapped her arms around him with a big hug, before pushing him away and looking back to the newspaper.

"Can I explain now?" Taking the microphone from Rachel's hand, Scott looked out to his classmates and spoke. "I should begin with an apology. You see, until I saw this newspaper, I was trying to figure out what was going on too. When I came back here, I wondered why hardly anyone recognized me. I assumed it was just the long hair and beard. I thought I would just wait and see how long it would be before someone saw me, as me. I think maybe four of you did." Scott took the newspaper and held it up. "I finally understood when Rachel came up here with this." He turned the paper so he could look at it again. "The reporting was technically accurate, but not so much for this area. Scott THOMAS Severson went by his middle name, so everyone up here knew him as Tom. Scott was his legal name, the name on his driver's license, and the official name on the accident report the newspaper used for this story."

Scott handed the paper back to Lois and looked around the room. "Things kind of fell apart for me in Wisconsin, so I went to New Mexico to see Dad. After the long drive, I really needed a shower. So, while I was cleaning up, Dad ordered a pizza and ran uptown to get it. I had parked behind his truck, so he took my car. That is why Scott Senior was driving Scott Junior's car, when that drunk driver killed him." Scott paused and took a deep breath. "I had Dad buried next to Mom. After that, I decided to just get away for a while. I had a friend who was always talking about Alaska, so I headed up there for a few years. The Griffin Gazette did publish a death notice for Dad, TOM Severson, but I imagine that was a week or two before they got this story from New Mexico. They must have missed the connection too. I'm sorry for the confusion." Scott handed the microphone back to Rachel and returned to his chair.

Rachel was still searching for words when Randy stepped up with his mic, and said in his announcer's voice, "This concludes our dramatic interlude for tonight. You may now proceed to the buffet line in an orderly fashion."

Nadine turned to Dave Masters, and asked, "Was that some kind of play, or was it real?"

"Back in high school, Scott had shorter hair than anyone in the class." Dave looked at Scott as he spoke. "After a fresh haircut, he came to school with white sidewalls. He also had zero facial hair, not even sideburns. His new mountain man look took everyone by surprise. I know I didn't recognize him."

"Okay, one more question." Nadine leaned close to Dave, "What is a buffet line?"

"Picture a restaurant, where instead of the staff dishing up your plate to make it look pretty, they bring the food out so you can pile it on your plate any way you like."

Nadine said, "You are kidding?" as Dave took her by the hand and led her to the buffet.

Chapter 11: Dinner and Dancing

The buffet tables included salad plates and a small salad bar, followed by dinner plates and the main meal. One roaster contained beef tips in gravy, followed by another with baked chicken. There was also a choice of scalloped or baked potatoes, green beans, and large homemade dinner rolls. Altogether, it was a totally new experience for Nadine, who had never even dished up her own plate before.

Nadine's greatest surprise was watching Bill Spencer, who was just ahead of her in line. Bill began by opening his baked potato and pouring the beef tips and gravy inside of it. He topped that with sour cream and added shredded cheese from the salad. Bill's method was repeated by others, and that was one of the best baked potatoes I've ever had. I suspect that the surprise on Nadine's face may have been hiding a bit of envy. Unfortunately for Nadine, she lacked the courage to try such a dish in public. She could try it at home, but that would require that she first explain it to her cook.

Most of us were still eating when Randy returned to the stage for pre-disco entertainment. He picked up his mic and began: "I really enjoyed talking to so many of you this afternoon. There are a lot of questions out there about how Rachel Davis got into radio, and why she married me. If you don't mind my talking while you eat, I'd like to answer those questions.

"At that party five years ago, your five-hour reunion, I offered to give Rachel a tour of the radio station. Later that week, she arrived to take me up on that offer. During that tour, we happened to come across Midnight Wally, who was complaining to the station manager about not having anyone to answer the phone while he was on the air. The manager told him that no one was available. Wally said, '*Hire someone!* So, of course, Rachel chimed in with, '*I need a job.*' Her timing was perfect, and Rachel was hired as Wally's assistant from midnight to five. She enjoyed it and began taking classes to learn everything she could about radio.

"Fast forward a few months. One night, Wally left his mic on after starting a song. During the song and after it ended, if you listened closely, you would have heard Rachel giving CPR to Wally, who had just suffered a heart attack while he was on-the-air. She got his heart started before the ambulance arrived, and she only broke one rib doing it. When Wally was on his way to the hospital, Rachel's voice was heard on the air for the first time.

"She apologized for the confusion and explained that Midnight Wally was having '*technical difficulties.*' She then stayed on the air to finish his shift. The next day, the station manager asked Rachel to continue doing Wally's show until he was ready to return. Wally recovered and decided it was time to retire. 'Midnight 'til 5:00, with Rachel Davis,' became a permanent show every weekday."

Looking over his audience, Randy asked, "Do any of you remember the busses and billboards with Rachel's picture and the words 'Midnight 'till 5:00, with Rachel Davis,' followed by the station's call letters?"

Randy saw several hands go up from people who remembered those ads. "You may be pleased to know that picture of Rachel was taken by your own Ray Ellis." Some applause went up for Ray who stood up and gratefully took a bow. "Ray shot those pictures by the light of tiki torches at your party five years ago."

Ray retook his seat and Randy returned to his story. "Schedules changed, and I ended up doing weekday mornings, so I arrived every day just as Rachel's shift ended. After a year of that, I was offered a job at a station in Denver. An old religious station had been purchased, and the new owners were preparing to start fresh with a whole new format. They made me an offer that was too good to refuse. I gave my notice, and eventually, I came in for my last broadcast in the Twin Cities." Randy pushed a button, and we heard the taped recording of that broadcast.

"Good morning one and all. It is five a.m., and this is Randy Richards in the morning. I have to say, I am a little disappointed. Since this is my last day here, I was hoping to talk with Rachel Davis before she stepped out. Unfortunately, she started her last song and was out of the booth before I could see her. Hey Rachel, if you can hear me, I would like to share a mic with you one more time before I leave." A song began to play but was edited out of the tape.

Randy's voice returned. "It looks like Rachel heard me. She's watching me from the door, but she's not coming in. This booth has a big glass door for a sound barrier. Right now, the lovely Rachel Davis is watching me from the other side of that door. Are you coming in, Rachel? No response. She's just standing there with a funny grin. I see she has her coat on already, so she must have been on her way out. Is that a new coat Rachel? I haven't seen that one before. It looks like a raincoat. It's not raining Rachel. Is that what they call a trench coat? Rachel, if you come in, I have a special song I'd... Whoa!!! Ahhh... Please excuse me... I am speechless. Ah... Rachel did manage to surprise me. I must say, that is a lovely outfit, Miss Davis. I have not seen anything like that since the mermaid sighting in the Apple River! Now please, Rachel, just open the door and come in here. I have something for you." A commercial began to play, but it was also edited out.

"We are back. The lovely Rachel Davis has agreed to come in and join me. Good morning, Rachel."

Rachel's voice said, "Good morning, Randy."

"I must say, I like your outfit. Did you wear that through your entire show?"

"No. I saved this for your show. Just a little goodbye to help you remember me when you're in Denver."

"Should I mention that you are barefoot?"

"I never wear shoes when I'm swimming. Your listeners should know, I modeled my favorite swimsuit, and it may be a bit too much for Randy."

"Too much is not exactly how I would describe that, but I do like it."

"You said you had something for me?"

"Yes, I do. First, let me start this song, since this is a music station." Tommy Roe's *Party Girl* began playing, but the mic remained on so they would still be heard.

Rachel's voice said, "You left your mic on."

Randy's voice replied, "That is because I am feeling incredibly brave this morning."

There was a pause in their conversation as Rachel listened to the song before saying, "You played that the morning after we met. You dedicated it to my class that morning."

As the song played, Rachel's voice said, "What are you doing?"

Randy's voice said, "You once said I had to do this on one knee."

Tommy Roe sang, "...I realize, there's fifty guys, that you've got on a string..."

Rachel asked, "What's that?"

Tommy sang, "...But I'm going to change all that, when I show you this diamond ring..."

Rachel's voice said, "OH MY GOD! IS THAT REAL!?"

The song played through to the end, with Tommy Roe singing, "...so dance, your last dance, Party Girl."

"Are you still going to Denver?" asked Rachel's voice.

"Denver heard your show. They said they have room for you too," said Randy's voice.

"I should talk to my parents about this."

"As of last Saturday, your dad said he is fine with it. If he knew what you're wearing, he might insist on it." A sound card was played with the sounds of whistling rockets and exploding fireworks. Randy's voice returned to say, "Ladies and gentlemen, what you have just heard is not a bit, and you heard it here live. Rachel does not seem to be talking now, but I believe the kiss I just received was a yes."

Randy stopped the tape and said, "And that is how I managed to get your classmate to marry me."

Rachel joined Randy on the stage with her microphone. "And yes, I do still have that swimsuit, but no, I will not model it for you."

Doris joined them on the stage, and together they gave out token reunion prizes. A classmate now living in Los Angeles received a U.S. roadmap for traveling the farthest to get there. For having the most hair growth since high school, Scott received a comb. Another award was given for having the most children, adding the ages of their children to decide the tiebreaker. The last prize was for the most pregnant girl at the reunion. The winner, who was four months pregnant, received a box of disposable diapers from Doris. Rachel asked her to wait, explaining that she had another prize for her as well.

Rachel held up a hardcover book. "This a first printing of 'What You Should Know About Fetal Alcohol Syndrome,' autographed by the author, Doctor Nomora Drinking."

Randy said, "She was a guest on our show last month, but I don't think that was her name."

"Maybe it was Keepya Sober. I just know the bitch made me give up stingers for the next six months." Rachel gave her the book and said, "I hope you enjoy it more than I did. I miss my stingers."

"Whaat?" A confused Randy turned to look at Rachel.

"She's a whole month ahead of me, so she gets the prize." Rachel gestured to Randy and said, "And that, my friends, is what a man looks like when he discovers that he's going to be a daddy."

With the award portion of the evening completed, the lights were turned down, and the Richards began playing music for dancing. Randy and Rachel played all the popular disco songs, mixing them with rock and roll, and other songs that were popular while we were in school. Randy also played songs that he could dedicate to classmates with matching names: Richie Valens *DONNA,* for Donna (Strong) Peterson; Tommy Roe's *CAROL,* for Carol Murphy; *Help me RHONDA* by The Beach Boys; and *JOY to the World,* by Three Dog Night. It seemed that for most girls in our class, Randy had a song with her name.

Rachel took her cordless microphone around the room so she could stop at tables to have brief talks with classmates between songs. Vanessa Winters joined the Peace Corps but delayed leaving for Brazil until after this reunion. Peter Baker explained that his degree in computer science originally got him a job with a large corporation, but he also works part time with a pair of detectives.

During one of those breaks, Rachel stopped at Dave Masters' table. "We now have our Valedictorian, the one and only Dave Masters. Who is this with you, Dave?"

"This is my fiancée, Nadine DeBraught. Nadine does some modeling, and I met her when she came to visit her father, who happens to be my boss."

"It's a pleasure to meet you, Nadine, and congratulations on your engagement."

Nadine leaned close to the mic. "Thank you. This is my first visit to Wisconsin."

"I do hope you are enjoying your visit, and how could you not at Masters' Manor?"

"Actually," Dave leaned close to the mic, "she hasn't seen my parent's house yet. They are on vacation in Mexico, and they won't be back until Wednesday. The house is locked up and empty, so we're staying at the Riverside Hotel until they return."

"Well, that gives you time to show Nadine some of the sights in this area." Rachel turned to face Nadine. "Before we give the show back to Randy, I do want to mention that Nadine's dress is one of the nicest I've ever seen."

Nadine leaned to the mic and said, "Thank you. I chose this one special for tonight. It's a Pierre Couture."

"Well, it is fantastic! Dave, you need to get her on the dance floor so everyone can see it."

Randy's voice came over the speakers. "And this is for the lovely NADINE." Chuck Berry's Nadine began playing as people got up to dance.

Rachel turned her microphone off and laid it on the table. "If you two want to dance to Nadine's song, I'll wait here, and we can talk without the mic when you get back." Nadine got up to dance, but Dave seemed hesitant. "Go ahead, Dave, you can do it. Just leave your coat and tie and loosen the top few buttons of your shirt."

Dave stood and removed his coat and tie while Nadine listened to the song with a look of confusion.

Rachel said, "This one isn't Disco, Nadine. It's pure rock and roll, and it's just for you."

Nadine took Dave's hand and pulled him to the dance floor as he was loosening his buttons. This may have been Dave's most casually dressed moment in years.

Disco may have been all the rage in the late seventies, but those of us in Griffin, Wisconsin still enjoyed rock and roll. It was not long before the dance floor was filled. Even though Dave was not dressed for dancing, he and Nadine were having a great time. As the song neared its end, Nadine nearly froze with shock when she saw Eve dancing with Danny.

Dave saw Nadine's expression and asked, "What's wrong?"

"That girl," Nadine looked around nervously, "she's wearing the same dress!"

Dave saw Nadine was looking at Eve. "That's Eve Johnson. It's not the same dress; yours is black and hers is red."

"It's a different color, but it is the same dress!" She grabbed Dave's hand and began walking to the table. "Quick, let's get off the dance floor before someone notices."

Dave leaned close to her and spoke softly, "No one will notice. No one here would even care about that. If anything, you can get together like mismatched book ends."

"How is this even possible?" she softly asked when they were near the table. "I didn't think anyone here could afford a Pierre Couture!"

When they reached the table, Rachel said, "You guys looked great out there. Why the quick return?"

Nadine quickly slouched into her chair. "I can't go back out there. It's too embarrassing."

Dave tried to explain, "Eve's dress is a different color, but it looks like the same dress to Nadine."

Rachel looked to see Eve on the dance floor and looked back to Nadine. "It's hard to tell, but that's not a problem here. You could just go out there together and make the best of it. Let's call her over here and see for sure." Rachel waved to get Eve's attention. "Eve! Come here for a minute."

Nadine wanted to hide under the table, but that would only draw more attention.

When Eve arrived, Rachel said, "Okay, Nadine, stand up so we can compare. We need to see you two side by side." Nadine was reluctant, but realized this must be as embarrassing to Eve as it was to her. She slowly got up and stood next to Eve.

"Wow!" Dave exclaimed when he saw them side by side. Both girls stood about the same height and had similar facial features. Nadine's blonde hair was quaffed and barely reached the shoulders of her black dress, while Eve's equally blonde hair was long and straight, covering the back of her red dress. The fit and cut of the dresses looked nearly identical. Both fit tight, revealed generous cleavage, and were eye-catchingly short. Dressed as they were, Nadine and Eve might have passed as sisters.

"Wow is right," Rachel agreed. "You two look great together. You're a matched set, in different colors."

Eve looked at Nadine and realized what they were seeing. "Has your father ever been to Griffin?"

"Never," Nadine assured her. "Why?"

"Never mind!" Eve blushed at the thought. "Just something that crossed my mind for a moment, but I do love our dress."

"Thank you. Where did you get yours?"

"Oh," Eve looked embarrassed. "I wanted something special for tonight, so I looked through some fashion magazines. I saw a dress like this and thought it would be perfect for me in red. I made a few changes, so it's not quite the same as the one in the magazine." Looking at Nadine's dress, Eve recognized it and said, "Oh my God! You have the real one. I'm so sorry."

"Don't be. You two look great together." Rachel assured them. "You should run with it for the night. Just act like you planned it this way."

"We're not completely the same." Eve turned and lifted her long hair off her back. "I made mine with a low back, so it would be cooler for dancing. You couldn't tell because my hair covers it." She turned to face Nadine again. "I cut mine a little lower in front too, and it's about an inch shorter." Eve blushed when she admitted, "I tried to make it a little sexier than the one in the magazine. I'm sure my fabric is cheaper too, but it looks right, and it is comfortable. Black looks great on you, but I like red."

Nadine felt better when Eve pointed out the differences. "You made that from looking at a picture?"

"I learned to sew when I was ten," Eve said proudly. "I can make or repair just about anything I set my mind to."

As *The Hussle* began playing, Dave rolled up his sleeves and asked them both, "Ladies, may I have this dance?"

Forgetting her embarrassment, Nadine agreed to go with the mismatched-set look and walked out to the dance floor with Eve and Dave. She realized that anyone who noticed the similarity would easily realize that she was wearing the original, and it was Eve who wore the knockoff.

As she watched the three dancing together, Rachel realized why Eve had asked about Nadine's father. Eve and Nadine did resemble each other, well enough to pass as sisters.

Chapter 12: Winding Down

With dancing and conversations, everyone was having a good time. Scott and Carol had their arms around each other as they walked to the front door. Once outside, with the door closed behind them, Carol let out a big breath to relax while still holding Scott for support. "Thank you for helping me walk. I was afraid I would fall flat on my face with everyone watching."

"Believe me, it was my pleasure." Holding her as he was, Scott was nearly carrying her as they walked.

"I'm blaming Rachel for this. I should have stuck to rum and Coke." Carol let out a laugh, "But those stingers sure can knock you on your ass."

Reaching Scott's pickup, he opened the passenger door and helped Carol inside.

When she heard Scott start his truck, she asked, "Are you taking me to my place, or yours?"

"You may need to throw up later, and I don't have indoor plumbing."

Carol nodded. "Better make it mine. It's closer anyway."

From the corner of the bar, Mike Burman watched as they drove away. Lois had been right when she said using the bathroom in their cabin was easier. Lois was entering the cabin as he was leaving, so Mike was certain she had not seen them leaving together. Pleased with his timing, Mike returned to the bar and ordered a can of Mountain Dew. He was expecting a long night, and extra caffeine should help.

On her way back to the bar, Lois noticed a 1965 Mustang convertible in the parking lot. She walked over for a closer look, fondly remembering the one Mike had driven when he first showed up in Eau Claire. Other than being red, this car looked just like the blue Mustang Mike had owned. The top was down, allowing Lois to get a good look inside. This car was more than familiar. Everything was exactly as she remembered Mike's car. It even had the same slice in the upholstery on the back of the passenger's seat. Lois went to the rear wheel of the driver's side. She knelt to see that not only was it missing the hubcap, but a spray of black paint covered a broken lug bolt, with the same overspray of paint on the wheel. Lois remembered breaking that lug, and applying black paint so it wouldn't rust. She had no doubt that this really was Mike's old car.   Lois headed back, remembering how Mike had told her that his Mustang had been totaled in an accident. Returning to the bar, Lois passed Eve Johnson on her way out. She turned to watch as Eve drove away in that same Mustang.

Mike had been watching for Lois and hurried to meet her when she entered the door. "Hey, Sweetie, something came up, and I have to leave."

"What?" Lois was confused and suspicious. "What happened?"

"I had a talk with Scott, and he wants to get together. He said he had a lot of time to think when he was in Alaska, so he wants to get together so we can talk things out. He knows he has a lot to explain and apologize for. He's getting gas and wants me to meet him at the station. I'll follow him to his place, and we can talk there. I think he's right. He's done a lot of things I never told you about, and it will be good to clear the air."

"Really?" Lois was surprised. Mike had always resented Scott for some reason, but he never said anything about wanting to clear the air. "Does he want me to come too? He still owes me an explanation."

"It will be just him and me this time. If he has any reasonable explanation, I'll let you know. I may be wasting my time, but I would like to get some things behind us."

"When will you be back?"

"Sometime tomorrow morning. I don't know how long this will take, but I'm sure it will be too late to drive back tonight."

"Okay, I'll see you tomorrow. Drive careful."

"Thanks for understanding, Sweetie. I'll see you tomorrow." Mike turned and hurried out the door.

Lois frowned with suspicion as she watched him leave. She doubted very much that Mike would ever go anywhere to meet with Scott. Not peacefully anyway. Still, with Mike gone, she could finally relax and enjoy the reunion. On her way back to the dance floor she met Rachel. "Why did Eve leave so early? I thought she was having a good time."

"She wanted to get home to her daughter. She also said something about not wanting someone else's man. I'm guessing some married guy tried hitting on her or something. She's coming back to visit tomorrow." Rachel looked back to the stage. "I better get back to work. I've left Randy alone for quite a while."

"Okay," Lois smiled to her cousin. "And congratulations on the baby."

"Thanks, Cousin." Rachel grinned and said, "You know, I like the sound of that."

* * *

Scott parked in front of a little white house on Maple Street. "Is this the right place?"

Carol turned to look out the window. "Home sweet home." She tried to open the truck door but was having difficulty.

Scott opened the door from the outside and helped her down. He held her up as they walked to the front door. When she had trouble getting her key into the door, Scott took the key and opened it for her.

"I'm so glad you got me out of there before I fell on my face." She clung to Scott for support as he helped her into the house and shut the door behind them. "I'm sorry I got so drunk tonight, Seve... Scott... Both of you! And I do mean both of you because that's what I'm seeing."

"Are you going to be alright?"

"If I can get to my bed, I'll be fine." Carol pointed to her bedroom door. "It's in there." She held onto Scott as he helped her to the bedroom. "You really surprised everyone. This was our first resurrection. I'm sorry I didn't recognize you sooner. You just look so different with that beard, and all that hair. But it's good. It looks so good on you, and I can't believe I didn't recognize you. And I looked right into your eyes." Carol stared into Scott's eyes. "I guess I just didn't get to look into your eyes enough when we were in school." She released him and turned to toss her sheet and blanket aside before sitting on the bed.

Scott knelt and removed her shoes and socks.

"Thank you." Carol began unbuttoning her shirt. "I think I need all the help I can get."

Scott tossed her shoes and socks by the foot of the bed and looked up, as Carol tossed her shirt toward a chair. Putting her hands on the side of Scott's face, she looked into his eyes. "You're both still here. I can't believe that I asked Scott Severson on a date, and now he's helping me take my clothes off. You know Scott, you were the biggest hunk in school, but you never had time for any of us." Carol pulled him close for a long kiss.

Scott put his arms around Carol and returned the kiss, moving with her as she lay back on the bed. As they kissed, Scott's hand moved down to unbuckle Carol's belt, and then he unbuttoned her pants. Ending the kiss, Scott moved over to grab the sides of Carol's pants and carefully began pulling them down. Carol raised her hips enough for her jeans to slide down. Scott grabbed the bottom of her pants' legs, gave a brief pull, and tossed her blue jeans to the chair.

Carol sat up and reached around to unfasten her bra.

Scott lifted the top of the blanket, bringing it forward to cover Carol as she lay back, extending her arm out to drop her bra to the floor. He leaned in to kiss her again as he pulled the blanket up to rest it over the top of her shoulders.

"You're not staying, are you?"

"No," he answered with reluctance. "But thank you for the best offer I've had in a very long time. Believe me. I am tempted."

"Then why are you going?"

"If I were to stay with you, it would have to be with you, and not Rachel's stingers. I don't think my ego could take it if I stayed, and you couldn't remember it in the morning."

"I don't think I could forget, no matter how drunk I am."

"There's another thing too." Scott brushed the hair from her eyes. "Danny's still a friend of mine, and I saw how he watches you. I know what it's like to feel like that."

Carol lowered her eyes with a sad expression. "I know how Danny feels. I feel the same way about him. That's why I waitress there on weekends. But Danny doesn't want to do anything until he can buy his uncle's resort. His uncle might never sell it to him, and I can't wait that long." Carol let out a sigh. "He can still work there. He lives in one of the little cabins, but he could stay here too. This house is big enough for both of us, and I can handle the rent." She looked at Scott and grinned. "Maybe if you don't go back tonight, Danny will realize that I won't wait forever."

Scott leaned down and kissed her on the forehead. "Maybe if I do go back tonight, Danny will realize that he shouldn't be waiting either."

Carol put her hands on the sides of Scott's head and pulled him close for another big kiss. "Thank you, Scott." She let go of him and pulled her arms under the blanket. "You were terrific."

"And so were you." Tucking the blanket back up to her chin, Scott stood, and turned the lights off as he let himself out.

* * *

Danny grew a big smile when he saw Scott back so quickly. "Scott old buddy, it's good to see ya' again. Can I buy you a drink?"

"I think you owe me one." Scott sat on the barstool. "Just a Dew though. I've got a long drive home."

"Good 'nuff." Danny laid a dollar on the bar and asked Pat for a Mountain Dew. "I didn't think you'd be coming back tonight."

"I was tempted not to." Scott took a drink from his can. "So why did you?"

121

"I'm asking myself that same question. I guess I still have ghosts of memories here. She wasn't who I really wanted, and I knew I wasn't the one she really wanted. I'd rather not be in the middle of something where I don't belong."

Danny drank from his bottle. "So, what does she want?"

"She wants to stop waiting. She wants someone she can count on. Someone who's there for her." Scott looked Danny in the eyes. "If you keep girls waiting too long, they'll stop waiting." Scott raised his can for another drink. "I learned that the hard way. I finally had the girl of my dreams, and I left to earn a big nest egg. After a while, she stopped writing. When I came back, she was living with and engaged to someone else. If I could do it all over again, I never would have left, and she wouldn't have had to wait."

Danny looked down, shaking his head. "I have a little cabin here. It's hardly big enough for one person."

"She rents a house in town that's big enough for both of you." Scott turned his can between his fingers. "You're waiting for your uncle to decide to retire, and she's been waiting for you. Everyone has a point where the goal is no longer worth waiting for."

Scott looked up to the ceiling as if in deep thought. "I should at least get electricity and indoor plumbing before I bring anyone to my cabin, but I bet she would put up with it as-is. She would probably pitch in to help fix it up." He looked over to Danny. "She seems like the type who would rather work on something than wait for it." He took another drink from his can. "Maybe in a week or two, I should call on Carol again."

Danny grinned back at him. "Maybe that will be too late for you."

Scott raised his can, touching Danny's beer bottle in toast to his last statement.

Scott stood and turned back to Danny. "By the way, would you be willing to pick her up tomorrow? She left her car here, so she'll need a ride back."

Danny nodded with a smile. "Consider it done."

Rachel and Randy laughed their way through the front door, both with dripping wet hair. Stepping up to the bar, Randy ordered two stingers, and Rachel added, "And one Diet Coke." As they waited for their drinks, Randy stepped back and shook his head, spattering drops of water on anyone close.

Rachel cried out, "You're worse than a dog."

"Hey, it was your idea!" he said with a laugh.

Danny looked to the dance hall. "I thought you two were on stage. I just heard you talking up there."

Rachel brushed her wet hair back with her fingers. "We had a tape prepared so we could both take a break together." Pat set their drinks on the bar, and Rachel picked up one of the stingers.

Scott said, "I thought you were off those for the next six months?"

"Unfortunately!" Rachel took the two straws in her fingers, using them to lift one of the hazelnuts. Rachel dropped the nut in her mouth and said, "I can still have the best part, and there's still one Filbert left for Lois."

"So let me get this straight," said Scott. "You're not drinking, but you still get stingers and just hand them off to your friends?"

"I still get the first nut, and more people get to experience the wonderful stinger. Some people really loosen up after a few. Also, the booze that soaks into the nut doesn't count." Rachel patted her belly. "Junior can handle that much. The damn prohibitionist." Grabbing her Diet Coke with her free hand, Rachel followed Randy back to the dance hall.

Danny watched as they walked away and asked, "Why is their hair wet?"

Scott grinned, "How's the swimming down by the dock?"

Chapter 13: The Morning After

Lois awoke to a chorus of bird songs, reminding her of just how loud morning birds can be. An ache in her head brought memories of Rachel, who had given Lois more stingers than she could remember. Beyond that, Lois's memory seemed to be blank. She was glad that they had rented the cabin, which was only a short walk from the bar.

Whatever Mike's real reason for leaving, it did give Lois this time to enjoy having the cabin, and this comfortable bed, all to herself. He had said that he would be back sometime in the morning, but Lois expected he would return closer to their noon checkout time.

Stretching under the blanket, soft flannel sheets seemed to hug her as she lay. It seemed odd that the resort would use flannel sheets in the summer, but they did feel good. Maybe even too good? Lois shifted slightly before lifting the blanket to see that she wore nothing but her panties. She remembered packing pajamas, but must have been too tired, or more likely too drunk, to put them on.

As she looked at the room, Lois realized something was not right. The cabin they rented had faded blue walls, but she was seeing white walls, paneling, and finished woodwork. This cabin even had a second bed, just a dresser width away from the one she was in. Holding the blanket against her, Lois sat up for a better look, confirming that she was not in the cabin they had rented.

Lois reasoned that she was drunk and must have walked to the wrong cabin by mistake. No matter how she came to be in this cabin, she had to get out before anyone saw her. Lois could see no sign of her clothes. She even looked under the blanket to see if she had brought them into bed with her.

Wrapping the blanket to cover herself, Lois got out of bed to search. She found her shoes by the foot of the bed, but nothing more. Looking in a closet on the other side of the twin bed, Lois saw that it contained men's shirts. The closet on the other side of the room revealed a hidden gun cabinet with hunting rifles. Lois realized that she was not in just another rental cabin, but a cabin some man was living in.

Danny O'Brian lived in one of the resort cabins. Could Danny have taken her home? Had she done anything with Danny? Had Danny found her in his cabin, and left to spend the night somewhere else? Lois thought of how badly Mike would beat her if he found her undressed in Danny's cabin.

Searching through the dresser, Lois pulled out a large T-shirt. She tossed the blanket on the bed and quickly pulled the T-shirt on. She returned to the closet and removed the longest shirt she could see and put it on over the T-shirt. The sleeves hung over her hands, so she rolled them up, making sure she did not roll them high enough for the bruises on her arms to show. In another drawer, she found men's blue jeans, but they were too big, and would only highlight that she was not wearing her own clothes. Looking in the mirror over the dresser, Lois decided that the shirts covered her well enough. If anyone were to see her, they would assume that the long shirt covered shorts or a swimsuit. Hopefully, she would get to her cabin before anyone would see her. Once in her own cabin she could change into her own clothes. At least her shoes were by the bed, so she would not have to creep across the resort barefoot.

Lois's only thought was to get to the cabin before Mike returned. When she stepped outside, panic set in anew. NOTHING looked as it should. There were no other cabins. There was no bar. Even the lake was missing. She could see a brown pickup truck and a driveway heading into the woods. Beyond that, Lois saw nothing but trees.

Walking around the cabin, Lois noticed a scent that reminded her of something cooking on a grill. She saw an old-fashioned hand pump near an open meadow. Near that stood a structure with steps leading to a high black metal box, and an area concealed by curtains in front of it.

The curtain opened, and Scott Severson stepped out. He was wearing pants but no shirt, and a bath towel rested around his neck. His hair was wet and combed back, allowing more of his face to show than it had last night. The long curly beard was gone, revealing the face she had known before.

Scott saw her and called out, "Good morning!" He hung the towel on one hook and retrieved a shirt from another. He put his shirt on as he stepped down from the concrete platform and sat on a wooden bench to put on socks and boots.

Lois hurried over to Scott, praying that there was a reasonable explanation for where and how she was.

After pulling his boots on, Scott looked to Lois and said, "If you like it hot, there should be enough water left for a fast shower. Or maybe I should add another bucket of water to be sure you don't get burned."

"A shower?" Lois looked around with confusion.

"That's my shower," Scott gestured back to the structure. "Ray made it while I was away." He stepped over to the hand pump and pumped the handle to fill a stainless-steel pail with water. Carrying the pail up the steps in the back, he slid back a black metal cover and poured the bucket into a high tank. After replacing the cover, he stepped down to point to a slide out tray beneath the tank. "It has a Crisco powered water heater. It's like a big muffin pan you fill with shortening, add wicks, and their flames heat the tank. There's no thermostat though, so if you wait too long you could scald yourself."

Watching him push the tray back in place, Lois realized that was the cooking smell she had noticed.

Scott set the pail down and returned to the shower to point out its features. "The shower wall has a caddy for soap and shampoo on the back. There's a small medicine cabinet with a mirror for shaving and combing." A small shower head attached to a narrow tube hung from a hook. Scott lifted it and pushed a button on its back to spray water onto his other hand. "On and off at the touch of your finger to conserve water. That pail cooled the water a little, but it is still warm. In about ten minutes, it should be perfect." He returned the shower head to its hook and gestured to the curtains. "Shower curtains on three sides for privacy or leave them open to enjoy nature. There are plenty of hooks on the outside wall to hang clothes and towels." Scott removed a clean towel from the back and hung it on the nearest hook, where it would be easy to reach from within the shower. Stepping down, he said, "There's not near as much pressure as a normal shower, but it's the next best thing."

Lois felt very confused as she looked at him and said, "Can I ask a question?"

"Ask away,"

"Where am I? And how did I get here? And where the hell are my clothes?"

"I haven't named this place," he looked from side to side as if thinking of a name, "but I suppose you could say you're in Scott's woods. That's the hunting shack I once told you about. You were in my truck when I left last night, and you asked me to take you away. As for your clothes..." Scott turned and walked to a clothesline in the open meadow. He felt to be sure her clothes were dry, as he took them down from the line and handed them to Lois. "You took them off and threw them at me last night. You said they smelled like bar smoke. So, after you fell asleep, I washed them and hung them out to dry."

"You told me something about a little hunting shack." She looked back to the cabin. "You never mentioned it was nicer than the cabins at the resort."

Scott gestured toward an outhouse beyond the shower. "In their defense, they do have plumbing and electricity. Also, Ray made some improvements while I was away."

Lois looked at Scott with fear in her eyes. "I don't know what happened, but I have to get back to the resort before Mike discovers I'm gone."

Scott looked up to the rising sun and back to Lois. "It's nearly an hour's drive, so I think we're already too late for that. Also, on the way here last night, you swore that you would never go back to him."

"I did?"

"You did. You were almost giddy with excitement when you said it. It was a promise, and you can't break it."

"I promised you that?"

"No..." Scott looked into her eyes. "You promised yourself. Don't you remember?"

"I remember drinking with Rachel and then waking up here." Lois looked up with watery eyes. "Everything else is a blank."

"It will come back," he assured her. "It's a long story, so take a shower and wash the smoke out of your hair. I'll fill you in on everything over breakfast. Do you have any questions about the shower before I go?"

"You want me to shower? Out here in the open."

"You have curtains for privacy. Also, you're in the middle of 160 acres of woodland. I'll be in the cabin, so the only ones to spy on you are the birds, squirrels, and chipmunks. If you feel claustrophobic, open the curtains, and enjoy nature. If you want to go first, the outhouse is over there. I'll be in the cabin with the windows open. Just call if you need anything."

Lois looked to the outhouse and decided going there before showering did sound like a good idea. "Okay." She stepped up and hung her clothes on the hooks before heading over to the outhouse.

* * *

Clean and dressed, Lois headed back to the cabin, catching the scent of wood smoke as she walked. Scott was in the kitchen area of the cabin, using a whisk to whip condensed milk in a stainless-steel bowl. He looked up when he heard her enter. "I'm not sure which works better, the eggbeater or the whisk. I usually end up going back and forth with them, depending on which muscles are getting tired." He set down the bowl, which appeared to be half filled with whipped cream. "Now that you're here, how do you like your eggs?"

"Over easy," she answered without thinking. "Or whatever you want to make is fine."

Scott set a fresh cup of coffee in front of her. "Over easy it is. Or my best attempt anyway." He spread butter and cracked four eggs onto the griddle. He removed his waffle iron from the back of the stove to the countertop before opening it to transfer a fresh waffle to a plate.

Lois sipped coffee as she watched Scott move within his kitchen. He seemed totally at home with the wood-fired stove and cast-iron cookware.

Scott explained, "This was the original wood-burning stove from my family's farm. My grandmother was still cooking with this when my parents got married. It went to the machine shed when Dad bought an electric stove. When we built the cabin, it came out here. So did the hand pump outside. A lot of this place came from the old farm. The furniture was made by my grandfather. We didn't need it at the farm, so it came out here."

When breakfast was cooked, Scott removed the pans from the stove, and replaced them with two buckets to heat water for washing dishes. He set a plate in front of Lois, with a Belgian Waffle topped with whipped condensed milk and cherry pie filling. A second plate with two fried eggs and sausages came next. He set two similar plates on the other side of the table and sat across from her.

Lois took her first bite before looking up to ask, "Did you build this cabin?"

"I helped. Dad bought the inner 80 acres years ago. We came here for hunting, camping, family picnics, berry picking, firewood, things like that. Later, the guy Dad bought the woods from decided to sell another 80 acres, between Dad's woods and the road. I drained my savings and bought that lot myself. It was a lot more than Dad had paid, but it was worth it. When Dad sold the farm, he gave me his 80 as a graduation present. That doubled my woodland, and it came with the cabin."

Scott ate a piece of waffle as he thought back. "I think I was in fifth grade when we started building the cabin. Dad drove a well and put the old hand pump from the farm on it. This became our hunting cabin and getaway retreat. Sometimes, I would take care of the farm so Dad and Mom could stay here. Mom loved it, and we didn't even have the shower back then. Ray came with us every hunting season. Sometimes we came here just to spend time in the woods."

After taking another bite, Scott said, "I left a key with Ray when I left. I told him to use it anytime he wanted. He left a journal telling me about every time he came here. He let me know what he did, and how everything was when he got here. He put a fresh coat of stain on the siding one year and built the shower another." Scott pointed to the large metal ice box on the wall across from the stove. "He found an old ice box, saved the doors, and made this one for the cabin. It looks big, but the walls and top are thick and super-insulated. Pour a few big bags of ice in the top, and it's as good as a refrigerator." Scott paused to take another bite. "Ray brought Samantha here while they were dating. When he saw how much she liked it here, he knew she was the one. This is where they spent their honeymoon."

When they finished eating, Scott began washing their breakfast dishes. "Do you remember what happened yet?"

"I'm not sure. I think some of it is coming back."

"I think you were one of the few people who recognized me. I saw it in your eyes when we bumped into each other, but you walked away like you wanted nothing to do with me. So, I stayed back and gave you your space. Mike didn't recognize me, but I had no desire to talk to him. I figured, if you didn't want to talk to me, there was no reason for me to talk to him. I didn't see

Mike after I took Carol home. I figured he decided to call it a night."

"I remember that. He said he was going to spend the night with you. He said you wanted to talk things over and put the past behind you. He said it was your idea."

Scott looked back with surprise. "That's news to me. I never even talked to Mike last night."

"Eve Johnson left just before him, and I got the feeling they were meeting somewhere. I recognized her car as the one he was driving when he came to Eau Claire. He told me it was totaled in an accident. It was repainted, but it's the same car."

"I don't know." Scott rinsed another plate and set it in the drainer. "I think Eve was hoping to see someone last night, but I don't think it was Mike. They have some history, but she figured him out and wanted nothing more to do with him. Also, she doesn't date married men. She wouldn't have gone with him when we were in school if he hadn't waved his ring around to prove you broke up with him."

"Wherever he went, he felt the need to lie about it. This wasn't the first time his story sounded fishy." Lois thought about that. "To be honest, I usually feel a bit relieved when he gives me a lame excuse to get away. It's even more relief when he leaves on his trips to Texas. Those usually keep him away for a few weeks."

"He takes trips to Texas?" Texas triggered a memory for Scott.

"It's sort of a side business of his. He buys antiques at auctions, garage sales, and things like that. When he has enough, he sells them in Texas for a huge profit. He said they're crazy for antiques down there." Lois noticed Scott's puzzled expression. "What's wrong with Texas?"

Scott shook his head. "I was just remembering something. Eve once told me about Mike's father being arrested. I mentioned it to my father, and he remembered the story."

"Mike never mentioned that."

"From what Dad remembered, Mike's father worked on a farm near ours. Supposedly, he was also buying antiques, like you said Mike does. He would occasionally take time off to sell them in Texas. The farmer let him store them in one of his outbuildings. The farmer happened to look in that building one day, and then he called the cops. The next day, they arrested Mike's dad. Apparently, the loot in that shed solved burglaries from all over the county."

"Did your mother have something to do with his arrest?"

"Not that I know of. Why?"

"Mike said something once about his father's troubles being your mother's fault. He just shut up when I asked him why, so I figured it was just more Scott-bashing. He does that when he's drunk."

Scott thought about that. "Did Mike's father go with him on those trips?"

Lois shook her head. "I never met him. He moved out of the area before we got married. His mother did too. I heard that she took off right after Mike left for the army. Mike has no idea where either of his parents went."

With his dishes finished, Scott pulled the plug to drain the sink. "It doesn't matter. You just triggered that memory when you mentioned Texas. Anyway, you did seem more relaxed after he left. You seemed tense and nervous before that. I didn't know why at the time."

"I'm remembering that now. Rachel was playing music, and Randy asked me to dance. He called me his cousin-in-law."

"That's right. I was talking to Ray and Samantha when you danced. I think my biggest regret is missing their wedding." Scott refilled their coffee cups and retook his seat at the table.

"I remember you talking to Ray. Then Doris got up and asked for volunteers for our ten-year reunion." Lois let out a laugh. "Dave Masters' fiancé raised her hand. Dave was reminding her that they lived in New York, but she didn't care. I don't know if she was just that drunk, or maybe she just loves throwing parties. I know they did put her and Dave's names on the list." Lois tipped her head and remembered more. "There was some disturbance in the bar, and you went out there."

"That's right. Some drunk started slapping his wife. I held him down until the cops came and took him away."

"I remember that! I saw him take a swing at you, and then he landed on the floor with his hand behind his back. You never hit him or anything. You just turned him around and put him down. I guess I'm not the only person you rescue."

"I have no patience for wife beaters. I could see old bruises on her face, so I knew that wasn't the first time. I wanted to take him outside and give him some of his own medicine, but he would have just taken it out on her later. At least now there's a record of his arrest, so it will be easier when she decides to leave him." Scott lifted his cup for another drink. "I didn't see you in the bar after that. I think you slipped out during the excitement."

Lois nodded. "I remember now. I heard what you said to that farmer and wondered if you would help me."

"The cops arrested him for disorderly conduct. After they took him away, I said my good nights and headed out too." Scott looked into Lois's eyes. "When I got in my truck, you were waiting inside."

"I remember now."

"I was surprised to see you. We hadn't talked all night. I started to ask what you were doing, and you asked me to 'just drive.' I pulled out of the parking lot and asked where you wanted to go. You said it didn't matter; you just had to go. At first, I thought you were crying, but when we were on the road, you sounded happy and excited."

Lois's face began to light up as she remembered, and the joy she felt in leaving began to return.

"I asked if you wanted me to take you home. You shook your head and said, 'No! I'm never going back!' When I asked if you wanted me to take you to your parents' house, you started to cry. You said that you could never go there, and they didn't want you."

Scott watched Lois's expression change with this memory. He could tell she was remembering more than the previous night. "I didn't know where to take you, so we came here. When we got past Balsam Lake, you started laughing. You said something like, 'I did it! I'm really doing it!' You didn't explain, but I could tell you were happy to be out of there."

Lois looked up, revealing the joy of escape once more. "I did it. I was worrying about what would happen when I got back, but I really left, so I can't go back." She was beginning to look excited again. "I got away, so I can't go back. I don't have to, and he can't make me."

"You said something like that last night too. After we got here, you wanted to use the bathroom. I got a battery powered lantern and showed you the outhouse. You smiled and said, 'That will do.'"

"That's right," she recalled. "You waited and walked me back to the cabin, so I wouldn't get lost or fall on my face. I think I was drunk enough that either might have happened."

Scott nodded. "I did laundry yesterday, so I put clean sheets on the beds and put my clothes away. I thought of making coffee so we could talk, but you were ready for sleep."

"And I took my clothes off in front of you?"

Scott sipped his coffee and nodded. "You sniffed your clothes and said they smelled like bar smoke. You said that Mike smokes, and you hate that smell. Then you took off your clothes and threw them. At first, I thought you might have been offering yourself to me. Then I realized why you wanted me to see you that way. You didn't say anything. You just held your arms out so I could see the bruises. You turned and raised your arm so I could see the bruises on your sides. I saw a lot of green stains from old bruises too. You've had a lot of bruises. You also pulled your hair back, so I could see where he had grabbed you by the neck. I put my arms around you and said I would never let him hurt you again. You just hugged me back and cried."

Lois sipped her coffee and looked up. "Did we...?"

"No. You just cried, and I held you. You held onto me too. I think you were feeling safe. I could have held you like that all night, but we both needed sleep. I let go of you and turned back the blanket. You said, 'Thank you,' and got into bed. I covered you with the blanket, kissed you on the forehead, and said, 'Good night.' If I had joined you, I think you would have let me, but I knew that wasn't what you wanted. You were just grateful to be out of there."

Lois bit her lip and nodded.

"You fell asleep, so I washed your smoky clothes in the sink and hung them out to dry. I got some rest on the other bed, but there was too much on my mind for any real sleep. The sun was coming up, so I got up and went outside."

"I never told anyone." Lois slowly rotated her coffee cup. "I couldn't. If I had, he would have killed me. I know he would. I wanted to leave so many times, but I had nowhere to go and no way to leave. When I saw you help that woman in the bar, I heard what you said, and I knew you would help me too. Make that, 'help me again.' This is the second time you rescued me from him."

"That's what I'm here for." Scott rubbed his bare chin. "When I kissed your forehead, my beard was tickling your face, so, I shaved it off this morning."

Lois let out a small laugh. "It is nice to see your face again." She looked around the cabin. "This is what you were talking about, isn't it? Back when you moved me into my apartment, I mean. Your farm was gone, and I said you were homeless, but you said you still had options."

Scott nodded. "I could have lived here then, and I am living here now. There are always options. I have other options that are more civilized, but I like it here."

Lois shook her head. "I can't think of any options for me. I don't dare go back to Mike. He would kill me; I know he would. I can't go to my parents' house." She looked up at Scott and said, "Don't ask. I have no right to ask you for more than you've done already. Do you think there's any place where he wouldn't find me? Somewhere I could start over."

"You see. You're sorting through your options already." Lois looked confused, so he explained. "Option of going back to Mike is out. I promised that I would not let him hurt you, and we both know he would. There's the option of going to your parents, but you said that's out. The option of living with me would be rustic for a while. You're still a married woman, but I won't rule it out. Running away and starting over comes with multiple options, but we need to do it right and be sure to close the door. Option: *Close the door on Mike,* is most important. That should be done no matter what you decide."

"How do I do that?"

"First, we'll go to the Sheriff's Office. We need to cancel any missing person report Mike may have filed. You can explain that you left him. Tell them about the abuse so they understand why. While we're there, I'll call the hospital in St. Croix Falls to see if we can get you a physical today, but we need to wait until tomorrow. We'll need documentation of your bruises and x-rays to show if he ever broke anything."

Scott noticed how Lois brought her hand up to her arm when he said that. "I thought he might have. From the bruises on your body, I'm guessing ribs may be a possibility too. I don't know of any lawyers open today, so we'll have to find one tomorrow. You need to file for divorce and get a restraining order. A lawyer can tell us where it's best to hide you until the divorce is final. He may want you in a shelter, or you may be safer here. I have another option where Mike won't find you, but it's out of state, so we'll have to be sure that won't interfere with the divorce." Scott looked into Lois's eyes and said, "This is all just off the top of my head, but how does it sound? Ultimately, this is all your choice."

Lois stared back with wide eyes. "Have you done this before?"

"No. I'm just thinking things out."

"But I'll have to get a job first. I don't know how long it will take to save enough to pay for this."

Scott covered Lois's hand with his. "That won't be a problem. The only important thing now, is keeping you safe."

PART 3: TEN-YEAR REUNION

Chapter 14: Riverside Hotel

Invitations for our ten-year reunion announced that it would be held in the banquet room of the River Side Hotel. For our dinner we had a choice of chicken cordon bleu or prime rib. The band was a bit of a surprise, as it played mostly ballroom-style music. They were good, but an odd choice for our age group in 1982. This reunion seemed to be a bit more formal, the result of Nadine Masters, Dave's wife, who was head of our reunion committee. It's not clear if Nadine took over the committee, or if the others simply stepped back and let her run with it, but in the end, this reunion was completely a product of Nadine's design.

The banquet room was a new wing the hotel had added a few years earlier. It included a separate bar and was available for all types of meetings, parties, or special dinners. The hotel kitchen had been remodeled and updated when they built the addition, making sure it could handle banquet needs along with those of the hotel restaurant.

As we arrived, we were greeted by Nadine and her committee members, who sat at a long table near the entrance. We were given a booklet of classmates which included senior pictures by our names, and updated information on everyone's lives. We also received one name tag to wear and a separate name card to reserve table space. The name cards were also to inform the waitstaff of our dining preferences. A red card for anyone who requested prime rib, and blue cards for those who selected chicken cordon bleu.

A large yellow banner hung over the bandstand, with green letters reading, 'GRIFFIN HIGH SCHOOL - CLASS OF '72.' The tables had yellow tablecloths and were set with coffee cups, water glasses, and green cloth napkins folded to hold the silverware. The entire hall was decorated in our school colors, green and yellow, along with large photos Ray Ellis had taken at previous get-togethers and other photos from school days.

* * *

Danny and Carol O'Brian arrived early and headed to the bar where Dave Masters was already waiting. Danny asked, "Shouldn't you be at the table with the rest of the committee?"

"I was on the committee in name only. This is Nadine's show, not mine." Dave paused to sip his drink. "I don't mind. It kept her busy, and she enjoyed doing it."

"Well, at least she got you here early this year." Danny turned to the bartender, requesting a draft beer and a can of Sprite.

Dave let out a small laugh and said, "I guess this is a record for me. I think I was the last to arrive at our last two reunions. It's kind of nice being first for a change."

Carol climbed onto the barstool and looked around the hall, admiring all the decorations. "It's hard to believe we get all this for only twenty-five dollars a couple. Will there be anything left in the class fund?"

"She ignored the class fund." Dave motioned to the bartender to put their drinks on his tab. "She is paying for everything and will use what you paid for partial reimbursement. Any profit will go to the class fund, and she will absorb any loss. She was talking a hundred dollars a person. I suggested she hold it to ten or fifteen, so she compromised at fifteen a person, or twenty-five per couple. She also said I should talk about my company tonight, so any loss can be written off as a business expense." Dave sighed and took another drink. "It's not so bad. She's spent more on parties in New York, and no one chipped in for any of those. Hell, she's spent more on dresses."

"Speaking of dresses," Carol grew a curious grin, "what are the odds of Eve Johnson showing up in a dress matching Nadine's?"

Dave shook his head. "Don't even say that in jest. Although, if that does happen, it will be because they planned it on one of Nadine's planning trips."

"Planning trips?" said Carol.

"Oh yes. She had to bring the committee here to check out the new room, and the food. She also had to take them to other places to sample their food, listen to different bands, and whatever else they could think of. I lost track of how many times she flew out here to work on this. They ALL had to research and agree on every detail."

Danny looked to the table where Nadine and her committee welcomed all arrivals. "No wonder they all look like buddies now."

"Each trip down here was a night out for the whole group. She considered it all a business expense for tonight's party."

"Just what kind of work do you do now?" Danny wondered how Dave could manage such an expense.

"I'm glad you asked." Dave pulled out a small notebook and wrote, "Talked to Danny O' about business." He looked back to Danny and Carol. "We are now talking business, so this an honest business expense. Chiefly, I'm still in acquisitions for the company Nadine's father runs. When they are interested in a company, I check them out and make my recommendation. They like to buy dying companies and sell them off in pieces for a profit. Sometimes I recommend some change or investment that may put a company back in the black. They don't show much interest in that, so I started my own company, Masters Enterprises. If they pass on my recommendation, I'm free to buy them with my own money, and make the investments myself. Nadine's father thinks he'll still be cutting them up for profit in a few years anyway, so he gave me official approval." Dave grinned, "I own five companies now, and each one has turned around with growing profits." He looked at Danny, "How is the resort going? Have you bought it from your uncle yet?"

Danny shook his head. "No, but he's got to retire someday."

Dave made a note of that in his notebook. "Good! That's even more business talk. Let the party begin."

"It sounds like you've done better than your dad already," said Carol.

"He still wants me to come home and work with him. He figures that since he owns so much of the town already, I should join with him and take over when he retires." Dave shook his head. "Businesses in Griffin are doing fine without me. The companies I buy are on their last leg and ready for the auction block. I like keeping them open and their people working. I can't do that if I'm limited to Griffin. I also make good money, so Dad's starting to come around."

Carol looked around the room again. "From the looks of this, if you're eating everything over ten to fifteen dollars a plate, this reunion must be costing you plenty. Even more when you add the planning trips."

Dave shook his head. "Costing Nadine, not me. She's doing all this with her money."

Carol asked, "Isn't that the same thing?"

"Not when she has her trust fund. Her father insisted on a prenuptial agreement stating that her money and my income are two separate entities. She is free to use her money in any way she wishes, and I have no claim or right to it. It also stipulates that my money and earnings are mine, so she has no special claim on them. I earn big bucks working for her father, but he doesn't expect my income to ever be as big as her trust fund." Dave grinned. "Her father never expected my company to take off either. I think he's beginning to wonder if separating our incomes was a mistake."

"Speaking of fathers," Danny asked, "are your folks on vacation again? Or did they stay home so you could stay with them this time?"

"We're staying here through tonight. Nadine needs to oversee everything for this party. My parents are a little vacation shy after our last reunion. Someone burgled their house while they were gone."

"That's right!" Danny said, "I remember reading about that in the paper."

"Some of Mom's jewelry was registered, so it set off a few flags when it turned up down south. That led to more being found, but they still took a big hit." Dave looked at Danny's name tags. "No fair. I only got one name tag."

"That's 'cause you married out of the class," Danny gloated. "See, I have gold letters on this tag for being Danny O'Brian, and green letters on this one for being Danny, Carol Murphy's mister."

Carol stood to show off her name tags as well, one read, "Carol (Murphy) O'Brian" and the other read, "Mrs. Danny O'Brian."

Dave noticed Carol's belly as she stood. "I see congratulations are due as well."

Carol proudly patted her baby bump. "Thank you. And in about five months, little Rebecca will be able to thank you, herself. This will be number three."

"That's right," Danny boasted. "The first was going to be named Shamus, because he came only seven months after our wedding. But she turned out to be a Katharine instead. Then came Sean. We will probably cease production after Becky."

"This one will be a girl then?"

"Just a feeling," said Carol. "I don't really want to know until she can show us herself. She, is just a working title at this point."

Danny added, "Any who come after this will be named Oops."

Ray Ellis and his wife, Samantha, arrived, along with Scott Severson and his wife, Roxanne. Roxanne's red hair was cut short, barely covering the top of her ears. Scott's hair was slightly longer than Roxanne's, with short sideburns as his only facial hair. They had just sat at the bar and ordered drinks when they were joined by Rachel and Randy Richards. Randy was clean-shaven with short hair, while Rachel's hair was a close match to Roxanne's.

"Add one stinger and one Diet Coke to that order, and it's on me," Randy said to the bartender.

Scott looked down at Rachel's round belly. "Are you still carrying that thing?"

"Not still, again!" Rachel complained, "This is number three. I think Randy likes to keep me this way, just to keep me sober."

Scott leaned close to Rachel and said, "I was talking to Randy... about you."

"Very funny. I think Randy likes that crib you made so much; he just wants to keep using it." Rachel tried to look grateful to Scott as she said, "Thank you again. It's fantastic and I love it. I just wish we could retire it to dolls."

Scott leaned close to Rachel and softly said, "So, I take it there'll be no skinny dipping at this party?"

Rachel looked around. "Does this place have a pool? How 'bout a hot tub? How big is the punch bowl?" Grinning, she said, "This is the *River Side* Hotel, isn't it?"

Scott put his arm around Rachel to hug her. "I miss you little sister." Turning to his wife, he said, "I'd like you to meet my wife, Roxanne - better known as Rox, because that must be what she had in her head when she married me."

"So, this is the famous Rachel." Roxanne stood to shake hands, only to change her mind and hug Rachel instead. "I'm glad I finally get to meet you, and Scott has never told me anything about you."

"It's nice to meet you too, and whatever Scott didn't tell you about me was a lie."

When the bartender brought their drinks, Roxanne stopped him and said, "I'd like one more please. Could you bring me a lowball glass of ginger ale on the rocks, with a splash of 7UP, two filberts, and two straws?"

When the drink arrived looking like a stinger, Roxanne gave it to Rachel. Rachel promptly used the straws to remove and eat one of the hazelnuts. After sipping it she said, "It's not the same, but it feels right in my hand. Thank you Rox." Holding her drink out to address it, she said, "I dub thee ... Stingless."

Rachel looked Scott up and down, studying the suitcoat and black pants he was wearing. "Damn, Scott, you clean up nice. No necktie though."

"Not now. Not ever."

"Is that a dress shirt?" Rachel reached to pet Scott's shirt.

"Flannel comes in solid colors too," said Roxanne. "As long as it's a solid color, it should be dressy enough."

Scott glanced at the door and saw Lois enter, wearing a tan dress with a pattern of curvy white lines. Her hair had bangs and some curls as it danced above her shoulders. He looked back to Rachel and said, "Hey little sister, your favorite cousin just came in, so Rox and I are going to the other side of Ray and Sam. Then you'll have room for her here."

Rachel was about to suggest that she and Randy just move over to make room for Lois, but she saw that Roxanne was already moving. Rachel assumed that Roxanne wanted to keep a distance from Scott's former girlfriend. "Okay. I'll just move in so I can still talk to you through Ray and Sam."

"Thanks." Scott was pleased that she understood, or at least thought she did.

* * *

Lois was crossing to the bar when Greg and Donna Peterson called to her from one of the tables.

"What's up?" Lois pulled out a chair and joined them.

Donna said, "At our last reunion, you told me about the letter you wrote to Scott, and how he reacted."

"Yes, I remember." Lois had hoped Donna would have kept their conversation secret, but she realized that she would not have kept anything from Greg. "That was the one thing I couldn't bring myself to discuss with Scott, but I can't hold that against him now. I'll never be able to repay him for all he's done."

144

Greg said, "I don't think there was anything for you to hold against Scott anyway."

This surprised Lois, but maybe Donna hadn't told him everything. "Well, it doesn't matter. Scott did so much to help me get away from Mike. He paid for the doctor, x-rays, lawyer, everything. He even set me up in another state so Mike wouldn't find me."

Donna asked, "Why did you need x-rays for a divorce?"

"In case we had to prove physical abuse. Mike broke my left arm and two ribs while we were married. The doctor also documented all my bruises."

Doris nodded with understanding. "Did Mike give you any trouble with the divorce?"

"He never even showed. His lawyer handled everything. I didn't want anything but my freedom, so I guess he was fine with that. I still worry about him finding where I live though." Lois looked at Donna. "So, why bring this up now?"

"Because Greg found these." Donna removed a stack of envelopes from her purse and handed them to Lois.

Lois began thumbing through them. "These are the letters Scott and I sent to each other."

"Those are letters Scott sent to you," corrected Greg. "The ones from you were never mailed. There's no postmark on them."

Donna asked, "Is there any way Mike could have intercepted your mail? You said he lived in the same building."

"You needed a key to open the mailboxes, but Mike was good with locks. He may have been able to pick the lock, or maybe even made his own key. I wouldn't put it past him." Lois looked through the envelopes and opened one. "This is the letter I wrote to tell Scott that I might be pregnant."

Greg pointed to the envelope. "There's no postmark. Mike got it before the mailman."

Lois looked and saw Greg was right. "That means Scott never knew. I believed Mike because he couldn't have known unless

Scott told him. But Mike was really the only one who knew." She looked at the envelope again, reconfirming the lack of postmark. With a puzzled expression, she looked at Donna and said, "If Scott didn't know, why would he have left a check to pay for an abortion?"

Donna reached to remove the next envelope in the stack and handed it to Lois. "I thought you might want to read this one next."

Lois took the envelope from Donna's hand, opened it, and began reading the letter. After reading the first half page, she stopped and reread it to be sure she had read correctly. She looked up to Donna and Greg and explained, "Back then, my biggest concern was saving enough to cover my college entrance fees. Admissions day was getting close, and I needed the first semester's tuition, and money for books. We had talked about that, so Scott knew I worried about it." She looked down at the letter again. "This says that he mailed a check to be sure it had time to clear into my account before registration day. There was a check sent with this letter!" She looked up to see Donna nodding to her. "That was the check Mike gave me. It was only for college costs. Scott really didn't know!"

Donna tapped the next letter in the pile. "In the next one, Scott says his job is almost done, and tells when he'll be back to see you. Mike knew when to have you away from your apartment to keep you from seeing Scott."

Greg said, "Scott told Danny that when he came home, the love of his life was living with, and engaged to another man. Mike must have snowed Scott as well as he did you."

Lois looked down at the letters, and back to her friends. "Does anyone else know about this?"

"No." Greg shook his head. "We haven't told anyone. I'm sorry for reading them myself. I was just going to throw them away, but I got curious. Then I talked to Donna, and she filled me in."

"How did you find these?"

"I was restoring a '65 Mustang convertible. I was removing upholstery from the passenger seat and found those stuffed inside. My guess is that he read these in his car and hid them in the upholstery."

Lois nodded. "I think I know the car. Mike was driving it when he got out of the army. He told me it was totaled in an accident, but I think he gave it to Eve Johnson."

Greg shook his head. "The car he had a title for may have been totaled, but that car really was Eve's. And Mike didn't *give* it to her. She used her savings to buy that car after graduation. I remember because she asked me to check it out when she bought it. Not long after that, she went shopping at Maplewood Mall, and it was gone when she came out. She hadn't even put regular plates on yet." Greg chuckled. "A few years later, she had it back, and had me paint it red again. She said some guy was flirting with her in the café and started bragging about his Mustang convertible. It had a crappy blue paint job, but she knew her car. That seat got cut when she was moving something to her apartment, and she remembered it. She still had the title, and the VIN numbers matched. She never told me who had it, but I figured that out when I found your letters."

"Why does that man still surprise me?" Lois shook her head. "Whenever I think I couldn't have a lower opinion of him, he digs down to another level."

Donna held up her class booklet. "According to this, Mike responded with a note that he would not be coming."

Lois nodded, "I called to ask about that before I decided to come. I didn't think he would try anything with other people around, but I didn't want to take any chances. He might find a way to get one of the booklets though, which is why I didn't say where I'm living." Lois looked at the stack of letters in her hand, and back to her friends. "Thank you so much. I can't tell you what this means to me."

Donna looked back to the bar. "Are you going to tell Scott?"

Lois looked to see Scott sitting with his wife. "No. He's married, and they look so happy. Telling him now would only hurt him; it could even cause problems with his wife." She turned back to Donna and Greg. "Can you both promise not to say anything, especially to Scott?"

"I won't mention it to a soul," promised Greg.

Greg and Donna excused themselves so they could mingle and visit, leaving Lois alone at the table. She knew she should wait, but she could not resist reading some of the letters.

* * *

There was no stated dress code in the invitations, but everyone did get the impression that this would be a semi-formal event. Many of the men wore suits. Others wore blue jeans, but they made sure they were clean and neat looking. Most of the women enjoyed the formal setting that gave them an excuse to dress up.

Nadine had looked forward to seeing what Eve would wear, guessing that Eve might have made a formal gown for the event. Imagine Nadine's surprise, when Eve entered wearing blue jeans, a stained T-shirt shirt, and sporting a large black eye. Nadine looked up to say, "Hello, Eve," letting her know that she recognized her.

"Hi, Nadine," Eve walked past her without stopping. "Don't worry, I'm not here. I just need to see someone for a minute." Eve surveyed the room, and hurried to where Lois was sitting. Taking a seat next to Lois, she asked, "Can we talk?"

Lois pushed the letters into her purse and asked, "What's up?"

* * *

Vanessa Winters walked past Peter Baker a few times before she finally recognized him. In school Peter had always kept his hair short, but it was now longer than any of his classmates wore their hair in the early seventies. She complimented his new look while climbing onto the barstool next to him. After a bit of small talk, she held up her booklet and asked, "Peter, is your occupation accurate in this thing? Did you really give up your computer job to become a detective?"

"Yes, and no," Peter said. "I am a private investigator now, but my computer still helps with a lot of my work."

"So, you're sort of a hacking detective?"

"You could say something like that, but please don't say it too loud. I like to think that it's still kind of a grey area."

Vanessa leaned close and spoke in a serious voice, "There's a big region of Brazil where I work. They're getting ready to clear-cut and burn it off. The tribes who live there have no rights, and they'll be run off, losing their entire lifestyle. I've been trying to find out who owns the land, but I keep running into dead ends. There are too many companies owning businesses, owning companies, and I haven't been able to find anything solid. My last lead pointed to England. I can't go there without knowing where it will end. Can you detect anything like that?"

Peter nodded with a look of interest. "I've never hacked anything International before. This might be interesting."

* * *

Rachel stepped onto the stage to use the band's microphone. "Good evening. I was asked to let everyone know that it's time to find their seats for dinner, and to please be sure to put their name cards on the table where the servers will see them. After saying that, I should keep talking, so everyone will break up their conversations and find a place to sit."

Rachel looked to where Nadine was busy talking to her committee members. Nadine did not seem to be paying any attention to her, even after *telling* Rachel to make this announcement. "On that note, I should mention that Randy and I are still on the air in Denver. Denver is nice, but their mosquitoes are different. They're real-tiny, and they hurt like tiny needles when they bite you. You can't knock them around with baseball bats or tennis rackets like we do here in Wisconsin."

Nadine still did not seem to be listening, so Rachel continued. "Things have changed here too. At my parent's farm, Mom told us to be sure to check for ticks when we come inside. We always had wood ticks in the past, but now they have tiny little deer ticks that carry something called Lyme disease. This really has me worried. I mean, I already knew mosquitoes spread malaria, and that sleeping sickness, but can they spread Lyme disease too?"

"Here's where it gets scary." Rachel tried to look serious. "Out at the farm, I caught a mosquito, and it had three ticks on one leg. I started wondering if I should send it in for testing, to see if it did have Lyme disease. Now I'm even more worried, because I only tied it down with some bailing twine, and this mosquito was too weak to break the twine." Rachel took a deep breath and went on. "I started looking at the ticks, and one was getting big and purple, like a grape. You know, like when they're getting ready to fall off your dog. Then the mosquito looked down at the tick... like it smelled blood or something. That's when the mosquito stuck his little pecker nose into the tick, and it started sucking its own blood back. So, the mosquito was sucking off the tick, at the same time the tick was sucking off the mosquito. I found myself wondering if they would just go on like that forever. You know, just feeding off one another." Rachel sighed and shook her head. "Then I got grossed out and smashed them both with Mom's skillet. Now Mom is mad at me for denting her favorite pan. Anyway, was this a good enough distraction? I'm satisfied. Now, everyone, go find a table and sit down!"

Dave laughed when Rachel returned to the bar. "She just kept talking with her group. I don't think she heard any of it."

Rachel shrugged. "In that case, remember the story; you can tell it at her next party. Let's find a table. Junior's getting hungry."

* * *

The tables in the banquet hall were round and large enough to seat six comfortably. Pitchers of water were set on each table, along with fresh carafes of coffee. The moment people began sitting, servers began bringing Caesar Salads and dinner rolls to their tables. Servers took note of the color-coded name cards, which told who would be eating which entrée. Cocktail waitresses began making their way among the tables and taking drink orders.

When all the salads had been served, they began serving entrées. Anyone with a blue name card received Chicken Cordon Blue, and anyone with a red card received a queen-sized Prime rib. Both entrées included a baked potato with sour cream and butter on the side. Servers were also quick to bring fresh water, or coffee as needed. The staff was fast and efficient, especially considering the size of our crowd. As our plates were cleared, they were replaced with dishes of white cake with '72 written in green over yellow frosting.

Dave and Nadine shared a table with Danny, Carol, Rich, and Doris. Rich told Dave how the district had built a new high school, and their old one was now being used for grades four through eight. He mentioned that they are now talking about building a new middle school and retiring our old high school completely.

Rich and Danny have been interested in those rumors. When public buildings are closed, they sometimes sell for bargain prices with the goal of getting them on tax rolls as fast as possible. Carol and Donna explained that the boys hope to buy our old school and turn it into a hotel and restaurant. Nadine thought that sounded like a grand plan, but she wondered if Griffin was big enough to support another hotel. Dave simply noted all of this in his notebook as evidence of more business talk.

Scott and Roxanne sat with Ray and his wife Samantha, along with Peter Baker and Vanessa Winters. From their table they could see that Lois was sitting with Rachel, Randy, Donna, and Greg. Lois felt that Scott might have been avoiding her and assumed that he did not want his wife to meet an old girlfriend.

As desserts were being served, Nadine and her reunion committee took the stage and awarded the usual token gifts to class members. Vanessa Winters had easily won the prize for traveling farthest to attend, having come from a Brazilian rainforest. She was given a world globe and said that she looked forward to sharing it with the people in her village.

After the usual awards, the girls on the reunion committee presented a special gift to Nadine, thanking her for all her hard work. Nadine glowed with their praise and was speechless when they gave her with an afghan and a quilt, which they had made for her. Nadine accepted the gifts, possibly with a hint of a tear in her eyes. Receiving gifts that were hand-made by the giver, rather than something with a price tag, was yet another new experience for Nadine.

With the awards completed, the band began to play, and many of us began to dance. The microphone was used only for announcements, as the band had no singer and was completely instrumental. The band included a drummer, an organ/keyboard player, and three others who played a variety of instruments. They began with old ballroom music but mixed it up with music from multiple genres. When the band played a polka, Danny O'Brian asked Nadine to dance, giving her yet another new experience.

When they were ready to leave, Scott and Roxanne stopped to visit Dave and Nadine. Remembering Scott from the last reunion, Nadine asked if he still lived in his little forest cabin.

"We're still in the woods, but Scott has upgraded. We now have electricity and indoor plumbing." Roxanne also told Nadine that living in the woods has its advantages; if she doesn't know what to make for supper, she can always ask Scott to go out and shoot something.

After more conversation, Dave asked, "Are you still doing construction work, Scott?"

"Carpentry," Scott corrected. "I have a nice workshop, and a small sawmill. My best projects come from lumber I harvest in my own woods."

"If you ever need anything," Roxanne handed Dave one of Scott's business cards, "Scott does amazing work. His cabinets and furniture go for a good price, but he might make a special deal for an old friend."

Nadine gave Dave a questioning look. "Maybe we should have Harold look at his work." Looking back to Scott, she explained, "Harold Tomlinson works with designers and decorators in New York. He often orders special or unique items from fine craftsmen. I had a desk made for Dave's home office. You could buy a new car for less than that desk, but it was worth it."

Dave nodded. "A desk like that would be setting your standards high. Harold's contacts are true masters in their craft. We could introduce you, but you would need exceptional talent to work with him."

"Sounds like quite a desk." Scott tried to look thoughtful. "Let me guess, solid oak lumber, no plywood or anything artificial. Maybe your initials, 'DM' embossed on the front. Lots of special built-in options. Maybe even a few hidden drawers and compartments."

"The initials were Nadine's idea," Dave said defensively. "But yes, like that. Also, the initials aren't fastened on. The whole board is planed down around them. The front is just one solid board with the initials coming out from it." Dave stopped talking and wondered how Scott had guessed about the initials on his desk.

Scott grinned and said, "We better be going. It's great seeing you, Dave. Nadine, this was a fantastic party. Thank you."

"That goes double for me." Looking back, Roxanne added, "When you get back to New York, tell Harold we said Hello."

Scott and Roxanne said a few more goodbyes as they made their way into the parking lot. After unlocking his car door, Scott stood up, tipping his head slightly as he listened. He handed Roxanne his car keys and said, "Wait here."

Chapter 15: Parking lot

Lois enjoyed visiting with her classmates, but she was unable to take her mind off the letters in her purse. She told Rachel that she would call the next day and said goodnight to other friends. As she made her way to the far end of the parking lot, Lois's only thoughts were of sitting in her motel room and reading the letters Scott had written a decade earlier. She had barely slid the key into the lock of her car door when a large fist struck the side of her head.

Lois found herself sprawled on the pavement with massive pain echoing between her ears. She did not remember falling, but the ache of her impact assured her she had. She could taste blood in her mouth, and could feel where blacktop had scraped her nose, cheek, and forehead. Still foggy as to what had happened, Lois turned and tried to get up. She had gotten to her hands and knees when she felt a large hand against her throat, with fingers and thumb squeezing the sides of her neck. She was jerked up and pushed back against the car.

The memory of being hit returned as Lois blinked away tears and found herself looking into the enraged eyes of Mike Burman.

"Keep it down," he warned in his softest voice. "We don't want any interruptions."

Before she could scream, Mike's fist struck between her stomach and ribcage. Lois buckled and dropped, unable to breathe. Mike slid his fingers into her hair, grabbing, and lifting to push her back against the side of her car.

"Just like old times, isn't it? Remember when your boyfriend hit my plexus?" Mike grinned as if he were getting revenge. "You'll be able to breathe soon enough, but I don't want anything louder than a whisper." Grabbing her throat to hold her, he pulled something from his back pocket with his free hand. "I want you breathing well enough to answer some questions." She heard a small click as the blade of his knife shot from the handle in his hand. "But if you start making noise, I'll slice your windpipe, and you won't say anything. Do you understand?"

Still fighting to breathe, Lois closed her eyes and tried to nod. Mike pushed the tip of his knife against the car door, retracted the blade, and returned the knife to his pocket. Lois let out a slight wheeze as the first bit of oxygen returned to her lungs.

"Okay, it's coming back. Just remember, nothing higher than a whisper, or your breath might not come back next time. You know what I mean?"

She gave another small nod while trying to bend forward, or turn, anything that might get her lungs working. Another small wheeze escaped as more air entered her lungs.

"Now," he leaned in close to her face, "just what the hell did you say to my wife?"

"Everything," she managed to say in a coarse whisper. "But... I didn't," she wheezed "...have to...." Her lungs were working more as she began to speak. "She already... saw you... herself."

"What do you mean, 'Everything?'" he asked in a slightly louder voice.

Tears were running down her cheeks as she was able to speak in faint whispers. "How you beat ... and controlled me." Her breath was short and painful, but she was breathing. "I was your prisoner...." She inhaled with a long wheeze. "I was trapped with no phone... and no escape." After taking another breath, Lois was able to say with tears, "You stole my mail!" Lois cried as she spoke, but at least her lungs were working. "You tricked us. You controlled us with lies." She took another big breath. "But you already showed her what you are. She already knew."

Mike drove his fist into her stomach, causing Lois to buckle forward and out of his grip. This strike was too low to take her breath, but the pain was intense. Another fist struck the side of her head, followed by yet another which caused her to fall.

Mike kicked once and was reaching for Lois when he noticed the reflection in the car window. He immediately spun with one arm up to block, while punching straight into Scott's stomach with the other. "No blindsided sucker punches this time." Hitting Scott felt like striking a heavy bag in a gym, but he did move back with the strike.

Scott continued moving back as Mike continued his attack. With open hands, he was able to slap most of Mike's strikes to the side, and those that did make contact had little effect; still, Scott continued his retreat. When Scott had backed all the way to the sidewalk, he stopped and brought his hands up with open palms facing Mike. "That's enough Mike. Just back off, and you can run away. Nobody needs to get hurt."

"Screw you, asshole!" Mike punched at Scott again, but his fist was slapped down as Scott's fist struck his cheek instead. His next attempt was knocked to the side, leaving him open for the blow which struck his stomach. He came at Scott with a series of punches, each of which was either blocked or stopped short because Scott's strike reached him before he could make contact. Mike tried kicking, but Scott punched down, striking the top of his thigh to make the leg feel numb and useless. As his foot came down, Mike moved in close and felt the force of Scott's right fist on the side of his face. Mike attempted to move back out of Scott's reach but failed to move his feet as fast as his retreat. Landing on his backside, Mike rolled back to gain distance before turning to face Scott.

Mike climbed to his feet, surprised that Scott had not attacked while he was down. Glancing back, Mike realized that Scott had not backed away out of fear but had been leading him away from Lois. Mike looked into Scott's eyes, seeing neither fear, nor worry. Scott's long arms had greater reach, and Mike realized he would not defeat Scott in a fair fight. He glanced back at Lois, who was leaning on her car as she watched.

Mike turned to face Scott, lowering his hands as if in surrender. "I was leaving on business when I realized that my wife had lied about the date. I told her we weren't going to this reunion, and she tricked me into thinking it was over. I found her at her mother's house, and she stuck a Ga' damn shotgun in my face!" He gestured back to Lois, saying, "It seems your bitch of a girlfriend has been telling her crap about me. It's not enough that she ran away with her old boyfriend while we were married. Now she tells my wife a bunch of crap, and she STICKS A GA'DAMN SHOTGUN IN MY NOSE, AND ASKS IF I'D LIKE HER TO BLOW IT!"

Scott fought the urge to laugh at Mike's words. "Looks like this just isn't your day."

"Where did you hide her anyway? She just disappeared off the face of the Earth." Mike turned as he looked back at Lois, trying to hide his hand going to his pocket. "You know what? You can keep her. Keep 'em both! I don't want 'em." Mike moved closer as he turned back to face Scott.

Lois had been watching from the car and called out, "He has a knife!"

With a small 'click,' the blade shot out with Mike's forward lunge.

Scott turned, blocking across his body with his left arm. His right hand slapped down to catch Mike's wrist, pulling it forward and up, while keeping his free arm tight to Mike's. When Mike's elbow rolled over Scott's shoulder, Scott turned to grip Mike's wrist firmly with both hands. Scott jerked down hard, while pushing up with his shoulder. Mike screamed as his arm snapped, and the knife dropped harmlessly to the ground.

Scott turned back to face Mike as he sent an adrenaline-powered fist to the side of his jaw. Mike spun to fall motionless on the pavement.

"Just so everyone knows," Roxanne's voice cut through the air, "the police have been called and they're on their way."

Scott looked at the unmoving Mike. "That's good. I think we're done." Looking back, he asked, "How's Lois?"

Roxanne looked at Lois's face as she took her arm to help her stand. "She'll live, but she's going to have extra color in that cheek tomorrow."

Scott looked down at the knife, resisting the urge to kick it away. It was best to let the police see everything untouched. Turning his back on Mike, Scott walked to Lois and Roxanne. Lois was bruised and shaken. The pain in her stomach made it difficult to stand, but at least her breathing had returned to normal.

A police car stopped by the hotel, and two officers were soon walking through the parking lot to meet them. Scott stepped forward to meet the officer and told them what had happened.

"He's over there." Scott pointed to where Mike had been, but he was no longer there. "Well, at least his knife is still here."

The police took pictures of Mike's knife before putting it into an evidence bag. They also took separate statements from everyone. Scott and Roxanne took Lois to the emergency room, where a doctor examined and reported her injuries. The police found no sign of Mike, but hospitals and clinics were notified to watch for anyone with a broken arm.

At Lois's request, the police also stopped at Eve's mother's house. When Eve saw it was the police, she set the shotgun aside before answering the door. She assured them that she was fine, and she doubted that Mike would return. She also assured them that if Mike did return, the next time the shotgun would be loaded.

At Roxanne's urging, Lois agreed to go home with them, if she could get a ride back to her car the next day. They stopped at the motel on the other side of town, where Lois picked up her belongings and checked out. Looking at the lightweight door of the motel room, they were all glad Lois would not be staying there while Mike was at-large.

* * *

On the way home, Lois explained what Eve had told her earlier. Mike had married Eve, and they had moved to a country home farther south. After seeing Mike's abusive side, Eve waited until he was out of the house and headed back to Griffin with her kids. After dropping her children at her mother's house, she went to the reunion to ask Lois about her life with Mike.

After their talk, Eve assured Lois that she would be getting a lawyer Monday morning. Lois warned that Mike could be dangerous and was glad to hear that Eve had been prepared.

Chapter 16: Lois and Roxanne

Lois awoke to the sound of a phone ringing somewhere in the house. Sunlight through the large windows lit her room, telling her that the day had begun. Examining herself in the large mirror over the dresser, Lois saw that Roxanne's predictions of extra color had been accurate. Her shirt would cover the bruises on her stomach, but the swelling and color on her face would be visible for some time. She dressed in denim jeans and a white button-up shirt before heading downstairs to meet her hosts.

"Good morning!" Roxanne was sitting at the long wooden bar that divided the kitchen and dining area. She closed her book and set it aside so she could visit. "I have coffee ready."

"A cup of coffee would be wonderful." Lois walked to the bar to join Roxanne.

"I'm sorry, but you'll have to put up with just me for a while." Roxanne brought a fresh cup of coffee and set it on a coaster in front of Lois. "A neighbor called this morning. Part of his fence is down, so Scott's helping him find his cows. He'll probably end up fixing the fence before coming home."

"That sounds like the Scott I know. When someone needs help, there he is."

Roxanne nodded. "I think he got that from his father."

"I am sorry for what happened last night. I guess I shouldn't have come after all. I really believed he wasn't coming."

"From what I heard; he only came because Eve got away. You just gave her moral support after the fact, so no one can fault you for anything." Roxanne sipped her coffee. "What happened last night was completely on Mike. Scott told me about him, but I had no idea how unhinged he really was."

Lois looked around, now seeing the house in daylight. She was in one large open room that made up the kitchen, dining area, and living room. It had a high vaulted ceiling and large windows. The wide stairway concealed part of a hallway to other rooms. Through the patio door, she could see part of the large wraparound deck she had noticed last night.

Roxanne watched as Lois surveyed the room. "Yes, it is a bit bigger than the little cabin he had last time you were here." Roxanne could see Lois was surprised. "Yes, I know about your past with Scott, and no, I do not hold it against you. I hope we can be friends."

"Thank you. I would like that." Lois lifted her cup for another drink. "Scott wrote to tell me he was getting married, but he didn't say anything about you. Not that I would expect him to keep writing after he was married."

"He would have told you more, but there were some things that we couldn't talk about... to anyone." Roxanne ran her finger around the top of her cup while deciding what to say. "Someone came to me with a problem. My job had very strict confidentiality rules, just like priests, lawyers, counselors, psychologists, and even U.S. marshals. Lots of jobs deal with secrets, and mine was one of them. Some secrets may seem trivial, but I know of one person who tried to commit suicide, just because someone learned her secret. We never know how important secrets can be to other people."

Lois thought of the letters in her purse. "I can understand that."

Roxanne brought her eyes up to look at Lois. "Someone came to me with a problem, but I couldn't help without looking into someone else's secret. The problem was serious, so I did what I could. I met Scott, and he was able to help. We were successful, but anything we said about that time could have exposed someone else's secret."

"I understand. I can only imagine what might have happened if Mike ever learned where I was." Lois took a deep breath as she thought about that. "He did try to find me. He said something about me dropping off the face of the Earth, so I know he tried."

"Scott told me about him, but he's even scarier in person. Rest assured; he will never hear where you are from us. On that note, how is New Mexico? I've never been there."

"I like it. It has warm winters, nice people, and I enjoy my work." Lois paused to drink some coffee before saying, "If you ever decide to get away for a bit, I would love to show you around. But be warned, Scott will want to bring some things back next time he comes."

"Oh?" Roxanne set her cup down with an inquiring look.

"When he brought me there, he said he would be coming back to get his mother's china."

Roxanne nodded as she remembered. "His *grandmother's* china. I do remember him telling me about that, and the cabinet he made for his mother."

Lois nodded. "He didn't want to bring it back until he had a safe place for it, but the cabinet will look good in this house. There are also things that belonged to his uncle. I'm sure he would want those too."

"Scott told me about him. I understand he visited a lot when Scott was young. Did you know him?"

"Not while he was alive," Lois shook her head, "but I did get somewhat acquainted while living in his house."

Roxanne opened her eyes wider as she looked at Lois. "You're not going to tell me you met his ghost?"

"No, but maybe the next best thing." Lois turned to face Roxanne. "There a box in the spare room labeled, 'THE PAST.' It has his metals from the war, a couple photo albums, and his journals."

"Journals... you mean like a diary?"

"Very much like a diary." Lois glowed with excitement as she explained. "His wife, Linda, got him to keep a journal and write about his bad dreams and memories from the war. Apparently,

Dale had problems. Linda used the journals to help him overcome them."

"Sounds like PTSD."

Lois nodded. "It's easy to understand when you read his first journal. You can see how well he overcame it over time. His later writings were more about his life with Linda, and how much they loved each other."

Roxanne looked up as she searched her memory. "Scott told me about some of Dale's wives, but I don't recall hearing about Linda."

"She was before Scott's time. The last time he was wounded, she was his nurse. She was the reason he moved to New Mexico."

"So, what happened to her?"

"Her first husband's plane was shot down over the Pacific. A few years after the war was over, they found him living on an island. He was alive again, so Linda had to choose."

Roxanne stared into her cup. "That couldn't have been easy."

"I can only imagine what she was going through. Dale wrote that she loved them both, but her first husband needed her more. Dale moved on with his life, but he never really got over her. When he was dying from cancer, he still wrote about how he wished she would come back someday."

Roxanne looked very thoughtful. "I wonder if Scott even knew about the journals. That might be a good way for him to know his uncle better. Maybe we should consider a trip to New Mexico. Would you mind if we dropped in sometime?"

Lois's face lit up. "I would love it. Let me know when you can come, and I'll have the spare room ready. Granted, it's not nearly as nice as this house, but it is nice."

Roxanne let out a small laugh. "Scott sees his little cabin as a vacation, so if you have electricity and plumbing, that's fancy."

Lois chuckled. "It has that. It is nice, far nicer than I deserve for the rent I'm paying."

"That's strictly between you and Scott. Your rent covers taxes and insurance, so you're saving him money. He feels better knowing someone is living there."

Lois looked around the dining room, picturing the china cabinet in different places. "Did Scott build this himself? I remember him talking about building a bigger house."

"He wanted to, but it would have taken too much of his time. He decided it was better to leave the building to professionals, so he could make a few pieces to pay for it. But he did make all the cabinets and furniture."

"It's beautiful." Lois felt the top of the bar with her hand. "He was having a pole barn built for his workshop when I left."

"He was living there when I met him. He had a little one-room apartment on one end. That was easier than trying to update the cabin before winter. He added a couple more rooms after we met. After we married, he started planning this house. He added a few more buildings too. One for his sawmill, one for drying lumber, and another for his machinery."

"The reunion booklet said you had a little girl."

"Randi's spending the week with some cousins, which is good. I'm glad we didn't have to bring a sitter home last night. Next week, her cousins will be staying here. They love spending time in the woods." Roxanne looked up the stairs. "We haven't filled the extra rooms yet, but they get a lot of use as guest rooms."

"Not all old girlfriends in distress I hope."

"No. My parents thought I was crazy for wanting to live in the woods. After we built the house, Dad decided he likes it here. He uses us like a B&B. Sometimes Sam and the kids stay here with me during hunting season, while Scott and Ray use the old cabin. Sometimes we get the kids, so Sam and Ray can have the cabin to themselves." Roxanne grinned. "Speaking of the cabin, it will have a visitor today. Rachel complained about not being able to skinny dip, and I mentioned the outdoor shower. She's coming to try it out this afternoon."

Lois laughed. "That sounds like Rachel. Once she tries that shower, you may never get rid of her."

"That wouldn't be bad. I like her. Scott told them he would grill something for supper, so I hope you'll join us for that too."

"I would love to. I didn't see much of them last night. I was planning on seeing them again today. Maybe they'll even give me a ride back to my car." Lois laughed. "Once last night, I mistook you for Rachel. I was about to grab her from behind, but it dawned on me that Rachel isn't that tall."

"I guess it's true," Roxanne laughed as she patted the bottom of her short red hair. "All redheads look alike. I asked for something short and different. I almost fell over when I saw Rachel with the same cut."

Roxanne looked up at the clock on the wall. "I should fill the shower tank and light the heaters after breakfast, unless Scott gets back in time to do it first. Otherwise, Rachel may be taking a cold shower. Speaking of breakfast, how do you feel about Belgian Waffles?"

"I love them."

"Good. They're Scott's favorite; I hope he gets back in time. If not, I'll..." Roxanne was interrupted by the ringing of the telephone. "Maybe that's him now."

Roxanne answered the phone and spoke briefly, before giving the phone to Lois. While Lois was on the phone, Roxanne went to the kitchen and began preparing breakfast.

After hanging up the phone, Lois explained, "That was the Sheriff's Department; they have Mike. They found his car and had it towed. When everyone was gone, he tried to get away in my car. I had dropped the keys when he hit me. With all that happened, I forgot all about them." Lois let out a small laugh. "He was trying to get away, but he couldn't drive a stick with a broken arm. He was still trying to get out of the parking lot when they caught him." She chuckled again. "The police said he wrote a note asking for a lawyer. He can't talk because the doctor had to wire his jaw shut. I guess Scott hit him harder than we realized."

Roxanne looked up from her mixing bowl. "Well, I guess that takes care of Mike."

"But for how long?" Lois's expression turned to worry. "My registration and insurance papers were in the car's glove compartment. Mike had them in his pocket when they arrested him. Now he knows where I live, and that I'm using Raine as my last name. I'll have to move and start all over. If Mike finds me again, he will kill me."

PART 4: FIFTEEN-YEAR REUNION

Chapter 17: Twin Pines Bar

The Twin Pines Bar and Supper Club sat near the shore of Crappie Lake, a couple miles northeast of Griffin, Wisconsin. Before going any further, I should point out that the A in crappie is pronounced like the "au" in aught, or like the "O" in crop. Crappie Lake is named for the pan fish, crappie, and not for a slang term that means excrement.

Back on topic, Twin Pines Supper Club is named for two large pine trees, one on each side of its long driveway. From the road, you cannot see the club, but the twin pines at the top of the drive stand tall and are easy to spot. Both trees hold a traffic-facing sign that says, "TWIN PINES SUPPER CLUB," with an arrow pointing down the driveway. The long blacktop driveway leads down through a patch of woods and ends in the supper club's parking lot. The majestic trees which give the club its name cannot be seen from the bar, although the bar and dining room have a splendid view of the lake. Owners of this establishment wisely chose to name their business after the two trees, rather than the lake, for obvious reasons.

As you enter the supper club, you see a long, neat bar across the inside wall, with multiple tables for fine dining. Extending back from the bar is a large room used for dances, meetings, swap meets, receptions, parties, and at least one funeral. It is not as large or fancy as the Banquet Room of the River Side Hotel, but it is nice, and its rates are affordable.

On the rainy last Saturday of July 1987, we gathered at the Twin Pines Supper Club for our fifteen-year class reunion. The separate bar in the back room was opened for us, complete with a bartender, cocktail waitresses, and busboys we would share with the main dining room. Our meal was prepared by the club and would be served buffet style. After our meal, music was supplied by a local band. I remember the band as being good, even though no one seems to recall its name.

* * *

Doris Lester was on the reunion committee again, so Rich was waiting at the bar when Dave Masters arrived early. "You beat the cocktail hour by forty-five minutes. I thought you had more pinpoint timing."

"At our last reunion, I learned that it's more fun to get here early." Dave took a seat next to Rich. "Also, I got a room at the hotel before I visited my parents. I now know that not staying at my parents' house when I'm in town is rude. That was made very clear to me today." Dave let out a big sigh. "I spent most of the day listening to both of my parents, non-stop. Need I say more?"

"'Nuff said. Can I buy you a drink?"

"I could go for a Manhattan. Thank you, Dickless."

"Just for that, I'll let you buy me one later." Rich ordered their drinks and looked back to the door. "Where's Nadine?"

"Nadine is in the past. We still run into one another, but our divorce is done."

"I'm sorry to hear that. Did she catch you boinking your secretary or something?"

"Very good guess, but it was my personal assistant. Also, it was me who walked in on them. Part of his job was to do things so I would not have to. My wife, however, was not on the list of things he was supposed to do. Long story short, she got her freedom, and he lost his job. As my personal assistant, he should have known my schedule well enough to know when I was likely to walk in on them. Such inattention to detail is unforgivable."

"Wow!" Rich shook his head. "I'm sorry to hear that."

"Well, it was coming. She was upset ever since I quit working for her father. She was afraid we would be destitute without

Daddy watching over us." Dave grinned. "Since I left, their stock dropped twenty points, and mine has doubled."

"Well, that's good anyway."

Dave sipped his drink. "It's all good."

"What's good?" Rachel asked as she and Randy stepped up to the bar.

Rich raised his glass. "Getting a sitter so you can step out early, and not listen to the kids."

"Getting out early so you don't have to listen to your parents." Dave raised his glass to clink against Rich's.

"How about, leaving your kids with your parents and getting out so you don't have to listen to either of them?" Rachel looked to the bartender and said, "Two stingers, each with two filberts and two straws."

Dave held his glass up in salute to Rachel. "She wins! This round is on me."

When their drinks arrived, Rachel used her straws to lift and eat the first hazelnut, before sipping her drink and saying in a sassy voice, "I can drink this year, because I'm no-ot pregnant."

Randy sipped his drink and said with a grin, "The night's not over."

Hearing that, Rachel looked to the bartender and asked, "Do you have a really strong rubber band? The kind they put on animal parts when they want them to fall off."

Craig Roberts entered the room, accompanied by a very pregnant young woman with dishwater blond hair.

Rachel leaned close to Randy and asked in a soft voice, "Does she look old enough, to have gotten drunk enough, to be that pregnant?"

Randy turned to Rich, "Is the drinking age still eighteen in Wisconsin?"

"It went back to twenty-one, unless accompanied by a parent, spouse, or guardian."

Randy turned back to Rachel, "Rich said yes, but only if he's her daddy."

Craig and his companion joined the others at the bar, brushing the rain from their hair as they walked. "Hi guys. I'd like to introduce my wife, Ruth. Ruth, this is Rich Lester, Dave Masters, Randy Richards, and his wife, Rachel Davis."

Ruth looked confused. "If she's his wife, why does she have a different last name?"

"I still use my maiden-name professionally."

"I've never been professional," said Ruth. "So, I guess I can stick with Craig's last name."

Craig looked at the bartender and asked for a Budweiser, before looking back to Ruth and asking what she would like.

"I don't know," she hesitated, looking at Randy and Rachel's drinks, "What are you two having? That looks good."

"This is a stinger, but in your case, I would suggest a stingless." When the bartender looked confused, Rachel leaned in and said, "It's the same as mine, only instead of brandy, you use ginger ale, and instead of white crème de menthe, you use 7up."

When her drink arrived, Ruth sipped it and said, "This is good."

Rachel quickly explained about using the straws as chopsticks to eat the Filberts, and how you must cut yourself off when you can no longer do that.

Ruth patted her round belly and said, "Craig's the one I should cut off."

Rich asked, "So, how long have you two been together?"

"We got married last January," boasted Craig. "We got together at an early Christmas party. The next thing we knew, we were getting married, and Junior was on the way."

Dave asked, "When are you due?"

"Late September," Ruth set one hand on her belly, "but early births do run in my family."

"First one comes anytime," said Rich. "My first came almost as fast as Danny's. Hey Danny!"

Danny and Carol joined them at the bar as Craig introduced them to Ruth.

"Are you okay?" Rachel noticed when Ruth tensed up, before relaxing with a big breath.

"I'm fine. I've just got the worst indigestion today."

Craig explained, "We got lunch at Taco Bell, and it didn't agree with her."

"I know what you mean." Carol had also noticed when Ruth tensed up. You'd better keep an eye on that. In your condition, if that indigestion starts coming and going close together, you may want to have it checked."

Rachel nodded. "Ditto."

"Oh, it's not labor. We have almost two months to go." Ruth remained firm on that answer every time she was asked.

Rachel leaned close to Randy and said, "I may have to switch to stingless after all. I might need some clear thinking before this night's over."

"I know what you guys are thinking." Craig set his beer on the bar. "Yes, there is a big age gap between Ruth and me, but Ruth says age is just a number, and we love each other."

Dave set his glass down and looked thoughtful. "When I got divorced, some friends were talking to me about the proper age gap for couples. One friend said to just be sure she was closer to your age, than that of your children."

"I turned 21 the day of that Christmas party. That's when Craig and I got together for the first time." Ruth wrapped her arm around Craig. "He was my Christmas and birthday present."

Rachel tipped her head to look thoughtful. "Scott's dad was older than his wife, and they were a great couple. And my great-grandfather was forty-two when he married Great Grandma, and she was only twenty-one. They had ten kids, and he still outlived her. Of course, he was getting on in years, so she was doing most of the work. Maybe that's what wore her out?" Rachel looked at Ruth. "Let that be a lesson. He may be older, but he can still do his share of the work." Rachel cocked her head and looked up. "Everyone always said how happy Great Grandma was. Of course, they also said Great Grandpa was hung like a mule, so maybe that's what wore her out."

Dave coughed and sprayed part of his drink into and over his glass.

"Get used to it." Randy laughed, "I think that's Rachel's favorite hobby."

"Really!" Rachel tried to look serious. "When my uncle saw Grandpa taking a leak behind the barn, he thought he was setting up a tripod. When his horse saw him pee, it ran away in shame." Rachel noticed Danny was about to drink. "Great Grandma was short, even shorter than me, and Grandpa was tall. Some said that when they did it the normal way, she still had to decide if she should spit or swallow."

Danny caught himself in time, and defiantly looked at Rachel as he swallowed his beer without coughing.

Chapter 18: Table Time

Cocktail hour was winding down and classmates began taking seats at tables, saving our places as it would soon be time to eat. Cocktail waitresses began making rounds, so a seat at a table was as good as sitting at the bar. There were round tables that seated six and banquet tables for larger groups.

Lois stopped by the round table where Scott sat with Ray and Samantha Ellis. "Is there room for one more?" When Scott looked at the empty chair next to him, she realized Roxanne might object to sitting with Scott's old girlfriend. "Or, I can find another seat," she raised her head to look for another seat. "It's alright."

"No!" Scott quickly stood to pull out the chair next to him. "I was just thinking, if you don't mind sitting next to me, there will still be room for one more couple." Pulling the chair out for Lois, he said, "I'm sorry. I'm a backwoods-savage who forgets his etiquette."

"Ah," Lois was confused as she looked and saw no sign of Roxanne. "Is it alright?"

Scott nodded as he held the chair for her. "Please have a seat."

Concerned, Lois sat and let Scott push the chair in for her. "Okay."

Scott sat and turned to face Lois. "Roxanne liked you. She would have wanted you to join us. We lost her to cancer a couple years ago. I would have let you know, but I never got your new address."

"Oh! I'm so sorry. I liked her too. I was looking forward to seeing her tonight. How's your little girl? This must be terrible on her."

"She doesn't like losing mothers, but she's adjusted to it. We take care of each other now. She even helps me in my workshop when she has the time. Being lady of the house keeps her quite busy you know."

"I imagine so. That's a big house for a little girl."

"I don't work her like Cinderella," said Scott. "A local girl has moved in to one of the guest rooms. She's sort of a live-in housekeeper and daughter companion. Between the three of us, we manage to keep the house in shape."

After more conversation, Ray asked, "Where are you staying Lois?"

"I'm staying at my parents' house this weekend." Lois grinned with excitement as she explained, "I had a falling out with my parents when I was with Mike. Part of it was something I had done, but I now learned that it was mostly lies Mike had told them about me. We had a big fight, and pretty much cut off all contact. I still sent them Christmas cards with letters, so they knew I was alright. Last Christmas, Dad wrote back. Now we call and talk to each other. They even invited me to stay with them this weekend. I never thought it would happen, but I have my parents back."

"That's terrific." Scott patted her hand. "I knew your dad loved you too much to stay mad at you. When I first met him, he asked me to look after you at our graduation party."

"And you did. That was the first time you came to my rescue." Thinking of the timing, Lois looked thoughtful, "It seems you rescue me every five years. I hope nothing happens tonight."

Scott said, "I think we're safe this time. They didn't even have an address for Mike. Bill Spencer told me he made a delivery to Mike in Iowa, but he's using a different name now."

Ray looked sad and turned his reunion booklet over for Scott to see. On the back page were two pictures of Bill Spencer, one from their senior yearbook and a more recent one of him by his truck. Above the pictures were the words, *"In Memory,"* followed by a brief obituary.

"Hi guys, have you got an extra seat?" They looked up to see Peter Baker asking to join them. Peter now wore his hair in a ponytail that reached the middle of his back.

Ray gestured to an empty chair, "Have a seat, Pete."

* * *

Rachel kept her reunion booklet in hand as she wandered among the classmates who had already arrived. When she saw Doug Paterson and his wife coming in from the rain, she hurried to meet him before he had time to wipe the rain from his glasses. After a brief conversation, Doug headed back out to his car. As Doug stepped out, another couple entered.

A well-dressed gentleman entered and began folding his umbrella. It took a moment for Rachel to recognize the finely dressed lady who accompanied him.

"Nessa!" Rachel stepped forward to hug Vanessa Winters. After a fast hug, Rachel let go and stepped back to study her old friend. "Damn Nessa. You clean up nice. I take it you didn't come from the jungle this year?"

Vanessa smiled politely before speaking with a hint of an English accent, "Not this time Rachel. I am no longer with the Peace Corps." Turning to the gentleman next to her, "Rachel Davis, I'd like to introduce my husband, Lord Maxwell Westford."

Rachel's eyes grew wide as he lifted her hand with a slight bow, and lightly kissed the back of her hand. "It is a pleasure to meet you, Ms. Davis."

Rachel's knees bent enough for a slight curtsy. "It's a pleasure to meet you sir."

Vanessa took his arm, "Let's get a drink from the bar before finding a table. I see some more friends I would like you to meet."

As they walked toward the bar, Rachel looked back to Vanessa and mouthed out the word "Lord?"

Vanessa nodded and mouthed back, "Yes, for real."

Ray Ellis recognized Vanessa as they crossed the room. "Whoa! Looks like we have a whole new Nessa. Who's that with her?"

Peter turned to see the new couple. "Wow! This could be good. I think we have someone here who is even richer than Dave Masters. And by richer, I mean by moving the decimal over a place or four."

Samantha looked amused. "It's too bad Nadine isn't here. I wonder what she's like around people who have more money than she does."

They began looking through their reunion booklets to see what it said about Vanessa's husband. Peter explained, "Vanessa asked me to find out who owned, and was preparing to destroy, the rainforests her village was in. I followed company to company and came to an English Lord, who looks just like that guy. From the looks of them, and the rock on her finger, I think our Nessa was successful in saving her rainforest."

* * *

At the bar Danny O'Brian asked, "So, Lord is a real title you use with your name?"

Vanessa's husband explained, "I realized noble titles are illegal in the United States, but since I am not an American, it does not apply to me. Although, that law seems to be somewhat meaningless. Your Congressmen and Senators seem to have simply replaced our titles with their own. I have met some of your Congressmen and Senators, who seem to think of themselves as being more royal than those who have actual titles."

"So," Rich tipped his head slightly, "do we need to call you by the whole thing, or can we just call you Lord Max, or something like that?"

"Vanessa said that you would be less formal here. Many of my friends call me Maxwell." Lord Westford smiled at Vanessa as he held her hand. "At this party, you may call me Max."

Carol reminded Vanessa, "When we were little, all the stories were about meeting a handsome prince. You said you didn't want

176

a prince. You said you were waiting for Tarzan. I thought that was why you went into the Peace Corps."

"How interesting." Lord Max looked into his wife's eyes. "Well, in the book, Tarzan returned to England, reclaiming his title as Earl of Greystoke. It seems Vanessa may have gotten her wish."

* * *

When we split up to find tables, Vanessa invited Dave, Rachel, and Randy to join her and Lord Max, while the Lesters and O'Brian's sat with Craig and Ruth at a nearby table.

When a cocktail waitress delivered a round of drinks to their table, Rachel ate her hazelnut, sipped her drink, and said to Randy, "It looks like I'm back to stingers."

"You've been drinking stingers," said Randy. "Remember, you're not pregnant this year."

"My last two were stingless." Looking over to the table where Ruth was sitting, Rachel guessed what had happened. "Well, at least there's no one with a look-alike drink sitting with her now."

The owner of the Twin Pines stepped onto the stage to use the band's microphone. "May I have your attention, please?" He paused for a moment and repeated his request. When everyone stopped to listen, he said, "I have some good news and some bad news. The storm outside is getting worse. One of the twin pines at our entrance went down in the storm and is now blocking the driveway. I have people with chainsaws coming, but until they are finished, we're all stuck in here."

Someone called out, "What's the bad news?"

"That was the bad news. The good news is your food is ready." He gestured to the buffet, "You may proceed to the buffet line at your convenience. Again, I do have people coming, and we hope to have the driveway cleared before anyone is ready to leave. Thank you, and please enjoy your meals."

When Rachel approached Carol in the buffet line to ask how Ruth was doing, she replied, "Her indigestion seems to hit her once every fifteen minutes, unless I'm missing some."

"She's also giggling a lot more," said Doris. "Her favorite topics are how she was once prom queen, how she met Craig at a Christmas party, and that was the first time she ever did it. I don't know if she's trying to convince us, Craig, or herself. Also, believe it or not, I think she's starting to giggle with a slur."

Rachel was not surprised. "Yeah, I think she switched a couple of her stingless for my stingers. If she does it again, she's in for a surprise. I switched to stingless."

Carol thought about that. "I wonder which Craig has been buying for her. He got her another drink after we sat at the table."

On the way back to the table, Rachel stopped to ask Scott if he had a chainsaw in his truck.

Scott said, "Yes, but I didn't bring the truck tonight. Why?"

"We've got a tipsy prom queen who seems to be nine months into her seven-month pregnancy, and her indigestion pains are getting closer by the minute. Now a big tree is cutting us off from the world." Rachel gave Scott a curious look, "Scott, have you ever delivered..."

"Not even a cow!" he said before she could finish. "But Doug is here and..."

"Yeah, I already talked to him. We've got him as a sober standby."

* * *

The meals were enjoyed, by most anyway. Ruth ate very little, as her indigestion pains were getting closer together. When she let out a loud moan and said, "Oh, I wish I could just fart and get this over with," Doris held up five fingers, letting Rachel know indigestion pains were now five minutes apart.

Rachel hurried to the bar and asked to speak with the manager. When the manager came, she explained what was happening and asked how the tree removal was coming.

When she looked back to the tables again, she said, "Great! Now that she's getting close enough to pay attention, we're trapped in here anyway." Rachel noticed one of the tables near the wall remained empty and asked them to put a reserved sign on that table. She also asked the manager about clean bar towels, and would he leave some on that table?"

Chapter 19: Special Delivery

When busboys from the restaurant started clearing dishes from the tables, the band began to play. They began with a rock and roll number. Some of us were still eating, and the rest had just finished, so the first few songs had no dancers. They played a slow dance, tempting several couples to the dance floor.

Ruth blew out a big breath, listened to the music, and asked Craig if he would like to dance. As he walked her to the dance floor, she was heard saying, "I shink ssome exzersize might help a liddle?"

As they headed to the dance floor, Rachel sat next to Carol and said, "Just don't stay out there for a polka, or that baby will be bouncing on the floor." Rachel dipped her finger into Ruth's drink and licked the finger. "That's not stingless; that's the real thing."

When the song ended, Ruth stood bent for a moment, exhaled, and put her arms around Craig's neck for the next dance.

Rachel said, "That's a three-and-a-half-minute song, and she had one on each end of it."

The band began playing another slow song as Ruth stood motionless, except for her eyes opening wide with surprise. Rachel grabbed a busboy who was clearing a nearby table and said, "Forget the table. Go get a mop!" She looked to Randy, holding her extended thumb and little finger to her mouth and ear, signaling that it was time for him to make the call.

Rachel joined Craig, and with her assistance, they walked Ruth to the empty table by the wall. Following Rachel's lead, Craig helped Ruth onto the table and eased her down to lie on her back. Rachel grabbed a layer of bar towels and set them under Ruth's head for a pillow. The lights had been dimmed for dancing, but the row of lights over that table were suddenly bright, at Randy's request.

"Wha's going on?" Ruth asked with a slur.

"Well," Rachel tried to sound cheerful, "the good news is that you do not have food poisoning, or indigestion. Taco Bell is in the clear. The better news, is you're about to lose several pounds, and you won't have to waddle anymore."

"But it's too early!" Ruth whined. "It's not due for two more months!"

"Well," Rachel thought of how to say this, "I have a feeling that math was never your strong point."

"But this is too sooon."

"Well, Junior thinks otherwise, and this is one time that Junior gets the deciding vote." Rachel noticed that people were gathering around them, trying to see what was happening. "Okay everyone, LISTEN UP! I want everyone who's over here to turn around and stand together with their back to me. Close together so this girl can have some privacy. You are now a wall, so make it a good one! We don't want anyone peeking through. Except for Doug Patterson. DOUG, GET YOUR ASS IN HERE!"

Everyone turned and stood together as Rachel instructed. Rachel turned to Ruth and began pulling her dress up above the hips.

"Why are you pulling my panties down?" Ruth was clearly much drunker than they realized.

"Because your water broke and they're all wet," Rachel explained, "and if the first thing Junior sees is the inside of your pantyhose, he'll grow up to be a bank robber."

Ruth moaned and grabbed her stomach as another contraction hit.

"Breathe!" Rachel turned to look at Craig. "Craig! Help her breathe. Hee-hee-hee, like that. Short quick breaths."

Craig began making the short breath sounds as Rachel commanded, and together they worked through her contraction.

When the contraction had passed, the confused Ruth asked, "Do bank robbers make a lot of money?"

Rachel promptly replied, "Not much. Their partners usually make more when they turn them in for the reward."

Fear was beginning to show on Ruth's face as she asked Rachel, "Have you done this before?"

"Four times, but only as a pitcher; I've never been a catcher."

"I think we need a doctor!" Ruth moaned as another contraction began.

Craig went, "Hee-hee-hee," reminding Ruth of the breathing technique.

"He's right here putting his gloves on." Rachel shifted her gaze from Ruth to those standing to form a wall. "Peter! Greg! Grab a chair and get over here." Rachel grabbed Greg's chair and placed it next to the table facing Ruth. She told Peter to go to the other side of the table and do the same with his chair. "Now straddle the chairs and sit!" she ordered. Rachel put Ruth's left foot between Greg's shoulder blades and her right foot, likewise in Peter's. "Congratulations. You've both been promoted to stirrups. Now sit strong and don't turn around, no matter what you hear. If one of you turns, her foot could slip, or you might faint, and the baby will land on top of you. Believe me. We do not want that to happen again." It was the *"again"* that truly scared us into not moving.

Rachel looked at Craig. "You hold her shoulders, so she doesn't push back off the table. And remember to help her breathe, except when she's pushing. When she's pushing, tell her to hold her breath for a stronger push. Then have her blow the old air out. Have you got that Craig?"

With a perfect deer-in-the-headlights expression, Craig held Ruth's shoulders and nodded.

Doug stepped in wearing a surgical mask and long sterile gloves, which covered his hands and arms, all the way up to his shoulders. Giving Rachel an apologetic look, he said, "I don't have any shorter gloves with me." Doug stepped forward so Ruth could see him. "Hello, Ruth. I'm Doctor Doug Paterson."

"Are you a real doctor?"

"My diploma says Doctor, and I have my own clinic." Doug looked to see Rachel's nod of approval to his answer.

"Have you delivered babies before?"

"Mothers and babies do all the real work; I just make sure everyone gets out correctly. I've helped plenty of babies into this world."

"Why are your gloves so long?"

"Sometimes I have to reach in and reposition the baby." Seeing Ruth's eyes begin to widen, he said, "Don't worry. You're already crowning, so Junior is lined up fine."

With her next contraction, Doug told Ruth to push. Doug leaned in, to guide, assist, or catch. Whatever it was he did, I really was not watching.

The band had been silent from the moment the lights turned up. When the first baby cry was heard, they began to softly play an instrumental version of Paul Anka's "Are You Having My Baby?"

Doug wrapped a clean bar towel around the baby and laid it on Ruth's chest for her to hold. Craig recognized the band's song and began to sing the words softly.

When Danny heard Craig sing, "Are you having my baby ..." he leaned down to Carol and whispered, "Not according to my math."

A pan of warm water was brought from the kitchen. Doug dipped a clean bar towel into the water and began cleaning Ruth, or the baby, or doing whatever doctors do. Really, I was not watching so I cannot explain anything. I had my orders, and a good stirrup does not watch.

Ruth made a cooing sound when she looked at the baby in her arms, "She's beautiful."

"He's beautiful," corrected Doug.

Ruth gently brushed her fingers over the head of her newborn son. "Look, he has red hair."

"Why would he have red hair?" Craig wondered aloud.

"Because... he's premature?" said Ruth.

"Recessive gene," suggested Rachel.

Ruth smiled at Rachel. "He did it for Rachel. Rachel helped, and she has red hair." Not the greatest logic, but if Craig was as drunk as Ruth, he just might buy it. Rachel may have been hoping that no one would make any stereotypical comments about a redheaded stepchild, or she may have been resisting the urge to say something like that herself. It's not every day that Rachel holds back on an easy punch line.

"This first hair is mostly fuzz, which is likely to change with time," said Doug. "And as Rachel said, there are recessive genes from past generations. His hair could come from a sixth great-grandparent."

Soon two men dressed in white entered the bar with a gurney, ready to take Ruth and the baby to the ambulance, which had finally made its way around the remains of the tree. Craig would follow them to the hospital, where she and the baby would be checked out and cared for.

Doug removed his long gloves before shaking Craig's hand. "Congratulations Craig."

Craig smiled proudly. "Should I bring him to your clinic for follow-up visits?"

"No, he should see a people doctor now. But when you get him a puppy, bring it to Paterson's Veterinary Clinic, and we'll take good care of it."

"Thanks, Doc!" Craig gave Doug's hand another strong shake.

As they slid Ruth onto the gurney, she reached to grab Rachel's arm. "Rachel, we couldn't have done this without you. When my sister got married, she had a wedding planner who handled everything. Now I can tell my sister, that bitch was nothing compared to you. You really kick ass!" Ruth looked back to Craig. "I want to name the baby after Rachel."

"But... Rachel is a girl's name?"

Ruth thought for a moment. "Ray Chill! We could name him Ray Chill Roberts."

Rachel could only imagine what life would be like for a boy named Ray Chill. "My married name is Richards, and my maiden name is Davis. How about Richard Davis? Or even David Richard?"

"David Richard Roberts." Ruth liked the way it rolled off her tongue. "I like that, and we named him after Rachel. And he'll have the initials D R, so we named him after Doctor Long-gloves too."

Craig grinned and nodded. "I like that." As he followed the gurney to the door, he looked back. "Thanks for everything, Rachel. You too, Doctor Doug."

As they made their way to the door, the band began playing Happy Birthday to you.

Rich Lester stepped next to Rachel to say, "David Richard Roberts. Of course, in Rachelese, they will call him D. Dick Bob. In the phone book, it will read Bob D. Dick."

Rachel gave that some thought. "Now it sounds like he was named for a circumcision. Maybe Ray Chill wasn't so bad after all."

Eve said, "People used to make jokes about me having a baby at Prom, but who'd have guessed that someone would actually do it at our reunion?"

"But it never happened to you," said Rachel.

"I was too good at math. I may have been easy, but I was smart enough to keep track of when it was safe to be that way."

Chapter 20: Post-Partum Party

After a brief mopping, a wet floor sign was set where Ruth had been standing when her water broke. The band resumed playing, but conversation was still more popular than dancing for the remains of their first set. It seemed we all suddenly had something to talk about. I hear the owner of Twin Pines has added, "Public Birthing" to the list of events that have been held at the club.

When the band stepped down to take a break, Lee Swenson stepped up to borrow the microphone. He apologized that they did not have any prizes for this reunion, but pointed out that if we had, Vanessa would have once more gotten the award for traveling farthest to join us. He then thanked Lord Max, for bringing Lady 'Nessa all the way from Somewherein, England. He also pointed out that Craig and Ruth should have gotten something for being either most pregnant or for *having* the youngest child. "On that note," he added, "Craig did call us with an update. David Richard Roberts weighed in at a full seven pounds, thirteen ounces, and is twenty-two and a half inches long. Mother and child are doing fine. Craig is certain that tonight's premature delivery is due to his son being very advanced for his age." Before stepping down, he announced that the driveway had been cleared enough for safe passage, but most of the tree would remain on the side of the driveway until sunlight and dryer weather allows them to complete the job. He said we should keep that in mind and drive carefully.

The band began their next set, but many of us preferred visiting over dancing. Peter got up and said he was anxious to talk with Nessa and her new Lord. Looking more to Lois than the others, he added, "I'll still be around tonight if anyone wants to talk, and I'm staying at the Riverside Hotel if anyone wants to see me tomorrow."

Lois gave him an understanding nod, while Scott and Ray wished him a good night.

As Ray and Samantha got up from their table, Ray said that they would be dancing and visiting with others, letting Scott and Lois know they could have some time alone.

Feeling almost like a couple again, they sat close enough to hear one another over the band. Scott spoke briefly of Roxanne's cancer, and talked about the portable sawmill Ray was helping him modify.

Lois's face lit up as she talked about her reuniting with her parents. She went on to tell of her job and apartment, showing great pride in having established her new life without assistance from anyone. She was about to answer Scott's question about where she was living, when Rachel set two stingers on the table and dropped into the chair next to Lois.

Lois looked at the lowball glasses. "Oh no. I'm driving back to my parents tonight, and I still remember the last time you fed me those."

"No... these are both mine." Rachel lifted one of the glasses and took a big drink. "I had to get away from the bar; too many people were buying me drinks." Rachel set her glass down and turned to Lois with an expression of pride. "I have been named, 'official birthing organizer' for our class."

Lois laughed. "How many of those have you had?"

"Enough, but even the mix is sixty-proof, so it doesn't take many. Besides, this is the first time I could drink at a reunion, so I'm making up for the last two." Rachel finished off the stinger in that glass and used her straws to lift the remaining hazelnut. "You should see Doug. This is his first time as a people-puller, so everyone's buying drinks for him too. But he's not Doug anymore. His new name is Doctor Long-gloves. It even says that on his name tag. It's a good thing his wife is driving." Rachel attempted to drop the hazelnut into her mouth, but it missed and landed down the front of her shirt. She looked up with a smile,

"I'm saving that one for Randy." She lifted her other glass and used her straws to eat one of its nuts.

Scott said, "I take it Randy is your designated driver?"

Rachel chewed her hazelnut and sipped her drink to wash it down. "That was our backup plan, but I think we'll stick with Plan A. Our van has tinted windows and reclining seats, so we'll camp in it 'til morning. We parked way back in the lot, so we won't disturb anyone if I get loud."

Lois let out a brief, unexpected laugh at that.

"Aw, my timing's off. You were supposed to be drinking when I said that." Rachel smiled when she saw Lois's hand resting in Scott's. "It's good to see you two again. I had high hopes for you. You're both like family to me. But not to each other, so it's okay, if you know what I mean?"

"I think so." Scott gently squeezed Lois's hand.

Randy pulled out a chair and sat next to Rachel, setting his half-empty stinger on the table. Looking at the three of them, he said, "Vanessa introduced Peter to Lord Max, and Peter asked him about Sum Warren. That's really the real name of where they live. Who knew?"

"Really?" Rachel was surprised. "I thought he was just being evasive when he said they lived, *'Somewhere in, England.'* And Peter knew about it?"

"Sum Warren," Randy said with an air of correction. "Vanessa told Max that Peter was the one who sent her to him. Max thanked Peter and invited him for a visit."

"Far out." Rachel looked to Randy, "I was going to ask Scott and Lois if they wanted to go swimming with us tonight, but it's raining so hard, and we'd get too wet." Rachel looked at Scott when she heard him chuckle. "You know what I mean. Our clothes would get wetter in the rain than we would in the lake. We would have to leave our clothes in the bar, and hope they were still there when we got back."

Rachel took a drink and looked at Randy. "Maybe we need to start a new tradition."

Randy set his drink down and faced his wife. "What did you have in mind?"

"Eve was talking to me about math earlier." She leaned closer to Randy. "Eve is very good at math, and it only let her down twice. Once when she got excited about a prime number and forgot all her calculations, and the other time, her math partner wouldn't listen when she gave him the right answer. So, I let Eve help me with my math." Rachel looked to see Scott and Lois were still with them. She looked back to Randy, "It's like, if you time it right, you can eat all you want and never get fat." She winked at Randy. "Eve says I can go to an all-you-can-eat buffet every night this week, and still keep my girlish figure."

Randy tried to wink back at Rachel, even though he looked confused.

"I think we should go to the van, so you can find something for me."

"Did you lose something?"

"No, but you can still find it. It starts with C and ends with my sign."

Randy looked up with wide eyes and a happy smile. "I think I can help you with that." He lifted his glass to finish his drink and stood as he set his glass back on the table.

Rachel downed her drink and looked back to Lois. "This may take a while, I hope. If the van is moving when you leave tonight... it just does that sometimes."

Lois laughed out loud as she watched them casually stroll to the door, before racing into the rain.

The band began another slow song, and Scott asked Lois if she would like to dance.

As they began moving with the music, Lois looked up and asked if he'd found a good tenant for his house in New Mexico.

Scott shook his head. "As much as I liked having that house, I decided to let it go." He could see the surprise in Lois's expression. "You moved before we could get away, but we finally made it there for a few weeks. I was packing Grandma's china, and Roxanne was reading journals, when an elderly lady stopped to ask if the house was for sale. She had aged, but I could still recognize her from pictures of Uncle Dale's fourth wife."

Lois pulled back slightly, looking up with excitement. "Linda came back?"

Scott looked down with a grin. "Her husband passed away, so she wanted to come home. I guess the feelings he put into his journals were the same for her. Somehow, I think Uncle Dale is happy now."

Lois pulled tight against Scott with a joyful hug, feeling like a sad story had just returned with a happy ending. She lessened her hold enough to continue dancing, moving together as they once did when dancing to the crackle of a campfire. Lois liked being in his arms again. She found herself wishing her parents were not expecting her home after the dance. She felt a warm blush as the music ended. Taking Scott's hand, they returned to their table.

Eve Johnson was waiting at the table when they returned. She asked if she could speak with Scott for a moment.

Lois excused herself to visit the restroom, leaving Scott to speak with Eve. As she passed by Peter, Lois stopped to ask if they could meet tonight, instead of waiting until tomorrow. As much as she enjoyed her time with Scott, she did have important business with Peter, and being with Scott made her want to settle that business even more.

While walking back to the table, Lois wondered how she would explain her need to talk to Peter alone. She saw Scott talking to Ray, and he hurried back with a look of concern.

Scott wrapped his arms around her with a hug, easing the worry she was beginning to feel. Releasing her, he stepped back to hold her hands as he looked into her eyes. "I'm sorry Lois, but something came up, and I need to leave. I don't want to, but this is important, and I think waiting might be a big mistake." Taking a business card out of his pocket, he put it into Lois's hands. "This has my address and numbers on it. If tonight was as special to you as it was to me, call me. Hell, if tonight meant nothing to you, call me anyway. I'm sorry for cutting the night short, and I'd really like to make it up to you."

"Okay...." Lois slid the card into the front pocket of her purse for safekeeping. "What's going on?"

"It's a long story, and I don't have all the details yet; I guess I'll get them on the way. Believe it or not, I'm going to see Mike." Scott could see her eyes widen with fear at the mention of Mike's name. "I'll be fine. I know how dangerous he can be. That's why I don't dare put this off."

"When are you leaving?" Lois glanced at the door and saw Peter returning with a briefcase in his hand.

"Right after I say goodnight to you." Scott took hold of her hand as they walked to the door. He hugged her once more before opening the door. "Don't forget to call me. We still have more to talk about." After opening the door, he turned back to quickly kiss her, and turned to head out into the rain.

Lois nodded and tried to smile as she watched him from the open doorway. "Me too." She continued watching as another car stopped in front of his SUV; the interior light came on just long enough for her to recognize Eve Johnson as the driver. Scott followed Eve's car out the driveway, followed by another car that was also leaving. "Me too," she repeated, before turning back to the bar and allowing the door to close behind her.

Chapter 21: Peter's Report

The main bar and dining room had one large wall of windows with a good view of the lake. Peter waited at a table by one of those windows, not for the view, but for the privacy it offered. Only a few restaurant guests remained, and the bar was on the other side of the room.

Peter sat at the end of the table so Lois took a seat at the side where she would be close enough for them to look at his papers together. A waitress told them the kitchen had closed but she could still bring drinks from the bar. While ordering drinks, Lois looked out the window to see that the restaurant really did have an excellent view of the lake, even at night with multiple lights aimed across the shoreline.

When Peter set his briefcase on the table, Lois rested her hand on it. "Before you begin, I would like to explain some things that I couldn't over the phone."

"That's not necessary." Peter tried to look reassuring. "I've had similar cases, and I've done some research on Mike before. I understand how things can happen."

"It took me years to understand what happened, and I was there."

"You were pregnant; everyone thought Scott was dead. Then Mike proposed when you were vulnerable."

"First, he offered to arrange an abortion," she corrected. "When I told him that wouldn't happen, he proposed. I turned him down. I thought I should go home to my parents, but Mike kept saying how disappointed they would be. He said it would be better to just get married. I began to think, if he was willing to marry me, knowing I was carrying Scott's child, maybe he really did love me. Mike can be convincing, and I finally agreed. I was barely showing when we told my parents we eloped, so I didn't think they noticed."

When their drinks arrived, Lois paid for them and waited for the waitress to leave before continuing. "We moved to a small farmhouse south of Eau Claire. When we were living out in the country, Mike changed. He became controlling, abusive, and made me think everything was my fault. When he suggested I put the baby up for adoption, I told him that if he didn't want my baby, I would just go home to my parents. He said we were married, 'TILL DEATH DO US PART!' The way he said it, I believed him. I was afraid to mention it again. Once when he was out of town, I tried to leave, but my car wouldn't start. I tried to call my father, but the phone was dead. By then, I was too big to run, and there was no one to run to. I was his prisoner, and there was no way out."

After taking a drink, Lois took a deep breath before she continued. "One day, he brought home a puppy. He never even mentioned wanting a dog. He just came home with the puppy. I didn't want one, but he said he would train it. It was a puppy, so naturally, it peed on the floor. Mike grabbed it by the neck and pushed its nose into the puddle, hitting it while yelling not to pee in the house. I told him, 'That is not how you train a puppy.' He yelled, 'You have to teach them young, so they'll understand.' He was hitting the wet floor with the puppy's nose as he yelled." Lois's eyes began to water as she looked at Peter. "When I told him to stop, he stood up to yell at me while holding the puppy by the neck. All I could do was stare at the puppy. I don't know if he strangled it or broke its neck, but the puppy was dead. Mike swore and went outside with the dead puppy. That's when I knew I could never bring my baby home if Mike was a part of it."

"I know it doesn't help, but I've had other cases like this," Peter assured her. "I've met more than my share of Mikes, and you're not alone."

"I was then. Mike broke me down. I was terrified. Every time he hit me; I was afraid he would hurt the baby. I never saw anyone without him. I couldn't say anything to anyone." Lois wiped a tear from her eye. "Two people from the adoption agency were there when she was born. There was an older man with a bad comb-over, and a girl with long red hair. He did the paperwork, and she took care of the baby. My only way of keeping her safe, was to keep her away from Mike."

"And your parents never suspected?"

"We stayed away until it was all over. Mike made up excuses for not coming home on holidays. I now know that he secretly visited them without me, telling them I refused to come. He said I was using drugs, and worse. He got them to believe him. Worst of all, he told them about the baby. He told them that giving it away was my idea; because I didn't know who the real father was." Lois raised her hand to wipe the corner of her eye. "When I finally saw them again, they were furious. They wanted nothing to do with me. Family was important to Dad, and he said he would never forgive me for giving his grandchild away. I was no longer part of his family, and he wanted nothing more to do with me."

Lois wiped a tear and looked up with a slight smile. "We see each other now. We went years without even talking, but I have my family back. We just don't talk about what I did, and everything is fine. That's one of the reasons I called you. I'd like to tell them what happened to her."

Peter looked at his briefcase and back. "You may not like everything I've found. Are you sure you want to know?"

Lois felt dread with Peter's words. "I need to know what happened. Did you find her?"

Peter removed a folder from his case, opened it, and put a small stack of papers in front of Lois. "The top page is my summary and conclusions so far. Next are duplicate copies of what I found. Please understand, some of these papers are confidential documents, which neither of us has any legal right to."

Lois nodded. "Like, if you hacked into someone's computer and copied what you found, it might be best not to mention it."

"Something like that. We have copies of the hospital records and the adoption papers signed by you and Scott..."

"Scott never signed anything." Lois stopped him before he could finish. "He didn't even know I was pregnant, because Mike stole my mail." Lois looked through the papers, finding the one she had signed. "I had signed first. When Mike saw that I had listed Scott as the father, he signed with Scott's name." She handed the paper to Peter. "Look! Mike even misspelled Scott's name: he only used one T."

"I did notice that." Peter looked at the papers. "We also have copies of the papers between Doctor Harold Michelson, his wife Victoria, and the adoption agency. And there's the final adoption certificate, making Dr. and Mrs. Michelson, parents of Miranda Alexis Michelson."

"Miranda Alexis." Lois smiled when she heard her daughter's name. "Do you know where they are?"

"They were in Madison at the time. Later, they moved to Highland Park Illinois, that's a suburb of Chicago. They were there for a few years, and then nothing. I finally found them in an accident report. In 1979, they were in a multi-car accident on I-90. Dr. Michelson was killed instantly. His wife was in critical condition, and Miranda was injured too. She had been in the back seat, buckled with a regular seat belt. The seat belt saved her life, but it also bruised and damaged both kidneys. With one dead parent, and the other close behind, the hospital thought they would have an instant donor for a transplant. Unfortunately, Miranda was adopted, so neither parent was a match. Her blood was AB negative, which made finding a donor a long shot."

"Did they find one?" There was fear in Lois's voice. "I would have gladly given mine."

"You're not AB negative either. They knew your blood type from the hospital birth records. There were newspaper stories about her, and the search to find a donor. The news articles stressed that she had very little time. There were no follow-up stories. I couldn't find any record of anyone named Michelson receiving a kidney transplant, or any other records with her name."

"So, did she die?"

"I can't confirm that. I couldn't find any obituary, but with the parents dead, who would have written one? I checked on the parents. The father was a doctor who was concerned about the lack of cadavers in medical schools. The parents' wills specified that when they died, their bodies were to be donated for that purpose. Before she died, the mother arranged to also have Miranda's body donated if she died too. She also specified that her sister in Chicago should get custody of Miranda if she survived. I checked school records. Victoria's sister has two children of her own, but their school has no record of Miranda. I did a search using her the sister's last name but found no hospital or school records for her with that name either." Peter reached forward to cover Lois's hand with his own. "I just found the information on the sister this week. I can go to Chicago and talk to her. That would confirm everything, one way or another. That would add a trip to Chicago, but if you want me to continue, I will."

Lois looked down, as if studying the table. "Do you think she could still be alive?"

Peter took a deep breath and sighed. "From what I have now, it would be highly unlikely. She lived longer than the parents, so she was not included in their obituaries. Her rare blood type made finding a donor unlikely. She was to go to her aunt if she survived, but she never registered in their school. I did this in a rush, so I may have missed something. It doesn't look like she survived, but I would have to talk to the sister to be sure."

Lois blinked several times, trying not to cry. "I think you're right Peter. Thank you for what you've done. You don't need to bother the aunt. She would have attended school with her cousins if she lived." Lois took a big breath and exhaled. "She would be fourteen years old now." She put the papers back in the folder, knowing she would go over them more intensely later. "I was looking forward to telling my parents what I learned. I thought I might even be able to tell Scott. It's better that I say nothing, but at least I know. Thank you, Peter."

"I'm sorry Lois."

"Don't be. You only did the research. You couldn't change what you found." Lois looked at the folder. "I'm going to put this in my car for safekeeping. I'll be back soon."

Their waitress returned to ask if they would like anything else. She seemed to be watching the shoreline through the window as she asked them.

"We've barely touched these." Lois looked but saw nothing unusual outside.

"Are you looking for anything special out there?"

"No." The waitress shook her head. "Someone thought they saw someone skinny dipping out there. In this weather, they must have imagined it."

Chapter 22: Scott and Eve

Eve had grown accustomed to the constant swish of the windshield wipers. When their southern trek took them beyond the rain, the change caused her to sit up and blink. "Am I dreaming?"

"You could be." Scott turned the wipers off. "You've been pretty quiet; I think you dozed off for a while."

"I'm sorry. I should be talking to keep you company. I just feel so warm and relaxed. I'm doing something I've only dreamed of. If I am dreaming, please don't wake me."

Scott kept his eyes on the road as he reached for the cup in his cupholder. "You know, my mother was from Iowa, but I've never been there."

"Neither have I. I've thought about this trip, but I never had a destination."

"We still have a couple hours. Why don't you use the time to fill me in?"

"I don't know where to begin."

"Well," Scott drank the last of his coffee and returned the empty cup to its holder, "how did you happen to marry Mike?"

Eve sighed with regret. "He called to say he was in town one night. He asked if he could buy me dinner at the Griffin Hotel. I told him that I didn't date married men, and he said that he divorced Lois after she ran away with you." Eve looked at Scott to say, "I was happy for you when I heard that."

"It was more a case of Lois escaping, and him not contesting the divorce. After that, she lived in another state to keep him from finding her."

Eve nodded, remembering what Lois had told her five years ago. "I told him I didn't date much anymore, and it wasn't a good night anyway. He said it would only be dinner and talking, and not too late because he had to leave in the morning. I hadn't been out for a long time, so I said we could talk over dinner, but nothing else." Eve's voice turned more serious. "I didn't date like I had in high school, but I still tracked my schedule. I was too fertile for anything that night."

Scott nodded with understanding.

"We talked over dinner, and it was nice. The restaurant was busy, so he suggested we free up the table and talk in his room. I enjoyed talking with him, so I agreed, but I made it clear that it would be TALKING, and nothing else." She paused briefly as she remembered the conversation in their room. "While we were talking, he poured himself a glass of wine, and offered one to me. We had wine with dinner, so I didn't think anything of it. A little more talk, a little more wine, and I got up to say goodnight." Eve turned to stare ahead at the oncoming road. "Mike got up to walk me to the door, but instead of opening it, he tried to kiss me. I stopped him and said, *'No!'* I knew where Mike's kisses could lead. He could kiss the shirt right off your back, and I was way too fertile for anything like that." Eve's eyes dropped to her lap. "Mike wouldn't take no for an answer, and I couldn't stop him. That was my first and only date rape. Afterward, he couldn't understand why I was upset." She looked at Scott. "I was crying, and he couldn't see why."

"Did you report it?"

Eve laughed. "Who would have believed me?"

"I do, but I stopped him before."

"I knew what my reputation was. I was just being Ivy's mom in those days, but let's face it; my high school days had more banging than Chuck Conner's rifle. Anyway, I knew my schedule, and I was right. When he was born, I named him Timothy Michal Burman, and listed Mike as the father. Child Support found Mike, and he came back to see me. He was Timmy's father, and I told him so." Eve turned to look ahead. "He decided to be a real father. He made support payments and visited Timmy. He invited us, me, Ivy, and Timmy, to his place. It was an old farmhouse, South-east of Eau Claire, but it was nice. He asked me to marry him and move there with the kids. He said we would be a real family. A family sounded nice, so I decided to give it a try."

Scott thought about that. "You never had a regular family, did you?"

Eve shook her head. "Just four generations of women living in the same house. My mother knew her father, but she wouldn't talk about him. I know nothing about my father. I think I understand that now; I'm sort of like that with Ivy. Sometimes, there are reasons for keeping secrets."

"So, you married Mike and moved away."

Eve nodded. "First, my car stopped running. Mike said it would cost more to fix than it was worth, but he promised to get me another car after we moved. He got me a '68 Plymouth Satellite. Nice, but nothing like my Mustang. Living in the country was nice at first. It was peaceful, and Mike was gone a lot with his work."

"What did he do for work?"

"He didn't talk about work much. He said he delivered things that were too valuable for the post office, or UPS, but not enough for an armored car. Expensive things that required personal delivery."

"I saw a movie about a guy who did that." Scott paused to think. "I thought you had to be bonded to do that. As a convicted felon, Mike can't be bonded."

Eve looked to Scott with surprise, "Mike's a felon?"

"I had Peter check him out a while back. He was convicted of burglary in Kansas. That's why he didn't show up for his divorce. He probably just got out around the time he visited you."

"That might explain his impatience."

"When they caught him, he still had some things from the Masters' house. He left our five-year reunion after Dave mentioned his parents were out of town. They couldn't convict him of that, but the possession was read in at his sentencing. Lois didn't know anything about his work, but it looks like burglary may have been his stock-in-trade. Something he learned from his dad."

"Interesting! Maybe that's another reason he got mad when I wanted to go to our ten-year reunion. He might have been afraid Dave would say something."

"I don't think Dave knew Mike was the one they caught. I doubt he would have let Mike into his house if he'd known."

Eve looked back in surprise. "Mike went to Dave's house?"

"Just long enough to destroy his desk and steal a pile of cash. That's why he was asking about Mike too. I told him I'd see if there was any chance of getting the money back. I also said I could replace the desk if he watched your daughter while we're gone."

Eve nervously turned to look out the window. "So why did you want Dave to watch her?"

"Your daughter shouldn't be left there alone. Also, if anything happens to us, Dave will feel obligated to take care of her." Scott showed a slight grin as he glanced at Eve before looking back at the road again. "Murphy's defense. If you prepare for things, they usually don't happen. Dave's a good guy; you can trust him. You left the note to tell your daughter who he is, so they should be fine."

"She has the note, but she doesn't really know who he is." Eve looked back to Scott. "What about your daughter? What if something happened to you?"

"She's at Ray's tonight. If I don't come back, he'll bring her to her grandparents. There would be some changes, but I'm sure everything would work out." Scott reached for his coffee, but remembered it was empty. "So, how was life with Mike?"

"Not bad at first. Sometimes he could be nice, but he mixed things up with what he learned from his father. He hadn't heard from him since graduation, but he was still trying to be what his father wanted. His father told him a real man is always in charge, so that's what he had to be."

"Did you ever meet his father?"

"No, but Mike often talked about him, like when he let Mike drive when they went bar hopping in his cool Trans Am. He wanted someone to race for titles so he could win Mike a car. Mike thought he was cool, but he sounded like an asshole to me. When Mike forgot about his father, he could be quite nice."

"So, he wasn't too bad?"

"Not bad at first. Better than it was for Lois anyway. I think Lois was his way of getting at you."

"You said something like that before. What did he have against me anyway?"

"He'd talk about you after he'd been drinking. It's hard to tell what was real, and what was just in his mind. He blamed you for everything. If something went wrong, somehow it was your fault." Eve turned to look at Scott, "He wrestled varsity, and almost went to State. They matched him against you in Phy Ed. You pinned him, and he never won another match. He was always competing with you, even when you didn't know it. When you won, it just made him want to beat you more."

Scott thought about that as he took the next exit with a gas station. Soon, they were once more driving South on I-35 with a full tank, empty bladders, fresh travel cups of coffee, and some snacks to help keep them awake. After setting his cruise control, Scott asked, "How was Mike as a father?"

"He was good with Timmy. With Ivy, he was mostly curious about who her father was. When I told him it wasn't anyone I'd dated in high school, he asked about you, because you brought me to the party *after* high school. I told him that *we* never happened that way, and he finally stopped asking."

"I imagine he was relieved to hear that."

"Definitely." Eve lifted her cup, drinking just a small sip, as the coffee was still hot. "After a while, he got more controlling. Like, he was the man of the house, and everything must be done his way. When I said I wanted to go to our class reunion, he slapped me and said we weren't going. The next time I mentioned it, he used his fist, and told me to never bring it up again."

"Returning to the man he was with Lois."

"He was getting there." Eve sipped her coffee again. "One day, my car wouldn't start. It only sputtered, like my Mustang did. I looked under the hood; everything was dusty, except for a couple plug wires on the distributor cap. It looked like he wiped dust off the wires when he switched them. I could see which ones he moved and put them where they belonged. Then the car sounded fine. I put them back, so he would think he fooled me; and told him we should take it to a shop. He said he would have it towed when he got back from his next trip. I wasn't to go anywhere anyway because I had a black eye."

Scott said, "Lois couldn't even use the phone."

"That too. Suddenly, the phone just didn't work. He said he would get it fixed after his next trip, but he didn't seem to be leaving."

"Was he waiting until the reunion to be over?"

Eve nodded. "That's what I thought. Saturday came, and I casually mentioned that it was a shame we missed last weekend's reunion. Suddenly, he was heading out for his next delivery. As soon as he was out of sight, I grabbed the kids and headed for Griffin. I left the kids with my mother and found Lois at the reunion." Eve shook her head slightly as she said, "Lois told me plenty. Monday morning, I filed for divorce."

"I remember that night."

"He stopped at my mother's house first, but I was prepared. I thought he was going to pee his pants when he saw my grandfather's shotgun." Eve looked to Scott, "I am sorry for what he did after that."

"That wasn't your fault." Scott glanced over to Eve and then looked back to the road. "It didn't turn out to be a good night for him either."

"That's right." Eve smiled at that thought but shook her head as she remembered more. "He must have had one hell of a lawyer. He barely got anything for attacking Lois."

"Part of that was my fault; his injuries made him look like the victim. I didn't have to break his arm. I could have held him like that until the police arrived. After I saw him hitting Lois, it was hard to hold back."

Eve looked at Scott. "He deserved everything he got. He tried to give me his side later. In his mind, he was just talking to Lois when you attacked him. I guess he forgot that I've seen his temper, firsthand." She looked ahead again. "It did help with my divorce though. He was given supervised visitation with Timmy. Once a month, and I had to approve in advance."

"That sounds reasonable."

"At first, his visitations were few and far between. When Timmy turned five, he started coming every month. He was nice on those visits. He almost always brought him a present, took him out for ice cream, and things like that. Timmy only knew him from those visits, so he thought Mike was great."

"I guess it's better that he didn't see his bad side."

Eve nodded. "When Timmy turned six, we had a big party for him. That was on a Saturday. Mike called the night before; he said he couldn't make it Saturday, but he would see him soon. The following Monday, a neighbor friend was walking Timmy home from school with her son, and Timmy saw Mike. Timmy ran to give Mike a hug. Mike told her that he had just left me, and I said it was okay for him to take Timmy for ice cream. Timmy was all excited, and she let them go. She went straight to my house to check, but they were out of town before she got there. I haven't heard from either of them since. I was hoping someone at the reunion would have heard something about him. I was really surprised when Ray said you knew where he was."

Scott nodded and said, "I can see where that would be a surprise. Bill Spencer made a delivery to me. He had recently made a delivery to Mike, who now goes by Burnard Michaels. He still had the invoice, so he gave me the address to pass on to the reunion committee."

"Do you think he's still there?"

Scott tipped his head with a shrug. "This wasn't long ago. Bill told him about the reunion, so he might worry about Bill telling anyone where he is. That could be reason enough for him to pull up stakes."

"But Bill died before the reunion."

"So, Bill's death would have kept his secret." Scott nodded and briefly glanced over to Eve. "But how would he know Bill died, unless he had something to do with it."

Eve looked down as she thought about that. "I hate to admit it, but I wouldn't put it past him. Now I wonder what he'll do when we show up to take Timmy."

Scott reached for his coffee and said, "We'll see soon enough."

* * *

Arriving in Des Moines, Iowa, they stopped for fuel and used the restrooms. Eve smoked her first cigarette since their last stop, while Scott picked up a map of the city. He found the street where Mike lived, in a southern suburb of the city.

It was close to 5:00 a.m. when Scott parked across the street from Mike's apartment building. Eve stepped back for another cigarette, while Scott looked over the street and neighborhood. Scott's SUV, and the white panel van he parked behind, were the only vehicles on the street. Scott assumed that resident parking must be available in the back. The van had darkened windows, and a row of accessory lights around its top. Eve joined Scott as he began walking past the van to cross the street in front of it.

Scott stopped to step on a cigarette butt, which was smoldering on the sidewalk. When the van blocked any view of them from the apartment building, Scott turned to Eve. "I don't think we'll need to contact the police yet. I'll go in to get Timmy. If I don't come out, or if Mike comes out instead, take my car, and find the police. Explain that Bernard Michaels is really Mike

Burman, and he's wanted for kidnapping Timmy in Griffin, Wisconsin. Let them know that you're Timmy's mother. Give them our names, Scott Severson, and Eve Johnson, because they'll want to check us both out."

"Mike would never give him to you, and Timmy doesn't know you. I have to go in."

"Okay." Scott seemed to be speaking louder than normal. "I just want to be sure everyone is on the same page. If we don't come out soon, we may need backup."

Scott could see Eve was confused as they crossed the street in front of the van. He leaned to her and said, "Murphy's defense."

* * *

Mike answered quickly when Scott knocked on the door. He looked surprised, if not horrified, when he saw it was Scott and Eve. "What the hell are you doing here?"

"Hi Mike, or do you prefer Bernard?" Scott pushed the door open wider so he and Eve could enter. "Timmy's sleepover has been long enough, so we came to take him home."

Mike glanced at the wall clock. "Not now. You two can't be here."

"It's kind of early to be expecting company, but I understand. We'll just get Timmy and be on our way." Scott followed Mike's eyes and pointed to the door. "Eve, I think Timmy's in there. Go wake him so we can get back on the road,"

From the way Mike glared at Scott, it was clear that he wanted to attack, but Scott could also see that he did not want any trouble. When Mike looked at a desk drawer, Scott could guess what was inside. Scott said, "I promise, we'll be as fast and quiet as possible. After all, we don't want to disturb any neighbors. We wouldn't want them calling the police or anything."

Mike looked hard at Scott. "Damn it! I don't have time for you this morning."

"I get that feeling. Soon as Eve gets Timmy, we'll be on our way. By the way, I promised Dave Masters I would ask about the money you owe him. If you have it handy, I can return it."

Mike let out a short laugh. "That's long gone. I had trouble with a delivery and needed that for reimbursement." Mike glanced at the bedroom door, and smiled slightly as he looked back at Scott. "I never got around to giving him the information we discussed, but I'll get it out in today's mail. I'm sure he'll think it's worth the price."

"I'll pass the word." Scott kept a close eye on Mike. He could tell that he really wanted to attack, but he was in too much of a hurry to get them out of there. His impatience was near panic level.

"I'll tell you what, Scott. I don't have time for you this morning, so how about if I come up and visit you, sometime soon?"

"I'll look forward to it. I've got 160 acres of woods and a backhoe. I'm sure we can find a place for you."

"Why are you here now? Why did you come this morning?"

"Just freak timing, I guess. Our class reunion was last night, so I had a chance to talk to Eve. I don't know what you've got going on here, but I can read you well enough to hazard a guess. Don't worry; we'll just take Timmy and be on our way." Scott looked at the bedroom door. "If he's in pajamas, just grab some clothes and he can change in the car. We need to get out of here."

Eve emerged from the bedroom holding the hand of her sleepy son. Timmy was still wearing pajamas, but also wore shoes, and had a bundle of clothes in his free arm. Eve said, "It's time to go home, Timmy."

Timmy let go of his mother's hand and began walking toward a small travel bag with a cartoon dog on it. He stopped when Mike yelled, "Just leave that Timmy. You don't carry it this time. Just, all of you, get the hell out of here." Mike hurried to the door, holding it open as they stepped out.

Eve stopped and passed Timmy's hand to Scott. "Just a moment." She stepped back to Mike. "We are done! I don't want anything from you. I don't ever want to see or hear from you again. In fact, there is one thing you gave me that I'd like to return."

Mike glared as he stepped through the doorway. "And what might that be?"

Eve launched her right fist into Mike's eye. Mike fell back, bouncing his head off the door frame, and falling into his apartment. Scott let go of Timmy's hand, expecting Mike to come charging out. Eve simply retook Timmy's hand and began walking to the stairs. When Mike did not emerge, Scott turned and followed, making quick glances back as they left.

Scott led them across the street in front of the van again. He looked up to Mike's window to see if he was watching them leave. Seeing no sign of Mike, Scott stopped them when they were once more on the blind side of the van.

"Okay. We've got Timmy, so we're leaving. We'll stop for breakfast at the restaurant by the freeway entrance. After breakfast we'll be heading back to Griffin. I think he has a gun in his desk drawer but didn't want to use it because he's expecting company. By the way, Mike didn't want Timmy to carry the little cartoon dog travel bag this time. I wonder what's in it." Scott stepped on another burning cigarette butt on the sidewalk. "Some people shouldn't smoke. It's like waving a flag." Eve gave Scott a confused look as they continued walking to his SUV.

Scott opened the back passenger door so Eve and Timmy could get in. Eve began changing Timmy's clothes while Scott climbed in and drove away.

* * *

At the restaurant near the freeway entrance, Scott was happy to see they had Belgian Waffles on the menu. They were only listed with strawberries, but for a slight upcharge he was able to get them with cherries. They relaxed and took their time over breakfast, while Scott kept an occasional eye on the door. They had nearly finished eating when a man in his early fifties entered and walked to their table. He asked, "Mind if I join you?"

Scott gestured to an empty chair. "I've been expecting you."

The man sat down and turned to the approaching waitress. "Just coffee for me." He turned to face Eve. "Good morning Ms. Johnson. I'm glad everything went well for you this morning. I'd like to thank you both for getting Timmy out when you did. His presence had us concerned. Your arrival had us worried, but with the child out of the way, everything went much smoother."

Eve looked confused. "Who are you?"

He thanked the waitress for his coffee and looked back to Eve. "I'm sorry." Removing a wallet from the breast pocket of his coat, he opened it, and slid it over for Eve to examine his badge. "My name is Williams, and I'm with the DEA. We were waiting for some men to visit your former husband when you showed up. Less than two minutes after you left, those visitors arrived. Your ex and his friends are all in custody. They may have had some disagreement before we arrived. Burman appears to have taken a good blow to the eye."

Eve gave an apologetic smile. "That may have been me."

"Deservedly so, I'm sure." He turned to Scott, "There was indeed a gun in the desk, but we didn't let him get near it. It will, however, give him an additional charge of felon with a firearm, as it was in his apartment. Also, thank you for your tip on his name. We were having trouble coming up with anything on Bernard Michaels. Running Mike Burman's name connected a lot of dots."

Eve asked, "Was there anything in the travel bag?"

"I'll just say that it was full, but there was no cola." He looked back to Scott, "Just how did you make us so easily?"

"I've been told that I have a good eye for detail. It helps in my work. A parked van isn't unusual, but cigarette butts dropped out the window suggest someone's inside. A cigarette burning on the sidewalk pretty much confirmed it. The lights around the top of the van look nice, but they're not practical for anything. But those lights could come in handy for hiding lenses for surveillance equipment. Knowing Mike, the thought of some type of surveillance seemed natural. I had no idea what it was for, but I was pretty sure it concerned Mike. Eve told me Mike had some sort of delivery job. I could only think of one thing of high value that someone with his record might deliver. His reaction when Timmy went to get the bag told me that he may have had Timmy helping when they traveled. Who would give a second thought to a little boy's travel bag?"

"Was the van the only thing of ours that you spotted?"

"Did you have more?"

Williams smiled. "Those in the van will get a good dressing down. Everyone else gets a gold star." When the waitress brought their bill, Williams picked it up. "I'll get that." He sipped his coffee and looked at them. "I'd prefer to leave you three out of this, but you were there just minutes before everything went down. I'd like you to come to the police station so we can get formal statements. If a lawyer learned someone else was there and we left it out of our reports, they would be all over it. Just be completely frank about why you came, and what happened. We have a recording of your statements before going in, and when you came out. If there is any problem, that will back up your story. Also, we'd like someone to talk with your son about his trips with his father. That may give him child endangerment charges as well."

Scott nodded. "If it keeps Mike out of our hair a little longer, it will be worth the delay."

Chapter 23: Dave and Ivy

Dave Masters did not sleep well, but sleep did eventually come. Eve had told him that he could use her bed, but the thought of Eve's daughter finding a strange man in her mother's bed did not seem right to him. He was not sure if a strange man sleeping on their couch would be much better, but he opted for the couch anyway. He had hung his coat, dress shirt, and tie on the back of a dining room chair. Still wearing his pants and undershirt, he covered himself with an afghan and went to sleep.

When morning came, Dave awoke with the uneasy feeling of being watched. Opening his eyes, he saw a teenage girl with short, blonde hair looking at him over the sketchpad she was holding. One of the dining room chairs had been placed directly in front of him, giving her a clear view of him as he slept.

"Don't move," she said when she saw his eyes open.

"Okay." Dave tried not to move while she finished her sketch.

Her hand began moving more quickly when she began shading around her drawing. "Okay, you can move now."

Dave stood and returned the afghan to the back of the couch before putting his shirt back on. He turned to face the girl while tying his necktie. "Good morning. My name is Dave Masters. I went to school with your mother."

"And you came here to sleep on our couch because Mom went to find Timmy and didn't want me to wake up alone." Eve held up her mother's note. "She pinned a note to a stuffed bear that watches me sleep. Tell me, do you think it's better for a girl to wake up alone, or to find a strange man sleeping on her couch?"

"I wondered about that too, but we didn't want to leave you alone. I suppose it depends on the girl and the man. What do you think?"

"I figure you must not be a scary stranger, or Mom wouldn't have even let you in the house. The last time she did that, she ended up marrying him, and that didn't work out. Also, you slept on the couch. I figure a creep would have jumped at the chance to sleep in her bed, even if she wasn't there."

"I like the way you think." Dave felt wiser with his choice and sat on the couch so he could face her. "Can I see your drawing?"

Ivy looked at her sketchpad before handing it to him. Dave studied the drawing, which was a very good likeness of him sleeping. "That's very good. I like it."

"If you flip back a few pages, there are a couple more of you. You're a sound sleeper."

Dave flipped the pages to see a close-up drawing of his face, and another of him on the entire couch. "These are good too. Are you an artist?"

"I don't know, but I enjoy drawing. Some schools give art scholarships, so that could be a way to go to college, if I'm good enough."

"A girl with a plan. I like that."

Ivy looked at his suit coat, which still hung on the back of a chair. "I get the feeling you went to college. Most guys around here don't wear suits unless they need to look important for their job."

"You're very observant."

"Thank you. By the way, I'm Ivy, but I think Mom already told you that."

"I'm pleased to meet you, Ivy. My name is Dave Masters."

"I know. Are you related to that Masters guy who owns half the town?"

"He doesn't own that much, but yes, he's, my father."

"I haven't heard about you. Are you like, the black sheep of the family or something? The one nobody talks about."

"I just haven't been around much since high school. I live in New York, but I came home for my class reunion."

"How'd you get talked into babysitting me?"

"A friend asked me to. Your former stepfather had taken something from me, and my friend was going to see if there would be any chance of getting it back."

"Do you really think there's any chance of Mike giving anything back?"

"Probably not, but I should at least make the attempt. My friend also said he would make me a new desk if I looked after you, and that's worth more than what Mike took."

"You can find a decent desk at the thrift store, so I think you got the short end of this deal."

"My friend makes very good desks. He's like an artist, only with wood."

"He's kind of an artist, and he went to school with my mom." Ivy gave this some thought. "What's his name?"

"Scott Severson."

"Doesn't sound right. But I'll check him out when they get back." Ivy paused with more thought. "Is he tough? Because Mike can be mean."

"Scott's a big guy. He cuts down trees and works with the wood, so he's kind of tough. He fought with Mike five years ago, and Mike didn't do so well that time."

"I heard about that!" Ivy grew a big smile. "I wish I could have seen it. That was right after we left Mike's house."

Dave grinned, "I think I would have enjoyed seeing that myself."

"Do you think they'll bring Timmy home?"

"I hope so. Scott had a lead on where they are, so they're checking it out."

"I hope so too. Timmy can be annoying, but he's still my little brother. I hate to think of any little boy staying with Mike. He's mean. He gave my mom a black eye, just because she wanted to go to her reunion. I don't like him, and I'm glad he's not my dad."

"I made the mistake of trusting him once," there was regret in Dave's voice. "I won't make that mistake again."

"What happened?"

Dave thought for a moment and decided it would be best to be honest with her. He didn't like the idea of dad bashing, but Ivy was only a stepdaughter and had already seen Mike for the man he was. "Mike came to my home and asked if he could stay the night. He said he had some information I would want to buy. I assumed he knew something about a company I was looking at. If there's a problem with a business, it's best to know before I buy it. I had to be somewhere, so I told him he could stay the night, and I would be back the next day. He said I should stop at the bank for extra cash, suggesting his information was very valuable. I told him not to worry. I kept cash on hand for such things."

Dave looked down with an expression of self-disappointment. "Thinking back, I may have subconsciously glanced at my desk when I said that. Either that, or he just searched everywhere else, and determined the desk was the only place left. That desk was special, with secret drawers you couldn't see. When I came home, there was a skill saw lying on what was left of my desk. Mike had cut it apart to find the hidden drawer. I had twenty thousand dollars hidden in that desk. The money was gone, and so was Mike."

Ivy's eyes opened wide. "Twenty thousand dollars? And you were going to buy a company? You really are rich, aren't you?"

"I do okay." Dave grew a slight smile. "I manage to keep people working, and sometimes that's better than being rich. But being rich is good too."

"Wow! We've never had a rich man here before. Is your middle name Lee? Or do you have a number with your name, like Dave Masters the Fourth?"

Dave let out a small laugh. "Hardly. Why?"

"Sometimes I get curious about my dad. Mom says she doesn't know who he is, but she slipped when she said that I was named for him."

"That's why you said Scott's name didn't sound right?"

"Yeah. Not that it matters. It's more like a puzzle I'd like to solve." Her face lit up again when she said, "But if my dad bought companies and kept twenty grand lying around the house, that could be a pretty-cool guy to have for a dad. Then I might not need an art scholarship."

Dave laughed. "I see what you mean. I'm sorry, but there's no Lee in my name. And as far as I know, I'm still Dave the first."

Ivy looked back with a crooked smile. "It's okay. Maybe your company will come up with a scholarship I can apply for. I've got a few years yet, so you've got time to think about scholarships. They're tax-deductible, you know, and scholarships make great publicity."

"I'll keep that in mind." Dave thought for a moment. "Do you have any other clues, other than your name?"

"Not really. I look a lot like Mom, so no real clue there."

"I take it Lee is your middle name?"

"Yeah. Only she spelled it L-E-I-G-H. That could be just to make it more feminine, or maybe it's an anagram for his name. Ivy could be a name, or his initials I-V."

"Or a Roman numeral 4, which is why you asked if I was a fourth."

Ivy nodded. "It's surprising how many possibilities Ivy Leigh can suggest. Lee Ivy. Mr. I. V. Higel. Mr. H. Giel, the fourth."

"Or the third. If he was Lee the third, and you were named for him, that would make you the fourth."

Ivy nodded. "I thought of that too. Also, if you type 49137 in a calculator, upside down it reads LEIGH. He could be from the 49137-zip code."

"Or numeric code. The fourth letter is D, nine would be I, then A, and C, and seven would be G. Diacg." Dave shook his head. "Somehow, I don't think that's the code."

"I couldn't even come up with an anagram for that one."

Dave thought before saying, "I don't know if I should be helping you with this. I mean... if your mother doesn't want ..."

"That's okay," she interrupted. "It's not like I expect anything to come of it anyway." She looked at Dave with a shrug. "It's mostly just something to be curious about. After fourteen years and never so much as a birthday card, I'm not sure if I want to meet him. Still, it would be nice to know. It's clear that he has no interest in me after all this time."

"If that's the case," Dave looked her in the eyes, "he must be a fool."

Ivy glanced over to the kitchen. "Mom's note said I should feed you breakfast. Are you hungry?"

"I could eat, but instead of you feeding me, would you mind eating at the hotel? I noticed that the hotel has a small arcade. If you wait for me there, I could run up to my room for a quick shave, shower, and a clean suit. Then we could eat in their restaurant, and you can eat anything you like."

"I was going to show off my cooking but going out for breakfast sounds better. I don't have any change for an arcade though."

"I'm sure I could get a couple rolls of quarters at the front desk. That should last you."

Ivy grinned at that thought. "Okay. I'll leave a note for Mom though, in case she gets back before us."

Dave looked at his watch. "We should have plenty of time, but you're right; you should always leave a note."

* * *

When they returned to Eve's house, Ivy unlocked the front door with her key. She did feel some guilt, as she had more than a full roll of the quarters left. After some thought, she decided that she would return them, if the subject came up.

Ivy spotted the light on the answering machine as soon as they walked through the door. In the message, her mother told them that they have Timmy, but there was some paperwork they needed to do at the police station. They would be heading home as soon as they finished.

They were relieved to hear that the trip was a success, and Ivy felt excited that her little brother was finally coming home. Dave reminded Ivy that she had promised to show him more of her drawings.

"Okay, you wait in the living room, and I'll get my sketchpads." Ivy hurried to her room and returned with a short stack of sketchpads. "You don't have to look at them all; I know it gets kind of boring."

"Nonsense!" Dave lifted the top pad from the stack. "But if you get bored with showing them to me, we can do something else."

"Okay. You just be sure to say something if I start getting bored."

"Deal. And I like the way you think." He opened the first sketchbook and began looking through it. "I recognize this. That's by the old dam."

"That's right," she said with pride. "Did you really go to school here in Griffin?"

"I was valedictorian for your mother's class."

Ivy gave a small nod. "It figures that you would have been valedictorian."

Dave looked at her and said, "I worked hard for that. It was one of my goals. I wanted that title on my resume for college."

Ivy nodded. "That would be a big help for scholarships and stuff."

"It would have, but not for me. The scholarship only covered state schools. My goal was to be accepted by one of the big Ivy League colleges. What I needed was an impressive resume. I had some tough competition too."

Ivy looked puzzled. "You had tough competition in Griffin?"

"Absolutely. Vanessa Winters was right behind me, and her only goal was to serve in the Peace Corps. In fact, I saw the list showing our class rankings, and your mother was almost an honor student too."

"Really?" Ivy was surprised.

"Really. She liked to play the dumb blonde in class, but your mother was well-read and a very good student. She just didn't like to show it in class."

Dave continued looking through the sketches and often commented on pictures. Ivy eagerly explained any picture he was not familiar with. Dave was looking through the fourth sketchpad in the stack when he said, "These are good. I'm no artist, but I think you have a good shot at going to art school."

"It doesn't need to be an art school. I just want to go to college. I'm not a jock, so a sports scholarship is out. I am smart, but I won't be valedictorian or anything like that. But an art scholarship gives me a chance. Unless, of course," Ivy looked into Dave's eyes, "there's a Masters Scholarship that can give me a full ride."

"I'll keep that in mind." Dave admired her conviction. "When I was your age, I had my sights set on Harvard, but I would have settled for Yale, or Columbia. I mostly just wanted something in the Ivy League. Any of them would have made me happy."

"How'd that work out?"

"After one year at Princeton, I was able to transfer to Harvard. I've seen a lot of people with wasted educations, but mine has served me well." He looked thoughtful as he picked up the next sketchpad. "But it did come at a price. In high school, I was only concerned about getting the perfect resume, so I never did anything fun until after graduation. For the most part, I wasted my formative years. I got to know my classmates more at reunions than I did when I was in school."

Dave opened the next sketchbook and looked puzzled when he saw the first picture. Ivy saw his confusion and asked, "What's wrong?"

Dave pointed to the girl in the picture. "I recognize her, but I don't know how you could have drawn it. You're too young."

Ivy looked at the sketch, "That's drawn from a picture."

"Oh. That explains it. Your grandmother used to babysit for us, so my father must have given her the picture."

Ivy looked confused. "What?"

"This picture is my little sister." Dave held up the sketch to show her which one he was talking about. "She's younger than me but still too old for you to have seen her at that age. If you drew it from a picture, my father must have given it to your grandmother. It makes sense now. It just confused me at first."

"That's not your sister." She let out a laugh. "That's me before I cut my hair short." Ivy retrieved a picture from the hutch in the dining room. It was an old school photo of her, but with longer hair. "I drew that a long time ago. It's not very good, but you can recognize it from the original."

Dave looked at the two pictures side by side. "You're right. It is the same picture. I'm sorry. It's just ... it also looks like my sister." Dave studied the photograph of the younger Ivy, amazed at the resemblance between her and his sister. He asked, "How old are you?"

"I turned fourteen last April. April tenth." She watched Dave study the picture in deep thought. "Counting back, I think I was conceived around the Fourth of July, in 1972."

Dave thought back, remembering the summer after graduation. That was a time when school was out, and colleges had already received his record. He had finally been free to enjoy his summer and reunited with an old friend. A friend he liked to say was his girlfriend in their preschool days. They dated throughout the summer, up to the day he left for Princeton. Dave turned to look at Ivy, now seeing her in a different way.

"OH MY GOD!" Ivy slapped her hand over her mouth in surprise. She lowered her hand to say, "You wanted an Ivy League school. That's why Mom spelled my middle name that way. Mom said I was named FOR my father, not AFTER him. I'm Ivy League!"

Dave felt like his eyes were about to water as he looked at Ivy. He held out his hand to her, "I'm pleased to meet you, Ivy Leigh. I remember the Fourth of July very well. It was one of the happiest times of my life."

Ivy took his hand and shook it, as if meeting for the first time. "It's a pleasure to meet you sir."

"If you enjoy drawing, please continue; you are very good at it. As for needing a scholarship, I don't think that will be a problem. Feel free to study whatever makes you happy."

Ivy stared at him in deep thought. "So, you really were seeing Mom that July?"

Dave nodded, happy with his memories. "Something upset her at our graduation party, so we sat in my car and talked. We talked and talked, until we both fell asleep. The next day, we went out on a date. We kept on seeing each other throughout the summer; all our free time was spent together. I found her first apartment and helped her move. I drove her to Wolf Creek so she could buy her first car, and I was the one she called when it was stolen. We did almost everything together that summer. I don't think she had time to see anyone else."

"Mom never told you?"

Dave shook his head. "She must have known by the time I left. She also knew how much college meant to me. I guess she decided not to say anything that might interfere with me getting what I wanted. It was five years before I saw her again. By then, I was engaged to someone else."

* * *

It was early evening before Eve, Timmy, and Scott returned. Ivy and Dave stepped out to greet them when Scott parked in front of Eve's house. Timmy ran to Ivy's open arms so she could lift him with a big hug.

Ivy said, "I missed you little guy."

Timmy overflowed with excitement as he returned her hug. "My dad's going to jail so he won't bother us again."

"That's okay," she whispered, "I'll share my dad with you instead."

"Okay," he agreed with a smile.

Scott said to Dave, "I'm sorry we took so long. We had to do some paperwork at the police station, and they had a lot of questions for Timmy. It doesn't look like you'll get back any of the money he stole. Mike lost a delivery and used your money to reimburse his partners. I did say I would replace your desk, so I will."

"Don't worry about the money," Dave reached to shake Scott's hand, "and I'll pay for the desk. We can discuss that later."

Eve looked at Dave. "Were you supposed to fly back today? Did you miss your flight because of us?"

Dave shook his head. "No. I hope you don't mind, but I made some calls on your phone. I'll be spending the rest of the week in Griffin, and I may do some rearranging after that."

Ivy looked at her mother and asked, "Mom, have you ever thought about moving to New York? Or Dad might be able to move things closer to us. His companies are all over the country, so he could run them from anywhere. Maybe even St. Paul. He'd only be like, an hour and a half away if he was there."

Eve's eyes opened wide as she looked from Dave to Ivy. She turned to Scott and said, "I think we have some things to discuss. Thanks for all you did, Scott. I don't know how I can ever repay you."

Scott grinned with understanding and hugged Eve goodbye. "I should get over to Ray's before my daughter starts to worry."

As he climbed back into his SUV, Scott could hear Timmy say, "Mom gave Dad a black eye. She knocked him out cold."

Scott let out a small laugh as he drove away. It looked like Eve and Dave really did have a lot to discuss.

PART 5: TWENTY YEAR REUNION

Chapter 24: Check-in Friday

The original school in Griffin was a long three-story building. Each level had a long hall with classrooms on each side. On the ground floor, they added a small gymnasium and cafeteria onto the south end. As the little country schools closed, their classes were moved to the city school in Griffin. A separate two-story high school was built across from the cafeteria. School needs grew, and a large gymnasium and commons area was built, connecting the previously separated buildings. The school's driveway ran alongside the earlier building, with a round cul-de-sac in front of the main door of the commons area. On the other side of the driveway was the school's parking lot, which led to the front door of the high school building.

Many years later, a new elementary school was built on the other side of town. Still later, a new high school was also built near that elementary school. Eventually, a new middle school joined that campus as well. After the new Intermediate school was built in 1990, our old school was finally put out of service. As Rich Lester had predicted a decade earlier, our old school was put up for sale, with a bargain price to speed it onto the tax rolls.

The Lesters sold their farm and pooled their money with funds the O'Brian's had saved. Hoping to one day buy the Pike Lake Resort, Danny and Carol had a sizable nest egg of savings. With some other financing and investors, they succeeded in converting our old school into The Old School Hotel. After a great deal of work and remodeling, they opened for business in September 1991.

The commons area became the hotel entrance and lobby. The former gymnasium became a banquet room, or event center.

Naturally the cafeteria was converted into The Old School Restaurant and Supper Club, which Doris and Carol ran together. The small gym became O'Brian's Pub, run by Danny O'Brian. Bathrooms were added as each classroom was converted into hotel guest rooms. When most of the remodeling was completed, parts of the school looked like they had never been anything but a hotel, while other areas managed to keep the appearance of an old schoolhouse. When money got tight, nostalgia was a reasonable excuse to cut spending and preserve the original appearance.

Our twenty-year reunion committee had Rich and Doris Lester, along with Danny and Carol O'Brian. They had volunteered to handle this reunion five years ago, hoping they would be able to purchase the Old School and convert it as they did. When invitations were sent out in the early months of 1992, everyone learned that our twenty-year reunion would be held in The Old School Hotel that coming summer.

For the weekend of the reunion and through the following week, any members of our class staying, or dining, at the Old School would receive a special discount. This encouraged some of us to extend our reunion even longer. To add even more incentive, Rich promised a Sunday afternoon cookout for all classmates.

* * *

Danny and Rich were spending their Friday afternoon at the front desk of the hotel lobby. Large windows along the front of the lobby gave them a clear view of cars and approaching guests. They both watched in admiration as a red Lexus convertible, driven by an attractive girl with long, blonde hair, parked in front of the lobby door. They continued watching the girl as her passenger got out to remove their luggage. Rich and Danny watched the blonde deliver her Lexus to the hotel parking lot and paid no attention to her passenger until Scott Severson carried the luggage into the hotel lobby.

Danny called, "Scotty!" when he recognized his old friend. "Glad you could make it. I haven't seen you since you put my bar together."

"It's good to see you too, Danny." Scott set the luggage down by the front desk and looked back to Rich. "Lex is parking her car and putting the top up. I believe we have reservations."

Rich slid a registration card over for Scott to sign. "Two adjoining rooms for Severson and friend. To make it easy for you, it's the old science rooms on the second floor. Right across from the study hall."

"In that case, I know my way. Are any other classmates here yet?"

"Lord and Lady Westford have a two-room suite on the top floor of the old school. That's the Principal's suite. Our nicest rooms, and a great view of the lake."

"And three flights of stairs."

"We have elevators now," boasted Rich. "You have one too. It's at the end of this hall. The Masters have reservations too. We have at least five more coming tomorrow. Those are just the ones with reservations. This reunion looks like our best turnout yet."

Scott gestured to the building around him as he said, "How could anyone resist coming *here* for the reunion?"

The door opened, and the slender girl with long blonde hair and a tight-fitting dress entered. Rich silently guessed her age to be somewhere between eighteen and twenty-two. When she got to the front desk, Scott said, "Lex, these are two of my oldest friends, Danny O'Brian and Richard Lester."

Lex nodded with a polite smile, "It's a pleasure to meet you."

Danny said, "I think we met once before, but I could be mistaken."

Lex turned to look around the lobby. "Your old school looks very nice now."

Scott picked up their luggage. "This is it. After we get settled, I'll give you a tour and tell you what it used to look like."

After Scott and Lex left for their rooms, two men wearing dark suits arrived. They told Rich that a friend had made reservations under the name Burtoni.

Rich looked at his book, "Yes. You wanted the three rooms on the top floor, in the Northeast corner."

"Yes. We're looking into some possible real estate investments. The view from those rooms may be of help."

Rich handed him the registration card. "You wanted three rooms, but there are only two of you?"

"A couple friends will join us later. We'd just as soon get all the rooms now and prevent any delay when they arrive."

"Very good. Now if you'll just fill this out, I'll get your keys."

When Danny and Rich were once more alone in the lobby, Randy and Rachel Richards entered with luggage in hand. Rachel looked to see Rich at the desk. "If this is The Dickless Inn, I'm going somewhere else."

"That's an old-school nickname, so you belong in the Old School Hotel." Rich pulled out a registration card. "I thought you were staying with your folks all weekend."

"With five kids running wild, the farm was getting too crowded. Mom suggested we let a couple of kids take over my room and let her handle them without us. Randy had our bags in the car before she was done talking." Rachel gave Rich an imploring look. "Tell me you still have a room."

Rich cheerfully handed her a registration card. "What type of room would you prefer?"

Rachel grinned. "Have you got anything by a pool?"

* * *

It was nearly five o'clock when Scott and Lex stepped into O'Brian's Pub. Scott wore black jeans and a grey flannel shirt, while Lex wore a white sleeveless dress, cut short with a tight fit. Lord and Lady Westford, also known here as Nessa and Lord Max, sat at the bar talking with Randy and Rachel Richards.

"Scotty Boy," Danny called with his imitation Irish accent. "We were just talkin' about yea." Scott and Lex joined the others at the bar, as Danny went on. "Lord Max was admiring my fine bar. I told him the top was made from a single slice of Oak, cut as long and wide as we see it today."

Scott was pleased with the admiration. "It helps when you have a portable sawmill and can cut it where the tree lands. It took a few cuts to get it right, but we managed."

Danny pointed to the tables in the bar area, "Scott made me tables as well. They look like four-leaf clovers, do they not?"

Lord Max walked over to admire one of the tables. Each one was made from four slices of large oak tree trunk, pieced together so their shape was like that of a four-leaf clover. You could still count the rings of the separate slices, although they now fit together as if they'd grown that way.

"They were somewhat of an experiment," Scott explained. "I got the idea, and wanted to see if I could make it work."

Lord Max ran his fingers over the tabletop, admiring the seamless feel. "I am impressed. I will be sure to remember you next time we need something made."

Scott gave him one of his business cards. "This has a much more rustic look than most of my work, but it fits when you consider Griffin began as a logging town."

Max asked, "Did you make all the furniture for the hotel?"

"Only for the bar. The bar and these tables were done more for the fun and challenge of it. The whole hotel would have been too big of an order for me. My business is more special-order, so I don't mass produce. It's easier to be picky and watch my quality that way. I think Rich ordered the rest of the furniture from some of Dave's companies."

As Scott talked with Vanessa and Lord Max, Danny was looking at Lex. "Now I know where I've seen you. You were helping Scott when he put my bar together."

"Guilty as charged," Lex laughed. "He does let me work with him sometimes. I can't help but remember, your Irish wasn't quite as strong back then."

"When your name is O'Brian, and ye own a pub, sometimes it's just more fun to put on the accent as well. And I should add, it is even more fun to put on the Irish, when ye have an actual English Lord sittin' at yer bar. Will ye be having anything, or are ye just waiting for the dining room to open?"

Lex looked at Randy and Rachel's drinks, and then back to Danny. "How about a stinger for Scott, and a stingless for me."

"A fine choice." Danny did not need to check Lex's ID for a stingless, but he was still curious as to her age.

Lex turned to Rachel. "Scott was showing me pictures last night, and you are Rachel." Turning to Randy, she added, "Which must make you Randy. Hi, I'm Lex."

"Hello Lex." Randy turned to shake Lex's hand.

Rachel smiled back at her. "It's a pleasure to meet you."

When Danny set the stingless in front of Lex she pointed to Scott and said, "He's paying." Danny simply nodded and brought the stinger down to Scott. Lex used her straws to lift and eat one of the nuts from her drink before looking back to the Richards. "So, Scott says you two are Disc Jockeys."

"I'm still a DJ at an Oldies station. I play music from the '50s, '60s, and '70s," said Randy. "Rachel has a talk show on another station."

"Awesome! I love oldies. Talk radio too. When Scott has the radio on in his shop, it's always on either talk, or oldies."

"Who are you calling oldies?" They turned to see Dave Masters, walking hand in hand with Eve.

"Dave! Eve!" Randy got up to shake hands with Dave, and hug Eve. "It's great to see you guys." Randy turned to Lex, "This is Lex. She's here with Scott."

Eve smiled politely, "How wonderful. How did you meet Scott?"

"Oh, he saved my life once. We've been close ever since."

Eve nodded. "Somehow, that does not surprise me."

After bringing Dave and Eve their drinks, Danny turned to Lex. "Scott tells me it was your car that you two came in. Nice."

"Thank you. My dad said he would buy me a new car if I graduated valedictorian of my class. Since I'm Lex, he got me a Lexus. I think it suits me."

Danny nodded. "It suits you well."

"Thank you." Lex turned to Eve. "Eve, I recognize you from your yearbook picture. Scott told me about you too." Eve felt slightly uncomfortable until Lex asked, "Did you really knock your ex out cold with a single punch?"

Eve laughed. "We left without realizing he was unconscious. It was later that we learned his friends had to wake him up. In my defense, he did have it coming."

"Scott told me that too."

Eve looked at Scott. "You know, she's young, but I like her." She looked back to Lex, "Do you sew?"

Lex stood and turned around. "I made this dress."

Eve laughed. "Be careful girl. Dave's first wife was ready to shoot me for upstaging her in a homemade dress."

Lex turned to face Dave. "You're Dave Masters, right?"

"That would be me."

"I read about you. I think it was in Forbes. I like the way you run your business. I even have ten shares of stock in Masters Enterprises."

"Thank you. I'm glad you have that much faith in me."

Dave looked at Danny. "So, does having your own bar mean you've given up on buying your uncle's resort?"

Danny shook his head with disappointment. "After years of him saying he'll sell me the resort when he retires, he started showing it to some guy from the Cities. He was talking terms, prices, and closing the deal. With that kind of loyalty, we decided to throw our savings in with Rich and Doris."

Dave looked around. "Impressive! You must have had some good savings."

"Carol and I saved more than we spent over the years, so we had enough socked away for the bar and part of the restaurant."

Small talk continued until Carol O'Brian opened the doors to let everyone know the dining room was open. Lord Max invited Dave and Eve to join him and Vanessa, while Rachel and Randy asked to share a table with Scott and Lex.

As Carol led them to their table, Scott commented that this year had the makings of a true 'Class of '72' event. "The hotel clerk, the bartender, and our hostess are all from our class."

As they took their seats, Carol said, "That's not all. Doris Lester is our chef, and there's still more to come." She handed them menus and said, "Your waitress will be with you soon. Enjoy your meal."

They were still looking at their menus when a waitress arrived and set glasses of ice water on the table before saying, "Good evening. My name is Lois, and I will be your server tonight." Scott looked up in surprise when he heard her voice. Lex noticed Scott's reaction and looked up at the waitress as well. Lex was speechless as she stared up to see Lois Vanderzee.

Lois asked, "Would you like anything from the bar before you order?"

"Hi Cuz," Rachel grinned. "Yeah, I think we could use another round. Three stingers and a stingless. Do you recommend anything special?"

"It's all good, but the walleye is our special tonight. Doris does a great job with that."

Lois looked to the others for more questions, as Scott simply smiled and said, "Hi."

"Hi." She returned his smile. "I'll be right back with your drinks." Lois left to place their orders.

Lex watched her leave before turning to Scott to say, "She's so pretty." She immediately felt embarrassed when she realized she had said that out loud.

"Yes, she is." Scott agreed.

"You see," Rachel nudged Randy. "I knew this would be fun."

Scott looked at Rachel. "You knew?"

"Hey, she's still my cousin. We've been keeping in touch with each other since she got away from Mike. Who do you think has been telling her about the reunions? Well, after the five-year anyway."   Rachel noticed the still surprised look on Lex, remembering that she was Scott's date. "Oh, I'm sorry Lex. It's... well..."

"It's alright," Lex assured her. "I know all about Lois. Scott told me everything, and I saw her pictures. I was just surprised when I saw her in person. It's fine." Scott put his hand on Lex's and smiled without needing to say anything. Lex looked back at the menu and said, "I think I'll have the Walleye."

Lois returned and set the drinks on the table before asking if they were ready to order. Scott looked to Lex, inviting her to order first.

Lex closed her menu and said, "I'll have the walleye, fried, baked potato with sour cream and butter, and ranch dressing on my salad."

"Very good." Lois smiled as she wrote it down. She looked at Scott. "And you?"

"I'll have the sirloin steak, baked potato with sour cream and butter, and Italian dressing."

"And how would you like your steak?"

Lex instantly answered, "Knock off the horns, wipe its ass, and throw it on the plate."

From the table behind, they could hear the spitting sound of someone surprised while attempting to drink. In other words, Lord Max had just sent part of his drink out his nose.

Scott smiled. "Like she said, rare."

Lex looked embarrassed and said, "I'm sorry, I just wanted to beat him to it."

Scott patted the top of Lex's hand. "And you did. It was fine."

Lord Max got up from his seat and stepped over to Lex. "Excuse me. Would you mind if I borrowed that line?"

"Help yourself." Lex tried to smile through her embarrassment. "I stole it from him," pointing to Scott. "I think he got it from his dad, so it must be in public domain by now."

"I've never had my steak rare before." Lord Max smiled, "This will be something new."

After taking Randy and Rachel's orders, Lois asked, "Will there be anything else?"

"I guess that's all for now." Scott handed Lois his menu, with numerous questions racing through his mind.

As Lois left, Rachel said, "I like you, Lex. You're young, but a lot better than last reunion's prom queen."

Lex laughed. "I heard about that. I can honestly guarantee, I will not be going into labor tonight."

"It sounds like Scott told you a lot. What did he tell you about me?"

Lex lifted her glass as she said, "You are like a little sister to Scott." She watched as Rachel lifted her glass and began to drink before adding, "And swimming stops when the fish nibble on your nipples."

This time it was Rachel who coughed into her drink.

Randy laughed and said, "There! How do YOU like it?"

Rachel wiped her mouth and nose with a cloth napkin. "I welcome the competition." Looking at Lex, she said, "How about it, Lex? First one to get Randy to shoot potato chips out his nose wins."

* * *

After their meals, they returned to the bar to relive old memories and discuss newer events. After the kitchen closed, the kitchen and waitstaff from the restaurant joined them at the bar. When Lex saw Lois enter, she turned to Scott. "I'm going to talk to Rachel or Sir Max for a bit. Feel free to sit there and look lonely. Better yet, why don't you grab one of the tables?"

Her statement puzzled Scott, until he too, saw Lois entering the bar. Scott looked back to say, "Yes dear. Have fun." He turned to Danny and asked if he knew what Lois would like to drink.

Lois was not sure if she should go to Scott or not. After all, he was with another girl. She watched as Scott picked up his stinger and the Tom Collins Danny had just made and carried them to one of the clover-shaped tables. When he pulled out a chair, inviting her to join him, Lois sat down and said, "It's good to see you."

"And you." Scott took his seat across from her. "You really surprised me tonight. Are you in Griffin for good or just helping with the reunion?"

"I have my parents back, so I decided I was done hiding. After going to prison, I'm sure Mike has a lot more on his mind than me. When I stopped to see the old school, Doris offered me a job. It's different work, but I enjoy it. I clean rooms during the day and wait on tables at night. I don't even have to commute; I have a basement apartment in the old Driver's Ed rooms."

"Really?"

"Yeah. The basement rooms couldn't be hotel rooms, but they're high enough, with big windows, so they make great apartments. It's small, but it's enough. The old wood shop turned into a nice apartment for the Lesters, and the O'Brian's made a home out of the ag rooms."

"I'm glad. I'm sorry I left so abruptly last time. I thought I might hear from you."

"I know. I wanted to call, but... something came up." Lois looked apologetic. "I often wish I had."

"It was my fault for leaving so fast."

"No! I heard what happened. You had to go. Rachel keeps in touch with both Eve and me, so she relayed the full story. I'm glad you did what you did."

"We just got lucky, and everything worked out."

Lois looked over to Eve and Dave. "They look so happy now. Who'd have guessed?"

"There were signs," Scott recalled. "I think we were all just too preoccupied to notice. I'm glad things finally worked out for them."

"So," Lois looked inquisitive. "When'd you get together with Lex?"

"She's been with me for a long time now. She asked if she could come, and it's hard to say no to her."

Lois looked to where Lex was talking with Rachel, Vanessa, Carol, and Doris. "She seems nice. The others sure seem to get along with her."

"She is special. You should get to know her too. She's looking forward to knowing you."

"Really? Why would she want to know me?"

"We talk a lot, so she knows everything about me. You were an important part of my past, so she wants to know you."

"Just how much does she know about me?"

"Only the things I can tell her, but I don't think I left much out. You were my first love, and I let you slip away. She finds you fascinating. She asks questions, and I never lie to her."

"Does she ask about Roxanne too?"

"She doesn't have to. Roxanne is the one who introduced Lex to me. She may have known Roxanne better than me."

They continued talking until Lex came to look down over an imaginary notebook, doing her impression of a cocktail waitress. "How is everyone doing? Would you like another round of drinks?"

Lois lifted her glass. "This one is still good."

Lex pulled out a chair and joined them at the table. "Good. Danny would just want to see my phony ID anyway. Your loss, this round would have been on Lord Max. He had his first rare steak tonight, and he's feeling very grateful."

Lois smiled and said, "He was pleased with it. He left a generous tip for me, and one for the chef."

Lex grinned at Scott. "I gave him a few more of your ways to say, *'rare.'* Vanessa can't wait until he orders one in England."

Lois laughed as she pictured that. "It's nice to meet you Lex, officially anyway. I'm Lois."

"You certainly are." Lex took a drink from her stingless, "It's a pleasure to finally meet you."

"Are you enjoying your stay in Griffin?"

"Very much. I was a little disappointed. I was hoping to buy a new dress for tomorrow night, but I couldn't find anything here."

Lois nodded. "We only have one clothing store in town, and it doesn't have much choice. You may need to run to Maplewood Mall or Rosedale to find any selection."

Lex grinned. "Mall shopping! Now that sounds like fun. Would you like to go with me? Malls are never much fun if you're alone, and Scott is a terrible shopper."

Lois laughed, "I wish I could, but I have to clean rooms tomorrow."

Lex's face lit up as she said, "I heard that. That makes this your first wish. Don't go away." Lex left her stingless on the table and hurried back to the other girls.

Scott turned to the confused Lois. "I think she's granting you three wishes. Be careful and use them wisely."

Lex returned with Doris, who looked at Lois and said, "Tina has been asking for more hours, so if you would like tomorrow off, it's not a problem. In fact, this is your reunion too. Why don't you take the rest of the weekend off? Tina will be thrilled at the extra work."

"Okay." Lois felt speechless. "Thank you. Thank Tina for me too."

Doris returned to the others as Scott said, "I told you Lex was hard to say no to."

Lex looked almost giddy with excitement. "I know we'll need time to get ready for the reunion after we get back, so we should leave early. We can stop for breakfast on the way, my treat. What time will you be ready to go?"

"I don't know..." Lois looked at her watch. "I suppose seven or eight?"

Lex thought for a moment, "That sounds good. I'll be ready by seven, so just call my room when you're ready. Otherwise, I'll come to your room at eight."

Lois laughed and looked to Scott, "I see what you mean." She looked back to Lex. "I'll call you after seven."

Lex picked up her stingless and got up. "Looks like I'll be getting up early, so I'll go say my good nights to the others." She started walking away but stopped to look back at Scott. "Good news for you. I'll be out of your hair, so you get to sleep in tomorrow."

Lois watched as she walked away. "I think I better call it a night too. Is she always like this?"

"When she's excited. Have a good time with her, and I'll see you after you get back tomorrow. Also, thank you."

"For what?"

"Now I don't have to take her shopping."

Chapter 25: Shopping with Lex

Lois and Lex left promptly at eight o'clock.   Drive-time conversation included Lex's talk of college in Madison, and Lois's talk of classmates they may see at the reunion. Lois warned Lex to beware of Rich Lester's flirtations. "He likes to make innocent flirts disguised as compliments. I always get the feeling he's hoping for someone to smile back and invite more. I just remind him that Doris wouldn't approve of him talking that way. Mentioning Doris usually shuts him up."

They stopped for breakfast in Stillwater, Minnesota, and proceeded on to Maplewood Mall, which was a little more than an hour's drive from Griffin. After exhausting the shops in Maplewood, they moved on to Rosedale Mall. If they found nothing there, they would move on to other shopping centers and malls in the Twin Cities area.

In one store, they found a variety of dresses that would have looked great on either of them. Lois held up a short red dress and asked Lex what she thought of it.

Lex said, "Fantastic!" but then she touched it and felt the material. "Polyester! You might as well put it back. Anyone wearing polyester will have no slow dances with Scott."

"Really?" This news took Lois by surprise.

"For Scott, polyester feels like fiberglass insulation. I don't know if it's an allergy or if he's just sensitive to it, but he can't wear it, and he avoids touching it. That's one of the reasons I make a lot of my own clothes. Some things look great, but if you want it in cotton, sometimes you have to make it yourself."

Looking through the next rack, Lex pulled out a short, black dress with an extremely low back, and held it up for Lois. "How about this one?"

"Fantastic again." Lois took the dress to hold, while Lex looked through the rack to see what else was available. Lois was holding the dress against herself in front of the full-length mirror when Lex joined her, holding another dress with a similar cut but with a higher back. Lois admired it too, and suggested Lex try them both on.

"I'll try this one on." Lex held up the second dress. "You try that one on and we can see how they look side by side."

Lois had not planned on shopping for herself, but this seemed a reasonable way to compare dresses. She was enjoying their shopping, and it wouldn't cost anything to see how it looked. They stepped out of the separate dressing rooms to admire themselves in the large mirrors. Both dresses were the same deep black, made of soft cotton blended with just enough spandex for a snug fit. The dress Lex wore had spaghetti straps and showed generous cleavage, while Lois's dress had short sleeves, showed some cleavage, and covered hardly any of her back.

They took turns modeling the dresses for each other. Lex reached to pet the soft fabric of Lois's short sleeve. "Now this feels better. A girl wearing that could dance with Scott all night."

"Do you want to try this one on, so we can see how it looks on you?"

Lex looked at the open back, "No. I have a scar that would show with that one, but you look great. But you'll have to lose the bra, or we can shop for one with no back."

Lois laughed. "I don't know about that."

Lex looked around to be sure no one was close enough to hear. "Go ahead. If top floor commando doesn't work, we can look for a push-up bra with no back strap."

Lois laughed and returned briefly to her dressing room, leaving her bra when she came out.

"Alright Lois! You can still pull that off. You look fantastic. I may need to get a push-up to keep up with you."

Standing side by side, Lois admired their reflections in the mirror. "They match, but they're different."

"Just a minute." Lex stepped back into her dressing room and returned moments later to admire their reflections again. "There, now we look like sisters." Lex moved her shoulders for a slow shimmy. "See! Going commando works for me too."

When they came out of the dressing room, wearing their own clothes again, Lois looked at the price tag on the dress, thought for a moment, and hung it on the hook to be returned to the rack.

"I heard that." Lex reached and picked up the dress.

Lois looked confused. "I didn't say anything."

"But you were thinking it. You were thinking, *'I wish I could,'* but then you put it back because of the price."

"So? That's normal."

"So," Lex laid Lois's dress over the one in her arm, "that's your second wish." When Lois tried to protest, Lex said, "There's no going back on wishes, even if you don't say them out loud. Didn't Scott warn you about that?"

After eating lunch in the mall, they found another shop with designer shoes to match their new dresses. In another shop, they found small matching handbags. Lex asked Lois if she wanted to shop for push-up bras too, but Lois declined. She said that she didn't want to compete with Eve in that area.

Lex laughed, "Without a backless bra, you'll be free and natural. Eve will be struggling to keep up with you. Strapless push-up or Mother Nature, either way, you're going to look great."

* * *

When they returned to the hotel, Lex sorted the bags to be sure she gave the correct ones to Lois. "Thanks for coming, Lois. It was fun shopping with you."

"Thank you. I had fun too, but you shouldn't have bought all that for me. I need to pay you back."

"Don't even try. You can't cancel wishes. It's all part of the service. Besides, I feel guilty enough for taking your time away from work. This was your workday, so I should have been paying for your time."

"That's where I would have to draw the line." Lois looked at her bags. "Thank you again, Lex, for everything."

"Thank you for coming. I can't remember when I had this much fun shopping."

Chapter 26: Gymnasium Party

Our reunion was held in the Banquet/Events Room, which we knew as the school gymnasium. Each classmate who worked at the hotel had someone replacing them for the evening. Of course, Danny would pop behind the smaller bar in the banquet room to work when needed. Danny did not mind working during reunions, as he felt most at home when behind the bar.

Over half our class attended, a dozen of which were staying at the hotel. All enjoyed the nostalgia of being back in their old school; some even joked that they had slept in the same classrooms twenty years ago.

Rachel hurried to Ray Ellis when she saw the camera hanging from his neck. "As long as you have that, can you get me a good shot of Scott and his new girlfriend tonight?"

"Scott has a new girlfriend?" Ray was surprised.

"Yeah! Just wait until you meet her. She's young, even younger than last reunion's prom queen, but she's a sweetheart and I like her. Of course, if he sticks with her, he won't be getting back with Lois. I still had hope for them."

Samantha tugged on the sleeve of Ray's shirt and pointed to the door. "Maybe he can have both."

"Oh my God!" Ray brought his camera up to zoom in for the picture.

Scott entered the room, walking between Lois and Lex. Scott was dressed in black denim jeans and a black flannel shirt, a good match with Lois and Lex in their new dresses.

"That's something I never expected to see!" Ray flipped the flash up on his camera and hurried over to shoot more pictures of the trio. Lois offered to step out of the picture, but Ray insisted that she stay. After a few pictures, Ray asked Lois to move to the other side, and took pictures with Lex in the middle.

When Ray stopped to change film, Lois said, "Ray, this is Scott's girlfriend Lex."

Ray nodded to Lex, "How nice to meet you."

Lex stepped forward and gave Ray a hug before turning back to Lois. "Ray and I know each other. He's Scott's best friend, so we see a lot of him." She looked back to Ray. "Lois is my new best friend, for the weekend anyway. She agreed to join Scott and me for the reunion."

Samantha looked at Lois. "How wonderful. We've known Lex for years. She babysat for us during the last reunion."

Ray stepped back to admire Lex. "Damn, L! You look sharp tonight." Ray snapped the film door shut on his camera as Lex pointed him back to Scott, who was still standing next to Lois. Ray quickly brought his camera up for a few fast shots of Scott and Lois together.

Lex leaned over to thank Ray with a kiss on the cheek. Ray noticed their new dresses. "How about one more of the girls? You look like a matched set." Scott stepped aside, allowing Lex to take his place while Ray snapped a few more pictures.

Lois gave Ray a puzzled look. "That's a lot of pictures of just us."

"That's because you're all good friends who I never get to see enough of."

Ray and Samantha shared the table with Scott, Lex, and Lois. Ray apologized for not knowing Lois had returned to Griffin, or that she now worked at the hotel. He explained that with work and family, he and Samantha did not get out nearly enough. After seeing how their old school had changed, he said that he and Sam would be back soon.

When most were nearly done eating, Rich Lester stepped up to the stage and took the microphone to address the class. He mentioned that they had a record attendance of sixty classmates at this reunion. He also named the five classmates who were no longer with them. One had died of cancer, another suffered a heart attack, and three in traffic accidents in their car, motorcycle, and truck.

Randy Richards was pointed out as the one-time speaker who never went away and was now an honorary classmate. Rich also pointed out that Mr. Opus, one of our class advisors, was in attendance with his wife. Mr. Opus declined requests to make a speech, although he enjoyed visiting with former students throughout the evening.

Rich finished his talk with, "...For those of you who have not been to any of our previous reunions, be warned, you never know what to expect. In previous years we have been held hostage by a giant tree, interrupted our dance for a live birth, witnessed a resurrection, and have had calls for both ambulance and police. This year we're getting back to school, so this should be a little less eventful."

Rachel softly muttered, "He didn't knock on wood. He probably just jinxed us all."

Rich concluded with, "...Have a good time, but be prepared for anything."

Instead of a live band, this reunion featured karaoke. There were lists of available songs to choose from. The DJ played an instrumental portion, allowing individuals to come to the stage and sing the vocals. A video screen displayed the lyrics with the music, which was a great help when we discovered we did not know the words as well as we thought.

Some of our karaoke highlights featured Rich Lester and Dave Masters singing *The Battle of New Orleans* in honor of Lord Max. Scott, Rich, Vanessa, Ray, and Rachel sang together, representing those from River Bend's one-room schoolhouse. Dave and Eve Masters did their Sonny and Cher impression with, *I've Got You Babe.* Since Scott lived in the woods, he put on his best Big Bad Wolf act as he and Lex sang, *Hey There Little Red Riding Hood.* Some chose not to perform, while others were up repeatedly throughout the evening. Whenever there was a break with no singers, the DJ played the background music so we could still dance.

Samantha went on stage to sing *Hey Jude,* leaving Ray without a partner for a long slow dance. Lex asked Ray to dance, leaving Scott and Lois alone at the table. Predictably, Scott asked Lois if she would like to dance.

Lois felt Scott's shirt as she put her arms around him. "Lex was right; your shirts really are soft. It feels nice."

"Yes, it does." As soon as Scott spoke, he realized his hand was on her bare back, due to the low cut of her dress. "The fabric, I mean," he added apologetically. "Okay, make that, the fabric too."

Lois gave a short laugh. "I know what you mean." Instinctively, Lois moved closer as they danced. "Lex said flannel was like wearing a hug. I think she's right."

"This does feel good too." Scott held her closer. Lois had grown her hair out, so it completely covered Scott's hand on her back. As Samantha's song ended, another classmate took the mic to sing, *You've Lost That Loving Feeling.* Happy for another slow song, Scott and Lois stayed on the dance floor.

Lois felt happy and comfortable as their bodies moved with the music. She laid her head against him as she had at their last reunion. That night, Lois's parents were expecting her home after the dance. This year, Lois had her own little apartment, only a short walk around the hall. She could feel Scott holding her tighter, with his warm hand on her back. She turned her head up to see Scott looking at her as he had when they danced near their campfire at the Polk County Campground. Lois found herself kissing Scott, as they moved with the music. A tingling sensation shot through her when Scott's hand moved higher on her back. Enjoying his touch, Lois felt even more grateful to Lex for buying this dress. Lois instantly pulled back when she thought of Lex. Looking around, she remembered where she was, and who she was with. She could see Lex smiling as she danced with Ray on the other side of the dance floor.

"I'm sorry." Lois stepped back from Scott. "I can't do this. I'm sorry." She turned and hurried back to the table.

"What's wrong?" Scott asked with confusion as he hurried after her.

Lois picked up her handbag and turned to face him. "It's just... you... me... I couldn't help it. I'm sorry. I really like Lex, and... I can't do this to her. I'm sorry." Lois turned and hurried out the door.

When Lex saw Lois walking off the dance floor, she knew something was wrong. She said something to Ray and hurried after her.

Entering the hotel lobby, Lex could see Lois near the end of that hall. Lois was about to turn down the side hall when she heard Lex call her name. She looked back and watched as Lex hurried to catch her.

"I'm sorry," Lois cried when Lex reached her. "I didn't mean to. I just ... we were dancing, and I couldn't help myself. It was an accident Lex, and it won't happen again."

"What was?" Lex was confused. "What happened?"

"I'm sorry." Lois could feel tears on her cheeks when she looked at Lex. "I was dancing with Scott... and I kissed him. It was my fault. It won't happen again."

Lex brought her hands up to hold Lois's arms. "It's alright. I understand. You two have history. It can happen."

"It won't happen again. I'm going back to my room, and I won't see him again."

Lex looked worried as she shook her head. "No. You don't have to. It's alright."

Lois brought her arms up and hugged Lex. "I'm sorry. I know Scott is yours, and..." Lois released her hug and moved back to take hold of Lex's arms. Looking into Lex's eyes, Lois could see worry and fear. "When I talked to Scott, I could see how much he loves you. After getting to know you... I understand. I really do. You don't have to worry. I won't come between you." As Lois let go, Lex looked as if she were about to cry.

Lex's bottom lip began to quiver. "No! Stop! That's not how it's supposed to go."

"I know, Lex. It was a mistake, but it won't happen again."

"No, Lois! That's not it. It's my fault. I messed everything up. You have to go back. It will be alright."

"I can't go back. I know that would be a mistake. You go to him, and I'll go to my room. Everything will be okay."

"No! It won't be okay. I ruined everything."

Lois looked into Lex's watery eyes, thinking she looked like a little girl trying to fight her tears. She grabbed Lex and hugged her again. "I like you so much, Lex. You don't have to worry. I promise I will NOT come between you." She released Lex to look into her eyes. "Go back to him, and I'll stay out of the way."

Lex's lip quivered again. "Stop! It's not supposed to be like this. Yes, Scott loves me, but he's not in love with me. It's not like that." Lex could see Lois's confusion. She grabbed Lois and hugged her. "Lois, please tell me I didn't mess everything up." Letting go, Lex wiped her eyes and said, "He's not in love with me, Lois. He's in love with you." Lex paused to look around, realizing that even though the lobby was empty, they were still in a public area. She looked at the tear streaks on Lois's face. "Maybe we should go to your apartment. I think we both need to wash our faces, and maybe we should talk."

Looking at Lex, Lois realized she must have the same puffy eyes. "I think that would be a good idea. Let's go to my apartment, and maybe I can figure out what's going

Chapter 27: Lois's Apartment

In Lois's small apartment, they took turns washing their tear-streaked faces. After drying their faces, Lois turned to look at Lex. "What's going on?"

"Scott is NOT my boyfriend. Yes, I love him, and he loves me, but we're not lovers. It's not like that. He's... he's Scott. He loves you, and he always has."

Lois shook her head with confusion. "So, you're not in love with Scott?"

"Not in that way. I could never in that way. Ewww! I love him in a different way. And in our defense, we never said we were lovers. We never said anything like that; people just assumed. We even got separate rooms for God's sake! Would we have done that if we were a real couple?"

"Then, what are you doing here?"

Lex took a deep breath. "I know how Scott feels about you, and I wanted to meet you. I thought that if I could see you, I might be able to give you both a little push, but I didn't mean to push you apart." Seeing surprise on Lois's face, Lex barked, "And you love him too, so don't deny it! Anyone can see it. Everyone can see it. Go back to him Lois, for both your sakes. Go back to him for all our sakes."

Lois shook her head. "Who are you, Lex?"

"I'm Lex. And that's all you need to know."

"So, Scott brought you here, thinking you could bring him and me together?"

Lex shook her head. "No, Scott brought me because I asked him to. I wanted to meet you, and he couldn't say no."

"Why do you even care?"

"I want Scott to be happy." Lex watched as Lois thought about this. "Lois. Do you want me to be happy?"

"I want very much for you to be happy."

"Then go back to Scott. Ask him to dance. Or just tell him you want to sneak off and be alone. Kiss him again. Kiss him, like the first time you kissed him. Don't even think about me. Just think about you and Scott. Bring him back here if you want. Talk, dance, kiss, or jump his bones. Do whatever feels natural. Whatever you do, just do it together."

"Will you come back with me?"

"I think I better. Otherwise, everyone will think you killed me and went back to claim your prize."

Lois realized it would look like that if she went back to Scott alone. "Okay. Let me check my face, and I'll go back. Are you sure about this?"

"More than I've ever been about anything in my life. I'll go back for a while; then I'll go to my room, where I'm out of the way. If I wake up because you two are in Scott's room bouncing the bed off the ceiling, it will be music to my ears. If he's not in his room, I'll assume you are both down here having the time of your lives. Not only will I not mind, I'll bring you breakfast in bed."

"Who are you, Lex?"

Lex grew a cocky grin and said, "I'm your ef'n Fairy Godmother."

* * *

Lois and Lex returned to the party together. When Lois felt like they were being watched, Lex leaned close to say, "The only reason anyone's looking is because we are smoking hot in these dresses. We're so hot; if these dresses were polyester, they would be on fire by now."

Scott was standing by the bar with Ray and Samantha when he turned to see the girls coming toward him. They looked happy, so Scott found himself smiling when they reached the bar. "I started to go after you, but Ray stopped me. He said that whatever was wrong, you two would work it out. It looks like he was right."

"Yeah," Lex faked a bit of a Brooklyn accent. Or was it a Jersey accent? "Turns out, we're pretty smart when it comes to figuring things out." Lex dropped onto a barstool as she looked at Scott. "You know what's wrong? I think she's got a crush on you, and she doesn't want to get in the way. You know what else? I know just how she feels. I noticed something else too. I realized that you're about twice my age. I'm startin' ta think you're too old to be my boyfriend. I think I should be dumping you."

"So, this is it. You're dumping me?"

"That's about the size of it. Now I know it will be hard to get ova' me, but maybe if you and Lois here talk it out, you'll be able to get ova' it. Capiche?"

Scott leaned forward and kissed Lex on her forehead. "What am I going to do with you?"

Lex smiled and continued with the fake accent. "Not a thing. Like I said, we jus' broke up." She kissed Scott on the cheek and returned to her natural voice, "I'll check on you to see how things went in the morning. If you bring anyone back to your room tonight, lock the door between our rooms, and I'll just go out for breakfast." Returning to the phony accent, she said, "But if she brings you back ta her place, I kind o' promised breakfast in bed. So don't get cocky if she invites ya' ova'; she's just doin' it for da waffles."

Scott gave Lex a quick hug. "Don't stay out too late." He turned to Lois and held out his hand. "I just got dumped. Do you know anyone interested in consoling me?"

"You poor thing." Lois took his hand and looked around the room. "I think I've seen everyone here. Would you like to go talk, or something?"

Scott squeezed her hand. "I'd like that."

"It looks like I'm a free agent again." Lex spun around on her stool to look at Danny, "Barkeep, how about a stingless?"

Lex continued using her phony Jersey Accent, or was it a Brooklyn accent? Come to think of it, I think she may have bounced back and forth between the two. This, of course, encouraged Danny to pour on his Irish even more. When Peter Baker came over, he joined in with a Swiss or German accent. Vanessa soon began ordering drinks in Portuguese while Lord Max surprised them with a Cockney accent. Rachel chimed in with a Scottish Brogue, and Doris began speaking high school French. A handful of other classmates went with our region, using Swedish accents straight out of the Ole and Lena jokes. Swedish accents were natural, of course, because many of us had grown up with elderly relatives who spoke with them. It may sound odd to you now, but each one of us who got into it had a great time. Of course, those who were not gifted with other accents, local or foreign, simply wondered what the hell was going on.

* * *

Lois held Scott's hand as they walked to her basement apartment. As she opened the door, she instinctively asked if he would like coffee.

"I don't think coffee would be good this late at night ... maybe a glass of water."

Lois took two glasses from the cupboard, added ice, and filled them with cold tap water. After setting the glasses on the table, she sat across from him so they would face each other. Neither was thirsty but holding a glass in your fingers can sometimes aid in conversation.

"Who is Lex?"

"She's... Lex. That alone is quite a bit."

Lois shook her head. "At first, I was surprised to see you with such a young girlfriend, but then I got to know her. You two seemed like a great couple. You're still a great catch, so I could see what she saw in you. Anyone could see what you saw in her. Then I got to know her, and I felt like I loved her too, and I don't know why. Now, she says that she is not, and never was, your girlfriend. So, who is she?"

"Who did she tell you she was?"

"She said she was my ef'n Fairy Godmother."

249

Scott gave a slight shake of his head as he grinned. "Sometimes I think she is my fairy godmother." He lifted his glass for a small drink as he thought. "I think I had another fairy godmother once. She came to me for help, and then she helped me. She lost her job for coming to me, but we saved a life, so it was worth it. I fell in love with her, so that was one reward."

Lois's fingers slowly rotated her water glass. "You're talking about Roxanne?"

"Yeah," he said with a nod. "She had a job that required keeping secrets. She didn't like it, but it was part of her job. She violated that rule once, with bad results. She learned that only the person with the secret has the right to share it, even when it involves other people."

Talking of secrets reminded Lois of the many secrets she had kept over the years. "And Lex has a secret?"

"No, but she's part of one. It was Lex's life that we saved. Lex remembers my part, but it never would have happened without Roxanne. There is a secret with Lex, but it's not hers or mine to share. When Roxanne died, she made me promise we would keep that secret. Neither of us likes it, but we made a promise. Also, we just can't risk hurting the person who has the secret. No matter how well you know someone, you don't know how they'll react if their secret is revealed."

Scott gently moved his glass from side to side. "I know this doesn't make sense. I can't explain Lex because she's part of a secret that I'm not supposed to know."

"So, someone else's secret is the real problem here."

"In a nutshell," he nodded. "I can tell you that Lex is very special to me, and I to her. I can't imagine life without her, but it's not a romance. She knows how I feel for you, and I think she wanted to bring us together. Also, she REALLY wanted to meet you."

"Why would she want to meet me?"

"She has her reasons."

"And there's no romance between you."

"To be honest, we never said she was anything more than my guest."

"How would she feel if you didn't want to be with me?"

"Lois, you know that could never happen."

"Wait here." Lois walked to her bedroom, returning to drop a thick file folder in front of him. "I understand about secrets. Keeping them may hurt, but sometimes there's a good reason for it. Sometimes we do things for good reasons, but we know people will hate us when they find out."

Scott looked at the file and began to open the folder.

"Wait!" Lois pushed the file back down. "Before you read that, will you hold me? Just hold me one more time. You might not want to afterward... and... I'm feeling selfish. Please... just for a moment."

Scott stood up and put his arms around her. Lois laid her head against his chest and hugged him closely. He gently brushed his fingers up and down her bare back. "I really do like this dress."

"It was a gift from my ef'n Fairy Godmother." Lois looked up as Scott leaned down and kissed her.

* * *

Scott watched the sleeping Lois beside him as his fingers softly danced about her skin. He realized how exhausted she must have been, both physically and emotionally. Lois and Lex were both up early for their shopping trip, and Scott knew that shopping with Lex could be an exhausting ordeal. It was no surprise that Lois was tired. Scott on the other hand, had a free day with little to do. Defying the typical stereotype of a man rolling over to fall asleep, Scott had never felt more awake. He carefully pulled away from Lois, rising from her bed without waking her.

Partially dressed, Scott sat at Lois's table and opened the file she had given him. He saw a bundle of envelopes and a small stack of papers, the top of which was a letter Lois had written to him. Scott set the rest aside, choosing to begin with Lois's letter.

Her letter began by explaining how Mike had intercepted their mail and used their letters to deceive them. She explained how she was thinking of the baby when she married Mike, and why she had given her away to protect her from him. She told how she had hired Peter to learn what had happened to their daughter, only to learn she had died, and did not even have a grave they could visit. Next, he read Peter's summary, and thumbed through the remaining papers from his investigation. He then went back to read Lois's letter again, beginning at the top, and not stopping until the very last line.

Scott looked to find Lois's phone, and quickly dialed the number for Lex's room. Having no answer, he looked at the time and saw that it was not yet midnight. The reunion would run until one or two o'clock, so many would still be there. Scott quietly grabbed the rest of his clothes, dressed, and closed the door behind him as he left.

Chapter 28: Sunday Morning

Lois admired the tiny life she had made. She marveled at the tiny fingers, with their tiny fingernails. That such a thing could have come from her was the most incredible feeling she had ever experienced. She felt her tears, as the nurse took the baby away and handed it to a slender girl with long red hair. Papers were placed before her, which she signed, and returned to the heavy-set, balding man. The red-haired girl looked at the infant as she followed the man out the door.

Lois could see the newsprint picture of a pretty girl with blond hair. She could hear Peter telling her that the aunt would have raised her if she had lived, but that never happened. Lex's voice seemed to take over, and Lois heard her saying, *"I'm your Ef'n Fairy Godmother!"* The words seemed to echo in her head. She heard Lex again, but now the voice was accompanied by a knocking sound.

Lois opened her eyes as the knocking on her door registered. The dream was over, interrupted by the knocking. It did not matter. Lois never enjoyed that dream anyway. She looked around to see that she was alone.

She called out, "Just a minute," threw back her blanket, and put her robe on while walking to the door. Lois wondered if Scott had stepped out and the door locked behind him. When she saw the papers lying across the table, she prayed that the knock was Scott, wanting to return.

Lois opened the door and Lex entered with a service cart, which held two covered plates, cups, and a carafe of coffee.

"I warned you that I would bring breakfast in bed," Lex cheerfully chimed as she pushed the cart to Lois's table. "I'll stop, and you can take it from here. If he's sleeping, you can bring the plate to him. Otherwise, I'll leave so you can both come to the table."

"Who?" Lois looked around, still seeing no sign of Scott.

Lex opened her mouth to speak, stopped herself, and then said, "Scott. His door wasn't locked, he didn't answer, so I checked. His bed hasn't been touched, so he must be here." Lex grinned at Lois as she reached forward to hug her. "I'm just so happy this morning. I know it's embarrassing, but I'm happy anyway." Lex lifted one of the covers to reveal a plate of Belgian Waffles with cherries and whipped cream. She whispered, "It's his favorite."

"Wait a minute." Lois checked her bathroom, and looked back to her empty bed again, before returning to Lex. "Scott isn't here."

Lex looked confused. "He was here, wasn't he? His bed hasn't been slept in."

"He was... last night anyway. I woke up to your knocking, and... he was gone."

"He must have snuck back to his room while I was getting breakfast. I bet he went there so he could make me think he was there all night. You put the plates on the table. I'll run up and send him right back." Lex hurried out the door and ran up the stairs.

Lois gathered her papers and set them on her kitchen counter, putting the old letters in a separate stack. She dressed in a hurry and was opening her window when Lex returned.

"Is he back?"

Lois shook her head. "I don't think he's coming back." She lifted the covers from the plates. "Would you like to join me for breakfast?"

"Of course, he's coming back." Lex opened her eyes as if suddenly realizing the obvious. "He must have left to get breakfast too. That means his plate is up for grabs. If we eat fast, I can be out of here before he shows up with the same thing, and you can have seconds."

Lois set the plates on the table as Lex poured coffee. "How did it go last night?"

"I'm not sure." Lois began cutting her waffle with a fork. "We talked. He tried to explain, or tried to explain why he couldn't explain. Something about it being someone else's secret, so he wasn't allowed to talk about it. I didn't understand, but in some ways, I could because I've had secrets too."

"So, did you give him yours? Sort of like, 'I'll show you mine, you show me yours.'"

"Sort of." Lois ate a piece of waffle before saying, "I wrote it all out in a letter, but I asked him not to read it yet. Then..." she paused.

"Then?" Lex looked at her with a big grin.

"And after that... I fell asleep. I woke up when you knocked."

"After that...?" Lex's grin grew wider.

Lois looked down at her plate. "I fell asleep. He must have come out here to read my letter. Then he probably went home so he wouldn't have to see me again."

Lex shook her head as she swallowed a bite of waffle. "First of all, he would not do that. Second, we came in my car. Third, Scott loves you, and nothing would make him walk out on you. If he's not here, I know there's a good reason for it. He must be out getting breakfast in bed for you."

They were interrupted by a knock on the door. "See! He's back." Lex opened the door, only to see Storm Vanderzee.

"Well, hello," Storm said in a cheerful voice.

Lex opened her eyes wide and said, "Hello! I'm Lex, Scott's friend." She quickly shook his hand and said, "We'd love to visit, but Lois and I are discussing something real important now. Okay?"

Storm looked at Lois and said, "Oh. Alright. I'll ... I just wanted to tell Lois that we'll be out of town for the day. She can call me later."

Lex closed the door, saying, "Okay, bye-bye Gramps."

"Lex!" Lois looked shocked. "That was my father."

Lex hurried back to the table. "And he could see we were in the middle of something. He'll call back."

"Why are you starting to remind me of Rachel?"

"Maybe it's because she's kind o' cool. I like her. Maybe it's because I'm excited." Lex took another bite of waffle. "So, you wrote Scott a letter about your secrets. Did he read it? Is everything out in the open?"

Lois stood up and got the stack of papers from the countertop. "They were on the table when I got up, so he must have read everything. He knows what I did, so now he's gone." Lois dropped the papers next to Lex. "You might as well see too. It doesn't matter who knows if he does."

Lex looked at the papers, and her eyes opened wide as if she had been given a sacred document. She pushed her plate aside to pull the papers in front of her. "Oh my God." She looked at Lois, "This is exciting. You go ahead and eat your waffle. I'm going to savor this."

Lois shook her head in confusion and began eating while Lex read.

Lex read Lois's entire letter, looked over Peter's summary, and thumbed through the other papers. She softly said, "R. Campbell," aloud while reading the signatures on the adoption papers. Stacking the papers back as they had been, Lex reread Lois's letter to Scott and looked back to Lois. "You were sleeping when he read this, and he didn't wake you?"

"No. He just left, and I don't blame him."

Lex thought for a moment. "I know what happened. He went to get me."

Lois looked totally confused. "What?"

Lex stood and walked to Lois's side of the table. "Stand up."

"Why?" Lois stood, feeling even more confused.

"Because I'm going to give you a hug." Lex wrapped her arms around Lois and squeezed.

When she let go, Lois stared at her in shock. "What was that for?"

"Because I'm alive! And now we need to find Scott."

"What?"

Lex hugged Lois again. "It's over. You showed yours, but Scott should be here before we show you ours."

"What are you talking about?"

"No more secrets!" Lex was starting to sound giddy. "You gave us your secret, so we don't have to keep it." Lex stared into Lois's eyes, "Who am I?"

"You're my ef'n Fairy Godmother."

"Okay, now make a wish." When Lois glanced at the papers on the table, Lex yelled, "Granted!"

"Can you explain something...? Anything?"

Lex grabbed the stack of papers and held them up. "Okay, but this is your third wish." Seeing Lois's confusion, Lex said, "You had Scott's baby, and you gave it away to protect it from your psychotic husband. Right?"

"Right."

"NOW, that part makes sense. I understand, and I thank you. Next, car crash! New-mom and dad are dying. Little girl will die without a kidney. Correct?"

"Yes. So, Scott's daughter is dead. Why are you happy?"

"No! Scott's daughter would die without a kidney. If she got a kidney, she would still be alive."

"And then she would have lived with her aunt in Chicago. She never did."

Lex grinned. "Maybe they let her live with the donor."

"Why would they let her live with the donor?"

"Because he never gave her away." Lex shook her head at Lois's confusion. Pulling up the side of her shirt, she revealed a large surgical scar on her side, which continued around to her back. "Scott has one too. Didn't I say that he saved my life? If Peter would have questioned Aunt Nancy, she would have told him that I'm alive."

Lois stared at the scar, frozen as Lex's words began to register. Her eyes slowly moved to study Lex's face. Seeing her own features in Lex, her eyes began to water. "You?"

Lex wrapped her arms around Lois again, only this time Lois returned her hug, wanting to laugh and cry at the same time. "You're her?"

Lex held her mother tight. "I'm me. I'm alive!"

"How?"

Lex let go of Lois to look at her as she tried to explain quickly. "I needed a kidney from someone AB negative. I got AB negative from Dad. Aunt Nancy found Mama's adoption papers. They were signed by R. Campbell, and she tracked her down. Roxanne tracked down Dad, but he wasn't the same Dad that was with you when you gave me away. She talked to Dad anyway ... because maybe he's related, so he might be AB negative too. Dad came, and figured out who I was as soon as he saw me. Real Dad never gave me away, so Aunt Nancy and Roxanne helped him get custody of me." Lex took a deep breath. "The problem was, they didn't know your reason for giving me away. They couldn't tell you unless you told us first. It was your secret, and we weren't supposed to know. Anyone who figured it out had to keep it secret too."

Crying with joy, Lois hugged Lex again. "Why didn't he say something?"

"Another girl came to Roxanne wanting to know her mother. Roxanne told her. She went to her mother. That mother told her that if she had wanted her, she never would have given her away in the first place. The mother's husband found out and divorced the mom. She had gotten pregnant and gave it away when he was in the Korean War. It was a mess for everyone. Another one of Roxanne's mothers tried to kill herself, just because someone discovered she'd been pregnant. Roxanne swore, never again. The problem was, I was going to die."

"And R. Campbell was Roxanne?"

Lex nodded. "She was afraid you might remember her. That's why she cut her hair and tried to avoid you at the reunion. She lost her job for going to Dad, but that was okay because I lived. She helped Dad take care of me, and they fell in love, making her my next mom."

"She called you Randi?"

"When she called little me, *'Miranda,'* it made me think of dead mom. Roxanne said I had a big name, and I could use part of it. Miranda became Randi. After she died, Alexis became Lex. Much easier than Miranda Alexis Vanderzee Michelson Severson, don't you think?"

Lois wiped the tears from her eyes. "No wonder I liked you so much. I wondered why Scott would have such a young girlfriend, but you were so easy to love."

"I told you it was a different kind of love. We had separate rooms for God's sake. Do lovers in Griffin ask for separate rooms?"

Lois thought for a moment. "I thought that you were the girl Scott had hired as a housekeeper. He mentioned her five years ago."

Lex laughed. "I was only fourteen five years ago. Laurie came shortly after Roxanne died. She was eighteen then. She kept the house clean and tried to help me with my homework. I usually ended up explaining things that she never understood when she was in school. She left to get married a few years ago, so now it's just Scott and me." Lex laughed at the thought of being mistaken for Laurie. "Okay, put your shoes on; we need to find Dad... Scott... we need to find him."

As they headed to the door, Lois asked, "Where are we going?"

"I don't know, let's try the front desk. Maybe someone saw him!" As they began to open the door, they heard a loud BANG through the open window.

Lois looked at the open window. "Did that sound like a gun?"

Chapter 29: On the Rooftop

For Scott, waking up was more of an act of regaining consciousness. When he finally began to wake, he could feel sunshine on his face. He was unable to move his hands, as a narrow rope was wound tightly around his wrists. Scott bit down on the gag in his mouth and tried to recall what had happened.

He was returning to the reunion in search of Lex when someone down the hall called his name. A man Scott did not know told him that his girlfriend had a problem and asked him to bring Scott for help. When he heard that Lex had a problem, Scott followed the man without question.

In the elevator, the man said that he could not explain her problem, but everything would be clear when he saw her. On the third floor, the man opened a door and led Scott up the stairway to the roof. As they reached the rooftop door, the man shook his head saying, "I tell ya' man, this is something you have got to see with your own eyes." When Scott followed the man through the doorway, everything went black.

"I think he's finally awake?" It was a voice Scott did not know.

"You shouldn't a' hit him so hard." It was the voice of the man who led him to the roof. "I was start'n ta' think he wouldn't eva' wake up."

Opening his eyes, Scott could see that he was on the roof, and there were other men standing around him. One of the men knelt to Scott, preparing to remove his gag. "I'm going to take this off so we can talk, but I don't want any yelling. Do you understand, Scotty Boy?" Scott recognized this man. His head was shaved, and he wore a full beard, but without a doubt, it was Mike Burman.

Scott nodded, and Mike removed the gag. Scott moved his jaw, licked his lip, and swallowed, happy to be rid of the gag. He said to Mike, "I thought you were in prison?"

"It wasn't a life sentence, and sometimes, they get flexible about time served." Mike stood up, and an older man stepped over to join him. "Guess who I met in prison? Scott, I'd like you to meet my old man. I hadn't seen him since graduation. I guess I should thank you for setting me up."

"Nobody set you up Mike. We just happened to show up on the morning they took you down."

Mike snapped, "You saw what was going on, and you said NOTHING! You even told them my real name." Mike paused to calm himself. "That turned out to be the best thing you ever did to me. I found Dad in prison. We talked, and we decided it was time for me to do some talking. I talked about my friends, and they were no longer a problem for Dad's friends. Dad's sentence was up, and I got out early. Between his contacts and mine, we made our way up together. Look around! Now we've got men working for us."

"So, you brought me up here so you could thank me?"

"No Scott. I brought you up here for payback, and you have it coming."

"I take it that means you're still blaming other people for your own mistakes. You have a long history of that. Where did that begin? Was it when you punched the wall in grade school?"

"I broke my hand because of you. Then I got home, and they took my father."

"So, you see me as the reason your father got arrested: as if his burglaries had nothing to do with it." Scott looked at the older man. "That's right. I had someone check on Mike a while back, and he looked up your record while he was at it. With a rap sheet like yours, you must be proud of your son. He grew to be so much like you. Car theft, burglary, assaults, not to mention all those drug charges. You two have so much in common. Do you think it's in the genes?"

"Maybe it is." Mike grinned. "Maybe that's why we do so great together."

"How about homicide by intoxicated use of a stolen vehicle? Have you got that one too Mike?" The look on the old man's face was as telling as a confession. "Yeah, I finally got enough little clues to put that together too." He looked back to Mike. "That's why you blamed my mother when your father stopped coming to Griffin. You went barhopping together, and people might remember the loudmouth trying to get someone to race him. Police found the car after a fatal accident, so you couldn't come back because someone might recognize you."

The old man glared at Mike, realizing he must have said something to someone. He looked at Scott. "How'd you come up with a story like that?"

"Just little details every now and then. Nothing made sense until I put a few pieces together, and they fit."

"Like anybody would believe any o' that now."

"After all these years, it wouldn't matter if they did." Scott looked into the old man's eyes. "At least now I know who killed my mother. Of course, Mike will still blame me anyway. He's like that you know. Did he learn that from you?"

Mike leaned close to Scott's face. "Every time something went wrong, it came back to you." Standing up again, he looked down at Scott. "Every loss I had in school. The hassles I got in boot camp. You stole my girl and knocked her up." Realizing how much he had said, Mike calmed his voice to gloat. "That's right, you have a daughter, and your girlfriend just gave her away."

"I'm sure she grew to be a wonderful person." Scott was glad Mike knew nothing about Lex.

"I got careless and went to prison because you took my wife. You broke my arm and my jaw, and they made ME go to anger management. You even took my son. The list goes on. You did it all Scott, and payback comes today!"

"You know, you're only drawing attention to yourself."

"Nobody even knows I'm here. I'm a big man now. Men are working for ME! I've almost got it all, but I still need to finish things with you." Mike looked back to his father. "Dad agrees."

The old man held his chin up. "A man has to settle his scores."

"So... what? You get your revenge on a man who's tied up and outnumbered? That doesn't sound very manly to me."

"No." Mike leaned close to Scott. "You and I will have it out one last time. No more blind-siding me when I'm drunk. No more sneaking in when a big deal is going down. No more running away with my wife while I'm working."

"No more pulling a knife on an unarmed man. No punching a woman when her back is turned. It's just five against one, and the one is tied up."

Mike stepped back from Scott. "Stand him up!" Scott felt two hands on each arm pulling him up to his feet. "I thought of dropping you off the roof with a suicide note, but that didn't sound good enough."

After last night's revelations, Scott imagined how Lois would have felt if he had been found like that.

"No, Scott. I'm going to break you into pieces with my bare hands." Mike nodded to one of the men behind Scott, who walked around to remove Scott's bonds. "You and I are going to have it out, Scott, and it won't go so easy for you this time."

Scott looked Mike over while the rope was being loosened from his wrists. Mike had gained a great deal of muscle since Scott had last seen him. Prison seemed to have increased his bulk and may have improved his fighting skills too. "So, you and I have it out. And what happens if I win?"

Mike laughed. "Not this time Scott. When we're done, I'll leave you to see how long it is before someone finds you. Up here, I bet they won't even smell you. Hell, they'll probably think you're just a left-over Halloween decoration."

Scott felt a pistol being held against his back as he was being untied. "So, if I'm winning, your goons shoot me?"

"That's just to make sure you behave until we get started."

Scott could feel the gun against his back. If the others were also armed, at least their guns were still concealed. For the moment, this was the only gun he was concerned with.

One man stood in front of Scott, removing the yellow rope which bound his wrists. Scott recognized the rope as the type used for water skiing, very narrow, and usually at least fifty feet long. The man who lured Scott to the roof now stood between him and Mike. Mike's father stood back closer to the door, blocking the only safe way off the roof.

Scott slid his foot back slightly as he turned to glance over his left shoulder. The only man behind him was pushing his gun into Scott's back. He also saw the short wall at the edge of the roof, just a short distance away. At this height, that would hardly be a safe exit.

Scott was expected to fight with Mike, but he had no reason to believe the others would not interfere if Mike was losing. The odds were not in Scott's favor. If he moved quickly, he might be able to lessen those odds.

The man in front of Scott finished removing the ropes. Scott wiggled his fingers to check his circulation. Everything seemed to be moving and working correctly.

Scott pivoted back against the gun, turning sideways as he gave an elbow strike to the gunman's wrist while his other fist struck the side of the gunman's head. By the time the gunman had squeezed his trigger, Scott was already parallel with the barrel. The bullet lightly grazed Scott's back as it cut through his shirt before hitting the man holding the ski rope.

Scott's elbow strike sent the pistol flying from the gunman's hand. Scott slid his hand down the gunman's arm to catch his wrist while dropping to one knee as he swung his free arm to arc up between the gunman's legs. Rising quickly, he lifted the gunman in a fireman's carry. Coming to a full stand, Scott threw the gunman, head down, into the wounded man with the rope. The rope man was still realizing he had been shot when the gunman flew into him. The rope man fell back as the gunman dropped headfirst onto the roof.

Mike's dad yelled, "Grab him!"

The third man charged forward with both hands reaching for Scott. Slapping down with one hand, and up with the other, Scott caught hold of both wrists while confusing his attacker's balance. Changing directions, he pulled the raised hand down, while raising the lower hand high, causing the man to rotate, turning with each step. When his back was to Scott and he was facing the ledge, Scott placed his foot on the man's backside to push him forward as he released his hold of the wrists.

Had the man simply bent his knees and dropped, he would have slid to a stop on the rooftop. Instead, he struggled to stay on his feet, stumbling forward until he toppled over the short wall at the roof's edge. His brief scream was silenced when he landed with a thump.

Scott turned to face the others. The gunman had landed on his head, his body covering the wounded man with the rope. Both looked to be unconscious, but Scott did not know how long they would remain that way. Mike's father stepped back to watch, still standing between Scott and the door. The odds shifted to even, provided Mike's father kept back and the other two stayed down. Scott had no time to worry about them, as Mike was already charging with ready fists.

* * *

Lois and Lex rushed out the back door, after hearing what sounded like a gun. Rich was across the yard preparing his grill. Doris, Carol, and Danny sat at a picnic table nearby. They had been discussing their plans for the afternoon's picnic when they also heard the bang.

Lois and Lex ran to ask about Scott, and about the bang they heard.

They were looking up when Lois asked, "Rich, did you just blow something up?"

"I haven't lit anything yet," said Rich. "I think it was something on the roof."

Carol let out a short scream as she saw a man stumble over the edge of the roof. They began running to the fallen man, but stopped when Carol yelled, "There's someone fighting up there!"

Danny continued running to the fallen man, but the others stopped to look up. The fight quickly moved away from the edge and out of sight.

"That looked like Scott. He's dressed in black like he was last night." Doris looked to the others and added, "It looked like he was fighting with some hairy bald guy."

Lois looked to see the fighting men again, but only for a moment. "That's Scott and Mike!" Grabbing the small fire extinguisher from Rich's grilling tools, Lois ran toward the back door of the building.

Lex looked to see them too. She screamed, "DADDY!" and ran to follow Lois.

Danny returned and said to Rich, "You better call the cops." He looked back to the man on the ground. "And an ambulance, but I don't think they can help him."

As Rich ran to make the call, a confused Carol asked, "Did Lex just yell Daddy?"

* * *

Lois led the way up and around the stairs until she emerged at the doorway onto the roof. Winded from running up the stairs, she stopped to catch her breath. Lex began to go around her, but Lois stopped her so they could assess the situation before they were seen. Scott and Mike appeared to be boxing, with an occasional kick being attempted and blocked. Most of their punches were blocked, while strikes that made contact seemed to have little effect. Other than the back of his shirt being torn, and half gone, Scott appeared to be holding his own.

An older man stood closer to the doorway, but still had his back to Lois and Lex. Another man knelt on one knee, examining someone who appeared to be unconscious. The kneeling man got to his feet and hurried to the other without looking back to the door. Lois heard him say, "Joey's shot, and I can't wake him up."

The older man looked out to the sound of approaching sirens. He looked at the other and said, "This is taking too long. Pick up your gun; it's time to end this and get out of here."

"What about Joey?"

"If he can't walk, put one in his head to keep him quiet."

The younger looked at a gun lying on the roof and began walking in that direction. The old man called, "Time's up! We gotta get out o' here!"

When the old man's hand went into the lapel of his coat, Lois was certain he was reaching for a gun. She moved close as she pulled the pin from the fire extinguisher. Stepping to the man's side, Lois pointed the fire extinguisher at his face and squeezed her trigger.

The old man let out a brief yell as he tried to shield his face, already covered with white chemical dust. Closing his eyes, he reached into his coat again. Lois could see the pistol when his hand came out from his coat. She swung the extinguisher around and down on his wrist, knocking the gun from his hand. As the extinguisher came down, Lois continued its movement, circling around and up to strike the old man in the face. With an audible moan, he fell back like a falling tree.

The second man was bending to pick up his gun when Lex tackled him, knocking him over and beyond the weapon. Lex landed on top of him and quickly scrambled back for the gun. The man rolled over and kicked at Lex's head, knocking her over.

Dazed from the kick, Lex felt the man grab hold of her wrist and twist the gun from her hand. Lex pushed into the man, grabbing the gun barrel with both hands, only to fall over backward when his free hand punched the side of her head.

With the gun in his hand, he looked up just in time to see a fire extinguisher swinging toward his face. He brought both arms up defensively and rolled back with the blow, hearing the words, "DON'T TOUCH MY DAUGHTER!"

Before Lois could look at Lex, she heard the word "BITCH!" yelled somewhere behind her. She turned to see the older man had retrieved his gun and was climbing back to his feet.

His face was still white, offering hope that his eyes were also affected by the spray. Lois stepped to the side to move away from Lex, while watching his head turn to follow her. Watching his gun come up, Lois had no doubts about his vision. At least she had moved away, so Lex was no longer behind her and in his line of fire. She wondered if another spray might create enough of a cloud to obstruct his aim. He might even bring his hands back to cover his face again. Lois would never know if that would have worked, as she found herself frozen in place when she heard the shot.

Lois was still staring at the old man when a red dot appeared and began to grow on his chest. The gun was still in his hand as his knees bent, and he fell forward.

Realizing that she was uninjured, Lois turned to see the man who had kicked and punched Lex. The smoking gun was still in hand.

"That asshole wanted me to kill my brother." Laying his gun on the rooftop, he said, "I'm done," and returned to his wounded brother.

Mike had ignored his father's call but turned to look when he heard the shot. He watched his father fall as Scott landed a solid fist to the side of his head. Scott followed with another fist to Mike's face and yet another, which spun Mike to see the rooftop rising to meet him.

Mike opened his eyes to find himself lying on his stomach, one hand firmly held behind his back, and Scott's knee on the side of his head to hold him down.

The sirens had stopped, and the first two policemen stepped through the doorway to the rooftop. Scott released his hold, stood up, and backed away from Mike. Scott held his hands up, allowing the officers to see that he was unarmed and not attacking anyone.

Mike surveyed his situation as he rose to his feet. Joey now lay on his back with his shirt open. His brother knelt to hold the cloth that had been Scott's gag against his wound. An officer beside them talked into his radio while the other shook his head and stepped away from Mike's father.

Mike looked upset and satisfied, as he faced Scott. "I had you. If they hadn't distracted me, you would be down."

"If you say so." Scott stayed back, while keeping his eyes on Mike. "Either way, it's over."

Lex was walking to join her father when a breeze blew the back of his torn shirt. When she saw a bloody line across his back, she called out, "Dad, are you alright?"

"I'm fine," answered Scott. "Thanks for the assist. You helped even the odds."

Hearing this, Mike instantly looked to see Lex for the first time. His gaze shifted from Lex to Lois and back again, as if reading signs which read 'mother' and 'daughter.' He looked down at his father before turning to lunge into Scott, pushing him back toward the edge of the roof. Scott bent his knees and dropped, sliding on the roof, and stopping when he hit the short wall at its edge. Mike stumbled over Scott, falling onto the ledge wall, and rolling over it.

Scott reached for Mike as he went over, managing to catch hold of his ankle. Scott held tightly as Mike's weight pulled his arm over the ledge. Scott held his body against the short wall, anchoring himself as he fought to maintain his grip on Mike.

Scott looked back to the others. "I can't hold him. We need that rope!"

Lex grabbed the rope and ran to Scott. Lois took one end of the rope and tied it to a metal vent pipe while Lex dropped the other end down to Mike.

Scott called out, "The rope is too small to hold. Grab it and wrap it around your hand and wrist, and then grab it again. Your grip will hold like a knot that way." With his free hand, Scott grabbed part of the loose rope, winding, and grabbing it as he had instructed Mike.

Dangling from one leg, Mike managed to catch hold of the rope and began rotating his wrist to wind it around as much as he could. As soon as he grabbed hold of the rope again, his ankle slipped from Scott's hand, and he began to fall. He had only dropped for a moment when he jerked to a stop, now hanging from the rope wound around his wrist.

Scott had the rope wound around one wrist and hand, while his other hand covered it so the two hands could pull together. He managed to pull high enough to get his hands over the ledge, gaining some leverage with the rope folding over the wall. Lois, Lex, and the police officers helped to pull Scott back into a seated position, until his legs were straight and braced against the wall.

Grabbing the narrow rope and turning their hands for grip, they were able to slowly pull Mike upward. When Scott got some slack in the rope, he wound it around his wrist to grip and hold, so they could all get a fresh grip to pull again.

Working together, they soon had Mike close to the top. One of the policemen was able to grab the back of Mike's shirt and pulled him up enough for Mike's free hand to reach the top of the wall. With that, they were able to pull him up, allowing Mike to roll over the short wall and collapse onto the rooftop.

One officer helped Scott up to his feet, while the other lifted Mike to stand. Scott attempted to loosen the rope which was still tangled and wound around his hand and wrist. He looked at Mike and said, "Okay, now it's over."

When Mike stood and walked around Scott, it was clear to all that he wanted to put distance between himself and that ledge. "Yeah, I guess it is over now." When he was past Scott, Mike looked across the roof, beyond them, and yelled "JOEY! DON'T SHOOT! IT'S OVER!"

Everyone looked back to where Mike had been looking. Having a moment of distraction, Mike skipped back with a powerful sidekick, which caused Scott to stumble back and over the short wall at the ledge.

Mike only had a moment to enjoy his victory, as the rope was still wound around their hands and wrists. Mike was pulled down in an instant, catching the ledge wall with a thump before the rope pulled him over as well.

Scott jerked to a stop when Mike hit the ledge, and again when the rope became tight between him and the vent pipe where Lois had tied the other end. Mike fell past Scott until the rope went tight between them. When Mike's fall took all slack from the line, the rope felt just enough additional tug to slide up and over the top of the pipe, leaving nothing to hold it as it slid over the ledge. Those on the roof attempted to grab the rope, but it was too small to hold and moved too quickly. The rope slipped through their hands, disappearing from the roof with a brief snap.

Chapter 30: Griffin Hospital

Randy Richards was seated in the hospital waiting room when Lois arrived. As she sat near Randy, Lois explained that she wasn't allowed to leave until she finished giving her statement to the police.

"Have you seen Lex?" Lois saw no sign of her in the waiting room. "Scott may need blood, so they let her go first. I told her I would catch up later."

"No.... I haven't seen her." When Randy spoke, Lois could hear the worry in his voice.

"That may be a good sign." Lois tried to sound hopeful. "Maybe Scott wasn't hurt too bad, and they let her see him."

"Scott? Oh, I'm sorry. I forgot about him. He was on top, so the ambulance took him first. The second one was already waiting; I think they put Mike in that one. We had to wait until the first one was back again." Randy seemed to be very confused. "Wait, one of those took another guy. I think he was from the roof?"

"We?" Lois was confused. "You're not here for Scott?"

"No... well, yes... him too." Randy was obviously distracted with worry. "I'm waiting to hear how Rachel is doing. They took her in the third or fourth ambulance."

"Rachel!" She wasn't even on the roof. What happened to Rachel?"

"Something happened to Rachel?" Randy and Lois looked to see Lex approaching with a bottle of water in her hand. Lex pointed to the bandage on her arm, "I had them take a pint of AB Negative, just in case he needs it. What happened to Rachel?"

Randy closed his eyes and took a deep breath, still seeing everything in his mind. "We went out with everyone else, to see what was going on. Doris was filling us in when the bald guy went over the roof. It looked like he was hanging by his foot. The ambulance arrived about that time, but Rich told them to wait because someone still breathing might need it. They said a second ambulance was already on the way, but they saw what was happening, so they waited anyway. The guy on the ground wasn't in any hurry."

"Yeah," Lois recalled, "he landed before Lex, and I went up."

"Anyway, they got the bald guy back on the roof, and everyone started to relax. Then Rachel yelled, *'That's Scott!'* We looked, and Scott was going over the ledge. Rachel was running like she thought she could catch him."

"She tried to catch him?" Lois looked at Randy with wide eyes.

Randy nodded. "Maybe it was her motherly instinct or something. Anyway, Rachel got there just in time for the bald guy to land on her. Then Scott landed on top of him. All three were unconscious, so the ambulance crews just started taking them from the top down."

"Technically," everyone looked up to see Rachel approaching in a wheelchair, which was being pushed by a male nurse, "I helped break their fall, so that should count as a successful catch."

In an instant, Randy was by his wife's side. He wanted to hug her but settling for holding her offered hand.

Lois asked, "Rachel, are you alright?"

"Nothing too serious. The X-ray dude took more pictures than Ray. Then they did a cat scan to see if my brain was still there. I did manage to break my leg again, but at least I'm conscious."

"Thank God." Randy let out a sigh of relief. "I can't believe you tried to catch them."

"By myself, I might add. Maybe if you had been there with me, we might have done a little better." Rachel looked at Lex, "It was cool though. I bet Scott never tried a catch like that before." Rachel took a deep breath and turned to face Randy. "I did get a thorough examination while I was here. Randy, would you believe their x-rays showed that I was pregnant, and I lost the baby?"

"Oh no. I'm so sorry." Randy knelt, squeezing his wife's hand.

"Not as sorry as you're going to be. We already have five, and that is enough." Rachel turned to the male nurse who was standing close by. "This nice man-nurse is going to lead you back to meet Dr. Snipes." Rachel grinned at Lex. "Isn't this great? With all that's going on, they still had an extra doctor on hand for Randy?" She looked back to Randy with a stern expression. "Dr. Snipes is preparing for a special operation, and you will be up and walking before dinner. Afterward, you get to relax and take it easy for a few days. Just think of how much you'll enjoy that." Rachel looked back to Lois. "His name really is Dr. Snipes too. With a name like that, he should open his own vasectomy clinic. Get Snipped by Snipes. Isn't that a great motto? I can see it on the billboards now."

Randy started to speak, but Rachel stopped him. "No backtalk! Follow the nice man-nurse, and I will be checking for a scar. It's Dr. Snips now, or I'm calling Doug Paterson tomorrow. No ifs, ands, butts, or vaginas. We already discussed this last time. Now get!"

"I guess I'll catch up with you guys later." Randy stood with a dejected shrug and followed the grinning male-nurse down the hall.

Lois looked at her cousin and said, "Rachel, I am sorry to hear about the baby."

"What baby?" Rachel began rolling her chair to join them. "Oh that. They had an intern on hand, and Randy needs incentive. I didn't really say there WAS a baby. I said, *'Would you believe?'* That throws it up in the air like, *bullshit or not?* Randy knows that by now. We've had a few scares this year, so I wasn't going to let this chance slip by." Rachel looked down and shook her head. "It wouldn't be so bad if he weren't so damn cute. He gives me those puppy eyes; the next thing I know I'm riding him like a mechanical bull. It's his fault for being so damn cute." She looked at Lois with a serious face. "Any word about Scott?"

"Not yet."

Unable to hold it, Lex let out a small laugh.

Rachel turned to look at her. "What are you laughing at?"

"I'm sorry, Cousin Rachel, just listening to you sometimes ... I really do think you're cool." Lex held two fingers up like scissors and made a snipping motion.

"What's with the cousin talk?" Rachel looked confused. "I'm cousin to Scott's other girlfriend, remember? And what was with that Daddy talk I heard about? Word back at the school is you're Mike's daughter."

"Okay." Lex thought and corrected herself. "You are my first cousin, once removed, and I'm no relation to Mike." She glanced back to Lois, "Just ask Mom. She'll tell ya."

Lois grinned at Rachel. "Rachel, I would like to introduce you to my daughter, Lex."

Lex looked back to Rachel. "Miranda Alexis Vanderzee Michelson Severson, alive and in the flesh. That's a mouthful, so just call me Lex."

Rachel looked from Lois to Lex and back again, "Are you shitting me?"

"Remember the morning after our graduation party? When I came back to the party wearing Scott's shirt?"

"Your hair was wet. I figured you both went skinny dipping."

"That was before we took a shower. And after ..." Lois motioned to Lex.

Lex shrugged her shoulders. "I missed that party by nine months."

"For real? And you didn't know until now? Just how drunk were you? I mean, every time I popped out a kid, I remembered it."

"It's a long story. I never said I was Scott's girlfriend." Lex set her hand on Lois's, "I wanted to meet my mother, and Dad couldn't say no."

"Does Randy know about this?"

Lois shook her head. "You're the first we've told. I just found out this morning."

Rachel grinned and looked at Lex. "Okay, if we time this right, we can probably get potato chips to shoot out Randy's nose again."

Lois suddenly stood up in surprise. "Mom! Dad! What are you doing here?"

Lex and Rachel looked to see Lois's parents walking into the waiting room. Her mother stepped over to hug Lois. "We got home, and the answering machine had a message from Lex."

"We came right away. Is there any news about Scott?"

"Nothing yet. Thanks for coming Gramps." Lex stood to hug Storm.

Lois looked at her parents and Lex with confusion. "You know Lex?"

"Why else would he have let me call him Gramps this morning?"

"I thought you were just being disrespectful to an older man."

"Okay. Explanations, round two." Lex took a deep breath. "Roxanne was dying of Cancer. We brought her to see an oncologist who came to this hospital. While we were here, Dad saw Gramps was here, so we stopped to see him."

"I had some heart problems at the time," Storm explained. "I was in my room, and Scott stopped to visit. The moment I saw Little Lex, I knew who she was." He looked at Lois, "She was the spitting image of you at that age."

"Dad couldn't lie. Remember I said anyone who figured it out had to keep the secret? Gramps was one of those people. Dad told Gramps a few things about Mike too. And he talked to him about seeing you again." Lex stood next to Storm with one arm around him. "I got my grandparents, so the only thing missing was Mom. Now I have her too."

Lois asked, "Who else knew?"

"Ray and Samantha visit Dad a lot, so he had to explain how he suddenly had a seven-year-old daughter. Also, there's Aunt Nancy in Chicago, but she doesn't count because she's in the adopted family. Now if Peter had checked with her, she would have sent him straight to us a long time ago."

"Damn." Rachel shook her head. "I should be taking notes. I could sell this family as a soap opera. But who would believe it?"

PART 6: TWENTY-FIVE-YEAR REUNION

Chapter 31: O'Brian's Resort

After our twenty-year reunion, it was assumed that all future reunions would be held at the Old School Hotel. It had become the in-place for class reunions. They even had reunions there for schools from neighboring cities. Fortunately, none of the other reunions came with the drama of our twentieth. When it was time for our Twenty-Five-year reunion, we were all surprised to learn it would be at O'Brian's Pike Lake Resort.

To save time, I will just give you a quick summary of what happened at the Old School Hotel. The hotel was doing well with its hotel, supper club, bar, and event bookings. Doris did have some problems with Rich's wandering eye, but she began keeping him on a shorter leash, and things were going well. That is, things went well until their mystery investor, or silent partner, came for a stay in the principal's suit. Nadine preferred life in the big city but felt the need to check on her investment from time to time.

Doris herself was doing housekeeping duties that day. The door did not have a Do Not Disturb sign on it, so Doris simply knocked before entering.

Rich and Nadine did not hear Doris's knock, nor did they hear when she called out, "Housekeeping!" as she entered. Doris later reported that Rich and Nadine were so preoccupied when she found them that she nearly had to throw cold water on them before they realized she was there. According to Dave Masters, his marriage to Nadine ended pretty much the same way.

The Old School was appraised for the dividing of assets. In its few years of operation, the hotel had done well, and was worth far more than their original investments. Nadine bought out the others' shares, making her the sole owner of The Old School. Since then, she hired a series of managers and consultants to run the hotel for her.

The retiring businessman who had purchased The Pike Lake Resort may have been good in his previous career, but he knew very little about running a country resort. When The Old School was being appraised, he decided it was time to cut his losses as well. His asking price was significantly less than he originally paid, but he bought the resort when it was a successful business. Nadine's purchase of the hotel included Danny's bar, giving Danny and Carol enough profit to purchase the resort.

A new restaurant was added to the bar, along with other improvements to the resort. Under Danny and Carol's management, the resort, bar, and restaurant recovered to become a successful business.

The Old School was still a great place for class reunions, but our reunion committee saw Nadine's affair as an insult to one in our class. Rather than giving their business to Nadine and her hired managers, they decided to bring the reunion back to O'Brian's Resort. For us, the resort inspired enough good memories to be nearly as nostalgic as the school.

The dance hall was decorated, a band was set up, and all was ready for the evening's reunion. Extra help had been hired so Carol and Danny would be able to take much of the night off to join in the festivities. Their restaurant was open to the public, as was the bar, but the dance hall was reserved for our reunion. Our dinner in the dance hall was handled by Doris Lester, who had left the hotel to open her own catering business.

* * *

Naturally, Danny O'Brian opened the bar on the day of our reunion and continued working for some time after other bartenders arrived to replace him. Fishermen and others were in and out, keeping Danny busy throughout the day. Dave and Eve Masters arrived to wait at the bar, while Danny was serving a pair of fishermen.

Danny hurried to greet his old classmates with, "Carol wins the pool. Let me guess, a Manhattan and a Tom Collins?"

"You have a good memory," said Dave. "What pool?"

"We were betting on who would be the first ones here for the reunion. Getting keys for a cabin doesn't count, so unless you want a cabin, Carol wins."

"No cabin. We're already staying in town." Dave paid for their drinks. "Has someone else rented a cabin already?"

"Randy and Rachel. They like to rent a room so they can tip back a few and not have to drive home."

Dave turned to look around the bar. "It's hard to believe our last reunion here was twenty years ago."

"I still remember that night," Eve turned to look at Dave. "I was so looking forward to seeing you. With your Ivy League schooling behind you, I was hoping you would want to pick up where we left off. I was hoping to bring you home to meet your daughter. Instead, you showed up with a fiancé and didn't even remember me."

Dave set his hand on Eve's. "I always remembered you. I was just trying to move on in a different life."

"Maybe you remembered more than you realized." Danny wiped off the bar in front of them. "As I recall, Nadine looked enough like Eve to pass as sisters. Did you ever wonder if her resemblance to Eve was what attracted you to Nadine?"

Dave raised his glass in salute to Danny. "That's a good possibility. It's even better if my wife buys it and loves me more."

"Not possible." Eve slid her hand from under Dave's.

"What's not possible? You buying his theory? Or loving me more?"

"That's for you to figure out." Eve rested her hand on Dave's leg and gently squeezed.

Dave looked at Danny. "So how many did you have in this pool? Most of our class is still up and active."

"Yeah, but there's a handful we can always count on. Those who never miss a reunion, no matter where they are."

The door opened and the Richards came in, followed by Lois and Scott Severson. Rachel called out, "Stinger time," as she climbed onto a bar stool.

Danny asked, "All around?"

"I'll have a Diet Coke." Lois seated herself on a stool. "The last time I had stingers in this bar, I woke up in a strange cabin wondering what happened to my clothes."

"You could use that as a testimonial for your bar." Rachel raised her hands, fingers up and thumbs out, as if framing an image. "I can see it on the billboards now. They'll be coming from miles around."

"Will Lex be joining us later?" Danny asked as he set the drinks on the bar. "We did make her an honorary classmate."

"She's home this weekend, but she decided not to come." Lois grinned. "She said she'd rather stay home and hang out with her little brother."

"Little brother?" Carol appeared from the kitchen, which was behind the back wall of the bar. "Remind me to ask the reunion committee if they have a *'Damn, they're still doing it'* award this year?"

Scott let out a small laugh. "Well, I am still younger than my dad was when I was born. I think he did alright."

"He was a bit of a surprise, but we are happy about it," said Lois. "He's four now."

"Four? Sounds like another reunion-baby. Didn't Lex show up just nine months after our graduation party? And let's not forget, Katherine was born just nine months after our five-year reunion." Danny looked at Scott, "As I recall, Scott drove Carol home that night."

Scott held one hand up as if taking an oath. "I swear, I only tucked her in and kissed her good night."

"I know," Carol said with a pout. "I was so disappointed."

"Well, Thomas Storm JUST turned four, so he was a few months AFTER the reunion, Baby." Lois reached to hold Scott's hand. "We were even married by then."

"Is that your souvenir from our last reunion?" Dave gestured to the cane Scott used while walking in.

Scott lifted his cane. "I don't really need it now, but it is still a comfort. Also, I thought I should keep it on hand, just in case I need a weapon for Mike and any goons."

In time, they were joined by a man wearing the dress uniform of an Army Major. As Danny served him, he recognized him as Carol's cousin, Alvin Murphy.

"First one is on the house," Danny said before Alvin could pay. "It's about time you showed up for a reunion. I haven't seen you since our graduation party."

"Thanks Danny. I haven't been home much since then."

"It's great to see you," said Eve.

"It's good seeing you, too, Eve. You haven't changed a bit."

"More than you might think." She squeezed Dave's hand. "Al, I've always wondered. You and Mike went into the army together. How did he get out so quick?"

"Mike Burman ..." Alvin looked up as he recalled. "Basically, the army realized that he was not a good fit. He was better at getting into trouble than taking orders. Trying to hook up with a Colonel's sixteen-year-old daughter didn't help either. By the time basic training was done, they had decided to demote him back to civilian. Otherwise, the Colonel might have had him shot."

After another round of catching up with Alvin, a lady entered the bar holding the arm of a thin, nervous-looking man, leading him as they walked to the bar. She helped him onto a barstool and asked for a 7UP and a kiddie cocktail. When Danny set the drinks on the bar, the thin man grabbed the tall glass and sucked on its straw.

He looked at Danny and said, "Thank you," with a childlike voice and expression.

Hearing his voice, Eve turned to recognize his features. "You have got to be kidding me." The others also turned to realize the thin man was Mike Burman.

The lady looked up and asked, "Do you people know Mikey?"

Lois nodded. "Oh yes. We all know him."

The lady smiled, "I'm so glad. I heard his class was having a reunion here tonight. I was hoping he might be able to see some old friends, even if he doesn't remember them. There is the possibility that someone will trigger a memory, and it's a nice outing for Mikey anyway." She held her hand out to Lois, "My name is Florence Crain. You can call me Flo. I'm one of the people who takes care of Mikey."

The surprised Lois shook Flo's hand. "I'm Lois. Mike was my first husband."

"Oh, how nice!" Flo turned to Mike. "Mikey, this is Lois. She was once married to you."

"It wasn't exactly nice. He beat me and killed his puppy. He's also the reason I spent much of my life hiding in other states."

Mikey looked at Lois, smiling as he turned to look at Flo and said, "She's pretty."

Confused, Eve got off her stool and walked to him. "I'm Eve. I was Mike's second wife. We got married after a date rape pregnancy. I escaped when he started hitting me. He also kidnapped my son and used him as his dope mule."

Flo turned to Mikey. "This is Eve. She was also married to you. She says you and she have a son together."

Mikey grinned wide again, and once more turned to Flo and said, "She's pretty too."

Using his cane as he walked, Scott stepped over to Mike and shook his hand. "I'm Scott. We've had a few fights over the years. The last one ended when you threw us both off a building."

"Oh, I'm so sorry," Flo said to the group. "I heard that he was quite unpleasant in his past life. That Mike is gone now. Mikey is, in a way, a whole new person. Like I said, I don't expect him to remember anyone, but I thought it would be good for him to get out."

Mikey shook Scott's hand and smiled. "Hiiee."

Dave stepped over to shake Mike's hand. "Dave Masters. You destroyed a valuable desk and stole a lot of money from me."

Mikey smiled and shook Dave's hand. "Hiiee." Turning to Flo, he said, "He wears a nice suit."

Alvin stepped over to shake Mikey's hand. "I'm Major Alvin Murphy. We went in the army together, but they let you go."

When he saw Alvin's dress uniform, Mike turned to Flo, saying, "His suit is neat."

"I suppose this is confusing to you." Flo looked from person to person. "The Mike you knew, in a way, he died five years ago. When he came out from his coma, his mind was a complete blank. He really is a whole new person. He doesn't know or remember anything from before he woke up in our care. He has improved a great deal since then. He talks some, and he's learning to do a lot of things by himself."

Rachel stepped over to shake Mikey's hand. "I'm Rachel. You once jumped off a three-story building, and I caught you. I was trying to catch Scott, but he stopped to ask directions on the way down, so you landed first. I guess you won that race."

Mikey said to Flo, "She has red hair, and she's pretty."

Eve looked amazed as she shook her head. "If I didn't see it with my own two eyes...."

Carol gave Mikey a pleasant smile. "I was Carol Murphy when we were in school."

Mikey grinned and said, "She's nice."

After finishing his kiddy cocktail, Mikey set his glass down and said to Flo, "I have to go."

Flo helped Mikey down from his bar stool and asked Danny where the restrooms were. She walked Mikey to the door and asked him if he needed help.

Mikey said, "I can do it," and went into the restroom alone. Flo waited by the door, listening in case Mikey called her with any problems.

When Mike came out, Flo asked him if he had washed his hands. He nodded with pride and returned to the bar with her. She explained, "Going to the restroom by himself is a big accomplishment. He is very proud of that."

After Mikey got back onto his barstool, he stared for a moment before rolling his eyes, and sat without moving for close to a minute. Flo saw this and held him to prevent him from falling. Flo explained, "It's hard to explain what's happening right now. It's sort of like having little stokes in his brain, and he's having them much more frequently."

When Mikey opened his eyes again, he looked around and said, "Hiiee." When he saw Lois smile at him, he said to Flo, "She's pretty."

Flo looked at him and said, "Mikey, you just had another event, so it's time for us to leave."

"Okayyy." He got up from his stool and took Flo's hand.

As they began to walk away, Scott said, "Have a good trip Mikey. Maybe we'll see you in five years,"

Flo stopped to look back. "I'm sorry, but I don't think so. These little strokes have been getting worse, and I don't think he'll be with us much longer. That is why I was happy to be able to take him out today. I'm just sorry he couldn't stay longer and see more of you. He may not show it, but I know Mikey was happy to see all of you."

Lois said, "I'm sorry to hear that. You have a nice trip home Mikey. And thank you for bringing him."

Listening to Lois, Mikey grinned at Flo to say, "She's pretty." Everyone watched in silence as Flo walked Mikey out the door.

* * *

At five o'clock, the bar began filling up with classmates. Doris arrived to set up the buffet. When all was set, and her roasters were heating, Doris went to the bar to talk to her friends.

Nadine, Dave's first wife, walked into the bar as if on a mission. She looked around and walked straight to where Doris was sitting. "Doris, you never return my calls. I was hoping I would find you here. Can we please talk?"

"I never return your calls because we don't have anything to discuss, Nadine."

"I know what I did is unforgivable, but I still wish we could get past it. I need your help, so tell me, what I can do to get it?"

Doris gave Nadine a stern look. "I have no interest in working under one of your managers. When Rich ran the hotel, I ran the restaurant, and nobody interfered. Then you took my husband for a test drive, and now the hotel is yours. I see no reason why I should work for you."

"I'm sorry about what happened with Rich. He smiled... I grinned... and I will always regret it. You are right about my managers. I'm on the third one since you left, and they are all idiots. I need YOU, Doris. I do not want you to work for me; I want you to work with me, or without me. What I need is for you to be there and IN CHARGE."

"I tried running the restaurant after Rich left. That didn't work!"

"That's because one of those idiot managers interfered. I know Rich didn't really run the hotel anyway; you did. Everyone working there said so."

"Why do you even care? With your trust fund, you could just sell it for scrap and forget about it."

Nadine shook her head. "Too much of my trust fund is invested in my father's company. It's been going down as fast as Dave's company has been going up. What's more important, Father laughed at me when I invested in the hotel. He LAUGHED at me. It was the same way that he laughed when Dave started his own company. I need it to be a success again. I need you, Doris. How about ten percent; is that enough?"

"Ten percent of what?"

"Fifteen percent of the hotel... and I mean all of it."

"You mean like partners?"

"Like partners. With me going back to being the silent one who can stay in New York. I know what I like, but I know nothing about running a hotel in Griffin. Neither do any of the consultants or the managers I've hired. They're constantly calling me to come back here; it's like they're proud of their incompetence and want to be sure I'm aware of it. If you own fifteen percent of it, you will be building it up for yourself, not just for me. Is there any way we can make that work?"

Doris gave it some thought. "So let me get this straight. You want to give me twenty percent of The Old School, so I run it as I see fit, and you still get eighty percent of the profit."

Nadine smiled. "I saw what you did there. Okay, you own fifteen percent now, and you run the hotel with no interference from me. You have one hundred percent control, and I remain a silent partner. After one full year of it running in the black, we turn your fifteen percent into twenty. Will that work?"

Doris looked pleased with this idea. "I'll think about it and call you back tomorrow."

"Deal." Nadine held her hand out to Doris.

Doris shook her hand. "I'll call tomorrow."

Doris hurried to tell Carol of Nadine's offer. "I hate it, but I think I'd like to take her up on it. The only problem is, I don't want to be competing with you guys. We've always been a team; I don't want us to be enemies."

Having heard it all, Danny said, "We wouldn't really be competitors you know. We have a resort, and you'll have a hotel. You'll have a supper club; we have country dining for the family. We're on the lake; you have a pool. Together, we fill two different needs. Sometimes people will be deciding between you or us, but there are enough customers for both. Some hotel guests might want to get away and eat here, and some cabin folk might want a fancier dinner from you. Do what you want Doris. Don't give competing with us a second thought. We could even work some promotions together."

Doris thought about that. "I wonder if I can raise my percentage higher over time. She might be willing to sell more of the business later. Maybe I can work with Nadine... if I'm working without her. I should hold a grudge for what happened with Rich, but he was as much the blame as she was. To be honest, I'm sure she wasn't his first. She was just the one I walked in on. Seeing it live kind of brings it to life."

Nadine was on her way out but stopped when she saw Dave with Eve. "I'm sorry, it would be rude of me to walk by without saying hello."

Dave said, "Hello, Nadine. I hope you are doing well."

Nadine glanced back to where Doris was talking with Danny and Carol. "Possibly? I do think things will be improving soon." She looked at Eve, "It's nice to see you again, Eve. I hope Dave has been taking good care of you."

"We take good care of each other."

Nadine studied Eve's face. "I do see it, you know. When you married Dave, people said he married you because you resembled me. I do see that. What my friends do not realize is that he knew you first. You had a child together. It hurts to admit it, but I believe he married me, because I was his doppelganger for you."

Eve took Dave's hand. "It doesn't matter. You can tell them he married me for being your doppelganger. Just don't let them say that I took him away from you. I kept my distance when you were with Dave. I didn't even tell him about Ivy. They figured that out all by themselves."

"I know, and I appreciate that. If Dave doesn't mind, I would still like to be your friend."

"Just don't ask Eve to talk me into working for your father again. That will never happen."

"I know. It's his loss, and I will not make excuses for him. He laughed when you left to focus on your own company; he's not laughing any more. He even tried to duplicate what you do, and he failed miserably."

Dave shook his head. "He doesn't duplicate what I do. When he gets a business, he looks at buildings, machinery, and customers. He never sees his most valuable assets. He decides to cut costs, so he eliminates the higher-paid workers who know what they're doing. He hangs on to dead weight because they look good on paper. He sees dollars and cents, but he has no eye for value. Do you remember when he said he would end up buying my companies anyway? I bought one from him last week. I'm going to enjoy turning this one around."

Nadine smiled. "I hope you do. Please don't tell Father, but since Masters Enterprises went public ... let's just say my trust fund has begun diversifying in that direction."

"I promise, he will never hear it from me."

* * *

Doris was still talking to Carol when Rich Lester approached to ask, "Can we talk?"

Doris turned to see him. "There's a lot of that going around tonight." Excusing herself from Carol, she walked with Rich to an empty table. "I don't see your girlfriend. I seem to recall losing a young waitress when you left for Florida."

Rich looked down sheepishly. "That ended when we got to Florida. A cute young chick may sound like fun, but when the fun is over, that's all it was. The last thing I want is another fling like that. Or any fling."

"So, you've seen the errors of your ways and want me to take you back?"

Rich looked at her hopefully. "I would like that. I do love you, Doris. I always have, and I always will. I've made mistakes, and I will always regret them."

"How many?" Doris waited for an answer. "How many mistakes have you made? How many more would you have made if you had only gotten the chance? I know Nadine wasn't your first, nor will that valley girl be your last. Your flirtatious compliments were never jokes. I know that you were willing to roll with anyone who responded with a smile. I tried to ignore it.

I tried not to see it when it happened. You always had little excuses when you were late, and I'm guilty of not calling you on them when I should have."

"I do love you, Doris."

"I know. I love you too, Rich, and I always will. For so many years, I wanted nothing more than to grow old with you. Unfortunately, I don't want to grow old alone because you're off chasing some side action when my back is turned. Since you left, I spent so many nights wishing you would come back, wishing we could give it another try. If you had come back sooner, we might have tried." Doris shook her head. "I can't believe I'm saying this, but I won't go through that again. I can't trust your promises because I know just how much they're worth. If you want my forgiveness, you have to earn it."

"I can change."

"Anyone CAN change, but we know they seldom do. Any promise of change is nothing but an empty promise. Now if you're interested in proving it, I may give you a chance." Doris took a deep breath and looked Rich in the eyes. "I will never settle for a promise, but I may consider something after I've seen results. You should get a job and move back to Griffin. Then you might even develop a relationship with your children. You should live by yourself and take care of yourself. Try to set a good example; become someone our children can be proud of. In time, if I see a real change in you, I may give it some thought."

Rich looked hopeful. "That sounds reasonable."

"Yes, it is. But don't think that means I'm going to sit and wait for you to prove your loyalty. I'm not looking, but if my shining prince comes along, I have a lot of time to make up for." Doris looked at the time and stood up. "Let me know where you land, and I'll pass it on to the kids. It's time I checked on the buffet." She began to walk away, but paused to look back and say, "Good luck Rich."

Chapter 32: Dave Sums us up

At six o'clock Doris removed the covers from her roasters, and it was announced that the buffet line was open. Our meal was excellent, and that would not be the last meal Doris prepared for us.

Danny and Carol's children, Katherine, Sean, and Rebecca, began bussing tables as we finished eating. The O'Brian children were regular helpers at the resort, but this night they were working for Doris. With the aid of the young O'Brians, Doris had everything cleaned and put away before the band began to play.

After completing his kitchen duties, 17-year-old Sean returned to Dave Masters' table, asking if they could speak for a few minutes. Dave pushed an empty chair out for Sean and asked, "What's on your mind?"

Sean sat facing Dave and explained, "I'll be graduating next year, and Dad says I should go to college. The thing is, I'm tired of school. I'd rather just get a job. Dad said I should talk to you because you know the value of an education."

Dave looked at Danny, who was sitting at the next table. "Are you sure you want him to hear what I say, Dan?"

Danny said, "I trust you. I figure you know more than either of us on this subject."

Dave turned back to Sean. "When I was your age, my only goal was to get an Ivy League Education. That was important to me, and I worked very hard for it. I got it, and it worked well for me. That was what I needed for the road I wanted. What matters for you, is what road you want to take."

"Doesn't college help you in every job?"

Dave shook his head. "Some people think so. Some think the only important thing is to HAVE a diploma, but they give no thought as to what they put into it. Some companies hire that way too. I've come across a lot of companies that are failing for just that reason. When I buy a company, one of the first things I do is look over the people working there. I almost always find someone who sits at a desk because they have a diploma, but their degree is no better for that job than a high school diploma. I've come across a lot of educated idiots too. People who know what they were taught, but never learned to think beyond that. They weren't educated; they were programmed. I do expect a degree in higher management positions, but I expect that degree to be good for what they're doing. I also expect management to listen to the workers, regardless of their education. Experience sometimes teaches things never dreamed of in a classroom."

Dave pointed to where Scott was sitting. "Scott's father offered to send him to college. Scott told him that he already knew how to think, and he was right. Give Scott any problem, and he'll find a solution. Scott likes working with wood, and he has a great eye for detail. He is a master at what he does, so his products sell for incredible amounts. His experience is his education. When he needs to, he does his own research to learn more."

Dave turned to gesture to Ray. "Ray Ellis started working at Griffin Metal Works right after high school. He just wanted a job. He got on-the-job training and learned to run most of the machines there. After a while, he took night classes and added machinist to his resume. Now, Ray can run every machine in the shop. He's also very creative with his personal projects, some of which we may find a market for. Scott tells me that some of his tools are things he and Ray designed and made together. I asked Ray if he ever thought about going to school to become an engineer. He said that he tried, but they gave him an I.Q. test and said his score was 20 points too high."

Dave looked out to the dance floor. "That's Craig Roberts and his wife Ruth. Craig went to college for a year. I think he majored in cannabis and beer pong. College was no more than extended high school for him. Craig had no real goal, and no real interest in higher learning. It was good that he dropped out to get a regular job."

Dave looked around and pointed out Vanessa and Lord Max as they walked to the dance floor. "Vanessa didn't plan on going to college, but she got a scholarship and went anyway. Her goal was to join the Peace Corps and help people in underdeveloped areas. She planned all her classes around that goal. She took a heavy load of courses, and she made good use of what she learned. She didn't care about the degree; she just wanted to learn what she needed to know. Vanessa was her own success long before she married her English Lord. She didn't need college, but she made good use of it."

Dave pointed to where Randy and Rachel were now dancing. "Rachel's real talent is her personality, but she is a lot more than that. Randy sparked her interest in radio, so she learned everything about that business. Rachel had some regular college. She also took night classes and correspondence courses. She got her bachelor's degree, but just being Rachel is her true talent." Dave leaned close and said, "You may be hearing more from her too. From what I hear, she and Randy are considering an offer from the Twin Cities station where they both started. If so, they may even become regulars at your father's resort."

Watching Randy and Rachel on the dance floor, Sean asked, "Why is their hair wet? It wasn't wet before we ate."

Dave grinned. "If they do move back, maybe you'll be able to figure that out."

Sean was confused, but he decided to drop that subject.

Dave gestured to Peter Baker. "Now Pete went to college and learned everything about computers. He worked with them for a while, until he found something he liked better. No one would have ever guessed Peter would turn into a private detective. That was just stuff on TV and movies, but our Peter is the real thing. He still uses computers in his work, but he does a lot without them too. Most of what he learned in college is outdated now, but he keeps up with the changes. College set him up for his first job, but he learned everything he needs for his present career without it."

Dave looked to where Danny and Carol were sitting. "Your dad had a dream of one day owning this resort. For years, your parents worked and saved for that goal. They learned by working and paying attention. What they know is not taught in college. That's why they're succeeding where that businessman failed."

Dave looked at Eve, who smiled silently as she listened to their conversation. "All through school, Eve played the role of a dumb blond. She was never dumb; she just didn't like the attention she got when people realized she was smart. She learned to read when she was three years old, and she's been reading ever since. She would have done fantastic in college, but she worked as a single mother instead. That was my fault. She grew up without much money, so she learned to live without it." Dave leaned close to Sean and said, "Now she can buy anything she wants, and she still makes most of her own clothes." Dave sat up and smiled, "She never had any extended education, but she always has something new to teach me."

Dave looked seriously at Sean. "If school is already boring to you, you wouldn't like the job a diploma got you anyway. You can go to technical school for a fraction of the cost and often end up with a better-paying job in a fraction of the time. Community Ed classes can teach you too. Also, never underestimate your own personal studies."

Dave pointed to Doris Lester. "Doris planned on going to college, but she married Rich to raise a family instead. She helped support her family by cooking in area restaurants. She learned from those jobs, and she took some cooking classes too. When your dad and Rich were remodeling the Old School, she read up on small business and the hospitality industry. She didn't get a degree, but she learned what they needed to know. Now Nadine wants her to run the hotel because she knows how to make it work."

Dave looked to where Rich Lester was sitting by himself. "Rich never thought of going to college. He did have some great ideas, but he didn't have the ambition to succeed alone. His success was getting the right people to help him. I don't know if college would have helped him or not. I suspect that Rich may have fallen into the college party crowd, graduating with nothing more than an empty diploma. It might have gotten him a job, but I don't know if he could have held on to it."

Dave looked at a table across the room. "And there's Greg, or Al; I hear he goes by his first name now. At our graduation party, he told me that he wanted to be a writer someday. He may have some good stories but getting them down on paper the right way is a lot of work, and further education would have helped. He may end up as just another man with an unfinished novel in his closet. Then again, he has managed to work past the odds with a few other goals, so he may surprise us."

Seeing Nadine earlier reminded Dave of his former father-in-law. "The man I used to work for is one who only sees education. He doesn't realize that education and knowledge are not the same thing. He doesn't realize that a man with experience in his job can be more valuable than a man who studied it in school. School does help, but they can't teach experience, and often fail to teach the need for it."

Dave looked into Sean's eyes. "Education is great. I couldn't do what I do without it. For a lot of jobs, you need to know what college teaches. But remember, a college diploma is not the magic token some people think it is. That diploma is only as valuable as you make it. If school is already boring you, and you want to work with your hands, don't waste your time. Do what you enjoy. Remember the old saying, *'A man who enjoys his job, never works a day in his life.'* The same way, if a diploma gets you a job that you hate, you may spend the rest of your life working to be miserable. Keep learning, Sean, but enjoy your life. Income and job title don't make you a success; being happy at what you do does. If you want a career that requires college, go for it. It all comes down to what you want."

Sean stood up, looking happy and satisfied. "Thank you, Mr. Masters. Dad was right when he told me to talk to you."

Dave smiled, "Your dad is a wise man. We can both learn from him."

* * *

The band that evening was good, and the dance floor was usually full. Rich Lester left after the first set, possibly because Doris had been sharing her table, and most of her dances, with Alvin Murphy. For the rest of us, dancing was fun, but visiting with friends often took priority.

Lois laid her head against Scott as they danced to *Pieces of April.* "This is nice." She lifted her head to look into his eyes. "You know, I really do love you."

"I know." The music stopped, and they were walking back to their table when he said, "You always did; you just didn't realize it for a while. I, on the other hand, always did know that I loved you."

"So," Lois dropped into her chair and looked at him, "just how soon did my love for you begin?" She expected him to say something about the night of their graduation party.

"I'm not sure, but it could have been the same day as for me. The country schools were closed, and we all started sixth grade in town. On that first day, I can't recall for sure if I walked in and smiled at you, or if I was sitting when you walked in to smile at me. The days went both ways, so it's hard to recall which came first. The thing is, every morning, we looked and smiled at one another. It had become a daily ritual for us. Unfortunately, we were both too shy to say anything at the time."

Lois looked into Scott's eyes as he continued with his memories. "We went from all grades in a single room, to multiple rooms for our grade alone. We even went to different classrooms for different subjects. They split our class up for one hour each day, so we boys could go to a shop class, while you girls went to the Home Ec room. That was so you could learn to cook and sew, all those things they thought only girls should know."

Scott let his mind drift back with memories of their first year of school together. "February came, and the class was going to have a Valentine's Day party. You girls had recently made Belgian waffles in Home Ec and decided to make them for our party. That's why the party was held in the Home Ec room. Everything you needed to make them was there."

Scott looked up as he recalled, "You all took up different tasks. Someone was mixing batter, some manned the waffle irons, someone was whipping cream, and someone was mashing strawberries to put on top. You had the task of putting them all together. You would put the waffle on the plate, then a big scoop of whipped cream, followed by a big serving spoon of strawberry topping. You piled the strawberries on heavy, almost like you were trying to run out. I was at the end of the line, so I got to you just as you ran out of strawberries. You smiled at me and said, *'Wait just a moment,'* and you opened a fresh can of cherry pie filling. You put a big spoon full of whipped cream on my waffle. Then, you scooped up the cherries. You tipped the spoon, pouring cherries in an arc as you moved it around. Then you did it again, going around in the other direction. When you handed me the plate, I saw that you had put the cherries on the whipped cream in the shape of a heart. I wanted to say something, but all I could do was smile. After I told my mother about it, she started making them that way."

Lois stared at Scott in amazement. "I remember that party. And I remember trying to make a heart with the cherries. I even remember returning your smiles. I had forgotten all about that. Why didn't we get together then?"

"I was still afraid to talk to you. Then another boy beat me to it. It was the age-old fear of rejection. Other boys took turns calling you their girlfriend, and I was just too scared to take my chance."

"I forget who was first to ask me to be his girlfriend, but I remember it always felt like he was my second choice. I had forgotten why. I think it was the second choice feeling that made me break up with him. Then there was another, and another. In junior high school, we just wanted to say we had a boyfriend. I think I even went with Rich for a day... until he tried to grab my boob and I kneed him in the nuts." Lois laughed. "Going steady didn't mean much back then. It was mostly just holding hands and talking at recess. That's what it was until high school anyway. In high school, all I remember was trying to get Mike to cool down. I had forgotten all about that sweet boy who always smiled." Lois thought hard to remember, "You didn't smile at me anymore."

"As I saw it, you belonged to someone else. I just had to wait and bide my time."

Lois looked out to the dance floor. "They're playing another slow song." Scott held out his hand to take hers. Hand in hand they walked onto the dance floor. Lois closed her eyes as they moved slowly with the music. "I'm remembering so much of those early days now. Thinking back now, I can still see your young smile." Lois smiled sweetly at the memory.

Scott held her close. "I always could see yours."

Lois nuzzled her head against him. "This been a long day. I think I'm just about ready for bed."

"If you're tired, we could rent a cabin from Danny and call it a night."

Lois looked up to Scott and curled up the corners of her mouth. "I didn't say I was tired." She laid her head against him again. "I don't think I want a cabin. I can wait until we get home. I would miss our flannel sheets." Lois looked up to see Scott smiling down at her. Resisting the urge to kiss, they simply smiled at one another until the music stopped, and walked hand in hand to their table.

Scott picked up his cane, gave a short wave of goodnight to Ray and Samantha, and held Lois's hand as they walked out the door.

Lex and her little brother would both be sleeping when they got home, but they weren't looking forward to any late-night conversation anyway. It would be some time before sleep overtook them tonight. In the morning, they will make Belgian Waffles together, and Lois will discover that she can still spoon the cherry pie filling into the shape of a heart.

* * *

I am tempted to simply end my story here, but I do not wish to give the impression that our story is over. I'll give this telling a rest for now, but the class of '72 is still going strong. Our twenty-fifth reunion was in 1997, which leaves us with just as many reunions remaining to be shared. I'm not done with these classmates either. There were 98 graduates in our class, each with their own story. We have many more stories to share. I just hope I will have the time to tell them.

* * *

The End

About the Author

Alexander Gregory is the pen name used by Alan Anderson, who lives in Amery Wisconsin. Becoming a writer has been a goal for Al for many years, but earning a living, raising a family, building a home, and life in general always seemed to come first.

After high school Al did not go on to higher education, other than a tech school welding class, some on-the-job training, and a decade of karate lessons. Still, his education did continue. When something caught his interest, he would look it up to learn what he could about it. When presented with a new task, he analyzed it and learned how to do it correctly. He gave himself many challenges over the years, and learned that if he worked at them, he could achieve them.

Al's main career was working in a metal job shop, which he did for 48 years. He has also worked in his father's service station, tended bar, and taught karate lessons. Remodeling his first home, and later building another helped him to develop a variety of skills, which earned him a reputation as a talented handyman. He learned that most goals can be accomplished if a person is willing to work at them. Now retired, Al looks forward to giving his writing the attention it needs and sharing his stories with you.